The
FORGOTTEN
PROMISE

Paula Greenlees has an undergraduate degree in English and European Thought and Literature, and a Masters Degree in Creative Writing. She spent three years living in Singapore surrounded by the history and culture that provided the inspiration for her novels.

Also by Paula Greenlees

Journey to Paradise

The
FORGOTTEN
PROMISE

PAULA GREENLEES

PENGUIN BOOKS

PENGUIN BOOKS

UK | USA | Canada | Ireland | Australia
India | New Zealand | South Africa

Penguin Books is part of the Penguin Random House group
of companies whose addresses can be found at global.
penguinrandomhouse.com

Published in Penguin Books 2022
001

Copyright © Paula Greenlees, 2022

The moral right of the author has been asserted

Set in 10.4/15 pt Palatino LT Pro
Typeset by Jouve (UK), Milton Keynes
Printed and bound in Great Britain by Clays Ltd, Elcograf S.p.A.

The authorised representative in the EEA is
Penguin Random House Ireland, Morrison Chambers,
32 Nassau Street, Dublin D02 YH68

A CIP catalogue record for this book is available from the
British Library

ISBN: 978–1–529–15839–7

For those we have lost

Chapter One

Malaya 1920

One hundred and fifty eyes stared back at Ella as the peacock spread its tail in a glorious arc.

'Do you think we can steal a feather from it?' she whispered, clutching Noor's hand, mesmerised by the iridescent vision.

Noor shook her head. 'If you want one, you'll have to wait for it to drop.'

The sun was beating down on them in the rose garden. Despite the fact Ella knew that her *ayah* would surely scold her if she dirtied her dress, or if her skin turned a darker shade from the tropical sun, today she didn't care. It was her father's birthday, and she wanted to surprise him with the card she had made. Earlier, she'd taken a sheet of white parchment, folded it in half and drawn outlines of the roses he loved so much, the ones that he had imported from England. Carefully, she had stuck on petals from the flowers she had pressed, re-forming the shape and depth of the blooms. At nearly eleven, she knew how to do this expertly, having watched her mother, who liked to collect and preserve exotic flowers from the gardens and landscape that surrounded the villa. The card was beautiful, but the problem was Ella wanted to deliver it to him at work, and she wasn't certain of the way to his office at the tin mine.

'Are you sure you know how to get there?' She looked at Noor for reassurance.

'Yes.' The younger girl stood tall and nodded. 'All the servants know how to get there, and my mother often takes your father food for his lunch, you know.'

Ella thought about this. It made sense. Her father would need to eat at work, after all, and Noor's mother was their cook. As Ella thought a little more, she realised that she had indeed seen Noor's mother carrying baskets of food through the garden and onto the jungle path. Usually, Ella didn't pay too much attention to what grownups, particularly servants, did once they had left her line of vision – they merely came and went out of her focus until she needed them. Besides, there were many rooms in the villa where the grownups went without her. She spent almost all her mornings in lessons, but in the afternoons was allowed to sit on the verandah with her *ayah*. Sometimes, though, when he'd gone to work, she hid in her father's study. She liked the soft leathery seats he had in there and the books that lined the walls. The room was different from the others in the house with strange paintings of a place called Scotland, which he had once explained was next to the country he had come from called England, but darker and colder with lots of castles and big lakes. Her father told her that he'd been born there before living in England and that one day, when she was a grownup, he'd take her there. She had wrinkled her nose, not because she didn't want to go, but because she couldn't ever imagine her father, who towered over everyone, with his big booming voice and red hair like fire, as a baby.

But now, her thoughts turned back to the task she had set herself. She needed to get to the mine. She'd been several times before, of course, once in the big black Rolls-Royce Phantom that Aati, their *drebar*, drove her mother around in, but never by herself. Ella recalled how she had sat on the back seat with the windows open while her mother stood outside the office talking to her father. Her mother held a parasol over her head and was dressed in a delicate cream lace dress that skimmed her ankles. Her jet-black hair had been arranged in a tight bun and held with a diamond clip that caught the light and sparkled like glitter. She had looked so small standing next to Ella's father. In contrast to his sunburnt skin and red hair, she resembled the servants and workers while he seemed to belong to a different world. Her mother brought to mind the dolls in Ella's nursery, with their delicate faces and beautiful clothes.

'Well,' Ella sighed, returning to the moment, 'if you're really certain you know the way, then I'll follow you.'

Noor took her hand. 'It isn't far,' she coaxed. 'I've watched where my mother goes – there's a path that leads from the kitchen to the back of the rose garden, then you follow a track through the palm trees and up there.'

Ella looked to where Noor was pointing and nodded, then she took Noor's hand. For twenty minutes, they pushed their way through the jungle foliage, parted bamboo canes and dodged the spiders that had spun huge webs across the path. Ella's cotton lawn dress stuck to her back as the sun beat down on her head and beads of perspiration formed on her forehead. Thirst gripped her and her courage evaporated. Fearful of being lost, she wanted to turn around; however, she pushed back the tears that were forming. How she envied Noor her loose-fitting *abaya* and the way her hair fell over her shoulders, shielding her from the burning sun. Then something rustled in the undergrowth, making her jump.

'It's all right.' Noor stopped. She placed her hands on her hips and said a little breathlessly, 'It's only a grass snake. Come on, it isn't far.'

They pushed on through the jungle path as monkeys chattered in the canopy overhead. Ella caught sight of a green stain on the hem of her white dress and saw that the lace had been torn. Her sash kept slipping from her waist and her shoes were rubbing her heels, while the card in her hand became limp in the humidity and she noticed that some of the petals had come unstuck and fallen away. She wished she hadn't come now and wondered how much trouble she'd be in for leaving the villa without telling anyone where she was going. It was different for Noor: she could do what she liked, whenever she liked. She didn't even have to go to lessons with the governess unless Ella asked for her to join them.

Meanwhile, the sounds of the mine grew closer and louder. She could hear the pounding of machinery that crushed the rocks that came out of the ground, the pounding of water as it dredged the ore clean. As she conjured up these images, the earth shivered, and a huge bang made her jump.

'It's just them using dynamite to open up the earth,' Noor said. 'It's finished now.'

4

'How do you know so much?' Ella demanded.

Noor shrugged. 'You are a funny one.' She grinned. 'Just think – one day, all of this will belong to you and I know more about it than you do.'

Ella stopped in her tracks. 'What do you mean?'

'Well, just that you'll be the mine owner eventually, won't you?'

Ella mulled this over. She didn't know if she wanted to own a tin mine like her father did. His skin was sunburnt and he was out all day and often tired in the evening. She'd rather be like her mother – wearing beautiful dresses and diamonds in her hair or sipping cocktails on the verandah and dressing up for dinner parties.

'I'm not sure what I really want do when I grow up.'

'Well, perhaps you won't have to. You might get married and move away, or your mother might have a baby boy.'

'I don't know. It's such a long way off. Do you know what you might want to do?'

'Not really. Perhaps my mother might get married again. Or I might be a cook like her. Who knows? Come on,' Noor urged.

But Ella didn't want to move. She turned and faced Noor full on. She'd been told that Noor's father had died when she was a baby, and that was partly the reason Ella had first taken to her. It didn't seem fair that this lonely little girl who followed her around the villa didn't have a father of her own. After that, they'd become firm friends.

'But you *can't* be my cook. You're my best friend. In fact,'

Ella paused then added, 'you're the only real friend I've ever had.'

And it was true. Every day of their lives they had spent together, and they loved each other like sisters. In fact, they knew each other better than they knew themselves.

Noor beamed. 'And you are mine. But things will change. You'll see, once you go to school in Ipoh, things will be different.'

'I know. But I wish you could come, too.'

'It's all right. I can go to the village school if I want to. We'll see each other in the holidays.'

A lump formed in Ella's throat. She didn't want to go away to school, and she certainly didn't want to leave Noor behind. It didn't seem fair that there was one rule for her, because her father, Mr Ferguson, was the mine owner, and another for Noor, just because her mother was a cook. Ella had always imagined endless days in which they'd be friends and couldn't bear the thought of them being parted.

'Well,' Ella picked at the hem of her dress where the lace had come even further adrift, 'let's be blood sisters then. I've read about it in a book.' She took the clip from her hair. The pointed end was sharp and glinted in the light. 'We have to make a bond by cutting our skin and mixing our blood together. It means that we'll be close, like real sisters forever. Ready?'

'All right.' Noor hesitated as she looked at the sharp clip, then she nodded and held out her hand. Ella jabbed the meaty part of her thumb and watched as a ruby bead emerged from Noor's flesh, then repeated the action on her own.

6

'I promise you will be my blood sister forever.'

'And you will be mine.'

Ella and Noor rubbed their thumbs together and, after their blood had merged, Ella spat on the palm of her hand. Noor did the same and they clasped hands, sealing their promise.

'Right,' Ella said. 'Wherever we both go, or wherever we end up, neither of us can break that promise. It's the strongest bond there is.'

They stood for a moment, encompassed by the jungle and their secret, before they linked arms and made their way along the remaining track until they reached the mine. A group of men, Chinese, Malays and Tamils, were loading rocks into carts harnessed to ponies. They turned their heads and watched as the girls approached the outlying huts.

'Your father's office is here.' Noor pointed to where a door stood wide open. The girls made their way inside. The room was just as Ella remembered it: a large fan turned overhead; shelves displaying rocks and minerals lined the walls; and in the corner there was the big desk and the leather-covered chair where her father usually sat. But today he wasn't there. She chewed her lower lip in disappointment.

'Perhaps I should leave this?' She made her way to his desk and placed the card in the centre. It looked a bit bedraggled after their journey through the jungle, and now that she'd achieved what she had set out to do, Ella felt tired and thirsty.

Footsteps sounded behind them and a man's voice spoke.

'Well, who do we have here?'

She turned. A man she recognised as Sid Collins, the mine manager, stood in the doorway.

'I've brought my father a birthday card,' Ella said. She felt a little foolish and embarrassed to see him standing there watching her, and she was suddenly ashamed of her dirty dress and messy hair.

Sid scratched his head as he took in the sight of them both. 'Well . . .' His voice trailed off. 'I'm really sorry, he's not here. He went down to Menglembu on business earlier. But he could be back any minute.'

Tears pricked Ella's eyes and she could feel Sid's gaze on her, detecting her disappointment.

'Don't tell me that you walked all the way here from the villa?' His voice softened.

Ella nodded. 'Noor showed me the way.'

'Well,' he came further into the room, 'I guess you can rest here a bit while you decide what to do . . . you know, wait for your father or not. But I'm thinking, you must be thirsty after your walk. Why don't you sit down and I'll get you some water? He should be back soon, you won't have to wait too long.'

'I'd like that, please.' Ella's throat was dry, and a headache had started pounding behind her eyes. 'If it isn't too much trouble.'

Sid went into the back office and she thought she could hear the murmur of his voice, then a moment later, the clatter of glasses. While they waited, Noor and Ella picked up the rocks from the shelves, attracted the most by the ones that sparkled with tiny crystals.

While they were looking at a black rock laced with copper, Sid returned with two glasses filled with water.

'Take a seat,' he said. 'I see you've found the ore samples. Would you like me to tell you about them?'

Ella sipped her drink and looked at Noor who had left her water untouched and was lifting each rock in turn.

Sid started to explain the different grades of ore to them. Ella sat in her father's big chair and half-listened, hoping that her father would appear soon. Minutes passed and her headache worsened. After a time, she heard the crunch of tyres and a car engine idling outside. It must be her father. She got out of the chair and made her way to the door, excited at the prospect of seeing him.

But it wasn't her father or his green Ford Model T pickup. It was the black Rolls-Royce Phantom with Aati at the wheel. Sitting in the back seat like a princess was her mother, her face clouded by a frown. Aati got out and opened the back door so that Ella could see her mother.

'Ella,' she called without moving from her seat. 'Get in the car, dear.'

Ella glanced at Noor, then took her hand and led her to the car. Reflected in the window she could see their misty figures, two pairs of brown eyes and their long black hair.

'Look at what you've done to your dress, dear,' her mother continued. 'You really shouldn't leave the villa without telling anyone where you're going. We've all been worried sick searching for you. I can't tell you how relieved we were when Sid telephoned.'

'You shouldn't have worried. I was with Noor.'

Her mother glanced at the other girl but didn't smile. In fact, she seemed to look right through her.

'Come on, Ella. Get in the car.'

She stepped forward, pulling Noor with her.

'No, dear,' her mother said. 'Not Noor. She will have to make her own way from now on.'

Ella stopped in her tracks. 'But if she's not coming, I'm not coming.'

'Ella, darling,' her mother sighed. 'Don't argue. Things are going to have to change. I know you're very fond of the cook's girl, but soon you'll be starting school in Ipoh and then you'll have to behave like your father's daughter. Now come along.'

Ella turned to Noor, tears burning in her eyes. 'I'm so sorry.'

'Don't worry about it,' Noor whispered. 'I can make my own way back.'

Before she could protest, Noor dropped Ella's hand and stepped back. Feeling like a traitor, Ella got into the car, then Aati closed the door behind her.

As the car drove off, Ella leant out of the window to call to her friend, but Noor had already left. Ella caught sight of her heading back to the jungle path, her long black hair flying behind her. It was at that moment Ella realised that Noor was right – and however much she wished otherwise, things had already changed between them.

Chapter Two

Ipoh 1941

The shop façade was no different from any other building in the vicinity. There were white shutters at the windows and the entrance was shaded by a canvas awning – the perfect sanctuary away from the tropical sun. Yet there had been something about it that had captured Ella's attention. Perhaps it was the noisy red-and-green macaw sitting on a perch that had first drawn her away from the dusty street, where bullock carts trundled along the bustling road while hawkers sat to one side of the pavement beneath the shade of the banana trees, selling peanuts. Their constant heckling for her to buy a paper cone of nuts was wearing, and she had been glad of an excuse to dart away from the cacophony of the street. The last thing she had been expecting, as she stepped away, was to find a sign on this building declaring that it was a music shop.

Despite her hat, the heat burnt the back of her neck as she stood before the doorway. In the window to her left, she caught sight of her reflection: her imported American sunglasses, her striped shirt-waister. All of it had been put together with care, and she was pleased to see that she looked as sophisticated as Ingrid Bergman. She shifted her handbag from her right arm to her left as she considered the wisdom of going into the premises – so many of the shopkeepers had accomplices who were pickpockets.

A couple of men brushed past her; tea planters, she guessed, from overheard snippets of conversation about second-flush tea and camellia bushes, and how the war in Europe was affecting prices. One of them touched the brim of his hat acknowledging her presence, while the other wiped his forehead with a handkerchief. She felt suddenly awkward and far too hot, loitering in her smart shirt-waister as though she belonged on a film set rather than a burning street in Southeast Asia, and before she knew it, she had stepped over the threshold into the shop.

A large fan turned above her and a wireless was playing. She had expected to hear Mozart or Beethoven, but instead the sound of Duke Ellington drifted through the air: the owner was clearly keen on listening to the latest hits. There was an upright piano at the back of the room, a cello propped up against one wall and a trumpet hung above the shop counter, which was to her right and stacked with music scores. The smell of fresh furniture polish hung in the air, along with the scents of jasmine and coffee. A small brown bird sang from a cage that hung behind the counter and a beautiful old gramophone with a highly polished mahogany base stood on a table in the middle of the room. It was like stepping back in time to how she'd imagined Victorian shops in the English story books her father used to read to her.

She made a beeline for the gramophone and ran her fingers over the brass trumpet then the handle. How she longed to place one of the vinyl discs on the turntable, to drop the needle into the groove and listen to the tune filling the room.

'It's very old,' a male voice said from behind the counter.

She turned to see a man with a full head of white hair observing her.

'Oh! You startled me. But, yes, it's beautiful,' she agreed. 'And you've got so many interesting things.' She indicated the cello and then the trumpet. 'Are you a collector or are they for sale?'

'A bit of both.' He tilted his head. 'And you – are you a musician?'

'No. But my husband is. He plays the piano.'

'Ah, I see. That would explain it. Are you perhaps looking for a gift?'

She hadn't been, but was suddenly taken with the idea of buying a surprise for Johnnie. 'If I were, what would you recommend?'

His gaze fell to the music scores lining the counter. 'Well, what about one of these? I've quite a few that are hard to come by.'

Ella made her way to the counter, her dress rustling. The man spread out the scores, and she noticed how gnarled with arthritis his fingers were, as well as being stained with ink. But he was right: there were piles of scores, and she began to sift through them.

'Do you live in Ipoh?' the shopkeeper asked.

'Not now. I used to come to school here, but these days I live up in the Kledang Hills. We own a tin mine and a small plantation.'

'Down for a few days, then?'

'Yes. Christmas shopping, before the monsoon arrives.' She shifted a pile of paper. But when her gaze fell on the title of the bottom score, it startled her: Liszt's *Liebesträume*. How long had Johnnie been trying to get hold of it? She lifted her head, fingering the flimsy paper in her hand.

'Do you know, I think that this would be the very thing.' She smiled at the shopkeeper. 'Please may I buy it?'

'Of course.' He took it from her.

'Thank you. My husband will love it. He's such an admirer.'

'And he plays, you say?'

'Oh, yes.' Ella smiled again. 'He's good, actually. Really very good indeed.'

'It isn't easy keeping a piano tuned in the tropics, is it?' The shopkeeper sighed as he placed the score in a sheet of tissue paper, which he wrapped lovingly around it. 'With the humidity, the strings tighten. It makes the pitch higher. Then of course, when the humidity falls, the opposite happens. But I expect you know all that?'

Of course she did. How often did Johnnie complain about the heat damaging the glue on the piano, insist that the servants keep the fans running constantly, or get annoyed when the blinds hadn't been closed all day? It was foolish to hope that the piano would remain unchanged, but she understood how it connected him to dreams of better days. She hadn't the heart to tell him that those times were over. And this man – she looked at him, his shirt frayed at the cuffs and collar, the stubble peppering his chin – was it the same for him? What

14

dreams had he once possessed, and still did for all she knew? Had he once been a musician himself?

'I do know,' she said, tapping the counter. 'Humidity is the enemy of the piano. My husband is constantly worrying about the wood cracking.'

The man nodded. 'I can't tell you how many pianos have been lost to the heat. Here.' He passed her the little packet. 'I hope your husband enjoys it.'

'Thank you.' She took the score and held it close to her chest. 'I know he will.'

She left the shop and followed the roads lined with palm trees that cast welcome shade all the way back to her hotel. At last, she had completed her errands and purchases: Liszt for Johnnie – the thrill of finding the perfect gift, combined with the anticipation of giving it, fired through to her bones. Although it was weeks away, she now had all her Christmas gifts organised and could relax a little in the last remaining hours before she returned home. Later, she would be meeting her old school friend Melody, who lived not far from the hotel, for a drink in the cocktail bar followed by an evening watching the latest cinema picture, *Dressed to Kill*. It was just what she needed before returning to the routine of domestic life.

In her mind, she ran through the gifts she had acquired: apart from the Liszt score, she had bought new polo shirts and a mallet for Johnnie, along with a copy of *For Whom the Bell Tolls* and a diamond tie pin. For Toby she'd found a dear little Steiff teddy bear and some picture books that she looked forward to reading to him when he was older. And for Grace she'd found a toy grand piano: the case was painted black and lacquered to look like the real thing. It even made a very convincing sound. Then there were boxed sets of Snakes and Ladders and Ludo along with a wooden doll's house complete with the most adorable contents: a mother and father and baby, all dressed in fine clothing, along with a dining table, tiny cutlery and plates, beds, even a bath. But best of all, a dressmaker had made for Grace a beautiful red silk frock trimmed with lace that would complement her pale skin and dark wavy hair. Just thinking about her daughter, the way her smile lit up her eyes and face, was enough to melt Ella's heart.

As she walked, a tremor of wind brushed her face followed by a drop of rain that plopped to the ground and was swiftly followed by another. She looked up and frowned. Blustery clouds were forming and she wondered if they were in for a storm.

The rain quickened. Ella darted beneath a walkway for shelter and, with a thrill of excitement, recognised where she was: the very place she and Johnnie had met for the first time. She had just turned nineteen and was on her way back from church when a downpour had forced her to seek cover. A young man, tall and slim with the blondest hair she had ever seen, stood inches from where she now sheltered, his face tilted towards the sky.

'Lovely weather for ducks,' he had said.

'I beg your pardon?'

'The ducks.' He had grinned. 'They must love this weather.'

He'd explained that he was a junior government officer in Ipoh. She'd liked his accent, the way it was interspersed with long vowels, but most of all, she'd loved the way he smiled and his rather offbeat sense of humour. They'd continued to chat long after the rain had eased, both seemingly oblivious to the passing of time. As she'd watched him light a cigarette with his long, sensitive fingers, she wasn't at all surprised to learn that he played the piano, nor that he really wanted to be a musician – a composer, in fact. She'd been startled by the current of desire she'd felt watching him, the way his eyes seemed to burn right into her soul. But now, as Ella leant against the same pillar she had stood against all those years ago, she pictured Johnnie bent over his desk today, the way his hair was thinning and his face was etched with worry. Poor Johnnie – the closest he'd ever got to his dreams were the waltzes and dances he'd written to commemorate their children's births.

The rain began to ease, so Ella decided to chance it. She darted towards the Imperial Hotel, where a small, dark-skinned Sikh held the door open for her.

'Can you see that this is sent up to my room?' she asked, giving him the packet. 'And please be very careful – it's delicate.'

'Of course, Mrs McCain.' The doorman gestured in the direction of a houseboy standing close by. 'Room twenty-four, boy, quick!'

'And can you get someone to run a note over for me to this address?' She dashed off a message to Melody confirming their arrangements for later, then placed a few cents in the man's hand and headed towards the dining room, longing for a cup of tea and a few more minutes on her own.

How glad she was that she'd insisted on this trip. Johnnie hadn't wanted her to spend such a long time away from the children, but if she was honest, she missed having time to herself, and now she was here she was so glad she'd been able to come.

'The baby is still too young,' Johnnie had told her when she'd first mentioned the trip.

'But he's four months old, not a new-born, and I'm not feeding him anymore. Lian is more than capable of looking after him for a few days.'

'But I'd worry about you.'

'Me? But Ipoh is my second home!'

'That's not what I mean. You know it isn't.'

'I'm not going to let those rumours about the Japanese worry me. Everyone knows they'd never dare attack. Besides, Ipoh is at its best at this time of year – you know how much I love it.'

And Ipoh, she thought as she took a seat, really was glorious. Despite the war in Europe, the shops were full of new stock, brightly coloured silks as well as toys for the children from as far away as America. Even the hotel dining room was looking festive with a Christmas tree in the corner and posies of red hibiscus flowers on the tables.

A waiter appeared at her side. 'Would you like some tea, madam?'

'Please. Orange Pekoe – with a twist of lemon.'

'Certainly, madam.'

A few moments later, another waiter, wearing the traditional Malay clothing of a white *baju melayu* and a *songkok* on his head, returned with a tea tray and a copy of the *Malay Tribune*. She watched him as he poured the amber liquid from the pot into her cup, then he gave a slight nod of his head and left. She took the newspaper and flicked through the pages: German forces had retreated from Rostov; Roosevelt had cut short his holiday and returned to Washington where he sent a message to Emperor Hirohito with an appeal for war between the United States and Japan to be avoided.

How far away it all seemed.

She leant back in her chair and observed the other people in the room: women who, like her, had come to Ipoh for their Christmas shopping; men in linen suits who'd left their plantations for business meetings. It was a world where Malays and Europeans lived side-by-side. Once, she'd heard it likened to pot-pourri – a description that she liked, for it seemed to describe everything she loved here: the mix of cultures, the fragrant spices, the vibrant colours. It was, she reflected, a good life, one to which as a Eurasian she truly belonged. But while she sat fingering the small gold crucifix at her neck, unease rippled through her: what if they were all so wrong and the Japanese were planning to attack Malaya, after all?

Two men were sitting at a table close by, and she realised that they were talking about a recent sighting of Japanese war planes flying close to the coast of Singapore. She lowered her paper and strained to listen to their conversation.

'Don't worry, Roosevelt will sort it out – Hirohito wouldn't bloody dare attack!'

'But what if he doesn't?' the other man asked. 'What then?'

'Look, this scare will pass. The Japs are always flexing their muscles. And anyway, the US doesn't want to enter into the war if they can help it.'

'But what if they're forced to? What if the Japs surprise us somehow?'

'How?' The other man laughed. 'The US have the best bloody communications systems in the world. I'm telling you – it'll just blow over. Besides, where are they going to attack us from? Singapore? They're on the ball there, with guns already pointing in the right direction. The east coast? Not bloody likely with the monsoon in full pelt. Take it from me, there won't be a single bomb dropped here by the Japanese and not a single Japanese soldier will ever set foot in Malaya.'

Ella wished she hadn't listened; all this endless uncertainty and speculation unsettled her. She closed her eyes and thought of Johnnie and the children. *Lord,* she thought, *I really do need to stop worrying.*

The men's conversation had turned to tin mining. The war in Europe had increased tin and rubber profits in Malaya, and she yawned as she listened to the men discussing the increase in value of their shares. She glanced at her watch and was about to go to her room when she saw the waiter coming towards her once more.

'Telegram, madam.'

She took it from him and read:

NEED YOU AT HOME STOP SENT MALIK STOP
BE READY AT FOUR J

'What on earth . . . ?' She frowned.

Something must be very wrong for Johnnie to send a wire. Whatever it was, she wished he'd said, because now she'd be worrying until she reached home.

After a moment, she stood and went to the concierge.

'Can I help you, madam?'

'Yes. I'd like to make a call to my husband – could you arrange that for me? Here's his office number.' She wrote it on a piece of paper.

'Of course, madam.'

She waited while the concierge telephoned, but he shook his head. 'There's no one answering, madam.'

'How annoying.' She bit her lip.

'Is there something wrong, madam?'

'I don't know. I'm going to have to check out early. Can you get my bill ready?'

She slipped a dollar over the counter then walked towards the hotel door. Bands of sunlight were easing through the grey clouds, lending an eerie quality to the light.

Ella turned back, went upstairs and began to pack.

Malik yawned as he placed her suitcase and shopping in the boot of the Lagonda. She noticed how his teeth and mouth were stained red with betel-nut juice. She slid onto the back seat, which even with the windows open was as hot as an oven, thankful that the concierge had given her supplies for the journey: a flask of water, some bananas and egg sandwiches, all packed up in a paper bag, which she placed on the floor next to her feet.

Malik coughed as he got behind the wheel – a deep chesty wheeze – then opened the door and spat onto the ground.

'I really wish you wouldn't do that,' Ella said. 'You know I don't like it.'

He shrugged as he started the engine and they pulled away. His eyes met hers as he looked in the rear-view mirror. Ella glanced away. Their driver must know why Johnnie had called her back but, despite her urgent need to know, she didn't want to give Malik the satisfaction of telling her. Instead, she stared out of the window at the shop fronts where groups of men wearing brightly coloured sarongs sat huddled on the ground. Some, like Malik, were chewing betel-nuts. But there were coconut stalls too to distract her, as well as others offering bananas and mountains of peanuts, and huddles of women, with their heads covered in brightly coloured scarves, who stood on the roadside chattering while their children chased each other among the slowly moving traffic. Bullock carts trundled along the streets together with rickshaws, while goats and the occasional car wove between them all.

As they reached the edge of New Town, she saw the now familiar sight of a group of civilian volunteers in a truck heading towards the racecourse, where she knew they would be practising civil defence, setting up training sessions, blackout practice or warden duties. Her thoughts returned to the conversation overheard in the hotel. She tried to convince herself that even with Japan allied to Germany, all this talk of invasion was just ridiculous and Malaya really had little to fear.

Eventually, the town gave way to the kampongs filled with flimsy huts made from bamboo and palm leaves, then after a time the kampongs dwindled away, revealing valleys and hills shrouded in cloud. Damn it, in the rush, she'd forgotten to tell Melody she was leaving; she'd have to contact her when she got home. In her mind, she began to compose what she would say, all the while observing scattered roadside shacks selling coconuts or papayas. The owners waved at the Lagonda, hoping to slow it down as it passed and to sell Ella their produce at highly inflated prices.

Finally, they reached the pot-holed roads that wound up through the limestone hills. They would follow these for miles until they reached home. A flock of red parakeets lifted from the jungle canopy and soared like a vermilion cloud into the sapphire sky. Ella caught fleeting glimpses of golden orioles glittering like flecks of precious metal between the leaves of the kempas trees. Her thoughts flickered back to the overheard conversations in the hotel. It was so hard to imagine the fighting in Europe, especially with all these miles of jungle around her. But it scared her to think that Japanese planes had been sighted so close to home and that war could be creeping ever closer, threatening them all.

The rhythm of the car and the heat made her drowsy but she fought the need to doze. When they reached a bend in the road, a truck full of soldiers overtook them at speed, forcing Malik to swerve. Ella was thrown forward, but still managed to catch sight of the rifles the soldiers were holding and the ammunition belts slung around their torsos.

'Madam, are you all right?' Malik turned to face her. A drop of red liquid trickled from his mouth; she couldn't tell if it was blood or betel-nut juice.

'Yes. Thank you. Are you?'

He nodded, checked the road in both directions, then pulled back out.

Whatever she felt about Malik, he was a good driver and now she was sorry she'd been annoyed with him for spitting in the road. How petty and stupid she could be; out on these roads, Malik wasn't just her driver – he was here to protect her, and she knew that underneath the driver's seat he kept a gun.

The bag of food the concierge had given her had spilt onto the floor. She picked up the scattered sandwiches, flask of water and bananas.

'Here.' She handed him the water and a banana. 'I don't know if you're hungry or thirsty, but there's more than enough here for me.'

'Thank you, madam.' He took the flask, opened it and took a big gulp.

'I wonder where that lot are going in such a hurry.'

'I saw lots of soldiers this morning, madam. Everyone's a bit jumpy. Some say the Kesatuan Melayu Muda and the Malayan Communist Party are hiding here.'

'The KMM, really? I thought that they'd arrested Ishak Muhammad and some of the other Kesatuan leaders ages ago.'

'KMM everywhere, madam. Some people say maybe the group is strong again. Everyone says that maybe they help the Japanese.'

Goosebumps prickled her skin.

'Do you think the Japanese will attack us, Malik?'

'I don't know, madam. Maybe yes. Maybe no. If they're coming – we can fight them. The British defences are very strong, but the local people will do everything they can to save our people from attack.'

'They're my people, too, Malik.'

'Yes, madam, I know. But you have a foot in two places. One with your husband, the other here in Malaya. But if the time comes to leave, I think perhaps you'd better not stay.'

'I couldn't leave my home, Malik.' She leant forward. 'But are you saying you think they might attack, then? Surely you don't think it will ever come to that?'

He shrugged. 'No one can be certain of anything anymore, madam.'

She sat back in her seat. Malik's words had unnerved her further: this must be why Johnnie had called her back. Looking out of the window, the jungle seemed suddenly hostile. It made her wonder what could be hiding amongst its shadowy leaves.

'Malik,' she asked, 'is there something you're not telling me? About why Johnnie wants me home?'

'Sorry, madam. I didn't mean to scare you. Better you wait to see Mr Johnnie, I think. I don't really know why he asked for you to come back home.'

They travelled in silence for a mile or two, Ella wondering what on earth was going on, until Malik slowed the car down.

'What is it now?' she asked, leaning forward.

'Roadblock.'

A soldier flagged them down and Malik unwound his window.

'Where are you going?' a Geordie voice asked. This was the same group of soldiers that she had seen earlier, and they were armed with machine-guns.

'The Kledang Hills. To the Wosterholme tin mine,' she replied.

'Open the door and step out with your identity papers, please.'

They did as they were asked. She watched nervously as they checked the car and roughly opened the bags of shopping in the boot, then searched through the glove compartment and even under the bonnet. One of the soldiers frisked Malik, gliding his hands lightly over his torso and legs.

'All clear.' The soldier nodded.

'You can get back in,' another man said, indicating the inside of the car with the barrel of his gun. 'Just take care up on the higher roads. If you see anything that concerns you, turn back. Failing that, pull over into the jungle – chances are a patrol will be out and about and can pick you up.'

Ella got back into the back seat, meeting Malik's gaze in the rear-view mirror.

'Don't worry, madam. I have a gun hidden in a special place. I'll take good care of you. Please don't worry.'

She nodded. 'I know, Malik. Thank you.'

But as they travelled the remaining miles, she clenched her hands, digging the nails into her palms, alert to every sound or movement in the jungle.

At last, they reached the boundaries of the mine. She heard a blast of dynamite as the ground yielded yet more ore to excavate, and she thought of the men working there, retrieving the ore then later washing it, all overseen by Sid Collins or Johnnie. Before long, they drove along the track that turned into the drive, and there, at last, in front of her was her villa with its shady verandah running all the way around the building. Farid the houseboy rose from his seat on a step as soon he saw the car.

'Thank God!' Ella's body finally relaxed. 'Malik, can you see to it that everything is unloaded? And you must be hungry after the journey – go to the kitchen and ask Noor to get you something to eat.'

'I will, madam. Thank you, madam.'

Farid opened the door of the Lagonda and she stepped out of the car, gave him a cursory nod, then made her way into the house.

A child's red-and-blue tricycle lay discarded on a Persian rug in the hall, but she couldn't see or hear anyone downstairs. She paused, listening for voices, but there was nothing other than the sound of her own breathing. She called again. Apart from Apollo, Johnnie's beloved spaniel, barking in the distance, the house seemed empty and still.

'Hello!' she shouted again. 'Johnnie? Is there anyone at home?'

Then she thought she heard movement: a door or a window banging. With her heart racing, she shouted again, 'Johnnie!'

And suddenly there he was, running down the stairs to stand in front of her in the hall.

'Ella!' He wrapped his arms around her and kissed the top of her head. 'I can't tell you how glad I am that you're back.'

She nestled into him. He smelt of sandalwood soap along with a hint of tobacco. She loved that scent: it made her feel safe and protected. At home.

'So,' she asked, looking up at him, wondering what he was going to say. 'What's so urgent that you needed to call me back?'

His Adam's apple rose then fell as he swallowed hard.

'I'm really sorry, Ella. It's Grace.'

Chapter Three

The blinds were closed as she crept into Grace's room, but there was enough light for Ella to see that a fan had been placed close to the bed. Lian sat on a chair pressing a cold flannel to the child's forehead. She looked up at Ella's approach.

'What's the matter with her?' Ella tried to keep panic from her voice.

'Madam—' Lian rose and stepped away from the bed.

'What's wrong?' she repeated. Grace's face was pink and feverish.

'I'm not sure,' Johnnie said. 'It came on very quickly yesterday.'

'Why on earth haven't you called Dr Gibbins?' She sat down on the bed and gripped Grace's hand. 'She's only seven, for goodness' sake. Look at her – she's burning up.'

'I did. But Dr Gibbins is in the Cameron Highlands. He'll be back later today or tomorrow.' Johnnie sat next to her, clenching his fists. 'You know that there's been an outbreak of diphtheria down at the servants' quarters, don't you? Do you think she could have picked it up?'

'I don't know.' She looked down at the small form in the bed and stroked her daughter's hair. It was damp and a loose curl stuck to her forehead. Instinctively, she moved it and kissed Grace's hot and sticky skin.

'I'm sorry, love, for calling you away. I know how much you've been looking forward to your trip, but I felt sure you would want to be here with her, and to be honest, I didn't know what else to do.'

Ella nodded. 'Of course I want to be here. You did the right thing.'

For the next hour or so she sat beside Grace, holding her hand, cooling her forehead or trying to make her take tiny sips of water while Johnnie called Dr Gibbins's house again to see if he had returned.

Darkness fell. Ella placed another cold flannel on Grace's forehead.

'Mummy!' she moaned. 'I'm so cold.' Her eyelids flickered but remained shut.

'I know, darling. Would you like something to drink?'

She held a teaspoon of water close to Grace's mouth, but she wouldn't drink. All Ella could do was wet her lips.

Later, after she had read to Toby and put him to bed, she sat near her daughter's bed with a book in her lap but didn't turn the pages. She could hear the rasp of Grace's rapid breathing and wondered if there was some swelling in her neck. In the distance, she could hear Johnnie playing the piano – she didn't recognise the music, but it was wild and passionate, like a storm. Much later, the music stopped and she could hear all the familiar sounds of the house shutting down for the night – Farid locking the doors and windows, followed by his footsteps on the stairs and the sound of him switching off the lights.

Around eleven, the door opened. It was Johnnie.

'How are you doing?'

'I'm fine. Noor brought me some dinner up on a tray.'

'That was thoughtful of her. I didn't ask her to.'

'I know. She's always so kind. And she told me not to worry about Toby. Between them, she and Lian will take care of him – I can spend all my time here with Grace.'

'How is she?'

'No change.' Ella glanced across at her daughter's face. 'I keep hoping that you're wrong, that she'll be a little better.'

'I really hope Gibbins will be back in the morning.' Johnnie gave her what she took to be a brave smile. 'Are you coming to bed?'

'No.' She paused. 'I think I'll stay here.'

'What? In the chair?'

'Yes.'

'Well, if you need anything, let me know.'

'I will, love. Good night.'

He closed the door, and she heard his footsteps fading as he walked along the corridor to their room. After, she made a quick visit to the nursery to check on Toby before returning to Grace's room, where she settled into a chair next to her daughter's bed.

Ella read for a while, but it was hard to with the dimmed lamp she had placed near her chair. A clock chimed downstairs. Midnight. She checked Grace's temperature – a hundred and four, the fever wasn't dropping. Her fingers touched her daughter's neck: there was swelling there and her nose was running, producing a worrying and strange grey discharge. Ella wiped her daughter's face with a hand-kerchief, then she placed more cool flannels on Grace's head before securing the mosquito net around the bed. Finally, she knelt by the edge of the bed.

'Dear Lord,' she began. 'Thank you for my children and the good life you have given to me. I pray now for my chil-dren, but especially for Grace and ask you to keep her away from danger. Lord, protect my family, keep this land safe and away from danger. Amen.'

She crossed herself and stood. Grace's breathing was extremely laboured. Ella paced the room then went to the window where she opened the blinds a little and looked out while a warm breeze blew in from the jungle. As she looked out, her eyes became more accustomed to the dark and she could distinguish the shapes of the trees and the distant hills. She listened to the monkeys calling, the buzz of cicadas and the chattering of macaws. All evening, she'd been focused on Grace, and now as exhaustion took hold, she wondered what secrets the jungle could be holding. The soldiers she had seen earlier on the road might well be out there, only feet away. And once more her thoughts turned to the conversation she had overheard in the hotel. What about the Japanese? Could they possibly be out there too? The dark, jungle-covered hills, as she well knew, could hide anything.

She watched as thunder peeled across the hills, followed seconds later by a flash of light. She listened, waiting for the thick, heavy monsoon rain to fall, knowing that when it did the downpour would last for days. But instead, the breeze nudged aside the sheer curtains and the mosquito net draped around Grace's bed. Ella shuddered as the cool air grazed her skin and another blaze of light rent apart the darkened clouds, yet still the promised storm gave up no rain. It could go either way now, she knew. The uncertainty stayed with her as she returned to her chair, plumped up the cushion, switched off the light and began to doze.

As the dawn light seeped through the curtains, she woke with a start. She sat up, her neck stiff. Grace seemed to be sleeping and Ella didn't want to turn on the lights, so she went to the window and drew back the shutters and blinds to let in the dawn.

A thousand years could pass and each day Ella would still love seeing the sun rise with renewed magnificence. Sunlight bled over the coconut trees, staining the wispy vapour clinging to the branches with orange, gold and pink. Light radiated through the sky, colouring the clouds with fingers of ruby. She listened to the nightjars singing and the macaques calling from the canopy that spread for miles into the Kledang Hills.

This was her favourite time of the day. There was nothing like watching her surroundings erupt into life, the mynah birds and howlers re-emerging from their nightly rest. However many times she witnessed it, the newness and promise of life brought by each fresh day always gave her hope.

As she absorbed it all, she waited to hear the familiar

movements of Noor. Every morning, just after dawn, she came out into the garden. She always left by the kitchen door to collect fruit straight from the tree for Ella's breakfast: mangoes, pineapples, rambutans, papayas, whatever was ripe or in season. Ella would watch her as she made her way across the rose garden and out onto the lawn, leaving a trail of silvery footprints in the morning dew. Today, a peacock strode across her path, its iridescent blue and gold feathers spread to dry in the early-morning sun. Noor stood still and waited a moment, then slowly she bent down and picked up a feather that had fallen to the ground.

It took Ella back to their childhood, to the days when they used to chase peacocks across the lawn together, hoping to catch a tail feather.

'It's bad luck,' Ella's *ayah* had called, 'to keep a peacock's feather.'

But the girls had merely laughed and continued with their game. From Ella's earliest memories, they had run across this garden playing tag or sitting on the verandah with her collection of dolls, playing at families, each believing that they belonged to the other and that Ella's toys were also Noor's. Sometimes, they'd eat noodles or curry out there, made by Noor's mother, whose face had faded to a vague memory in Ella's mind. All she could remember was her ethereal beauty, the aroma of bread and cakes cooking in the kitchen or her wandering the gardens in the early morning or at dusk, just as her daughter now did.

Noor lifted her face to Ella's window and slowly raised her hand while her fingers clasped the tail feather so that Ella could see it. *'It's bad luck,'* her *ayah's* voice echoed, but Ella hadn't believed her then and she certainly didn't now.

'Mummy.' Grace had woken and her voice was croaky. Ella turned. In the morning light, she could now see there were small blisters on the child's hands and feet.

'My God!' She placed one hand on Grace's head – it was scorching. They had to get a doctor as soon as possible. She rushed to call Johnnie.

He was fast asleep when she entered their bedroom. She sat on the bed and gently shook his shoulders.

'Johnnie?'

'Mmmmn.'

'Are you awake?'

'No.'

'Well, you'd better wake up now.'

'What time is it?'

'Around seven.'

He tried to pull her close to him, but Ella resisted. 'Johnnie, please, wake up.'

'What's the matter?'

'It's Grace. She's got strange blisters on her hands and feet. I think you're right. It's diphtheria.'

He sat up and switched on the bedside lamp.

'I've got a meeting at the accountant's this morning, but I can take a look before I head off to the mine offices if you like.'

'Yes. Please. I'm worried.'

He got out of bed, and she followed his sleepy form to Grace's room.

'Her temperature is really high,' Ella said, checking

35

with the thermometer again. 'And she's hardly drunk any-thing. I've tried giving her water from a spoon, but she's not taking it.'

'Look—' He rubbed his hands sleepily over his face. 'Her body is a bit pink and seems sore, too. I'll give Gibbins another call before I head off. If he's not back, someone else must be able to give us some advice, surely? Why don't you get us some tea while I'm on the phone?'

The last thing she wanted was tea, but she knew Johnnie couldn't come to without it. In the kitchen, she asked Noor to make up a tray, and as Ella carried it to the dining room, she passed Johnnie's study door where she could hear the murmur of his voice on the telephone.

The table was set for breakfast: silver cutlery, bone-china plates and linen napkins, a plate of papaya and limes. Noor had placed the peacock feather she had found by Ella's side plate. She could see it clearly as Farid had already opened the blinds. Through the open window, the scent of a frangi-pani bush filled the room, and it seemed for all the world like a perfectly ordinary morning, but as she placed the tray on the table, it seemed to Ella that something had shifted, some-thing that could never be changed.

Footsteps fell along the corridor. She looked up – it was Johnnie.

'Dr Gibbins is back. He'll be here right away.'

'Thank goodness.' Ella glanced at the tray on the table. 'Shall we take this tea upstairs? I really couldn't eat any breakfast, and I'd rather the servants didn't see us like this.'

They sat in Grace's room, sipping their tea and waiting.

At last, there was a knock on the door and Farid showed in a man in his fifties. He had a white beard and was wearing a pale linen suit.

'Dr Gibbins!' Ella stood, trying to keep the anxiety she felt out of her voice.

'Now then, my dear, tell me what's the matter?'

'We think Grace has diphtheria,' Johnnie said. 'It came on rather suddenly.'

'Let me take a look.' He took off his jacket, rolled up his sleeves and sat on the bed next to Grace. 'Could someone switch on a lamp? I need to examine her.'

Johnnie obliged and light flooded across the room, grazing Grace's face. She stirred and opened her eyes.

'Grace, it's Mummy. Dr Gibbins has come to see you.'

Her daughter rolled towards her. 'My head hurts.'

'I know, sweetie.'

Dr Gibbins took a stethoscope and a thermometer out of his bag.

'Now then, Grace, can you sit up and open wide for me, that's a good girl?'

Ella watched with Johnnie as Dr Gibbins placed the thermometer in Grace's mouth and listened to her chest before examining her back. He looked at her arms and legs, then took out the thermometer and examined the inside of her mouth.

'What do you think it is?' Ella asked.

'It's definitely diphtheria.' He tilted his head on one side. 'There have been a few cases recently – mainly amongst the locals.'

'Oh.' Ella sank into the chair next to the bed and reached for Johnnie's hand.

'There's been a case of it down in the workers' bungalows.' Her husband frowned. 'But how on earth did she get it – she doesn't go anywhere near there, does she?'

'Could easily be through the house staff, but we'll think about that later.' Dr Gibbins looked at them both. His expression had turned very grave. 'Look, I don't want to worry you unduly but it's extremely dangerous. You'll need to keep everyone here safe, especially Toby, you really need to stop it from spreading. But for now, we ought to get Grace to the cottage hospital in Menglembu – keep her safe and in isolation until the danger has passed for her.'

'No.' Ella shook her head. 'It's miles away – I can't allow it.'

'Darling,' Johnnie squeezed her hand, 'honestly, it's the best place for her as well as keeping everyone else safe. I really don't see that we have any other option.'

Ella looked up at him and saw the resolve in his face.

'But she'll be gone how long – a month? Two? And I know we won't be allowed to visit her in a fever ward.'

He put his hand on her shoulder. 'It's for the best – you have to think of everyone else, especially Toby.' Johnnie's voice trailed away.

Ella took Grace's hand. How hot it was. She knew that Johnnie and Dr Gibbins were right, but couldn't bear to be parted from her daughter when she was so ill and needed her mother the most.

She could hear Dr Gibbins packing up his bag, the snap of the clasp as he closed it, then water running at the basin in the corner of the room while he washed his hands. Sunlight brushed the top of Grace's head, highlighting her rich brown curls, and Ella stroked them, wishing there was more she could do to help her daughter.

'I know it won't be easy,' Dr Gibbins said, drying his hands on a towel. 'But the time will quickly pass and soon it will be Christmas. Having everyone alive will be the best present you ever have, believe me. Now, I'd better call them at Menglembu. May I use your telephone, Mr McCain?'

Johnnie took Dr Gibbins to the study while Ella sat waiting. Grace had fallen back to sleep and her breathing was more laboured than before. A dull ache formed at the base of Ella's stomach, then it spread, numbing her entire body. She wondered if Johnnie was feeling it, too. A moment later, he returned to the bedroom.

'They'll be here as soon as they can.' His voice was hushed. 'Diphtheria,' he continued. 'I can't believe it. Dr Gibbins said he's going to the workers' bungalows next. I'll guess we'll have to put them in quarantine.'

She nodded. Everyone was going to have to be careful and pull their weight if they were to save lives, but right now her thoughts were only for Grace.

Ella groaned at the thought of being parted from her daughter, perhaps for months.

Johnnie sat down on the bed and took both of her hands in his.

'You know this is extremely serious, don't you? If there are more cases, we've a real problem on our hands – no one can leave this area until there are signs that the infection has stopped spreading.'

Grace stirred and her eyelids flickered open.

'How are you feeling, darling?' Ella asked as she let go of Johnnie's hands.

'Horrid.'

'I know. I'm sorry.' She took the child's hand in hers and squeezed it tight. 'I've got something to tell you. An ambulance is coming to take you to the hospital where they're going to make you better.' Ella bent down and kissed Grace's forehead and smoothed her hair. 'Mummy and Daddy love you very much, you know that, don't you?'

'Can't you come with me, Mummy?'

'No, darling. But it won't be long before you get better, I promise, and then you'll be back with us again.' A tear fell onto Grace's cheek. Ella brushed it away. 'Now, shall I pack your things?'

But Grace had fallen back to sleep.

'They'll be here soon.' Johnnie stood up and gave his daughter a kiss. Ella watched as he stroked her hair, then said, 'I'd better go. I'm cancelling all my meetings for the day. I must go with Gibbins now and find out what's what down at the servants' quarters. Try to stop this wretched thing from spreading.'

When he'd left, Ella forced herself to stand and found a small suitcase that she filled with four of Grace's cotton lawn nightdresses, a toothbrush, her hairbrush and comb. She picked up a toy rabbit from the top of a chest of drawers, kissed its head and placed it on top of the pile in the case, then closed it.

Time passed as she sat in the bedside chair waiting until in the distance she could hear the low hum of a vehicle approaching. It grew louder and closer. She went to the window and saw an ambulance pull up outside the front door, then two men and a nurse stepped out. Her hands tightened on the sill, then she turned and went downstairs to meet them.

'Mrs McCain?' the nurse greeted Ella.

'Yes.'

'We've come for Grace – is she upstairs?'

'Follow me.'

The nurse took Grace's temperature, felt her pulse, then nodded to one of the attendants to carry her downstairs to where the other man stood waiting. Ella could see he'd wheeled a trolley into the hall. When Grace was placed onto it, Ella pulled the blanket over her daughter, stifling a sob.

'Sleep now, my angel. Rest and get better. I will come and visit you in the hospital as soon as I can.'

Her mind and body were numb as she watched her daughter being loaded into the back of the ambulance. How could this possibly be happening?

'We'll take good care of her,' the nurse said. 'I know it's hard, but hospital really is the best place for her, and it won't be long before you're all together again.'

When the ambulance had pulled away, Noor came and stood beside her mistress. She placed her hand on Ella's arm.

'Madam, are you all right? Can I get you anything?'

But Ella stood with her fists clenched at her sides until she could see the retreating ambulance no more. Still she waited, listening long after the sound of the engine had faded away and all she could hear was the beating of her empty heart.

Chapter Four

The day passed slowly once Grace had gone. Ella returned to her duties in the house with a heavy heart while Johnnie tackled the problems of stopping the infection spreading.

Ella spoke to Noor about the menus for the week: beef *rendang* or *laksa* for Johnnie's lunches.

'There are plenty of tamarinds in the garden,' she said, 'and perhaps we could have *nasi lemak* on Friday?'

Ella enjoyed the little parcels of banana leaves filled with coconut rice and spicy *sambal*. And, of course, *roti* for breakfast. Always *roti* – they all loved the flaky-doughy flatbreads eaten with dhal or curry and accompanied by mango *lassi* – it was the only way to make sure Grace drank plenty of milk.

'That just leaves the other days to think about,' Ella continued, brushing aside the image of Grace sitting down with a glass of *lassi* and wiping away the thin line of froth from her upper lip as she finished the drink. 'How about some chilli crab and fish-head curry in the evenings, and we can have spicy omelettes for lunch if there are enough eggs?'

Noor nodded, but Ella noticed she was more subdued than usual and put it down to her concern for Grace.

'She'll get better soon,' Ella said, placing her hand on Noor's arm. 'And the hospital is the best place for her.'

'Yes, madam. But I worry, maybe it's my fault she's ill in the first place.'

'Why?' Ella tilted her head to one side as she studied the face of the young woman standing beside her, its features as familiar as her own.

'I hear people are sick in the kampong. I visited my cousin Omar's house there. Maybe I brought it here and gave it to Miss Grace?'

'Unlikely, and you can't think like that.' Ella placed her hand on Noor's shoulder. 'Something like this . . . who knows where it comes from? The important thing is for Grace and all the others who are ill to get better and for us to try to stop it spreading.'

Noor nodded, but she didn't smile.

'Come on,' Ella said, forcing herself to be jolly. 'How about you make some *bubur cha cha* for Mr McCain? You know how much he loves it as a snack. We've got enough yams and coconut milk, haven't we? I bet he'll be hungry, having had such an early start this morning riding around the estate with Manager Sid.'

She left Noor, who had started to chop yams and sweet potatoes into tiny cubes ready to add to the fresh milk from the king coconuts that grew in the garden, and headed to her desk in the sitting room where she began to attend to some of the estate correspondence.

Later, she would run through the accounts with Johnnie.

She pictured him out riding with Sid, both men explaining to the workers the gravity of the situation. How easily her husband had taken to this life of hers, managing the estate as though the ability had always lain in his veins and all that was needed was the right set of circumstances to awaken those dormant skills. She smiled at the memory of him arriving here all those years ago, the frown that had marked his face for weeks as he shadowed her father until he had learnt to understand the workings of the mine. Others might have doubted his ability, but she never had and never would, which was why she'd been happy to make him a partner in the mine.

Now she turned her attention to her mail. There were statements from the bank showing a healthy balance. Their shares in rubber were doing well. That was the only good thing about the war in Europe as far as she could see – the need for more and more tin and rubber was making them all rich. She sighed, for this she knew was the reason why the Japanese had their eyes on Malaya: sixty per cent of the world's tin was produced here, along with forty per cent of the world's rubber. No wonder the locals were keen for the British to leave, and the colonialists were even more determined to stay. Ella felt a sense of conflict, if she was honest, for being Eurasian, didn't she have, as Malik had reminded her, a foot in both camps? She'd heard other rumours, too, of how the Japanese had planted spies in the villages, and how these people not only helped the communist rebels undermine the status quo but drip-fed vital information to their masters on how to navigate the jungle, rivers and unreliable roads. If she thought about it, she couldn't really blame them, although it deeply unsettled her.

All these ripples of local dissent were one reason why Johnnie had made her place her shares and investments with Lloyd's of London, Burma Oil and other blue-chip companies whose profits were soaring. However, it didn't always seem right to Ella that they were growing so rich when others around them were not. She'd often spoken to Johnnie about how she could help their workers more, even suggesting expanding the local school that her father had founded, but as yet her plans had come to nothing. She smiled as she thought of her father: such an honourable, kind man with a strong sense of charity and social conscience, always doing the right thing. When times were tough, she reflected on his sense of duty and how it had got him through the most trying situations. She was so proud of him: the way he'd set up a school for the local children, the food parcels he had given to the hungry, the way he had offered the cook's job to poor orphaned Noor. He was an example to them all, and she was determined to continue his legacy as best she could by making the tin mine and the surrounding plantation as profitable as he had always dreamt of them being – something that, as a Eurasian woman, she knew could meet with opposition from a white- and male-dominated society. Thank goodness for Johnnie's support and the fact that she would always have him by her side.

She stared out of the window. While it was reassuring that their finances were doing well and she had plans for how to help others, nothing could make up for the emptiness of the house and how much she was missing her daughter. She wondered what Grace would be doing now and glanced at the clock. After two, she would telephone the hospital to check on the child's progress, but she already knew the call wouldn't be enough to make up for the emptiness she was feeling. She sighed again, then flicked through her remaining correspondence.

There was an envelope addressed to her in Melody's handwriting.

Ella ripped it open.

Hey, you!

What happened to our little get-together? When I arrived at your hotel, they told me you'd already checked out. I know I didn't get the day wrong as you'd sent me a reminder. Anyway, I've tried telephoning you, but there's no reply. I do hope everything is fine with you. Must admit, I've been a little concerned. Anyway, I'll be calling by your way in a few days. Edward is at a medical jolly in Singapore – he goes to one every year (yawn!) – and I thought I'd go down the coast for a while. I've got some commissions I need to fulfil, and I've always loved sketching and painting the sea. My last sea studies sold really well (through a great contact in London), and I need to get some more work done for that slave-driver of a gallery owner!

Despite her downcast feelings, Ella smiled. Melody was like that. She could always raise her friend's spirits when she was down, just as she had all those years ago when, aged thirteen, they had first met at boarding school in Ipoh.

'Hey, I'm Melody!' she'd said as she sat down at the desk next to Ella's. 'My folks have just arrived from the States. Isn't this place simply the best?'

'Do you mean school or Ipoh?'

'Malaya, dummy!' Melody teased. 'Everything's so different and there are monkeys and parrots *everywhere*!'

'I know.' Ella smiled. 'I've lived here all my life.'

'Really? But I should have guessed that.' Melody grinned. 'With your dark hair and fine features, you could pass for a native.'

'That's because my mother is.'

'Really? I bet she's a beauty.'

Ella had paused, considering this: it seemed that apart from Noor, this was the first time a child her own age or anyone else at the school had not judged her for being half Malay and half British; the first time that someone hadn't made her feel like she didn't belong in either country. Instead, Melody had made her feel special, unique even. From that moment on, they had become inseparable. Ella's father called her 'Snow White' on account of her dark hair, and Melody 'Rose Red' because she was blonde. But that wasn't the only contrast between them. Ella was studious and precise, a natural mathematician; Melody was creative and dreamy, her rich inner fantasy world revealed in her artwork and stories.

And it was Melody who had been there for Ella just a year later when her mother had died, comforting her in the terrible days that followed, listening while Ella had cried all night, her friend holding her and trying to soothe the pain.

Now, Ella placed the letter on the desk in front of her. Melody always seemed to know when something wasn't quite right – even though they were both now married and lived far apart. It was as though they were the other half of each other's soul or the sibling neither of them had ever had. It would be lovely to see her, not only to fill the void that Grace had left, but to lighten Ella's spirits. She dashed off a quick note explaining her reason for leaving Ipoh so suddenly, and saying that it would be wonderful to see Melody – why didn't she stay for a few days? Ella managed to get the note to Farid just in time before he left to post the mail.

Afterwards, she checked on Toby, who was having his morning nap. Lian was tidying the clothes in his room, folding small polo shirts and shorts into a pile from a laundry basket and placing them neatly in a pale blue chest of drawers.

Lian gave her a hesitant smile as she came into the room. Ella placed her hand on the nursemaid's shoulder, then went to the side of Toby's cot, which was covered in a mosquito net, and watched him sleeping.

'He looks so peaceful, doesn't he?' she said.

'Yes, madam.'

Ella fingered the cross at her neck as she watched him. *Please, Lord, don't let him get sick, too.*

She turned and quietly left the room to the sound of Lian gently opening and closing drawers.

In Grace's room, the bed had been made up with fresh sheets and the windows were wide open. It must have been Lian who'd done it all, and Ella was grateful – it would have broken her heart to see the slightest dent still left by Grace's head on the pillow or the faintest impression of her body on the sheets.

She went to the window and looked out, half-expecting to see Grace running across the grass or throwing a ball for Apollo to catch. How she longed for the sound of her daughter's chatter, her squeals of delight as Johnnie picked her up and spun her round and round. Ella picked up a cushion from the bed and sank down on the chair, where she clutched the cushion close to her chest as though it could somehow stem the pain that was twisting her heart.

She heard footsteps entering the room and looked up. It was Johnnie.

'I thought I'd find you here.' He hovered by the door. 'I came back to see how you were doing.'

She stretched out her hand to him and he stepped into the room. He sat down on the bed beside her.

'What did Dr Gibbins say about the workers?' she asked, smoothing the back of his hand with her thumb. She sensed him tense and he cleared his throat before he spoke.

'Well, the incubation period for diphtheria is three to four days. He suggested that, in the meantime, we limit contact between people as much as we can. If after three days no one else shows any more symptoms, we're probably all in the clear. I've given instructions that the servants should try to keep apart from each other as much as possible, not that it is going to happen as they live and work so closely together. I've also suspended work in the mine for the next three days and prohibited the men from mixing. They've been warned in no uncertain terms what will happen if anyone breaks the rules. Dr Gibbins said he'd come back every day to check on the situation. Meanwhile, we need to report any new cases and get them to hospital.'

Johnnie let go of her hand and ran his hand through his hair. 'To be honest, it's Toby I'm most worried about. You'll probably think I'm being over-anxious, but he's only a few months old. Please can you make sure that everything that could come in contact with him is sterilised or washed in carbolic?'

'Yes.' She nodded. 'Of course. I'll make sure the servants know.'

'Obviously, I've been in contact with the workers – there's a new case of it, unfortunately, so I'm going to stay away from Toby until we know everyone is in the clear. Hopefully, this way we can contain the infection.'

'Do you think the miners and their families will do as you say?'

'I don't know. I'm going to get a whole load of supplies in, and I've also told them that I'll fine those who disobey my orders and give a bonus to those who obey them. I don't know what else I can do.' Johnnie sighed. 'I'm going to telephone Menglembu to see what supplies I can order for everyone and get them dropped off. Remember, don't go out and don't let anyone in. It's only for three days.'

Ella nodded. He stood up and she heard him going

downstairs to his study. It was then that she remembered the letter from Melody saying she was on her way. Three days . . . Ella calculated that was how long it would take for the letter to reach her friend – surely she wouldn't arrive before the three days were up?

Fear slithered down Ella's spine at the thought of those three days and of the infection possibly spreading. She pictured it like a pool of dark liquid seeping unchecked into every corner and space, covering every surface, and then, like water, condensing in the air and spreading all over again. She imagined them inhaling it and the disease festering in their lungs. Had she been careless while handling Grace? And what about Toby? She paced the floor wondering whether, in the early days before the diphtheria was diagnosed, Noor had passed the infection on to Grace or whether now Lian might pass it on to Toby. They must be in the clear now surely? There was nothing for it, though. However hard it was going to be, they must do their best to stay uninfected and wait.

All that day and the next Ella anxiously watched for any signs of the illness in Toby or herself. As the morning moved towards midday, she was sitting reading with her son on her lap when she heard a car approaching along the drive. Still holding Toby, she looked out of the window. It was a red Daimler sports convertible with the hood down, and sitting in the driver's seat was Melody.

'Damn!' Ella pursed her lips. Melody had arrived sooner than expected and Johnnie would be annoyed that she was here before their self-imposed quarantine had passed. Still,

Ella was excited at the prospect of seeing her best friend – some good company to relieve the slowly passing hours.

'Lian,' Ella called, 'can you look after Toby?' Ella handed the baby to her then ran downstairs to the hall and threw open the door.

Melody was standing next to the Daimler. She was wearing cropped trousers, a white shirt tied at the waist and a wide straw hat with a bow at the back that made Ella think of Vivien Leigh in *Gone with the Wind*. A large brown leather suitcase stood on the drive beside her, along with a box of paints and a foldaway easel leaning against the car door.

Melody waved to her.

'Ella!'

She rushed to her friend and they clasped each other in a tight embrace.

'Oh, my goodness, it's so good to see you!'

Melody stepped back and observed Ella at arm's length. 'I'm so sorry to hear about Grace – as soon as I got your letter, I thought I'd come straight away. You do look tired, darling. Come on, let's go inside and you can tell me everything.'

'Farid!' Ella called the houseboy.

'Yes, madam?'

'Can you please take Mrs Fielding's luggage up to the guest room? And please tell Mr McCain that we have an unexpected visitor.' Ella wondered if he'd be cross that Melody was here before the three days of quarantine were up. She could imagine his annoyance, telling her what kind of message did it send to the servants, and didn't she realise

53

it would undermine his authority if they told the staff one thing and themselves did another? Well, it was too late now. Melody was here and Ella certainly wasn't going to send her away.

On their way to the drawing room, they passed Farid who was on his way back down.

'Can you ask Cook to bring us some fresh lemonade and *kuih*?' Ella knew that the sticky rice pudding was Melody's favourite and that Noor had made a batch earlier in the morning.

'Oh, Melody, it's been so awful.' Ella flopped down onto a chintz-covered chair. The fabric had been imported from England especially for her: Colefax, and it had cost a fortune. Melody sat beside her. 'Can you believe it? Diphtheria! And my darling Grace will be in the fever hospital in Menglembu for at least a month.'

'My God, Ella, I'm so sorry. That's awful.' Melody took a cigarette out of a silver case and lit it with a tortoiseshell lighter.

'I know. But that's not the worst of it – it seems to have spread amongst the mine workers and their families. A baby died yesterday.'

'Shoot! I don't know what to say.' Melody shook her head. 'You must be going crazy.'

'We're doing what we can. Johnnie's taken a firm hand with them all, putting them in quarantine. We've been holed up in the house for the past couple of days until the danger has passed.'

'Which is how long?'

54

'About now.'

Ella glanced around the room and her gaze fell on a silver-framed photograph of Grace in her christening gown. She pulled out a handkerchief and wiped her nose, aware that Melody was watching her with concern.

'There's something special about your first,' Ella sniffed. 'But I'm so worried about Toby, too.'

And perhaps it was because Melody was here that the fear she'd been suppressing for the past few days overwhelmed Ella and she started to cry: big sobs that threatened to break her heart in two.

'Oh, Ella!' Melody placed an arm around her shoulders and squeezed. Instead of comforting her, it made her cry all the more, but eventually her tears were spent and she lifted her face to Melody's.

'It might not seem like it,' she gave a weak laugh, 'but I'm awfully glad that you're here.'

They stayed in the drawing room, drinking lemonade at first then gin, chatting about the children and looking at photograph albums of Grace and Toby. Ella's composure returned and she opened other albums that took her back to her childhood. They smiled over photographs of her as a child playing with Noor, her father chasing them around the garden with peacock feathers, her mother looking elegant in a long white linen gown and white gloves that reached up to her elbow.

'Do you remember this?' Ella opened a blue album trimmed with gold. 'It's the day we left school and you won the art prize.'

'And you won one for maths, I remember. Along with the form prize *and* the one for deportment.'

'Was I insufferable?' Ella rested the album on her lap.

'No. Never.' Melody grinned. 'I think I was a little minx, though. Don't you?'

'A bit.' Ella grinned.

'Do you ever wish you could turn back the clock?' But then Melody froze, realising her mistake. 'Oh, Ella, I'm sorry. I shouldn't have said that.'

'Don't worry about it,' Ella said. 'We can't change the past.'

But, of course, she wished she could. Then she would have stopped her mother from taking that ill-fated car journey not long after she'd visited Ella at school for the last time. Her father wouldn't have taken a mistress out of grief, then died a few years later from a heart attack after trying to keep up with the whims of a woman half his age. At least she and Johnnie had enjoyed a couple of years living in Ipoh as newlyweds before, at the age of twenty-three, she'd inherited the tin mine and all its responsibilities. Fate would throw what it would at you, she'd realised when she was too young, but somehow you simply had to grit your teeth and battle on.

'Are you getting hungry?' she asked, looking at her watch. 'It's almost lunchtime. Perhaps you'd like to freshen up before we sit down?'

She showed Melody to a room that overlooked the rose garden. It was the one that had been hers before she was married, decorated in pastel pink and green silk with wispy white voile floating at the windows, softening the blazing morning light that flooded in. It was one of her favourite rooms in the house. Lian had already unpacked Melody's case and folded back the mosquito net around the bed.

'My father always loved roses,' said Ella, standing by the window. 'It's foolish keeping them growing here when the climate isn't quite right. Any day now, the monsoon will dash them to smithereens, but I can't quite bring myself to get rid of them. I love the red ones the most, the gallicas, but also those pink tea roses.'

Melody joined her by the window. 'They're all beautiful. I'll enjoy looking at them and I can almost catch their scent from here.'

'I'll get Farid to cut some for you. There's a little bathroom through here.' Ella opened a door that led to a tucked-away bathroom where pink and green Malacca tiles echoed the colours of the bedroom decor and the roses outside. 'Well, if you have everything you need, I'll see you back downstairs, shall I?'

'Perfect. I'll be about five minutes.'

Ella made her way to the dining room. She wasn't hungry and the air was more humid than usual, making her listless. She wondered if the monsoon storms were closer than she had first thought. Sunlight streamed through the open windows onto the dining-room table, making the crystal glasses glitter and the Murano chandelier sparkle overhead. Johnnie was already sitting at the head of the table reading the paper. A glass of water was at his side, and he lifted his head at his wife's approach.

'So,' he said, frowning. 'An unexpected visitor, Farid tells me. Honestly, Ella, I'm trying so hard to get the workers and servants to stay away from other people. We should be setting an example.'

He spoke just as she had imagined he would: with a hint of annoyance. But she knew that if she slid her arms around his waist and hugged him, it wouldn't last for long.

'I know, darling, but what am I to do? I can't send her away, and to be honest, Melody could be just the distraction I need right now, with Grace in hospital.'

He kissed the top of her head, and she could feel his mood lifting like a cloud of butterflies rising. 'Well, she's here now. Just make sure you stay as close to the house as you can – no adventures further afield until we're in the clear.'

'Of course,' she said, kissing him back. 'It's not long now anyway. We only need wait until tomorrow – what's another day?'

'As long there aren't any new cases.' He folded the paper as she sat down opposite him at the long mahogany table.

'Do you think I should be checking on the miners' wives to make sure they have everything they need?' Ella asked. 'They always suffer the most, I think, and I wouldn't want anyone else to go through what we are with Grace.'

'I'm not sure I agree with you there.' He paused. 'Look, I really would rather you stayed away from them, for Toby's sake. Let me do what's needed up there, and I can update you as we go along.'

After lunch, Melody went for a lie down while Ella telephoned the hospital to find out that Grace was doing well and had settled into the ward.

'Please tell her that Mummy is sending lots of love,' she instructed the nurse. 'Do you think there is any chance we might be able to visit, at all?'

'I'm afraid not,' the nurse said. 'Seeing you might upset her, and it's not fair to the other children who are not allowed visits from their parents, either.'

'Not even a peek through the window?' Ella asked. 'Surely that can't hurt anyone?'

'No, Mrs McCain. You'll just have to wait until she's better, like all the other parents.'

She knew the nurse was right, but it annoyed her nonetheless. She decided to walk out her irritation by taking Apollo to see Johnnie's ponies, but he too seemed listless as he followed her and when they reached the stables, he curled up in a shadowy corner with a heartfelt sigh.

'I know.' She stroked his head. 'Nothing feels right, today, does it?'

When she got home, Melody was sitting on the verandah overlooking the rose garden, drinking tea. She had brought out a sketch book and some watercolours with her and was already at work with them. Ella had always admired her ability to set up camp anywhere, just like a nomad.

'It is lovely here,' Melody said, putting her sketch book on her lap. 'It can get so hot in Ipoh, even with the monsoon, but here it's that much cooler. I do envy you.'

'There are times when I really miss Ipoh.' Ella fiddled with the edge of her sleeve. 'And when the monsoon comes, it has such a detrimental effect on the mine. It worries me so. Last year we had a terrible flood. I ought to be up there now, checking that everything is safe for the miners' families, but with this outbreak, Johnnie won't let me.' She made a face. 'I usually run over the accounts at this time of year, too.'

Melody tapped her pencil on her sketch book.

'I've been thinking . . . Why don't we have a break down on the coast? I don't have to meet Edward in Singapore – he could get the train back to Ipoh when he's finished there. A few days by the sea could be just what you need.'

'No. I couldn't. I need to be near Grace.'

'But I thought they wouldn't let you see her – it could be for a good month, you know.' Melody picked up her pencil and started to sketch again.

'You could always stay here instead. I don't know how you dare drive all that way on your own. Doesn't it scare you?' Ella asked. 'Not just the roadblocks, but all these rumours about the Japanese?'

Melody lifted her head. 'I've never had trouble before and I don't think about it all that much. I suppose I should, but I can't see these pathetic attacks continuing, can you?'

'I hope not. But shouldn't you hire a driver or a guard, just in case?'

'I'll be fine.'

Ella pinched her lips and didn't say any more. Melody had always been lucky and far too independent for her own good. One day, Ella was certain, her friend wouldn't get away with it – no one's luck could last that long.

At six, they changed for dinner. Ella put on a red silk dress and a pair of diamond earrings that Johnnie had given her for her birthday. Melody wore a vivid iris-blue dress, and they met outside for cocktails. Farid had lit tea lights and arranged them along the edge of the verandah between the citronella mosquito coils, and he'd brought the chick blinds down to shield them from the blinding light of the setting sun.

Ella and Melody sat down on rattan chairs that faced across the lawn towards the hills; the peaks had turned golden in the reflected light of the sun. On the horizon, flashes of light exploded. Another electrical storm, Ella thought, that would precede the imminent monsoon. She'd learnt over the years to look for the signs: the dip in the heat, the overwhelming humidity followed by a picking up of the wind that invaded the villa like an unwelcome guest, banging doors and rustling curtains, finally followed by the sudden downpour that could last for weeks.

Farid returned with a tray of Gin Fizzes. Ella took a glass and handed it to Melody then another for herself. Melody lit a cigarette and they sat and enjoyed the view. The sun was an intense orange with a fainter halo and bled veins of pink, orange and yellow into the troubled sky. A clock chimed in the house and Apollo crept onto the verandah before curling up at Ella's feet and resting his head on her lap. She patted his head, wondering if he was missing Grace as much as she was.

Ella looked at her watch. 'Johnnie should be back by now. I can't think where he is.' She nodded at Melody's glass. 'How about another while we wait?'

Thunder rumbled. Then again.

'It's getting more regular every night,' she mused. 'Any minute now, I expect to hear the downpour.'

'I suppose I ought to leave before the rains begin in case the roads are flooded.'

Ella pictured the rivulets that would obstruct them, causing landslides and goodness knows what. She didn't think Melody was at all wise to be driving alone and made a mental note to speak to Johnnie about it – either to find her a driver or to persuade her to go to Singapore by train.

And just as she thought of him, she heard his footsteps ringing across the tiles in the villa, his voice as he asked Farid where she and Melody were, then a moment later he joined them. She smiled to see him, but quickly noted that his face was clouded with concern.

'Everything all right?' she asked.

'No. Not really. Another worker's baby has just died,' he said, flopping into a chair. 'He was four months old – imagine, Toby's age. Their other child had gone down with it, too.'

'That's awful,' Ella said.

'Poor things,' Melody echoed.

'I've asked Dr Gibbins to come back – I don't know how we can contain it,' Johnnie said. 'It's pretty much touch and go right now.' He gave them both a warning look. 'Please don't go too far from the house until we know this situation is under control.'

None of them felt much like eating and only picked at the food Noor had prepared for them. It was a shame, Ella thought, as the cook had made such an effort, decorating the dishes of rice and curries with hibiscus flowers and vegetables that had been sculpted to look like petals. The only thing any of them had been enthusiastic about were the bowls of *ice kachang*, the bean-and-sago pudding that Ella knew Melody loved.

'How about playing us something on the piano?' she asked Johnnie when they had eaten what they could.

He shook his head. 'Sorry, darling, I'm not in the mood tonight. Besides, there are a couple of things I need to finish off in my study.'

He poured himself a whisky from the drinks cabinet.

'Ladies, may I offer you one?'

Ella shook her head and Melody also declined.

'Right. I'll see you later.'

Ella listened to his footsteps retreating then turned her attention to her friend.

'How about a game of cards?'

'If you insist. But you always beat me.'

They played for the next hour: rummy, briscola, piquet – all the old games her father had taught her, and which Ella easily won.

'You know, I think I might just have an early night,' Melody said with a yawn. 'I've got such a headache forming.'

'Poor you. I've aspirin somewhere if you want one.' Ella was used to the headaches that the pressure of the air created when a storm was imminent.

Around midnight, rain began to hammer on the villa's roof. Ella crept out of bed. As sheets of lightning lit up the sky, she watched water pouring off the roof and the jungle shivering and shimmering under the onslaught, while thunder exploded like bombs overhead.

The following morning, the air was cooler and mist hung over the valley as clouds formed ready to lift and fill the sky with more rain. Ella shivered, her skin covered in goosebumps as she searched the greyness in vain for any sign of blue.

Chapter Five

The following day, there were two more cases of diphtheria. Ella looked out from an upstairs window; in the distance there was a fire. She could see plumes of smoke and assumed that clothing and bedding were being burnt. She watched the thin trail of smoke and listened to the sound of crackling until she heard the cries of a woman. It sickened her, guessing that this must be the mother of the child who had died. She longed to go out and comfort her, but Johnnie's warning and fear for Toby's and her own safety kept Ella indoors.

As she watched, she heard footsteps behind her. It was Melody.

'Hello, you,' Melody said. 'Terrible, isn't it?'

Ella nodded her head. 'I can't bear it. I keep wondering what if Grace or Toby . . .'

'Don't even think about it.' Melody's arm was around her shoulders. 'It really does no good dwelling on things like that.' Her tone was sharp, and it startled Ella; Melody was usually light-hearted, a party girl really, rarely so firm.

'Those poor children.' Melody nodded in the direction of the fire. 'They weren't as lucky as Grace, I know, but Johnnie has done all he can to help them. Worrying won't bring any of them back or make Grace better.'

'I know it won't.' Ella paused. Although she had initially been hopeful that the outbreak would stop soon, now she feared that it wouldn't. Melody's company had been the perfect distraction over the past few days, but Ella was certain she'd go mad if she sat here much longer, watching the situation worsen when she should be helping.

'I really wish you weren't going tomorrow,' she said, turning away from the window. Now that the rains had started in earnest, Melody had decided to set off before the monsoon proper set in. 'It's been such a relief to have your company. I really do wish I could come with you.'

'I don't understand what's stopping you. Think about it – Toby would love the beach, all that sand to play in.'

'Oh, Melody. I can't simply pack up and run away. What happens if there's a change in Grace's condition or a terrible outbreak here? You know, you always were a temptress.' Ella laughed. 'But the answer's no. Come on.' She linked arms with her friend. 'We've only got today left, so let's make the most of it.'

They went downstairs together. Although Ella made light-hearted conversation, Melody's suggestion had stirred a desire within her. Melody always had that effect on her: the need to let her hair down and literally run barefoot along the sand. The more she tried to dismiss the idea of going away for a few days, the more the longing within her grew.

All that day, Ella's mind kept straying back to Melody's invitation. As they sat on the verandah batting away mosquitoes, her thoughts kept returning to the idea of the gentle breezes on beaches she'd visited in the past. As they ate *nasi goreng* for lunch, she remembered the fresh prawns and crabs she'd eaten on the beach with Johnnie on one of their weekends away before the children were born. While Toby cried in the afternoon, miserable with prickly heat, she thought of the cooling water and gentle sea breezes that would soothe his irritated skin. She pictured the rock pools where he could splash in the shallows, his body healing from the incessant itching heat, and her longing to get away grew and blossomed. But then she thought of Grace, lying miles away in an unknown hospital bed. She could not abandon her daughter . . . and felt torn all over again.

The afternoon sun cast long shadows across the lawn while she and Melody sat on the verandah playing with Toby.

'It won't be long before he's crawling now, I guess.' Melody sat back on her knees and stretched out her arms to him. 'Come on, Toby, come to Auntie Melody.'

He beamed and stretched his arms towards her.

'You love children, don't you?' Ella asked.

'Absolutely,' Melody cooed. 'I'm going to miss him when I'm gone.'

Ella wondered again why Melody and Edward hadn't any children of their own. Her thoughts turned to Edward then and her friend's plans to join him.

'I still don't think you should travel alone,' Ella said. 'When Malik and I returned from Ipoh recently, there were roadblocks everywhere. Don't you worry about the rebels – people like us are such obvious targets?'

Melody lifted her head. 'Sometimes, but call me stubborn, I'm not going to let anything stop me doing what I want.'

'And what if the Japanese invade – don't you worry that it might happen?'

Melody shrugged as she played peekaboo with Toby. 'I don't think they will. They don't have the resources to start with and where would they land? Not Singapore or the east coast, not when the monsoon gets to full pelt, and certainly not the west coast. You need to stop worrying – we're well defended.'

Ella pressed her thumb and forefinger to the bridge of her nose. Now it was her turn to have a headache forming, and she could feel it pulsing in her temples. Melody was right. All this worrying wasn't going to solve anything. As she watched Melody blowing on Toby's tummy and listened to his squeals of delight, she wished once again that her friend weren't leaving.

That evening, as she lay in bed with Johnnie, the emptiness Grace had left seemed darker and deeper. It threatened to engulf Ella, and she knew she had to resist; the prospect of going away for a few days might just be the answer.

'I wish Melody weren't going tomorrow.' Ella nestled into her husband. 'She asked me to spend some time down on the coast with her. Suggested Toby might enjoy it too. Can you believe it? She can be so reckless and headstrong at times.'

'No.' Johnnie pulled her close to him and kissed her on top of her head. 'I can't. But I guess that makes two of you who are reckless and headstrong.'

'Honestly, you never let an opportunity pass, do you?' Ella shifted her arm and rested it on his chest. 'Did you know that she and Edward have a little beach hut down near Lumut?'

'Toby might love it there. Do you want to go?'

'I don't know.' She pressed her lips together as she thought. 'Part of me does, and part of me doesn't. I'm scared about Grace. What if something happened and I wasn't here? It would be very negligent of me.'

'I don't think you need worry about that. I'm here, and it wouldn't take you too long to get back.'

'But I worry about the journey. There are so many road-blocks these days. Malik said that the KMM have recruited many more supporters recently. What if there were an ambush?'

'There's no more risk of that than on any other journey. You could be attacked on your way down to Menglembu just as easily.'

'I suppose.'

'If you wanted to go, you could always take Malik with you.'

'It would be nice. Oh, I really don't know. Perhaps I should sleep on it?'

'I would go if I were you. Make hay and all that.'

'I'd miss you, you know.'

'And I you.' Johnnie slid one arm around her and drew her close. They kissed and embraced, her head resting on his chest. He stroked her hair, then his kisses grew stronger and she responded with a passion she hadn't realised she felt. After they had made love, she ran her finger over his profile, which she could just make out in the dim light.

'I love you, Johnnie, so very much.'

'I love you, too.' He drew her closer to him and after a

time they lay together, coupled like two spoons. 'You make me feel like the luckiest man alive.'

'Well, you are,' she laughed.

After a time, the pattern of his breathing changed and she too began to doze and to dream, but her dream was unsettling and mysterious.

It was as though she were entering a dark room or a cave, and as she walked, she noticed the silhouette of something walking just behind her. Fear washed through her as she tried to fathom what it might be; she couldn't tell whether it was something to be frightened of, or whether it was something good. In the darkness, she heard voices chanting and realised that there were people gathered around a fire singing, but was surprised to discover that they were attached by long chains to a wall. She could see their shadows dancing behind them – she wanted to reach out and touch them, free them, but as she raised her hand a burst of light filled the cave and a hole appeared in the wall behind them. The world of darkness was suddenly filled with the most exquisite light, and she knew that the presence behind her was benign.

She woke, shaking and covered in sweat, and was disappointed to find that Johnnie had already risen and his space in the bed beside her was cool to the touch.

At breakfast, Ella told Melody that she'd like to join her after all.

'Oh, my goodness!' Melody hugged her. 'What do you think you can manage? Two weeks?'

'No more.'

'I'm so excited!'

'Me, too,' Ella said. 'But Johnnie insists we take Malik with us, and I'd really like to bring Lian.'

'Of course.' Melody's face showed excitement. 'But what about my car? We won't all fit in that.'

'We can take the Lagonda – leave your car here until we come back.'

'Good plan. Now, do you need me to help you pack?'

Ella asked Noor to look after Toby and told Lian to pack a few things for him. Then she and Melody gathered together Ella's belongings. Sun hats and dresses, shoes, dinner dresses, wraps for the evening, Nivea sun cream for Toby. As she and Melody went through Ella's wardrobe, the Christmas presents that she'd bought in Ipoh were revealed.

'Wow!' Melody said, opening the door of the doll's house. 'You've really gone to town.'

'I ought to wrap them up.' Ella picked up the Steiff teddy she had bought for Toby. 'But I think I might take this with us.'

'What's this?' Melody pointed to the package containing the Liszt score that Ella had bought in Ipoh.

'It's a piece of music I bought for Johnnie. I was wondering about giving it to him now.'

'Well, you know how he loves his music.'

'Yes, I think I will.' She put it to one side and continued examining the dresses on the rail before selecting several that she liked and packing them in her case.

'Right. I think that's me done. I'm just going to finish off a few things, then I should be ready.'

She collected her toiletries, then picked up the Liszt score

71

and went to her desk. She stood gazing out of the window while she thought of how soon Christmas would be upon them when she returned in two weeks' time, and how it wouldn't be so very long then before Grace was able to leave the hospital. A flash of blue flitted through the leaves of the banana tree opposite: a kingfisher – she loved watching the birds here, especially bee-eaters and golden orioles. Once she'd seen a hawk-eagle sitting in the branches opposite the villa, as bold as brass, and their eyes had connected for a few moments until the bird turned its head away disdainfully. She started to write a note to her husband.

Dearest Johnnie,

I meant to give this to you at Christmas, but I've decided to make it a leaving present instead. When I'm away from home, I'd like to think of you playing it, practising for us all to hear on our return. You can pretend that we're in another room listening, that way we won't seem so far away.

Next time I see you, I will stand next to you as you play, turning the pages. I look forward to that more than I can say.

She kissed the paper, then sealed the letter in an envelope and tucked it under the string around the package before making her way to the piano. She ran her fingers along the edge of the score, then across the keyboard, tracing the places that she knew his fingers had touched. Despite the prospect of the holiday, leaving home now made her feel hollow. The idea of him playing the piece she had bought for him, fingers dancing over the piano keys, *allegro, adagio, forte,* seemed to reflect the changing tempo of their love. She longed to watch and to listen, to feel roused by the passion she saw in him when he played.

Later, she thought. And smiled at the memory of their love-making the previous night and the prospect of their reunion.

When it was time to leave, they all congregated in the hall; everyone, that was, apart from Johnnie. Lian was waiting with Toby while Malik was loading their cases into the Lagonda. Noor hovered in the doorway to the kitchen, and Ella smiled goodbye to her.

'Where's Mr McCain?' she asked Malik.

'He says he's just coming.'

Five minutes passed, then another. The heat was rising, Toby had been settled but now he started crying – the last thing she needed when they were starting on a long journey. Melody paced outside on the verandah; the aroma of her cigarette smoke crept into the hall while Ella's impatience mounted. What on earth was keeping him? He knew that they had to get going. At last, she heard his footsteps as he entered the hall with their passports in his hand.

'I knew you'd forget them.'

'Honestly, Johnnie, we're only going down the coast,' she snapped.

'You'll need them for the roadblocks.'

'Really?' she sighed. 'Sometimes I think you don't trust me to do anything by myself.'

She noticed a nerve twitch in his cheek as she took the

documents from him and pushed them into her handbag: Johnnie hated it if she ever challenged or contradicted him in front of the servants.

'I'm sorry – it's just a bit stressful setting off with Toby. He's all restless now, not the start I'd been hoping for.'

'I'm sure it won't take too long before he falls asleep.'

'I know. But that's not the point.'

'Look, I'm sorry I flustered you,' her husband whispered as he wrapped his arms around her, 'but I'm only looking out for you. I wish you wouldn't speak to me like that in front of the servants.' His mouth brushed the top of her head.

Well,' she whispered back, 'will you stop worrying about me, then? I'm perfectly capable, and it really is unlikely that we'll be stopped.'

She pulled away and, after Johnnie had ruffled Toby's hair and kissed him goodbye, made her way to the car, but all she could hear as she concentrated on settling down inside was the sound of her heart thudding. She sat in the back, holding Toby close to her, and waited for Lian to climb in the front. Malik slammed the boot then sat down in the driver's seat, turned the ignition and double de-clutched. As the Lagonda started to move off down the drive, Ella turned to look back.

She had wanted to imagine Grace standing on the steps with Johnnie, holding his hand and wearing the red dress Ella had had made for her for Christmas, both of them laughing and waving. But the image quickly faded and she was annoyed with herself for the cross words they had exchanged on parting. It was too late now for her to do more than mouth to him, 'I'm sorry. I'll miss you.'

Johnnie waved and smiled as the car drew away and she wondered if he'd understood what she had been saying. He was always so forgiving, and she wanted to preserve that image of him forever: the deep blue of his shirt, his blond hair shining like gold, how the skin around his eyes crinkled when he smiled. Just a hint of sandalwood and tobacco made her think of him, conjuring up in an instant all that he meant to her and instantly transporting her back home.

'Oh, my goodness!' Melody said again. 'I still can't believe that you've agreed to come. You'll simply love it. There's nothing but the sea for miles, and this little fellow,' she bent to kiss Toby on the head, 'will have the time of his life.'

'I'm so glad, too.'

'There are plenty of books to read. And a gramophone – I've a load of records there that you'll simply love. You and Toby can sit on the beach while I paint.'

'I've always wanted to draw and paint. Do you remember how hopeless I was at school?'

'Thing is not to over-think it,' Melody said. 'And to focus on tonal values. I can teach you if you like?'

'I'd love to be able to paint the children.'

'Children are hard. Start with something easier. The sun and the sea are perfect, especially if you get to grips with watercolour. And then, there's all this . . .' She indicated the blue-green foliage and bright orange blooms of a strelitzia, the flower Ella always thought resembled a bird of paradise. 'There's so much colour here, it's hard not to let it fire the imagination.'

Toby fell asleep and they chatted about the plants and

trees they passed, the people selling coconuts, eggs, chickens, even old bits of newspaper, on the side of the road. Ella wondered what on earth the old paper was for. When Toby woke, they stopped at a roadside stall where they ate *nasi goreng* and papaya and drank ice-cold Tiger beer from the bottle. As they journeyed through the afternoon, the beer and the heat made Ella doze. When she woke the sky had turned vermilion. Melody had unwound the window and held a Leica in her hands.

'Love a good sunset,' she said.

'Does it take colour photographs?' Ella asked.

Melody nodded. 'It's not brilliant, but my imagination makes up for the rest. I find it useful as a reference, really.'

Toby stirred in Ella's arms. For a moment, she wondered: if she hadn't been a mother, what would she have done with her life? Melody was so lucky being an artist, so free and independent and able to follow all the whims of her heart. Then Ella felt bad for thinking that. She had the tin mine and two wonderful children, whereas Melody had none of that. But still, it would be wonderful to have something of her own; something creative. She wasn't any good at sewing or needlework, perhaps painting was the answer. Once, she'd written poetry, but now the idea of painting and drawing appealed to her more. She looked out of the window and tried to see the world as Melody did – the layers of colour, the movement of the light, the harmonious tones, the contrasts and contradictions in colour and shape.

'Do you think anyone can paint?' she asked.

Melody turned to her. 'Of course. But the question might be better phrased: can everyone paint well?'

'You know, I think I'd like to take you up on the offer of teaching me.'

'Good.'

The road began to wind downhill and a gap appeared in the coconut trees ahead, revealing a golden cove fringing a cobalt sea.

'We're nearly there,' Melody said.

Ella leant forward as they edged down towards the shore. Set a little way back from the beach she saw a single-storey bungalow with a verandah running all around the outside.

'I can't imagine anything more idyllic,' she sighed.

Malik pulled up outside the bungalow. While they got out to explore, he unpacked the car. Lian looked after Toby as Ella walked barefoot along the sand with Melody, admiring the evening light kissing the waves.

'It's wonderful,' she said. 'So peaceful.'

'It is a long way from reality, isn't it? Up along the coast,' Melody pointed ahead of her, 'there are fishermen most days. We can get fresh fish whenever we want and have a barbecue in the sand.'

When they returned to the bungalow, Lian had lit mosquito coils and tiny lanterns glowed along the verandah steps. Inside, candles and lamps flickered, illuminating a sitting room with large rattan chairs covered in blue cushions. Vast canvases that Melody must have painted hung on the walls. A telescope stood close to a large window, and there was a gramophone with a stack of records on a table set against one of the walls.

'Gosh – it's so cosy. But how do you keep it looking so nice when you're hardly ever here?'

'Oh.' Melody had found a bottle of gin and was busy sloshing some into glasses. 'One of the fishermen has a wife who lives in the nearby kampong – between them, they look after the place for me.' She handed the gin to Ella then poured another for herself. 'There's tonic somewhere – let me go and find it.'

Ella sank down into one of the chairs and her thoughts turned to Grace. It still seemed wrong to be excited about being here at the beach while her daughter was in the fever hospital, and guilt threatened to spoil the moment. When Grace was better, she decided, she'd bring her here, and that was a promise.

They spent the next few days walking along the sand or swimming in the sea. Melody taught Ella how to sketch by using landmarks to plot her drawings and squinting her eyes while lining up a pencil, to gauge distance. At first, perspective eluded her, but then it suddenly clicked. She began to draw anything she could find: shells, starfish, driftwood, palm trees on the horizon. With each exercise, she saw the world in a different light, examining the details of objects she might otherwise never have looked at twice. Her world became more tactile, tonal and connected to nature.

She began to experiment using colour – Melody had some Caran d'Ache pencils, which she washed over with water. Later, she showed Ella how to prepare paper for a watercolour, the best way to create a wash, how to layer up colours and how not to overwork her painting.

In the evenings, they'd sit on the verandah with a gin and tonic while sea breezes gently moved the gauzy blinds as they listened to the Andrews Sisters or Glen Miller. They ate jumbo prawns and pomfret fish, and when Ella went to bed, she snuggled up with Toby next to her, devouring book after book by gentle candlelight – *One, Two, Buckle My Shoe; The Power and The Glory; The Waste Land*. Eliot's poem made her want to write her own again, and she found her mind wandering back to the words she had written before she'd met Johnnie, and wished once more that she had the energy to do something creative like Melody.

As the days passed, she could feel her whole body relaxing and her worries unravelling. At the end of the day, as they sat on the verandah reading or sipping a gin and tonic on the beach, she could hear the thunder of waves as the sea reclaimed the shore. However much the shoreline changed during the day, she realised, water always returned to the same place, leaving everything clean and restored. It was as though everything in nature was predetermined; however hard you tried to fight, you had to give in to it because you simply couldn't resist what the changing tide would bring.

Chapter Six

Noor swept the kitchen floor with forceful strokes. It had been several days since Mrs McCain had left with Mrs Fielding, and even longer since Grace had been taken to the hospital. How could Mrs McCain go away like that when her daughter was so sick? she thought. There was no way she would do it herself if she had a child; she'd stay by their side, refusing to move until they got better. And as for Mr McCain . . . why he didn't call his wife back, she simply didn't know.

Noor blamed Mrs Fielding for the change in her relationship with Ella. When she and Ella were young, they were like sisters – they had even taken a blood oath and sworn to be the best of friends for the rest of their lives. They had shared everything, vowing to be there for each other during all the most important moments. But that had changed as soon as Melody – Mrs Fielding now – arrived on the scene. Once Ella had started at her school in Ipoh, there had been a change in her – she'd become aloof and dismissive of Noor, brushing away her overtures of friendship. And Noor could see that Melody was a bad influence in other ways of which she disapproved. Not only had she introduced Ella to makeup, parties and drinking when she was only sixteen, but she'd made Ella think that the servants were beneath her and laughed outright at the clothes Noor wore as being old-fashioned or, worse, said that she dressed like a peasant.

Noor could never forget or forgive Melody for taking that special place in Mrs McCain's heart and pushing her old friend aside. Suddenly, the person who had once been as close to her as anyone could be was nothing to Ella. Instead, Noor became a figure of fun, someone to mimic or tease. No one knew how much it pained her, how Noor had tried to keep up by continuing her own education as best she could: reading books and newspapers that were discarded around the house, listening to the wireless. But Ella's education and Noor's own position had made the gulf between them impossible to cross. Well, Ella might have forgotten the promise they had made each other all those years ago, but Noor hadn't. If only Melody hadn't shone so brightly, Noor's life would have been very different from the way it was now.

She stopped sweeping and leant against the broom handle. If only she could find a way to improve herself, perhaps Ella might remember that promise and then they'd be friends again. Life had changed so much when her mother had died suddenly, some rumoured from a broken heart. Her aunt had taken her in and they all lived in the kampong for several years before her aunt too had died. Then Noor had returned to the villa again, aged eighteen, appointed as cook in honour of her mother. It had been wonderful returning, at first, as she had hoped her friendship with Ella might be rekindled. When it hadn't, disappointment roiled through her once again. For now, she was stuck with being a cook and couldn't see how to escape it. At least it was the end of the day and she could forget about the drudgery for the night. There was a clay-pot chicken bubbling on the stove, and she had almost finished clearing away the remnants of Mr McCain's supper, so there wasn't much left for her to do. It wouldn't be long until she would be eating with Omar and Farid – if the houseboy chose to come along, that was. These days, after he'd closed the house for the night, he seemed to disappear to she didn't know where, and she'd found him falling asleep on duty on more than one occasion recently. She was beginning to think that he had a sweetheart.

The household was so much quieter without Lian and Malik, she reasoned, it was hardly surprising that her own thoughts became more pressing. Lian was such a distraction; she knew all the gossip and Noor missed their stolen conversations about what was happening in the village. At least Omar, her cousin, would be able to fill Noor in when he arrived this evening. Her gaze fell on the papaya she had collected this morning. Papayas always made her think of Miss Grace: how she often used to come into the kitchen for a slice or to ask for a small taste of sago pudding with a piece of papaya mixed in. Noor tutted to herself once more, picturing Ella on a beach somewhere, drinking with Mrs Fielding, while her daughter was so sick. 'Disgraceful,' she muttered as she placed the broom back in the cupboard then banged the door. 'That woman has a lot to answer for.'

At the kitchen table, she picked up a sharp knife and cut into the papaya, revealing meaty, orange flesh and small black seeds. She scraped these out and pushed them into a pile. She sliced the papaya neatly and laid the sections on a plate, then quartered a lime, her thoughts still on Mrs McCain and Grace. It was hard to stay angry with Ella for long, even though over the past years Noor had hoped in vain for the glow of their old friendship to be rekindled. Despite everything, she knew that Ella needed her, if only as a servant; after all, wasn't it Noor who had been there the night before Ella had married, and Noor who had watched over her during the sleepless nights after Grace was born? She had hoped that Ella might ask her to become Grace's nurse, but she had given that position to Lian, which had really hurt. The difference was that Lian was apologetic about it, didn't flaunt her position, and was always very appreciative of the things that Noor did for her. Although Noor had known for a while that the closeness between Ella and herself might never return and realised their relationship had developed in a different direction – as mistress and servant – she still held on to the hope that their old camaraderie might one day count for something; that Ella would at least remember it from time to time.

Noor sighed. Perhaps it was best for her to move away, find a new kitchen to work in or, with her ability to read and write, she might be able to better herself. Omar was always suggesting that she could help in the village school, teaching the children to read. 'Shouldn't you be thinking about getting married and having children of your own?' he'd said.

'Rather than wasting your life on a family to whom you don't belong.' Much as she loved Mrs McCain and Miss Grace, Omar was right, it was time to think of her own needs and future while she was young enough to change it. She'd talk to him about it – he knew everyone and everything so he might be able to find a new position for her.

She decided to listen to the wireless as the chicken simmered on the stove. Old Mrs Ferguson had given it to her, and as the only servant who owned one, it had become her habit to relate the news to the other servants while they ate their evening meal. Lately, she had heard more about the progress of the war in Europe and how it seemed to be creeping like a thief in the darkness closer to Malayan shores. Only this morning, before she had taken Mr McCain's newspaper through to him at breakfast, she had read how the Chinese guerrillas in Malaya had joined forces with the Malayan Communist Party. She had been puzzling all day about why they would do such a thing.

As she listened to the wireless, she heard footsteps outside. She lifted her head and turned to face the kitchen doorway. It was Omar arriving.

'Hello,' she said. 'You're early. Look at you, you're wet. Has it been raining?'

Omar's clothes were damp from the light rain. He inclined his head in greeting and took his *songkok* off his head, folded it and placed it in his pocket. Noor wiped her hands on a cloth, switched off the wireless and smiled as he approached the table.

'How are you?' she asked. 'You look tired.'

'Well, you know,' he said. 'There's so much to organise.'

'There'd be less if you weren't so involved with the party,' she teased. 'You need a wife to look after you properly, to keep you in line.'

'That's the last thing I need.' A frown flickered over his face. 'Especially now. Have you heard the latest?'

'You mean, how the Communist Party are joining forces with the Chinese. So, it's true?'

'Yes.' Omar pushed a piece of papaya left on the table with his finger. 'And in turn, they will join forces with the British Military Alliance against the Japanese. Our leader Lai Teck is rumoured to be in Singapore even as we speak, to negotiate an alliance with the British military.'

'Oh.' Noor swept the papaya debris destined for the compost pile onto a tin plate. 'But I thought you wanted Malaya to be free from British rule. How does allying the MCP with the communist rebels *and* the British achieve that?'

'You're right,' he said. 'But although I'm a nationalist through and through, and I want the British to hand back control to Malaya just like others in the party do . . .' he looked her straight in the eye as he continued '. . . if the Japanese invade, which is looking increasingly likely, I have a horrible feeling that instead of freeing us from the British, they'll send all our natural resources back to Japan. I for one don't want to make their emperor richer. So, I'll ally myself with the British forces if I have to. Once the Japanese are defeated, we can think again about taking back power.'

'The situation is getting complicated, isn't it?' Noor moved to the sink and rinsed her hands before returning to the table. 'Do you really think the Japanese will invade?'

Omar shrugged. 'Whatever happens, Noor, my advice to you is to be prepared and to look out for yourself. If you need me, remember, I'm always here.'

'I know.' Noor nodded. He hadn't always been though, she remembered. It was only after her mother died that Omar's mother and he had come into her life. Noor had been thirteen when her aunt had arrived on the doorstep, offering to take her in. Before that, she'd hardly known them, but she was glad to be embraced by them as close family. That was until her aunt had died, and now it was only the two of them left.

She went to the clay pot where the chicken was cooking and released the aroma of garlic as she lifted the lid and dipped a spoon in to taste the sauce. 'It's ready. Shall we wait for Farid or make a start?'

Farid was always unpredictable but this evening it was as though he had heard his name being spoken because just as she put the lid back down on the pot, he tapped on the door and came in, bringing a gust of air and the hint of rain with him.

'I see the rain has picked up. Just the three of us tonight,' she said. 'I made some clay-pot chicken. I hope you're hungry.'

Farid sat down next to Omar, and Noor served the chicken out of the steaming pot. It was tender and the sauce was thick with aromatic and sticky rice. Although it was traditional for women to eat after the men, she had long ago told them all that if they wanted any food, they'd have to get used to her eating with them. The other servants had grown accustomed to it, and they would share news and conversation as they ate their evening meal together.

'Been out again, have we, Farid?' she asked. She turned to Omar. 'He is so secretive these days. I think he must have a girlfriend.'

But Farid didn't blush as she had expected. Instead, his gaze fell to the table before he looked back at her, his expression stony. 'I haven't got a sweetheart.'

'So where do you go all the time?' she asked as she spooned out chicken for him into a bowl.

'Just out. It's none of your business really, but if you must know, I've been meeting with friends. People who know what's really happening in this country.'

'Such as what?'

He picked up a spoon and tapped it on the tabletop. 'They say that Japanese planes have been sighted near Singapore and it won't be long before they land here.'

'Who are these people?' Noor glanced at Omar then back at Farid. 'Are you mixing with Mr and Mr Yamamoto in the village? I told you to be careful, everyone thinks they could be spies.'

'Why are you so anti them?' His voice rose. 'I don't understand it. They're good people. But if the Japanese invaded, it wouldn't be such a bad thing, would it? They'd liberate us from the British. It's only then that Malaya, that Asia, can be united and strong again.' He leant forward, the spoon still gripped in his hand. 'Just think how prosperous we could all be if we kept the wealth from tin mines and rubber plantations for ourselves. The Japanese will make Asia strong again – Asia for Asians, right? That's what they've been saying. I really don't understand why you don't support them.'

Omar gave a gentle cough to clear his throat, then said, 'I agree that we must get rid of the British stranglehold on us. But allying ourselves with the Japanese isn't necessarily the answer. I think the wiser course is to do exactly what we're doing – the MCP and the communists join forces with each other and the British. The British forces don't have the expertise to navigate through the jungle and fight the Japanese the way the guerrillas can. It's in this way that we can defeat the Japanese and then the British will owe us and respect us, and in due course they will give us more power.'

'Do you really believe that?' Farid glared at them both.

'Come on, Farid.' Noor had finished serving and picked up her own spoon to eat. 'I don't know what to think,' she said. 'The Japanese don't have a good record, do they? Remember what happened in Manchuria, how they murdered all those poor people who trusted them?' She thought about the huge numbers of women who'd been raped and shuddered at the memory of similar outrages when the Japanese had invaded China. 'The Chinese thought the Japanese could help them shake off the American sanctions, but look what happened. You can't trust them, Farid. Once they're here, it doesn't bear thinking what might happen next. Surely Omar's way is better?'

Farid's face flushed pink. 'But they'll never do it,

don't you see? The British don't care about anyone but themselves.'

Noor pursed her lips. She could understand both arguments. 'I don't think it's the right course of action,' she said, turning to Farid, 'to remove the British at any cost – think what could happen to Mr and Mrs McCain and their family if the Japanese invaded. It's too risky to ally ourselves with them.'

'It might be too late to avoid it,' Farid snapped at her. 'Everyone says there are Japanese ships off the coast. When you take that into account and the sighting of planes close to Singapore, my guess is that any day now, something significant is going to happen.'

'How do you know all this?' Noor tried to catch his eye. A sense of unease crept over her.

'I don't think it will come to that,' Omar put in. 'The Japanese really don't have a chance of landing here with the British army on full alert. It's monsoon season, too,' he added. 'They'd be fools to invade now.'

'But what if they do, Omar? What should I do then?' Noor asked.

'Well,' he placed both elbows on the table, 'if they do, Noor, you must leave this place at once and hide up in the hills for safety. There will be plenty of people up there with you – the jungle hides everything – and there are many caves that MCP members know about and no one else does.'

'What about you, Farid? What will you do?'

But he didn't answer. Instead, he dug his spoon into his rice, staring at something only he could see on the table, and she wondered if he would ally himself with the Japanese; if he was capable of being a traitor.

Silence fell between them, and she listened to the rain pounding against the window. Then a flash of lightning cut across it, making her jump. For the first time, a Japanese invasion seemed a distinct possibility and she wished, yet again, that Mrs McCain would hurry up and come back for Grace.

Chapter Seven

Ella woke early. The monsoon seemed imminent and there was a restless charge to the air, making her skin prickle with heat. She got up and poured herself a glass of water, then went out to the verandah where she sat in the darkness, listening to the nightjars singing and waves crashing on the shore.

Around seven, a semi-circular disc of orange appeared across the horizon, then the sky filled with red as the sun's rays spread into the void above the sea. In the distance, she noticed fishermen pushing their boats away from the shore; six small and brightly-coloured vessels with their bows curving upwards like the trunk of an elephant.

The sunrise was always so swift and sudden. She remembered Johnnie once telling her how Malayan sunsets were very different from British ones: those were slow, he'd said, and lingering, and sometimes you didn't see them at all. She found it hard to picture a place where the sun didn't rise and set like it did in Malaya, or those long winter months he described with snow and cold along with biting rain. No wonder her father had settled in the tropics, although before he had died he'd started to get homesick for Europe and had promised to take her to see the temples and theatres of

Athens, Delphi and Olympia; the Colosseum, Uffizi Gallery, St Mark's Square, Paris in the springtime – a promise he had not been able to fulfil. As she'd never been to Europe, she wondered if she'd ever see those sights now.

Instinctively, her fingers reached for the space next to her where she could imagine Johnnie sitting. An ache formed in the pit of her stomach; just a week and then she could hold him, hear his voice and his comforting words. She would show him her paintings and imagined his pleasure as she laid them out on the table for him to admire. And then, at last, he'd play for her. She would stand by the piano as he played Liszt's *Liebesträume* for her, watching his fingers dance across the keys while she rested her hand on his shoulder, feeling the softness of his breathing and the rise and fall of his chest.

The sun climbed higher and birdsong filled the air – she listened: pigeons kept company with a cuckoo, while gulls screeched out at sea. A troop of monkeys crept along the boundary where the jungle met the sand. One of them turned and looked at an oystercatcher before scurrying away to join its family.

And now, with her newly awakened painter's eye, she longed to capture this moment. She saw for the first time a spectrum of colours she had never noticed before: the bands of red and orange at the horizon; prisms of pink and yellow that the sun threw across the sky; light reflected by the water in tones of blue, grey, green, silver. A curlew flew across the waves, dipping its beak momentarily in the water before heading back to land.

After a time, she could hear stirring in the beach hut,

followed by Lian's voice as she spoke gently to Toby, who was cooing. She went inside. Lian was sitting on a chair with the baby on her lap, giving him his morning milk.

'Good morning, madam.'

'Good morning, Lian.' Ella raised her arms towards her son and Lian stood up and let her sit in her chair, with Toby on her lap.

'Would you like to have breakfast on the beach this morning?' Ella jiggled Toby, who ignored her, focusing on his bottle of milk instead. 'What about it, Lian? A picnic perhaps? Can you pack some *roti* and *sambal*? We could have papaya, too. Why don't you go and get everything ready while I get dressed?'

She placed Toby on her bed while she pulled on her bathing-suit and dragged a sundress over the top, then undressed her baby and rubbed Nivea everywhere that she thought the sun might burn. She scribbled a note to Melody explaining that she had headed off to the beach. As an afterthought, she threw a sketch pad and some pencils into the rucksack where she kept Toby's toys: a bucket and spade, and a rubber-ring that she'd need to blow up.

Thirty minutes later, they had set up camp in the small cove they liked to frequent. She sat down, noting that their footprints were the only ones on the fresh sand. This was what she liked the most about the coast; the freshness of a morning beach that was a clean slate. No one else had as yet passed over it, the day's history had still to be written. By the end of today, the sand would be marked with the comings and goings of all those who had crossed it; moments in time that would soon be washed away by the incoming tide so that the whole process could start anew the next morning.

She placed Toby on a blanket in a patch of shade and pulled out his toys while Lian unpacked her bags and spread out their picnic. Then she gathered pieces of driftwood to make a fire. Ella helped her place a circle of stones in the sand, then Lian made a pyramid of sticks before striking a match and blowing gently on the flame to encourage the wood to kindle.

Once the flames caught, Lian placed a small pan on the fire. After a time, she was able to heat the *roti*. When they had warmed through, the women sat on the rug with Toby, eating the *roti* or dipping their fingers into a bowl of dhal, before nibbling slices of papaya that Lian had brought in a bag, and drinking warm coffee from a flask.

When they had finished, Ella leant with her back against a coconut tree and watched the fishermen she had seen earlier. They were way out on the water and she could only just see them casting nets or hauling them in. She knew that they'd be out all day but wondered how far they would travel and what they would capture in their nets.

'Perhaps we should see if they catch any crab – what do you think, Lian?'

The nursemaid nodded as she tidied away their break-fast. Ella gazed out towards the boats once more.

'It's hard not to like the sea, isn't it, Lian?'

'Yes, madam.'

'But you don't swim?'

'No, madam.'

Ella noticed the flush of pink on Lian's face.

'Do you ever want to try?'

'Oh, no! So cold! I much prefer walking on the edge. Finding shells. When I was small, my grandmother used to walk along beside the sea with me. She looked for anything the water washed up – fish sometimes. Once we found shark's teeth, other times small pieces of glass or shoes, but I always prefer to search for shells. One day, my grandmother made me a bracelet from mollusc shells. They're very small. Tiny.' Lian held up her hand, crooking her index finger and thumb a quarter of an inch apart. 'It was my favourite thing.'

'That's a lovely memory.' Ella dug her fingers into the sand. 'Why don't you go down and search for shells now? I'll sit here with Toby. Here, take his bucket.'

Lian smiled, and Ella watched her making her way to the surfline then bending down to pick up shells and examine them. Some she tossed away, others she placed in the toy bucket.

Toby lay on his back on the blanket. Ella took out her sketch book and, with quick movements, traced out what lay ahead of her: the line of the ocean, the curve of Lian's back as she sifted through shells, a cormorant striding through the waves. When she'd finished, she chose a selection of coloured pencils, matching the hues of the waves and the sand as best she could.

Time slipped away. Toby fell asleep and Lian edged along the waterline, the breeze tugging gently at her skirt. Ella pressed her lips together as she focused on her work, then in the distance saw a figure moving towards them. It was Melody, waving her arms at Ella.

Ella smiled and waved back. She glanced at her watch: ten o'clock – Melody certainly had the ability to sleep. She packed away her pencils and sketch book, made sure Toby was still covered by shade then leant back against the coconut tree as she waited for her friend to arrive.

But as Melody drew closer her pace quickened, and Ella could see lines of worry etched across her face. She stood. Could there have been a message from Johnnie? Was it Grace?

'What is it?' she called. 'What's happened?'

'Oh, Ella!' Melody shouted. 'The most awful thing. You'll never believe it.'

The hairs on the back of Ella's neck prickled and fear struck a chill down her spine as she tried to make sense of the words Melody was uttering.

'I've just been listening to the wireless. Last night, Japanese soldiers landed on the beach close to Kota Bharu. There's been horrendous fighting – bloody awful casualties on both sides.'

'Jesus Christ!'

'I know. But that's not all. Around the same time, Japanese warships bombed the American navy's ships and base in Pearl Harbor. Hundreds, if not thousands, of people have lost their lives.'

Ella listened, trying to compute the information.

'I'm not sure I fully understand.'

'Oh, Ella, it's dreadful. America has declared war against the Japanese.'

'Bloody hell! Really?'

Melody nodded. 'I can't believe it, can you?'

Ella shook her head. 'No. It's not possible, surely?'

'Come on. Let's go back to the bungalow and listen to the wireless to find out what's what.'

Ella beckoned to the nursemaid, who was still collecting shells. 'Lian,' she called, 'come here.'

She raised her head and returned to them as Ella and Melody gathered up belongings from the beach.

'Lian,' Ella said when she was close. 'There's some dreadful news – the Japanese have invaded at Kota Bharu. We're going back to the bungalow to find out exactly what's happening now.'

Lian's hands flew to her face.

'I know.' Ella placed a hand on her arm. 'It's unbelievable. They've also attacked America, bombing Hawaii.'

'America?'

'Yes.' Ella lifted Toby from the blanket and settled him on her hip. 'Come on. We'll find out more from the wireless.'

They walked back, their feet heavy as they trudged across the sand. When they approached the hut, Malik appeared by the front door, frowning.

'You heard, madam?'

'Indeed. It's very, very bad news.'

Outside, they discarded their belongings, then gathered in the house as Melody tuned the wireless. Ella settled on a rattan sofa, Lian on the floor with Toby, and Malik stood behind them, leaning against the door jamb. Ella drew her legs up and wrapped her arms around her knees as she listened to the wireless crackling into life and, finally, the newsreader's voice.

'Just after midnight last night, Japanese naval ships landed off the coast of Kota Bharu, leading to a ferocious battle with the British Indian Army. Heavy losses have been reported on both sides. Simultaneously, a vicious attack was launched against the American naval bases in Pearl Harbor. President Roosevelt has responded to this unprovoked attack by saying:

' "Yesterday, a date which will live in infamy, the United States of America was suddenly and deliberately attacked by naval and air forces of the Empire of Japan . . . No matter how long it may take us to overcome this premeditated invasion, the American people in their righteous might will win through to absolute victory – so help us God." '

No one spoke for a moment, but then a dog barked in the distance, breaking the silence.

'So, what now?'

'I don't know.' Melody switched off the wireless. 'But it sounds like they damn well mean business.'

'Surely it's not so bad here. The army should be able to repel them without much effort.'

'True. But America—'

'The goalposts have certainly shifted. But I'm sure we don't need to panic yet.'

'What do you say to going into the kampong to see if we can get some more information and supplies?' Melody nibbled her thumb nail. 'We could go to the hotel and telephone Eddie and Johnnie at the same time.'

Ella nodded. 'Yes. Good idea.'

'Right.' Melody stood up. 'I'll get ready, then we can set off.'

The newsreader's words kept playing over in Ella's mind as she waited. It was unbelievable. The war that was ravaging Europe seemed very much closer to them now, and it terrified her.

No one spoke as the car wound through the jungle tracks, but as they passed women walking along to market, men cycling or leaning against the walls of houses chatting, it seemed impossible to believe that on the other side of the peninsula the enemy had landed. It was far away, Ella reasoned, and the army so well prepared that there was no doubt in her mind that this was a simple skirmish and the Japanese would be defeated before the day was out.

'Malik?' Melody leant forward and pointed to a stand selling newspapers. 'Can you pull over here?'

He nodded and parked the car. Ella followed Melody, who was already picking up a copy of the *Malay Tribune* from a stand.

IT'S WAR! the headlines screamed.

Ella's stomach turned as Melody dropped a few cents into the hawker's hand then spread the paper over the Lagonda's bonnet so she could share the news with the rest of them.

As she stood next to her friend, Ella's eyes scanned the page.

'"Just after midnight,"' Melody read aloud so that everyone could hear, '"Japanese ships had been spotted by fishermen off the coast of Kota Bharu. Indian and British soldiers fought them, but despite their resistance, a bloody battle ensued with heavy losses on both sides. It has been impossible to maintain the airport runway at Kota Bharu, which has now been evacuated. A working runway, along with recently stocked stores of petrol and bombs, is simply waiting for the Japanese, who it is believed are heading that way."'

'Bloody hell.' Melody lifted her head, the shock visible on her face. 'And if that does happen, then there is a chance Malaya will fall.'

Chapter Eight

'Look, there's no need to panic,' Johnnie said as Ella clutched the receiver. The air in the telephone cubicle was stale: it smelt of cigarette smoke mingled with sweat, and there was no fan to cool the perspiration that slithered down her spine.

'But don't you think we should come home?'

'There's no point. It will be over before it's even started. And what about Melody? She's not going to want to come back all this way if she's planning on getting to Singapore.'

'There's always the train.' Ella twisted the telephone cable around her index finger. 'We could take her to the station.'

'Like I said, I don't think there's any need. Stay put for now. Carry on with your holiday. I honestly believe this will blow over in a couple of days and then you'll have cut short your trip for nothing.'

His words didn't convince her. 'What if it doesn't, though? Melody thinks the Japanese are heading for the airports. That if they capture them, they'll bring their planes right in. What then?'

'They won't do it.' Johnnie's voice was firm. 'We have three times as many soldiers as they do, to start with.'

'But isn't it a possibility?' Now she held the receiver with both hands, as though it would bring him closer to her. 'If the truth be told, I'm frightened.'

There was a pause and she pictured him trailing his finger or a pen over the blotter before him on the desk.

'Darling, they're over on the east coast. If they do invade further, it will be days before they manage it. I can't see them attempting to, really. Honestly, it's best if you two stay put. But if the situation did deteriorate, I suppose I could come and get you, perhaps even head off to Singapore. I'd bring Melody's car.'

'And what about Grace?' Ella whispered, her heart racing.

'I'd pick her up on my way. The more I think about it, this makes the best sense. Stay where you are for now, we can assess the situation later.'

Relief washed through her.

'I suppose it would be better to head for Singapore if the situation got worse.'

'I guess. But, darling, you really do need to stop worrying about it. If for one moment I thought there was the slightest danger, I'd let you know. Now promise me that you'll stop worrying?'

'I'll try, but I wish I'd never come away. I feel as though I've abandoned Grace.'

'That's no way to think, love.'

'It's hard not to.' The thought of her daughter lying ill in a hospital bed miles away made something catch in Ella's throat when she spoke.

'Come on, sweetheart, you're meant to be enjoying yourself.'

'I know.'

'Call me again tomorrow?'

Ella hung up and sat in the cubicle, mulling over their conversation. Was Johnnie right; were they panicking for no good reason? The Japanese were miles away and the British army would most certainly repel them. Everyone was saying that there was no way Malaya would fall to the Japanese, and perhaps she should listen instead of worrying.

'What did he say?' Melody asked when Ella joined her in the hotel lobby.

'To stop worrying. But it's hard not to. Now that the Americans have joined the war, the scale of it has suddenly escalated massively. I'm sorry.' Ella gave Melody what she hoped was a reassuring smile. 'You must be worried about your relatives back home.'

'I don't know anyone out in Hawaii.' Her face fell. 'But it's awful to think about all those poor people who've been killed.'

'Come on.' Ella tucked her arm under Melody's. 'There's no point on dwelling on it too much.'

Her friend nodded, but they were both subdued when they returned to the beach armed with books and newspapers. They lay on the sand, reading or chatting, but despite the brightness of the day, their mood was downcast.

'I really can't concentrate on this book.' Ella closed the pages of *Maigret in Exile* and sat up. 'I know it's ridiculous but all I can think about is Grace in hospital, Johnnie miles away, and Japanese soldiers creeping through the jungle to murder us in our beds.'

Melody raised her head and looked at her, shielding her eyes from the sun with one hand. 'Or those poor people in Hawaii. One minute they're living and breathing, the next . . .'

'Don't.' Ella arched her back and shuddered. 'You know, it just doesn't feel right for us to be here, pretending nothing's happened.'

'Do you want to go home?' Melody lowered her hand and fixed her gaze on Ella.

'If I'm honest, yes.'

'And I'd really like to get to Singapore to be with Edward.' Melody glanced at her watch. 'It's too late to do anything now, but we could pack up tonight and set out first thing?'

'I don't think I'll have any peace of mind until I do.'

'I'll get the train from Ipoh and make my way to Singapore by rail.'

'I guess in that case, we have a plan.' Ella sat up, wrapped her arms around her knees and watched the waves rushing onto the shore from the endless ocean. The unpredictable body of water always fascinated her; you didn't know what it hid or where it might lead you. Sometimes, with its storms and waves, it was as powerful and destructive as a monster, while at others it was calm, a giver of life, a way to connect with foreign lands and adventures. Right now, it could be hiding the enemy or it could be their best means of escape, and that thought unsettled her.

She sighed then looked at Melody.

'Shall we go and pack?'

Melody nodded and gathered up her book and sunhat.

Together they walked back to the hut, their footprints sinking deep into the sand.

Later, they sat on the verandah watching the sun go down. Golden-orange and red light bled across the horizon and spilt into the silver waves, staining them like blood. Although she had experienced it many times, this evening, when the daylight suddenly disappeared and they were wrapped in darkness, unease churned through Ella as she viewed the shadowy forms around them in a new and malevolent light.

The following morning, they left just after dawn.

'Well, that's it then.' Melody slipped the key into her bag and got into the back of the car with Ella.

'Everyone got everything?'

'I think so.' Ella clutched Toby to her, inhaling his powdery scent as she kissed the top of his head.

'It's a long journey, but if we can manage a couple of hours, we can stop for a breather in one of the kampongs, then after that halt for a late lunch. Does that sound fine to you?'

'Absolutely.' Ella nodded, but the heat in the car was already overpowering and she wondered how long they'd last before everyone demanded a break.

Malik tuned the radio and found a local station that played American music. For half an hour or so, they sang along to Billie Holiday, The Andrews Sisters and Duke Ellington. Ella clapped Toby's hands in time to the beat and he gurgled with pleasure before falling asleep on her lap.

Halfway through 'Boogie Woogie Bugle Boy', a voice interrupted the music.

'*This is a news bulletin,*' said the announcer '*Reports are* coming in that the military aerodromes at Alor Setar, Sungei Patani and Butterworth have been badly hit by Japanese dive bombers. Elsewhere, we have reports that the British squadrons at Kuantan have been withdrawn to Singapore. There will be further announcements on the hour.'

'Jesus,' Melody said.

A chill settled over Ella. 'Won't that leave the east coast wide open to attack? Who the hell's in charge round here?'

Melody raised an eyebrow. 'But surely it's a good sign. The army wouldn't leave somewhere like that exposed if they thought there were any risk of attack.'

'It's better that the planes are in Singapore,' Malik said. 'To stop any attack before it reaches here.'

Ella bit her lip. This was worrying. 'But it hasn't stopped them taking over the airports, has it?'

They travelled on for another mile or so, discussing how best to stop the Japanese if they did decide to carry out more attacks, but then the Lagonda came to a halt as smoke spewed from the bonnet.

'Malik? What on earth's happening?'

'I don't know, madam.'

'For Christ's sake. That's all we need,' Melody groaned.

Malik got out and lifted the bonnet, an expression of concern on his face.

'Oh, God. I can't believe this.' Ella opened the door and joined him. Smoke was gushing out and there was a terrible smell, a cross between rubber and metal burning.

'What is it?'

'Maybe the gasket.'

'Can you fix it?'

He shook his head. 'No, madam.'

'So, what are we going to do?'

Malik glanced up and down the road. 'Wait for help. Then we will take the car somewhere to get it fixed. Maybe you'd better wait over there.' He pointed to a large oil palm close by. 'Until someone stops.'

They placed a sarong on the ground and sat in the shade of the palm; the ground was prickly with ants and ancient leaves that had fallen and turned crisp and brown. Toby started to cry, his face now pink from the heat and stained with his tears. Melody tapped the cloth with her fingers, looked at her watch and tapped the ground again. Ella wiped sweat and tears from her son's face with the edge of the sarong, while Malik tinkered below the bonnet of the car. He touched something in the still-hot engine and cursed.

The sun inched higher in the sky. Ella collected a bottle of water from the car and helped Toby drink, then took a glug herself before handing the bottle to Melody. Lian had wandered off and was poking about on the ground beneath a king coconut tree looking for fallen coconuts to split.

At last, something moved far down the shimmering road. Ella squinted to make out that it was a truck carrying watermelons. She watched as it drew closer. A moment later, Malik flagged it down. The truck slowed and Malik walked across to the open window. Ella watched as he spoke to the driver and tried to listen to what they were saying.

Malik came back to them, his skin glistening from the blistering sun.

'He says he can give me a lift to the next village, then I can get someone to collect the car. You can come with us, but you'll have to sit in the back of the truck.'

'What, with all those watermelons?' Melody said.

Malik shrugged.

'Looks like we have no choice.' Ella brushed off an ant that was crawling up her leg. 'You can stay here if you like, but I'm going in that truck with Malik. Lian?' she called. 'Are you ready?'

They grabbed a few essentials before locking the Lagonda. Malik climbed over the scorching sides of the truck before helping the women scramble over the watermelons, where they made themselves as comfortable as they could. The driver set off, bumping along the pot-holed road.

'At least there's a breeze,' Melody said as she leant against the side of the truck. 'And we can always crack open a watermelon if we feel like it.'

'They're not the most comfortable thing to sit on, are they?' Ella winced as they hit another bump. 'What do you think, Toby? Do you like your ride in a pile of watermelons?'

Eventually, they arrived in the outskirts of a small town. Everyone they passed stopped and stared with amusement or curiosity at Malik and the women in the truck. At last, they stopped outside a hut where a hawker was selling pineapples and mangoes, hot spicy chai and *laksa*. Malik helped them all scramble down.

'Christ, I feel black and blue.' Melody grimaced as she rubbed her legs and stretched out her arms.

'So, what's the plan?' Ella asked Malik.

'The driver is going to take me to a garage. Then maybe we can get the car towed and repaired later. It could take all day.'

'Well, in that case, shall we wait here and you can let us know?'

'Yes, madam. I'm sorry, but I think this is the best place for you.'

Ella nodded. 'Well, just get it sorted as quickly as you can and then we can head off again.'

They sat at a rickety wooden table underneath a canopy of woven palm leaves. Ella watched the truck disappear in a cloud of dust.

'I hope he won't be long,' she said, as the palms rustled overhead.

'I could kill a beer,' Melody said. 'I'm absolutely parched.'

'But it's only eleven.'

'I don't damn well care after the morning we've had.'

'Well, in that case . . .' Ella flopped down on a chair and ordered two Tiger beers and a mango juice for Lian.

They sipped from the bottles as they watched a farmer driving a team of oxen along the street. Lian jiggled Toby on her lap as she attempted to feed him bits of banana.

Half an hour passed. Then another hour. The sun had reached its highest point when the heat was inescapable. Ella looked at her watch.

'Shall we eat something?'

Melody nodded. 'And another beer wouldn't go amiss.'

They ordered bowls of *laksa* from the hawker. As they ate their spicy bowls of chicken soup laced with coconut, a maroon Ford De Luxe pulled up. The car was rammed with suitcases, and they noticed tennis racquets and a teddy bear stuffed in amongst the chaos.

The doors opened and a man and a woman followed by two children got out.

'Afternoon.' The man touched the brim of his Panama hat as he sat down at a neighbouring table while the woman gave them a nervous smile. Ella and Melody smiled back.

'What's the food like?' the woman asked.

'It's good, actually,' Ella said.

The man nodded at his wife and she and the children sat down. He took off his Panama and placed it on a chair next to him. His eyes met Ella's.

'I'm Jim Blackstock and this is my wife, Lindsey. On your way south, too?' he asked.

'No. Back north.'

'Really?' Lindsey's pale blue eyes widened as she stared at Ella. Her face was dominated by a long thin nose; her skin was pale, almost translucent, and dusted with freckles. 'But haven't you heard?' A pink tinge flushed her cheeks as she spoke.

'That we're at war?' Melody joined in the conversation. 'Of course. We thought we'd get back to Ipoh to find out what the situation is there.'

'I can tell you that,' Jim said. 'Everyone's packing up and leaving. No one in their right mind would go anywhere near that place.'

'There are roadblocks being set up everywhere,' Lindsey added. 'Everyone's being advised to head to Singapore.'

'I don't suppose you've heard the latest?' Jim interrupted.

'No.' Ella glanced at Melody who was focusing on Jim's face.

'About the *Prince of Wales* and the *Repulse*?' he continued.

'Go on.' Ella glanced at Melody, anticipating more bad news.

'Torpedoed in the South China Sea – over eight hundred men lost.'

'Shoot!' Melody whistled.

'That's unbelievable.' Ella shook her head as she tried to picture it.

'It's worse than that. It's a bloody catastrophe. And now there are no British or Allied naval ships in the entire Indian Ocean or the Pacific. There's no holding back the Japs.' Jim dabbed his forehead with a handkerchief. 'I hope you don't mind my saying, but you'd be fools to go back north – word is that the Japs are trying to make it to Penang. Head south – you can follow us if you like.'

Fear took hold of Ella. It rose from deep within her core and radiated throughout her body like cold, making the hairs on her arms prickle. The Blackstocks' prediction of victory for the Japanese had to be wrong, but surely even if Jim was right about their advance, there would still be time to go back to Menglembu and collect Grace and Johnnie? She glanced at Melody for reassurance, but she was taking a cigarette out of her case and listening intently to Jim Blackstock as she lit it. Ella shook her head, her whole body trembling.

'I don't know what to say,' Melody said. 'My husband's in Singapore, but Ella's is still in Ipoh.'

'I doubt he'll be there for long – look, take my advice, carry on south as soon as you can before the roads are flooded with refugees.'

'And they will be,' Lindsey broke in. 'People are really panicking. It won't be long before they're choc-a-bloc with cars.'

'Petrol's hard enough to get now, as it is,' Jim interrupted. 'Imagine what it will be like when there's a stream of people escaping. Get ahead of the game, I would, if I were you.'

Ella glanced at Melody who was rolling her cigarette between her fingers; her features were screened by the smoke, and it was hard for Ella to work out what she was thinking.

'I can't do that,' Ella said, a lump forming in her throat. 'There's no way I can go south. I must go back to Ipoh. You see, my daughter's in an isolation hospital there. I can't possibly leave her. I need to make sure she's safe.'

'Oh, you poor thing.' Lindsey's voice softened. 'But your husband's with her, right?'

'Yes.'

'So, he'll bring her with him.'

'Yes, I suppose, but I'm her mother. She needs me. I have to go and get her.'

Panic seized her. Ella glanced from Lindsey's face to Melody's. Tears forming in her eyes, she wondered if there was any way the Blackstocks could take Melody with them, but their car was so crammed it didn't look possible.

'Well, if you change your mind, you really should head for Singapore,' Lindsey said. 'Before there's nowhere left to stay there.' She sighed. 'Well, I suppose that's that. And I suppose we'd better eat. Never know what you'll find on the open road.'

Ella pushed her bowl of noodles away and leant her elbows on the table, digging the heels of her hands into her forehead. 'This is a nightmare, a bloody nightmare.' She glanced up at Melody, who was leaning back in her chair observing the Blackstock children chasing each other underneath a patch of coconut trees. 'What the hell am I meant to do?'

'I don't know.' Melody shrugged. Her gaze was distant, as though focusing on something just out of her line of vision. 'But we're not going anywhere until that damn car is fixed.'

'I knew I should never have come away,' Ella said. 'I should never have left Grace when she was so ill in hospital. Please, we have to get back as quickly as we can. There must still be time.'

Melody shook her head. 'I don't know. I think heading north is a bad plan. Besides, I'd like to join Eddie as quickly as I can.'

They sat for a few moments. Ella's thoughts swung in all directions. True, Johnnie was still at the villa, he could collect Grace and meet them where they were now, then they could make plans for what to do next. But what about Melody? If she headed off south, Ella would be alone. Thank God she had Toby with her. And Malik. If they could get the car fixed, then they could either take Melody to the nearest train station or she could squeeze in with the Blackstocks and head off home. Perhaps that was the best thing. She glanced at Melody.

'You might think this is a daft idea, but why don't you get a lift with the Blackstocks? It would be a squash, but you could pick the train up in KL or somewhere.'

Melody pursed her lips, then said, 'No. Don't be dumb. I'm staying with you.'

'You don't have to.'

'Of course I do. It's my fault you're here in the first place. I can't abandon you.'

There was a hint of exasperation in her voice. Ella decided not to push things. She was grateful Melody was staying but couldn't guess what she was thinking – and yet she had made no suggestion about heading straight for home.

'Good.' Ella nodded. 'I'm glad.'

When the Blackstocks had finished eating, Jim settled up with the hawker who was sitting in the shade of his hut.

'I do hope you decide to go to Singapore,' Lindsey said as she stood up to leave. 'You've got the little one to think about, too.' She indicated Toby with a nod of her head.

When the Blackstocks had finally piled back into their car and driven off, Melody placed her hand on Ella's wrist and squeezed it.

'Everyone seems to know everyone else's business better than their own, don't they? Listen, whatever happens, we need to stick together. They seemed the worrying kind to me, especially the wife. The situation probably isn't as bad as they think it is. When the car is fixed, we can decide what to do. Let's fix one problem at a time, hey?'

Ella nodded, but uncertainty, fear and guilt still churned within her. She got up and took Toby from Lian – as she held

114

him, she kissed the top of his head, squeezing his little body as close as she possibly could to her own.

The sun had shifted further west and longer shadows started to form when Ella spotted Malik walking along the dusty street. Ella's spirits lifted a little, but as he drew near, he raised his head and there was something in his expression that worried her.

'What is it, Malik?' she asked.

'Madam, they cannot make the car better today, maybe tomorrow. I am very sorry, but we are going to have to stay in Sungai a little longer.'

Chapter Nine

A combination of dust, sweat and tiredness made Ella want to cry with exasperation, and Melody's look of despair didn't help.

'Excuse me,' she called to the hawker who was sweeping watermelon skins and coconut shells into a pile. 'Is there a hotel nearby?'

'*Ya*.' He indicated left with a nod of his head. 'Ten minutes' walk up the main street.'

Ella paid, then they all gathered up their belongings and trudged along the scorching road. Ella's head was pounding from the heat and the beer, and the dust from the pavement seemed to have slipped under her clothes and into her eyes. The hotel was tucked away from the main street; a low, timber-framed building with a small garden where a pair of banana trees supported a hammock. She wondered if they had made a mistake.

'This can't be it – it looks like someone's house.'

Melody strode ahead of Ella. 'As long as it's got room for us, I don't bloody care.'

Once inside, they quickly agreed with the owner that they'd take the last available room while Lian would have to sleep in the servants' quarters at the back.

'What about you, Malik?'

'I can stay with garage owner,' he insisted. 'You're best not to worry about me. I will find you in the morning.'

Ella and Melody followed the owner to their room. The sheets were clean and white, but the space was tiny and, along with the drawer Ella had to use for Toby's makeshift cot, she and Melody were soon falling over each other.

Ella flopped down on the bed with her son. A sour smell escaped from his nappy. She hoped that Lian had put some clean ones and clothing for him in the bag. As she bent down and reached across to drag it to the side of the bed, her heart sank when she realised her own clothes were still in the Lagonda.

Melody had opened the window and stood looking into the courtyard.

'You should have gone with the Blackstocks,' Ella said, rummaging in the bag.

'We are where we are.' Melody sighed. 'At least the room is quiet. And hopefully it will only be for one night.'

'And it's not too hot.' Ella glanced above her at the lilting fan.

'I don't know what I want first,' Melody said, still staring down at the courtyard below. 'A large gin, a cigarette or a bath.'

'Perhaps you should have all three. But I must do something about Toby.' Ella lifted him to her and sniffed his bottom. 'I haven't got a clue what I'm supposed to do with his dirty nappies, though.'

Melody faced her. She looked smaller. Diminished.

Although she knew she wasn't to blame for the situation, guilt tugged at Ella's conscience.

'Really, why don't you have a soak in the bath?' Ella lowered her voice, hoping it might soothe her friend. 'I can try and wash Toby in the sink over there. Perhaps we can have a drink after or explore the rest of this town?'

Melody nodded and took a towel off the bed. 'Do you mind? It might make me feel more human again.'

'I noticed the bathroom at the end of the corridor when we came up. Take as long as you like.'

Melody left, closing the door behind her. Ella listened to her footsteps fading along the corridor. Was her friend really resigned to their fate or did she have a plan forming, one that she'd articulate to Ella on her return? There was no way of telling. After all the years they'd known each other at school and shared a dorm or a room, she'd learnt that when Melody went silent like this, it was best to leave her alone until she was ready to talk. But right now, despite her tiredness, Ella wanted to talk. She needed certainty, and she didn't want to be left alone in this empty room, a bleak reminder of all the comforts of home and her family who were all too far away.

Toby gurgled in her arms. She stroked the down on his head.

'Right, little man, let's get you clean.'

She laid him on the bed. In the bag there were towelling nappies folded ready for use, a set of Toby-sized clean shorts and a T-shirt. She took them out and placed them on the bed next to him, then spread out one of the towels on the bed before running water in the sink, testing it with her elbow to make sure it wasn't too hot, undressing him and removing his soiled nappy.

'Here we go.' She picked him up and cradled him close to her as she carried him to the sink. There was a bar of Coal Tar soap on the side, and after she had placed him in the water, she carefully washed him, marvelling once again at the softness of baby skin, the folds of flesh on his arms and his delicate toes, how something so precious and perfect could exist in such a terrible world. He gurgled as he splashed in the water, then lifted his face to her and smiled.

When he was clean, she wrapped him in a towel and kissed his forehead. Johnnie and Grace might be miles away, but soon they would all be together again. It wasn't the end of the world, yet, and she persuaded herself that nothing worse could happen.

She dressed Toby and sat with him on the bed playing Round and Round the Garden, and he squealed afresh every time she tickled him under the arm.

The door clicked open. Melody had returned, wrapped in a towel with her cheeks glowing pink and another towel around her hair.

'I thought you might be longer.' Ella blew on Toby's tummy as she spoke. He squealed again, drawing up his legs in delight.

'Couldn't keep awake.' Melody sat on the bed, unwrapped the towel from her head and rubbed her hair to dry it. 'I think I need forty winks.'

Ella picked up Toby and sat him on her lap.

'I'll let you sleep if you like. I need to find Lian, or at least

discover what to do with these nappies. Then I thought I'd
see if we can find some clothes to buy. All mine are in the car
and I thought anything fresh would be better than nothing.'

Melody was brushing her hair. Water dripped onto the
floor with every stroke.

'If you like but I don't know what you'll find around here.
We could have a drink when you get back.' She put the brush
down and ran her fingers through her hair, shaking the residual water out.

'I'll look anyway.' Ella picked Toby up, hitching him onto
her hip as she gathered up her wallet and sunglasses along
with the dirty nappy that she'd placed in a small bag. 'I'll
see you in a bit.'

She walked along the corridor. From behind the closed
doors, she could hear the murmur of other people's voices,
and when she reached the foyer, the owner was explaining
to an English couple that there were no more rooms left. The
exodus had begun just as Jim Blackstock had predicted it
would and another wave of fear took hold, one that she tried
hard to push away.

Ella caught sight of Lian, who was sitting outside chatting
with a group of maids. They squatted on their haunches and
one of them was tracing something in the dust as she spoke.
Ella watched for a moment, but Lian lifted her head and saw
her. She stood and took the nappy bag Ella was holding.

'I need to get some provisions,' Ella said, putting on a
brave face. 'Some clothes, really. Can you carry Toby? We left
his pushchair in the car. I'd like you to come with me to look.'

'Yes, madam.' Lian disappeared for a moment to get rid

of the nappy, then returned and gathered Toby in her arms and the two women walked in the direction of where Ella hoped there might be some shops. If she could find an *abaya* or two, the robes would do as long, loose-fitting dresses. Even wearing a long skirt would be better than the grubby shirt and slacks she was in now.

Perspiration slithered down her throat and back, sticking her shirt to her skin. The sun had cracked her lips and her throat was as dry as desert sand. Men were smoking or chewing betel-nuts as they stood and chatted in the doorways of shops, their teeth and lips stained red. Scattered along the road were fish traps. Fishermen recently returned from the sea were cleaning their catch ready to sell. She wished she'd brought a hat to shield her face as their curious eyes followed her. Thank goodness she had Lian with her, although the girl was walking too slowly, as though something were troubling her.

'Is everything all right, Lian, you seem very quiet?'

'The other maids tell me things that make me worry. They say the Japanese soldiers are everywhere now – in the jungle. Maybe soon they'll attack Ipoh, then also Penang.'

'I'm sure they won't, Lian. People always tend to panic.' She paused, wondering if she was saying this more for herself than for Lian. 'But there's something else, isn't there?'

Lian nodded. 'I'm very frightened, madam. I'm here and I worry about my family.'

Ella realised that after all the time she'd known the nursemaid, she had never asked her about her relatives or where they lived.

'Are they in Ipoh?' she asked.

'Some,' she said. 'My parents live in Penang.'

'And you're scared for them?'

Lian nodded again.

'I'm sure you don't need to worry, Lian. Penang isn't even on the mainland. And it's a garrison. I can't imagine the Japanese will be able to do any harm there.'

But Lian's face crumpled. 'I'm sorry, madam,' she sobbed. 'I don't know what's best I do. It's better I'm with you, but also I want to be with my mother and father.'

'Oh, Lian. Please. I'm sure you really don't need to worry.' Ella placed her hand on the girl's shoulder. The truth was, she didn't know what to do for the best either; one minute everything was fine, the next the world seemed to be falling apart. It really was so unsettling, the way the pendulum swung continually between doubt and fear.

'Look,' Ella said. 'We're all tired right now and we've had a difficult day. We'll probably just laugh at all of this tomorrow.'

Lian nodded and wiped her nose with her sleeve. Ella handed her a handkerchief. As she waited for Lian to gather herself, she noticed a shop selling Chinese porcelain and next to it a shop with *pua kumbu*s, the traditional woven blankets that she loved. Brightly coloured sarongs hung from a rail outside.

'Lian, look! There's a fabric shop there. Let's see what they have. I'll get you something new, shall I? I think we all need something to cheer us up.'

A small woman in her late forties dressed in a brown

abaya appeared from the shadows at the back of the shop and beckoned to them to enter. There was so much inside – bolts and bolts of *batik* and Ella fingered the fabric, noting the quality of the pattern on both sides; the exquisite gold *songket* brocade that ran through the more expensive cloth she knew would be made into sarongs or *abayas* for those with the money to show off. There were shirts made from *batik* as well as plainer *abayas* in yellow, green and pink. She turned her attention to the cheaper garments. The fabric was flimsy, but pretty: florals or geometric patterns that looked like they'd been printed rather than the more expensive hand-blocked fabrics. Ella chose a pink *abaya* for Melody, a green one for herself and traditional blue for Lian. They looked to be the same size and she guessed they were all the same fit.

She paid the shopkeeper, who folded the garments and wrapped them in a layer of tissue.

'*Terima kasih*. Thank you.' Ella took the package and she and Lian returned to the street.

'I've been thinking,' Ella said as they walked. 'You shouldn't listen too much to what the other maids say. There's a lot of gossip and uncertainty. I'm sure our chaps will sort the Japanese out.'

And then, right on cue, there was a low humming of aeroplanes overhead.

'See, I told you, Lian. Look – planes, off to fight the enemy.' They both swivelled around, and Ella could just make out three black spots heading along the coast from the south. They were small with a single propeller each. 'Thank goodness! I expect they're on their way to Butterworth airport. Can you see them, Toby? Wave like Mummy.'

They waved at the planes and Lian's face broke into a smile as she raised her hand. The shopkeeper joined them and beamed as she nodded at Ella, but then the planes flew lower and closer, and Ella's pleasure shifted to fear when she saw a large red dot painted on each side of the plane's fuselage.

'Good God!' she shouted. 'Those aren't reinforcements. They're the bloody Japanese.' She held her hand to her eyes to pick out any further details, and a moment later three more planes flew past heading north. 'Hell!' she murmured, following their line of flight. They all watched, rooted to the spot, until the planes had gone.

Her mood was lower than ever when she arrived back at the hotel. Lian returned to the maids in the servants' area. Ella found Melody sitting on the hotel verandah with a cigarette in one hand and gin and tonic in the other. The rattan chairs were bleached and worn, and the blue and yellow chintz cushions faded. On the table in front of her there was an open newspaper and a map of Malaya that she had spread out and weighed down with a packet of Lucky Strikes, a box of matches and an ashtray.

'Any luck?' She raised her head as Ella approached.

Ella nodded and placed the package of *abayas* on the table, but the pleasure of having found them had long-since diminished. She sank down into a chair opposite Melody's and placed Toby on her lap.

'Did you see the planes?' she asked.

'No.' Melody shook her head. 'But I heard them.'

'They were Japanese. On their way up north.'

'Christ.' Melody's eyes fixed on her. 'Where do you think they're going?'

Ella shrugged. 'Wherever it is, it can't be good, can it? I'm worried that it might be Penang. That makes some kind of sense, right?'

'They won't,' Melody stubbed out her cigarette. 'Surely?'

'I don't understand what they're doing. They seem to be attacking in the most random fashion – the east coast, now the west. It doesn't make any sense.'

'Well, that's reassuring then, they can't last long if they don't know what they're doing.'

'Let's hope so. Meanwhile, I think you could do with one of these gins.'

Ella couldn't sleep that night. Every sound that she heard, she imagined was another plane flying overhead. She got up before dawn and sat by the window, watching the mist rising in the distance, the rose-tinted clouds that hung like veils between the sky and the earth.

Around seven-thirty, Toby stirred. She pulled on the green *abaya* and picked him up, then crept out of the room, glancing with more than a little envy at Melody who still slept.

She made her way to the telephone cabins to speak to Johnnie, but the operator couldn't make a connection. It was, she realised, still early and he might well be asleep.

A waiter was setting up breakfast in the garden, so she sat in the lounge where a woman was sweeping bougainvillaea leaves from the painted tiles on the floor. She nodded as Ella sat down, and a moment later the waiter brought her a pot of tea. He poured it without speaking – Malay-style, from a height, making the milky liquid froth and bubble in the cup.

'*Terima kasih.*' Ella picked up the cup and he backed away as silently as he had arrived.

She was grateful for the sweet, milky tea, and sipped it with both hands cupped around the warmth radiating from the porcelain. Toby sat propped up on the floor, a bougain-villaea leaf in his hand, babbling and inspecting it as though his life depended on it.

Outside the lounge windows she watched a peacock bath-ing in the sun. In the morning light, the blues and greens of its plumage glowed like iridescent jewels, then he turned away from her and slowly fanned out his tail feathers. The beauty of the sight never failed to impress her. She listened, lost in memories for a moment, as the peacock called out a long, haunting *keow, keow, keow!*

But then the waiter returned and placed a copy of the *Malay Tribune* on the table in front of her, and what she read on the front page sent shockwaves pulsing through her.

The Japanese had launched a devastating air attack on Penang.

Chapter Ten

A shadow fell across the newspaper. It was Melody, dressed in the pink *abaya* that Ella had bought for her. She sat down in the chair opposite, and Ella slowly pushed the newspaper towards her. Her heart was racing, but she didn't speak.

'My God!' Melody read the article without lifting her head. 'This is appalling.'

'I should have guessed when I saw those planes heading north. It's unbelievable.'

Melody scrutinised the front page as though it would yield more information. The waiter arrived and hovered close to them, but Melody still didn't raise her head and so Ella waved him away. Another couple arrived on the verandah; their heads were close and their voices low as though they were sharing a secret. They glanced over at the two women then sat in a nearby corner, their voices still lowered. Ella guessed that they, too, had just heard the news.

'Well, that's it. We can't go back home now.' Melody looked up at Ella.

'But—' she started. Melody interrupted her.

'Remember what the Blackstocks said. There will be chaos everywhere. Other than the fact that there'll be roadblocks, we won't be able to get very far. As far as I can see, we have two choices. Stay here or head south to Singapore.'

'It might not be as bad as all that. We might find a way through.'

'Perhaps.' Melody lowered her voice. 'But I was thinking it out when you were shopping yesterday. Look.' She pulled the map and a pen out of her bag and spread it across the table between them. 'The Japanese landed here, right.' She pointed to Kota Bharu, and Ella nodded in response. 'Then they've moved across to Jitra, and after that they captured Alor Setar, Sungei Patani and Butterworth, here. I think they're going to move down like this.' She indicated along the east coast towards Kuantan and south towards the Perak River, sketching a pincer movement with her pen. 'If Penang completely falls, which it probably will, and the defence lines don't hold at Perak, my feeling is that they'll head down the Slim River then try to get to KL. And after that . . .'

'They'll head straight to Singapore?'

Melody nodded. 'See, all along here.' She swept the end of her pen over the east coast. 'We know that there are Japanese war ships and that the *Prince of Wales* and the *Repulse* were torpedoed, here, right? I bet the attacks will be stepping up. It's time to get to safety – perhaps we should go to Singapore before we're trapped and think about getting a passage to England before it's too late?'

Ella didn't want to believe it, but the evidence that Melody had just presented was too convincing. Nausea rose within her.

'But what about Johnnie and Grace?' Her voice cracked as she spoke.

'Darling, I know it's hard for you to hear this, but it won't be long before Ipoh is surrounded, too. If Johnnie leaves now, there's a chance he'll get out before the peninsula is completely overrun with soldiers.' Melody took her hand and squeezed it gently. 'Ella, we've got time and geographical constraints to consider. We need to head to Singapore now.'

'No.' She shook her head. 'I can't! It's impossible. I need to get back to Grace.'

'You have to, Ella, for Toby's sake if nothing else.'

Ella pursed her lips and wrestled with the impossible choice. Confusion and uncertainty rendered the decision even harder: Melody's argument was crystal-clear, but when Ella had spoken to her husband, his point of view had been so different.

'I want to try telephoning Johnnie again. I need to hear what he thinks is the best thing to do.'

She stood up and her footsteps ricocheted across the tiled floor as she headed for the telephone cabin. She focused on each tile as she walked, the vibrant blue and green mosaics that looked like trailing vines set within geometric shapes. She picked up the handset in the cabin and waited to be connected, then counted the dialling tone ring four, six, eight, ten times until at last the connection was made. When she heard Johnnie's voice, she struggled to keep at bay the tears that threatened to overwhelm her.

'Ella, is that you?' he asked. His voice caught, as though he were suppressing a cough.

'Yes.' She could picture him at his study desk, the morning light falling on his hair, the colour of his eyes, as clear and as blue as the sky at first light.

'Thank God. Have you heard?'

'It's dreadful, isn't it?'

'Unbelievable.'

He coughed again.

'You've got a cold,' she said.

'I'm fine. It's nothing. I'll shake if off soon.'

'Get Noor to make you a tisane with plenty of chilli and ginger. You need to sweat it out.'

'All right. If you think that will help. Now tell me, what are you going to do?'

'Melody thinks we should head straight to Singapore.'

'Yes.' He paused. 'I think that's a good idea. I'll get the train from Ipoh and meet you there. Where is Edward staying?'

'Somewhere near Kent Ridge. I've got it written down, hang on a minute.'

She heard him writing on a piece of paper as she gave him the address. She imagined his forehead furrowing, the way it always did when he was focusing on something.

'But, Johnnie, what about Grace?'

'I've already rung the hospital. I'll collect her later this afternoon, and then we'll be on our way. We might even be in Singapore before you.'

Her spirits lifted. This was certainly the right thing to do. In a few days they'd all be together in Singapore, and then hopefully the whole situation would blow over and it wouldn't be long before they could all be back at home in the villa again.

'And Apollo? You'll bring him, too, won't you?'

'Oh, Ella, of course I will. Everything all right your end?' He coughed again.

'You mean, apart from the car breaking down?'

'Oh, no. Is it fixed?'

'Malik is still sorting it out.'

'Well, for heaven's sake, let me know when it's done.'

'Don't worry, I will. I'll speak to you soon. And take care of that cough, won't you?'

When they'd finished talking, she pulled a handkerchief from her pocket and blew her nose, then stood up and went to find Melody.

'What did he say?

'Head to Singapore.' Ella picked up Toby. 'He's going to get the train from Ipoh with Grace and meet us there. All we need now is for the car to be fixed, otherwise we'll have to stay here another day.'

'That's if we can keep the room.' Melody glanced about her. More guests were appearing on the verandah and sitting at the tables set for breakfast. Newspapers were being read accompanied by the murmur of voices.

They decided to eat: dhal and *roti* served with frothy, milky tea and large slices of watermelon. Afterwards, they searched for Malik and Lian and found them in the hotel courtyard sitting in the shade of a king coconut tree. Ella was relieved to see that the Lagonda was there.

'Well, that's brilliant news.' Melody smiled. 'We should

settle up and check out. Get a head start before the heat of the day. It will be hours and hours before we reach even KL.'

'Malik – I didn't think the car would be ready today. This is splendid.' Ella made her way towards them. 'But we've had a change of plan. We're heading to Singapore.'

Malik glanced at Lian who gave him a slight nod. He coughed, then looked at his feet, then over Ella's shoulder.

'Madam.' He scuffed the dust with his shoe, then pulled himself up and looked her in the eye. 'I sorry to say, we have also decided to change our plans.'

'What do you mean?' Ella glanced from Lian then back to Malik. 'I'm not sure I understand.'

'Lian says after the attack on Penang, she wants to go back to find her mother and father, and I must leave you, too.' His voice was gentle, as though he were giving bad news to a child. 'You see, madam, a long time ago I joined the Malay volunteer soldiers. Now the time has come to fight – the Japanese have attacked our country and I must go and stop them.'

'Oh, Malik!' She looked at Lian, seeing now that she had been crying. 'How can you leave us when we need you most? How are we going to manage this if we're going south and you're going north?'

'Madam, I have thought about it for a long time. If the Japanese come, I must do this. I have arranged with the garage owner that he will help Lian and me get back to Penang. Here.' He placed the car keys in Ella's hand. 'My mind is made up.' The keys were heavy and still held the warmth of his hand. A moment later, he was offering her his gun. 'I also think it's best if you take this, too.'

Ella recoiled. 'No, Malik, I can't. It's yours and I wouldn't know what to do with it. Surely you'll need it more than we will?'

'Don't be so damn stupid,' Melody hissed. 'If he wants to go, let him, but take the bloody gun!'

Ella's hand wavered. Malik had always been there – her father's driver before he was hers – and as for Lian, she had been with them from the day Grace was born. Like layers of an onion, her old life was being peeled away.

She nodded and took the gun.

'Thank you, Malik. Both of you, thank you for everything you've done.'

She hugged Lian, the gun hanging like a deadweight from her hand. 'I'll miss you. I hope your parents are safe. And please, if you can, let us know you are, too.'

'Thank you, madam. I will try.'

'We'd better go now.' Malik picked up a bundle from the ground – a sarong Ella recognised as Lian's that held all her belongings.

Tears blistered her eyes as she watched Malik and Lian turn and leave. They walked out of the hotel grounds together until the dusty road and the shimmer of heat rising from the surface hid them from Ella's sight. She wanted to run after them, to order them to come with her. Not just because she was frightened of the journey, of driving a big car alone through hostile territory, of the uncertainty that roiled through her. No. It was because in that moment, she realised how rapidly life was changing and that she might never see either of them again.

In a blur, she packed up her own belongings. They had decided that Melody should drive, so she took the wheel while Ella sat in the passenger seat with Toby on her lap. As they drove, Ella kept thinking she could see Lian or Malik walking along the road, but each time they passed the figures, she realised it wasn't them and disappointment and fear flooded in.

Memories flashed through her mind of the twelve years of her marriage and her life before she'd met Johnnie. She thought of the villa and the first time he had taken her back there as his wife; the time he had spent learning how to run the tin mine with her father; the day Grace was born, her christening, their first Christmas as a family. The villa was their home. Malaya was home. Everything she knew was anchored here in Malaya, but she had a presentiment of changes to come that would be irrevocable.

Chapter Eleven

For the next two days, they took it in turns to drive. They hugged the west-coast roads towards Singapore, but the paddy fields and tea terraces passed by in a blur, and they didn't stop for long in Malacca. Under different circumstances, Ella would have loved to have lingered in the spice markets or to visit the Dutch graveyard as well as the Chinese quarter for which Malacca was famous. Instead, they grabbed *roti* from street vendors; the flatbread stuffed with eggs, onions and chicken was now a welcome staple of their diet. From time to time, they were stopped at army roadblocks, the queues and questions endless.

During the hottest parts of the day, they pulled over and rested, sometimes tying the corners of a sarong to a tree to create shade for Toby. One night, they stayed in a tea house on the fringe of the jungle. Ella was glad of the gun Malik had given to her, lying with it under her pillow as she listened to the cicadas and the trees rustling in the breeze, fearful that they disguised more sinister activity.

At last, they reached Johor Bahru: the tip of the peninsula where beyond shimmered the shoreline of Singapore that was reached by the causeway. They joined the line of dusty cars making the crossing as the sun disappeared and the sky darkened.

As they left the mainland, Ella wondered when she would ever return to her home, and prayed beyond any reasonable hope that Johnnie and Grace had made it here ahead of her on the train.

'Singapore at last,' Melody said. 'I can't believe we've done it.'

The other cars peeled away from them as they travelled on and all Ella could see was the inky silhouettes of trees flickering by and the occasional blur of lights from distant buildings.

She read the map by torchlight as she tried to make sense of their surroundings. They drove along eerily deserted roads covered by overhanging jungle and haunted by the shrieks of monkeys until the canopy of trees gave way to streets lined with houses. Eventually, they arrived at Kent Ridge and Melody stopped the car outside a three-storey building bathed in darkness.

'This must be it. Stay here for a minute while I check.' She picked up the torch before heading towards the building. Ella listened to her knocking on the door. A light came on, flooding the grounds with brightness. She heard Melody's voice, then Edward's. Ella tried to open the car door, but Toby wriggled in her arms and she was worried he'd wake. A moment later, Edward and Melody were walking down the path towards her. Tears of relief pricked Ella's eyes at the sight of Edward's tall, bulky figure. But there was no Johnnie following behind, and her heart sank.

She'd always liked Edward and his no-nonsense approach to life. He was ten years older than Melody, with a rugged charm that was reassuring; the type of man with whom you instinctively knew you would be absolutely fine. She was relieved when he opened the passenger door for her.

'I can't believe we made it,' Ella said. Her back was stiff and damp with sweat from the journey, but she didn't care. It didn't matter. They were here. They were the lucky ones.

Edward held out his arms to her and never had a hug felt so good.

'Have you heard from Johnnie at all?' she asked. 'He said he'd try to join us.'

'No. Not yet. But come in,' he said, letting her go. 'We can talk inside.'

Ella carried Toby as she followed them up the path. She could see frangipani bushes in the light from the house: sweet scent from their yellow and white star-shaped flowers flooded the humid air as she climbed the stairs to an open door.

'It's pretty basic – nurses' accommodation really – but I'm lucky enough to have two bedrooms. Ella, why don't you use this one?' Edward ran his hand through his hair as he spoke.

The room contained a small double bed with a sheet and a thin blue cotton blanket over it. A mosquito net hung from the ceiling. In one corner stood a chest of drawers with a fan and a pile of towels on top of it, plus a small basket containing soap and a bottle of shampoo. 'There's a bathroom along the corridor.'

'You're a star,' Ella said, placing Toby on the bed, where he rolled over onto his side.

'I suppose you'd both kill for a shower and some clean clothes. If you leave your washing out, the *amah* will do it in the morning,' Edward said. 'When you've had a chance to freshen up, I thought we could head out for a bite of something to eat. Somewhere along Beach Road, perhaps?'

As Ella showered all she could think of was Johnnie and Grace. Where were they? They should be here by now surely. But the trains might be too busy, she told herself, they might not have managed to get tickets yet. She kept reassuring herself that they'd arrive soon, maybe even tomorrow or the day after. Surely Johnnie wouldn't let her down.

That evening, all she could think of was her home, so many miles away. She kept wondering what lay ahead of her. For the past few hours, her only goal had been to arrive safely in Singapore, but now that she had, what on earth was going to happen next?

The following morning, before Edward and Melody were up, a telegram arrived for Ella:

STILL IN IPOH STOP TELEPHONE HOME STOP
JOHNNIE

There was a telephone in the hallway and Ella sat on a low stool with Toby on her lap as she waited for the operator to connect them, each ring of the dialling tone echoing the rapid rhythm of her breathing.

'Hello, caller, this is a collect call from Singapore, will you take it?'

'Yes.' Johnnie's voice had an unfamiliar tremor to it.

'Johnnie, why aren't you here?' she said immediately.

'Ella, I'm sorry,' he began. His voice rasped and his breathing seemed laboured.

'Johnnie, are you all right? You sound terrible.'

'I'm fine. I'll shake it off.'

'It doesn't sound like nothing. Have you seen Dr Gibbins?' Ella asked.

'He's left.'

'Oh, Johnnie.' She clutched the handset and a knot tightened in her stomach. 'Tell me that you've got Grace?'

'Yes. She's here with me.'

'Thank God. May I speak to her?'

She waited, then a moment later heard a tiny, faraway voice.

'Mummy.'

'Oh, my goodness, Grace! I'm so glad that you're home with Daddy. Are you feeling better?'

'A little bit.'

'That's good. You know that Daddy is going take you on a long journey, don't you?'

'No.' There was a trace of excitement in the child's voice. 'Where to?'

'You're coming to Singapore to meet Mummy and Toby.' She imagined Grace nodding and a smile stole across her own face. 'I can't wait to see you.'

'I can't wait to see you, too, Mummy.'

'I love you, Grace. You know that, don't you? More than anything else in the world.'

'I know, Mummy.'

'Bye for now, sweetheart. See you soon and then we can have so many hugs.'

Johnnie picked up the receiver again.

'Can't you just leave now, get someone to drive you here? Use Melody's car, for heaven's sake,' Ella insisted.

'I can't today. I'll be better tomorrow. I'll set off on the train then.'

'Promise?'

'I promise.'

'I'll wait to hear from you then.'

'I'll see you soon.'

'Look after yourself. And take good care of Grace.'

Ella put the handset down in the cradle and sat there for minutes. Her whole body felt cold, as though chilly fingers had run down her spine, and she shuddered, trying to shake off the sensation before going to the kitchen to make herself a cup of tea and warm some milk for Toby.

While she sat at the table, sipping tea, she heard a door click open and light footsteps coming towards her. It was Melody, her hair rumpled and her face still puffy with sleep.

'Morning,' she said, nodding at the pot of tea Ella had made. 'Is there enough for a second cup?'

Ella poured her one.

'Johnnie's still in Ipoh,' she said. 'I had a telegram this morning.'

'Shoot! What the hell's he up to?'

'He doesn't seem well,' Ella picked up a teaspoon, focusing on the movement of the liquid in the cup as she stirred. 'I'm worried he might have diphtheria.'

'Jesus. Surely not?' Melody sat down at the table and put her hand over Ella's. 'Are you sure it's not just a cold or something? You know what it's like when the monsoon strikes.'

Ella lifted her head. 'Maybe. I hope you're right. I suppose the only thing we can do is to wait until tomorrow and hope he's better then.'

'He will be. I'm certain of it.'

They sat for a while sipping their tea. Ella listened to the kitchen clock ticking. Eventually, Melody stood up. 'Shall I put the wireless on, see if there's any news or something cheerful to listen to?'

She fiddled with the dial on an ancient cream and brown Bakelite wireless. The handle was made from leather and humidity had eaten away at it, making it look moth-eaten and old. Ella half-watched as she toyed with Toby's fingers. He had curled up in her lap, a comforting bundle that she never wanted to let go.

The reception was poor. Melody continued to turn the dial until she found a Malay station playing music.

'This is hopeless,' she sighed. There was a packet of cigarettes next to the wireless. Melody picked it up along with the box of matches that had been resting beside it. She struck a match and Ella watched as the tobacco glowed red.

There was a crackle from the radio and a whoosh of

high-pitched vibrating sound interrupted the music, followed by a strange, highly accented male voice, speaking fast
and laughing. Ella jerked up her head and looked at Melody,
who was frowning.

'What the hell was that?'

'I don't know.'

The strange voice started speaking again. 'Hello,' it
resumed in broken English. 'Good morning, Malaya, this
is Penang calling. How do you like your bombing?' More
laugher echoed over the radio waves.

Ella froze. Melody stood perfectly still with her cigarette
unsmoked in her hand. It burnt down, leaving a long tip of
ash that fell to the kitchen floor.

'What the hell was that?' she said.

'I don't understand,' Ella said.

'Nor me.'

'Do you think it's a prank?'

'I don't know.'

The Malay station came back on air and a moment later
a newsreader announced that, after heavy bombing, Penang
had fallen to the Japanese.

Melody's face went pale. 'I don't believe it.' They both
listened hard and learnt that the whole garrison island had
been decimated, the number of casualties unknown. 'How
could that happen?' Melody asked. 'Why weren't they better
prepared?'

Ella clasped her hands together and dug her nails deep
into her palms. Lian. Malik. Where were they? Had they
managed to avoid the bombardment? And Johnnie . . . he

must surely come tomorrow with Grace; they'd get the train, wouldn't they?

The next morning, she rang the villa as soon as she woke, but her heart sank when her husband answered. He sounded terrible.

'Did you get tickets?' she demanded. 'For God's sake, why haven't you left yet?'

She held the receiver away from her ear as he started coughing.

'Tomorrow,' he said. 'We'll come tomorrow.'

'Well, make sure you damn well do.' The line began to crackle and she thought she'd lost him. 'Johnnie? Are you still there?'

'Yes. Now listen.' His voice was weak, and she could tell he was struggling to speak. 'We need to form some plans, just in case. Have you got a pen and something to write on?'

'Hang on a moment, yes.' There was a pad on the telephone table and a pen, which she picked up.

'I'm going to give you some contact details. I want you and Toby to get back to England as soon as possible. Try to get the first passage out that you can, then go to my parents – I'm coming to Singapore, but it's best to have a back-up plan. I can always meet you in England if all else fails.'

Ella balanced a piece of paper on her knee and the telephone receiver under her chin while she wrote down the address: *James and Polly McCain, Seymour House, Wood Eaton, Oxfordshire, England.*

'I'm going to wire you more money. I'm going to the bank

today to sort out our affairs. Keep it safe. We're going to need it.'

'Yes.'

'Now, about the Lagonda, Ella. Sell it. Try to get American dollars – easier to exchange than sterling.'

'But, Johnnie, you are coming, aren't you? You promised me that you were coming tomorrow.'

As she waited for him to reply, the line crackled again and went dead.

'Hello? Hello?' she called, pressing her finger down on the dial button and hoping in vain for a reconnection. There was so much she still wanted to say to him – that she was sorry about their stupid row before she left, that she loved him – he knew that, didn't he?

She sighed and put the receiver back into the cradle before she called again. But however many times she tried, to her utter despair, the operator couldn't connect them.

Chapter Twelve

There were voices in the hallway. Noor rested her ear against the crack in the door and listened. Earlier, she had heard car tyres crunching on the drive, Mr McCain shouting at Farid, footsteps thundering up and down the stairs. There had been a gunshot, followed by another, then voices she didn't recognise shouting to each other in a language she didn't understand. Instinctively, she knew these were Japanese soldiers.

Her breathing quickened as she concentrated on working out what to do; the suddenness of the enemy's arrival had shocked her. She turned away from the door and surveyed the kitchen. There was a clay pot of chicken simmering on the gas stove; a collection of kitchen knives and silver teaspoons drying on the draining board; papayas and coconuts in baskets next to the larder door where she kept large hessian sacks of rice and baskets of *kai-lan*, eggs and onions. There was also a glass jar with the odd coins she had saved from the housekeeping money that Mrs McCain had said she could keep as a bonus.

She had to run away. Omar had warned her to get to the jungle at the first sign of trouble – and this was it. In a panic, she tried to think what she should take – some provisions and a weapon would be best.

She hurried to the sink, picked up the silver cutlery and a sharp knife then rushed to the big walk-in larder. There was a large hinged and bracketed shelf set before a concealed cupboard where valuables were stowed: the best silver tea-pots and candlesticks, the silver cruets and cutlery that Mrs McCain used for best. Noor dropped down the shelf and opened the cupboard behind it. Along with the household valuables, she had hidden her savings here and with them the only photograph she had of her mother. Someone had set it in a silver frame, but she couldn't remember where that had come from. Her mother's beautiful features stared back at her as she picked up the photograph and placed it into a sarong she had grabbed from the laundry basket. She threw the knife, the cutlery, a small silver teapot, a pair of scissors and a con-tainer of rice into the pile, then tied it with a knot and lifted the sarong-bundle onto her shoulder. She was about to head out of the back door when the main kitchen door opened.

She froze. It was Mr McCain with Grace.

'Noor!' His voice was a desperate whisper as he pushed the child into the room before him. Her face looked startled and pale.

'Yes, Mr McCain?' Noor's heart was pounding like a hunted animal's, the longing to escape searing through every fibre of her body.

'Please,' he said with a panic in his voice, 'hide her for me. Whatever happens, don't let the soldiers find her.'

Noor didn't know what to do: Omar had told her to escape, but she loved Miss Grace like her own. Her gaze shifted from the child to Mr McCain, while the weight of the bundle hung as heavy as her conscience. If she hid the child here, she would have to stay with her, and then all hope of escape would be lost.

'I—'

The voices in the hall were getting louder and closer. 'Quick!' Mr McCain pushed Grace towards her. 'Noor, please,' he hissed. 'You must do whatever it takes to keep her safe. I'll remember it forever. Remember that – and you must do anything, anything at all, to protect her.'

As though sensing the danger she was in, Grace let go of her father's hand and ran to Noor. Her tiny hand slipped into Noor's, who slowly placed her bundle on the floor.

'Thank you,' Mr McCain said.

'OK. Now, Miss Grace, you'd better come this way with Noor because she's going to hide you.' She led the girl to the cupboard behind the larder shelf. 'Wait there for now, that's right, until I tell you to come out. Don't move, don't cry, and for pity's sake, don't say anything, all right?'

Grace nodded and Noor upturned a basket for her to sit on, closed the cupboard door and dragged a large hessian bag of rice in front of the shelf.

And not a moment too soon: Mr McCain had now been joined by two Japanese soldiers, who blustered into the kitchen as though they owned it.

The sight of these men sent fear stabbing through Noor as they paced about the kitchen, jabbing ingredients, pots and pans with the large swagger sticks in their hands. The taller of the two came towards her and lifted the hem of her *abaya* with his stick.

'You cook?' he asked in broken English. There was a sneer to his expression that she didn't like, but she nodded, trying not to show her distaste. 'Very good. Very good,' the soldier continued. He spat on the floor. 'You must cook for us. I see you have plenty of rice here.' He opened the larder and indicated with his stick the sack propped up against the shelf that hid Grace. 'Enough for many weeks.' He left the door open then walked to the stove and peered into the pot where the chicken was simmering. 'Chicken. Good! You give this to us to eat. Yes?'

She gave a reluctant nod.

'So, what are you waiting for?' the taller man barked at her, pushing his face into hers. His breath was sour and instinctively she stepped back, but not quickly enough. He brought his stick down on her arm with such force she thought it might break.

'Is that necessary?' Mr McCain stepped forward, but the stick came down again, this time on his arm followed by a blow to his back. Noor looked at Mr McCain, her eyes tearful with pain, but she turned and went to the larder as instructed. She scooped a bowlful of rice from the sack then poured it in to the sink where she rinsed it under the tap to wash out the starch and weevils.

Two more soldiers entered the kitchen. They shouted and opened cupboards and drawers, pushing Noor roughly as they continued their search. Her mouth went dry as she saw them approaching the larder, but she focused on rinsing the rice. To distract them, she dropped some on the floor, scattering grains everywhere. The soldiers turned and shouted at her, then one of them pulled her by the hair, indicating she should clear up the rice with her hands. She gathered up the grains, not daring to lift her head as she heard them continue to open drawers and cupboards. As they left, one of them kicked her.

When they had gone, she lifted her head to see all the cupboards and drawers were open, but worst of all, her precious wireless was gone.

She hauled herself up and crept to the open back door to see what was going on. In the distance, she saw two soldiers frog-marching Mr McCain with the barrel of a gun held to his back as they pushed him along the path. She watched with increasing fear as the soldiers pushed him towards a group of people: Farid was one of them. Some of the men had their hands tied behind their backs, while others had their feet bound. They were divided into groups: Chinese, Tamil, Malay, and then Mr McCain alone. The soldiers shouted words that she didn't have to understand to guess the meaning: 'Stand up! Walk! Over there!' Her gaze travelled towards an open-topped truck. She saw that the prisoners were being loaded onto it.

Her thoughts turned once again to the jungle and the safety that Omar had promised she would find there, but the child was still hidden and even if it meant Noor risking her own neck, she couldn't leave Grace. She was about to turn around when she noticed Farid being pulled away from the main part of the group. He attempted to speak to one of the soldiers, and she watched him waving his hands. One of the soldiers raised his arm and Noor saw the flash of a blade as a sword swished through the air.

She gasped as her hands flew over her eyes, unable to take in what she had just seen. Farid. Poor, poor, Farid. Her instincts kicked in again and she wanted to run as far away as possible, but her legs threatened to buckle beneath her and she knew that even if she did, she wouldn't be able to get very far before she turned back for Grace. Although it terrified her, she'd promised Mr McCain that she'd look after his child and that was what she was determined to do, even if it killed her.

Besides, as she made her way back into the kitchen, she realised that apart from Grace, there were many more precious things in the house that the soldiers might take, and she was damned if she was going to let them. It was bad enough that her wireless had been stolen. She would try to hide what she could before it was too late.

She opened the door to the hall and listened for voices. Nothing.

She was certain that the house was empty, so tiptoed into the hall. She froze when she heard a door bang and footsteps, but it was only Apollo, Mr McCain's dog, who was looking at her with his tail swinging.

He cocked his head to one side and sat down. She could feel him watching her as she made her way up the stairs. When she reached the landing, she stood to one side of the window and looked out. The soldiers were still there, pushing the men about. Poor Farid lay where he had fallen, and a soldier was standing next to Mr McCain with a gun pointing at his head. He pushed Mr McCain towards Farid. Noor watched as he and another man dragged the body away.

She moved past the window, then made her way to the master bedroom.

How many times had she been here as a child? It was difficult to say, but she knew the contents of the room so well. She opened the cupboard to see madam's dresses and the secret hiding places that contained her jewellery.

In a panic, she pulled out silk dresses and threw them on the bedcover. The pile grew as she added shoes, madam's emerald earrings, her pearl necklace, her diamond pendant, a jade bracelet, and finally a pair of beautiful diamond earrings. Her breathing was rapid as she ran back down the stairs and into the hall, where Apollo was now lying, his eyes following her as she made her way back to the kitchen and the larder cupboard.

She pulled aside the bag of rice then the shelf to reveal Grace. Her pupils were wide and dark. She looked like a startled mouse that had just been discovered. The girl tucked her hand into Noor's and wrapped her other arm around Noor's leg. She placed her hand on the girl's head and patted it. How could she explain to the child that it was just the two of them now?

'Miss Grace,' she said very quietly. 'Do you know what is happening?'

The child shook her head.

'These soldiers are bad men and I think they have taken your father away.'

'No, not my daddy!' Grace's voice broke and she wrapped herself more tightly around Noor's legs. Her shoulders were shaking, and Noor held her close.

'Shhh! I promised your father I'd look after you until he comes back. I'm sure it won't be long. You'll be fine.' Noor's thoughts raced: if the soldiers realised this was the master's child, they might take her too. She had, besides, heard terrible things about what the Japanese did to young women and even girls as young as this. She had to act quickly if she were to save Grace from such a terrible fate. 'But it would be better if we dressed you up as one of the servants. Maybe as a boy.'

'Why?' Grace sobbed.

'Well – it's safer for you.'

Grace continued to cry.

'Come, you need to be brave. Do you think you can do that?'

Grace nodded slowly.

'We have to be quick.' Noor spoke in a low tone as she smoothed Grace's dark curls. 'Let's get you out of this dress and—' Noor ran her fingers through the child's long hair. 'I'll need to cut this.'

Grace's hand flew to her hair. 'No!'

'Yes. Shhh! Now, sit quietly . . . there, that's it, and then you must take off this dress, I'll bury it in a pile of washing. Wear this for now,' she said, handing her a sarong and shirt from the laundry pile. 'You'll look more like a boy this way until I can find you something more suitable.' Noor could see tears forming in the child's eyes. 'Don't cry, *bayi perempuan*, baby-girl. This is for the best, honestly.'

'But I want my daddy.'

'Remember, he said you must do what Noor says is best

for you, Grace. Now I am going to be your auntie until he returns.'

Noor handed the child the sarong, which she wrapped around her waist, then cut Grace's hair, which fell to the floor like dark question marks. When she had finished, Noor brushed the fallen hair to one side with her foot, then they made their way back into the main part of the kitchen.

But standing by the stove was one of the soldiers, spooning rice from the pot into his mouth. He turned and their eyes met across the room. In that moment, Noor knew they would never be able to leave the villa now.

Chapter Thirteen

The soldier's eyes connected with hers. Noor's lids shut tight as a clam shell, but it didn't stop her from hearing him shouting. A moment later, he grabbed her by the hair and pushed her to the floor where he kicked her again and again.

She feared that her life was about to end, but the sound of rapid gunshots from the drive interrupted his assault. He spat at Noor and then at Grace, who was cowering by the larder door, before looking about him. He grabbed the ball of string that she used for trussing chickens and tied Noor's hands together behind her back then left, muttering incomprehensible words.

Noor looked at the sobbing child who stood trembling in the larder doorway.

'I'm all right, little one. It didn't hurt. Listen, *bayi perempuan*, you have to help auntie undo this string, do you understand?'

'I want *my* mummy and *my* daddy.' The girl's crying grew louder.

'No, Grace. Keep calm. You must help me before the soldier comes back. Come on, see if you can help me undo this silly string.'

Grace moved timidly towards Noor and pulled on the

string, which unravelled after a couple of tugs. After that, she curled up in Noor's lap and they sat on the floor clutching each other.

All kinds of thoughts raced through Noor's head. Should they make a run for it now? But the soldiers had seen her and after what had happened to Farid, she guessed that if the men saw them running, the odds were they'd both be killed. To protect Grace, she would have to take her chances on remaining in the villa, act as their cook as the soldier had demanded earlier. Again, she recalled the fate of the women in China, what she'd heard of the mass rapes of women and young girls, the murder and pillaging. If she were to prevent such a terrible fate from happening to Grace, it was important to keep up the pretence that she was a boy and kowtow to the Japanese, however hard it would be.

'Remember what I told you,' Noor said, stroking Grace's head. 'We'll make it a game – you can be my nephew. Have you got that?'

Grace nodded slowly.

'And if anyone asks, your name is Jaza. I know it won't be easy to do these things, but your parents will be proud of you when they know how brave you've been.'

Noor didn't know how long they sat there, sheltering from whatever terrible things were happening outside. But after a time, the soldiers returned and she could hear them shouting orders to each other. One of them came into the kitchen and Noor trembled, not knowing what was going to happen to them.

'You must stay here now.' His voice was kinder than the

other men's. 'You will cook for us. And the boy, too.' The soldier nodded in Grace's direction. 'We are hungry. There is chicken there, yes?'

Noor glanced across at the chicken that had been simmering for too long on the stove and at the pan of rice that the soldier had discarded in the sink. As she stood, pins and needles pulsed through her feet. She made her way silently to the sink. The soldier turned away and left them to it.

'I'd better do as he says before those *babis* – those pigs – return. Why don't you sit there on that stool for now?' Noor said to the girl. She fetched fresh rice from the larder and poured it into a pan without rinsing out the weevils then added just enough water to cover it. As she placed it on the stove to boil, she spat in the pan then placed the lid on top with a bang.

Next, she fetched her broom – the one with the long bristles that spread out like a fan – and swept Grace's hair into a pile. 'You have been a good girl. And very brave.' She leant on the broom handle and studied the child's tear-stained face. 'But I think it's best you don't speak to anyone unless they speak to you.' She put the severed curls in the bucket that she used for kitchen scraps and covered it with the lid. 'I'm sure it won't be long until these barbarians have gone. Just stay with me. I will tell you what to do.'

And so, over the next few days, Noor worked harder than she had ever done before: cooking meals for the half-dozen senior officers who had taken over the villa, making beds, washing sheets and clothes, cleaning rooms, all the while terrified that if she didn't do what they said, they'd beat her, rape her or, worse still, tie her in chains and leave her in the sun to die. All the while, she was listening, thinking, planning, waiting, hoping for an opportunity to escape that always seemed to elude her.

As Grace played in the yard, where she collected fallen coconuts, Noor saw that the soldiers were making the prisoners erect a high fence. It ran further than she could see, but she worked out that it must stretch around the entire perimeter of the property. The days passed, the fence grew higher, and she realised that she, too, was now a prisoner, just like the men who were constructing the fence.

Noor worried constantly about Grace. The child was still so young to cope with all this. She was just seven. Noor watched helplessly as the girl started to turn in on herself – she spoke little or not at all, and the smile had completely disappeared from her face. Her eyes seemed larger and her skin paled, although she spent so much time outside that the sun ought to be darkening her like a ripe berry.

So it surprised Noor when one day the girl tugged at her *abaya* and demanded, 'Where is Apollo?'

Noor pursed her lips. She hadn't thought about the dog, but now that Grace mentioned it, she realised that she hadn't seen the animal for several days. He always used to hang around in the house or sunbathe in the yard.

'I don't know. He's probably hiding somewhere or found his way to the stables to be with the ponies. Why don't you leave a bowl of water out for him, hey? Or some scraps of food?'

Grace nodded and filled a bowl with water from the tap,

then scooped a small handful of cooked rice that was cooling in a saucepan into another. Noor watched as Grace placed both bowls outside the door.

For the rest of the day, she kept returning to the bowls and scanning the yard. The following morning, there was still no sign of the dog, but the food had gone.

'Look!' Grace smiled as she pointed to the empty bowl. 'He's eaten it. But where is he?'

'Perhaps he is frightened of the soldiers,' Noor said. She wasn't convinced that the dog had eaten it – there were plenty of monkeys around or rats who would quickly have finished off the rice. In her opinion, the dog had either run off into the jungle or else the soldiers had shot him, but for the first time in days she spotted a glimmer of a smile on the girl's face when Apollo was mentioned and didn't have the heart to tell her what she really thought. These days, they all needed to hang on to as much hope as they could.

Noor wiped her hands on her apron and examined the contents of the larder as Grace looked for something else for the missing dog.

There was still a good amount of rice and sago, but their supplies weren't going to last forever. And there wasn't much fresh meat either. A few of the chickens from the yard had been slaughtered by the soldiers, who seemed to take delight in cutting off their heads. Yams and tamarinds grew in the garden, and Noor could always revert to using palm oil for cooking, although in her opinion it tasted disgusting. She wondered how long it would be before all the fresh food ran out.

The days were endless, but whenever she could, Noor

would slip another item of value from the house and conceal it in her hideaway or bury it in the rose garden. Although she was worried that if the soldiers found out she would get the same treatment as the decapitated chickens, the more she could hide from them, the better she felt.

At night, she and Grace slept on mats on the kitchen floor. The child found it difficult to get to sleep, but Noor told her stories about her parents and her past. She was not only trying to console her, but also wanted to keep memories of Grace's parents alive for her.

'Do you remember your fifth birthday?' she asked as they attempted to sleep one night. The mosquitoes kept them both awake and a flying cockroach kept returning through the open window. 'Your mother had bought you a pretty blue dress with a huge white sash and a doll with a matching outfit.' Grace snuggled up to Noor as she listened. 'I made you a chiffon cake with blue and yellow icing for your birthday tea. Really, I've lost count of how many people came, but we had finger sandwiches, *lompat tikam*, my special jelly dish, and there was an entertainer.'

'Tell me more.'

Noor put her arm around Grace and pulled her a little closer. 'Well, your mother looked like a real princess. She had her diamond earrings on, which caught the sunlight and sparkled like a hundred rainbows. She wore the most beautiful pale pink silk dress, and everyone must have thought she was a princess. After, your father played the piano, and everyone clapped so loudly it sounded like the thunder echoing across the jungle.'

'Even Apollo, did he clap?"

'Yes. By wagging his tail, which is the doggy way to show approval.'

Yet, as the days rolled into each other, Noor longed to creep into the kampong to see her cousin Omar. Much as she loved Grace, she needed to find out more of what was happening in Malaya. Now she had no radio or paper to tell her what was going on, and if anyone knew, it would be Omar with his web of connections throughout the peninsula.

As she went about her daily chores she thought and thought in vain for a way to escape this prison.

One morning, just as the sun had reached its hottest and the monkeys were resting in the boughs of the king coconut trees, she thought of a plan for a way to leave the villa safely. She approached a soldier called Naoki, the one who had been kindest to her, with a proposal.

'We are running out of rice – of everything really. See here?' She indicated the larder with her hand. 'What do you want me to do about it?'

'The soldiers will get it from the village this afternoon. There's no need for you to worry – we take what we want.'

'Wouldn't it better if the boy and I went to the kampong to get it? You have more important matters to attend to here. There are plenty of other things we need – things I'll see once I'm there.'

Naoki looked at Noor as though weighing up the situation. Then he nodded and glanced at his watch 'Quick, quick. I will walk you down to the kampong, then you must hurry back.'

Noor picked up her basket and gestured for Grace to join her. They walked ahead of Naoki to the high fence that now surrounded the property. They waited while he spoke to the soldier on sentry duty, who eventually let them through a small wicket gate, then Naoki led them to the village where they collected the goods Noor wanted. She didn't enjoy the process much; Naoki simply had to walk into a house or a store and the owners handed over whatever he demanded without asking for payment. The people who were formerly her friends looked at her with distrustful eyes.

Over the next few days, they repeated their expeditions in much the same fashion, but then Naoki was either too busy or else seemed to trust Noor because he told her she could go on her own.

'I'll take you to the gate, but you must make your own way to the kampong and come straight back. Otherwise . . .' He made a gesture as though cutting her throat.

When Naoki was out of sight, she scribbled a note to Omar asking him if he could think of a way to get her out of the villa. She had to get away, she hated working for the Japanese pigs, she wrote. Please, could he find a way to communicate with her? She explained how much she longed for information or news about what was happening in the country, please, please could he send a message to her?

'Jaza,' she called Grace. 'Please can you collect some duck's eggs for auntie? I'm going to take them to my cousin Omar.'

Grace did as she was asked. Noor carefully tapped the shell of one with a needle and produced a small hole. She let

the white and then the yolk slip out before she rolled up her
note and carefully pushed it inside the shell. She arranged all
the eggs in her basket and smiled to herself. No one would
be able to tell what she had done, and Omar would eventually find her note.

'Right,' she said. 'Let's go.'

Naoki walked them to the fence, and she tried to hide her
nerves. The duty soldier checked her basket then nodded
her through, allowing the two of them to walk to the kampong alone. How glorious it felt, to be free even for such a
short time, but she knew she had to be careful in case she
was being watched.

'Look!' Noor pointed to the boughs of a kempas tree. 'See
the monkeys? Nothing seems to bother them, they are as bold
and as naughty as ever.'

Grace lifted her face but didn't smile. Noor squeezed the
child's hand.

Although she tried to reassure her charge, Noor was
increasingly nervous at the sound of each footfall, the
creaking of the trees and the shadows dancing across the
path. For a moment, she was anxious about the wisdom of
this journey. What if she were being followed? Then she
would be leading the Japanese to Omar's door. That would
be the death of them all if he were having an MCP meeting
at the time. Perhaps she should turn back, but the desire to
see him was overwhelming. When at last she saw his palm-
roofed house in the kampong ahead of her and breathed
in the gentle smell of woodsmoke, she could have cried
with relief.

'Omar!' she called quietly by the door. 'Omar!' She waited until she saw his shadow precede him.

'Noor!' he said, surprise reflected in his face. 'What are you doing here?' He looked over her shoulder, checking the empty roads. His skin was a deep brown and his hooded eyelids seemed more than ever to give his face the look of an owl.

'Omar, I have brought you some duck eggs,' she said in a tone that she hoped hinted at a secret, but gave nothing away. 'They're very special. If you like them, perhaps I can bring you some more on my next visit?'

She sensed that he was puzzled, but he thanked her then took the basket, glancing around him once more before returning inside his home.

On the next visit she brought him a papaya. As she handed it to him, she felt him press something into her hand and realised that it was a piece of paper. Her heart raced as she kept it in her grasp until she could slip it into the sleeve of her *abaya*, saving it for when she could read it unobserved.

That night, when everyone including Grace was asleep, Noor got up and unfolded the letter to read Omar's news by the light of a full moon.

He told her that the Japanese were everywhere, how the peninsula was completely overrun. She learnt that many towns had fallen and the Japanese army was heading further south, possibly even to Singapore. The soldiers were unmerciful, he wrote, especially to the Chinese.

All the local Chinese who weren't taken as prisoners or who didn't escape to the jungle are dead. There is chaos everywhere,

Noor, but there are many Chinese and British soldiers hiding in the jungle ready to free us when the opportunity arises. Meanwhile, my hope is that we will be able to undermine the Japanese as best we can. I know it is terrible to work for them, my dear cousin, but it might be providential. Stay where you are and you might hear something – anything to the MCP's advantage would make a huge difference to us. Go through everything – rubbish, pockets. Listen at doorways. Any information you can find, let me know about it even if you think it's nothing. We must do all we can to get rid of the Japanese, however long it might take. My dear Noor, the soldiers are suspicious of everything, so I urge you not to continue sending me messages like this. I don't know how, but we must find another way.

When she had finished reading, the enormity of what he'd asked filled her with apprehension. As Noor burnt the letter on the stove, she chewed her lip, mulling things over. She decided that she would do it despite the terrible danger.

If she were to get more information for her cousin, she would have to find a better and more reliable way of communicating with him. Fortunately, she didn't have to wait long for the ideal opportunity to present itself.

Chapter Fourteen

Every time she tried to call Johnnie, the phone-line went dead. Had he already left? Ella wondered, biting her nails or pacing the floor. She couldn't sleep or eat for worry and still no news came, while her feelings swung from hope to desolation and back again to hope. Then the day she'd dreaded came: Ipoh was bombed, and the British army withdrew across the Perak River.

'I'm frightened,' she said as she and Melody sat in a covered area outside their building. Toby was sleeping inside, lying back on Ella's bed with his limbs splayed out, completely oblivious to anything in the world. 'I mean, really frightened.' She watched a cockroach scurry across the ground; it was huge, with large menacing pincers. 'It's been days and days now with no news. I'm beginning to think the worst.'

Melody swallowed. Ella could see the way her eyes darted away from meeting her friend's, as though making that connection would give away her true thoughts.

'You can't give up,' Melody said. 'Not yet. People are still coming across the causeway, aren't they?'

The cockroach had disappeared, and Ella wondered where it had gone so suddenly.

'All I want is some certainty.' Her hands were in her lap and she clenched her fingers together. 'If I knew they were on their way, then at least there would be hope.'

Melody turned her face towards her friend's. Her pupils were large, making the blue of her eyes look darker and more intense. 'Ella, we've really got to make some plans, you know. Edward and I were talking about it last night. If the Japanese get any closer, things could turn pretty grim.'

Ella shook her head. 'Not yet. Let's give it a few more days.'

'Fine.' Melody stood and brushed away some ants that were nibbling at her ankles and had left angry red bites. 'But you need to think about it.'

A moment of hope came when news arrived that the British had inflicted a huge defeat on the Japanese at Perak, but it proved to be a false rumour. Selangor was attacked, then KL bombed, and more and more refugees poured into Singapore by car, motorboat, freighter, cattle truck or whatever mode of transport they could find, bringing with them tales of battling through the mountain ranges in monsoon conditions as food, oil, tin and even petrol were destroyed, to keep resources out of the invading army's hands.

Christmas came and went. Ella lay in bed hugging her pillow thinking of the presents she had bought in Ipoh, all wrapped and waiting in her bedroom wardrobe. She tried to drive out images of them all sitting in the drawing room, Grace in her new red dress opening all her gifts, the carols that they'd sing at church, their Christmas dinner of roast chicken and vegetables that Noor really couldn't get right, and the games they'd play afterwards: Charades, Tiddly-winks. It felt like too much to bear.

But then KL fell completely and the last train to Singapore had left Prai and now the only way out of Malaya was by sea. Ella was desperate, phoning all the people she knew, visiting the embassy and ports, but there were still no reports of Johnnie or Grace. Rice started to run out in Singapore, then petrol. Fear-filled whispers spread over the island that turned into a wave of panic as defence line after defence line fell in Malaya and the Japanese progressed further south.

'I know that you're waiting for Johnnie but we've got to leave as soon as we can, Ella,' Edward said one morning while they drank tea in the kitchen. 'I'm going down to the quays to see if I can get us a passage home. I suggest you two get as much shopping done here as you can before there's nothing left.'

'I don't know what to do.' Ella lifted her eyes from the latest copy of the *Straits Times*, which brought more news of Japanese aircraft seen swooping over Singapore Island and strafing buildings in unrelenting waves. 'Where on earth is Johnnie? Why hasn't he contacted me?'

Her shoulders shook as she struggled to contain the tears she could no longer hold back. Melody wrapped her arms around her and kissed the top of her head.

'I don't know,' she whispered. 'All we can hope is that they'll be here any day. But Edward's right. We must think about getting away. If the Japanese arrive here, we're done for.'

'I'm going out to see what news I can get,' Edward said.

'I thought I'd head down to the Swimming Club, there's bound to be some talk down there. And then I thought I could try the ports again.'

'Well, good luck.'

Ella sat at the kitchen table for half an hour making a list of people she had known at home who might have got to Singapore and have news of Johnnie. They could be staying anywhere, she reasoned, hotels, club houses, with friends. It was an impossible task and the last time she had tried no one was interested in helping her. There were too many other incomers crowding Singapore for anyone to take much notice of a single woman with a baby in a pushchair.

But then the Japanese flew over the island, dropping bombs that hit the Alexandra Military Hospital, killing fifty staff. Planes were seen off the east coast and the bombing crept closer inland.

'I can't believe it,' Edward said, returning from the Golf Club. 'The Japanese are off the east coast close to Pulau Ubin! I've spoken to a Red Cap down at the port. Last night, the naval base around Kota Tinggi was blown up and there are fears for the causeway. He also told me that a Japanese observation balloon was spotted above Johore followed by artillery fire trying to shoot it down.'

It was as though a cold hand had touched Ella's heart.

'They're just across the causeway,' Melody said. 'It's not going to be long.'

'Not that you'd believe it from the chaos at the club,' Edward said. 'There are people drinking like billy-o. Apparently, the governor's banned the sale of alcohol from tomorrow and everyone's going mad. There was a group of Australian soldiers absolutely plastered in Orchard Road.'

'Christ!' Melody's hands flew to her face.

Her words sparked something within Ella. The days of hoping were over and as she heard another plane flying overhead and the *ack-ack-ack* of defensive gunfire, she was propelled into action. She sold the Lagonda for half its worth, annoyed with herself for not having done it before, then Melody dragged her through the street markets as in a panic they bought provisions for their journey back to England.

Like someone in a dream state, Ella bought what she thought they needed for Toby: packets of powdered milk, biscuits, coconuts and peanuts, muslin nappies. But she couldn't concentrate. With increasing desperation, she kept trying to picture Grace and Johnnie, but the images of them were fading and the more she seemed to focus, the harder it was to hold on to the details of their faces. She struggled to remember exactly how Grace's cheeks curved, how the curls of her hair fell as she brushed them. Was it the scent of lavender or jasmine that clung to her skin? And Johnnie . . . she fought to memorise the contours of his face, the line of his jaw and the shadow of stubble on his chin, though they seemed to disappear like the morning mist.

Ella's fear deepened: what if they couldn't get a passage home, or the ship was bombed at sea and all the passengers lost? And England, what was it like there? She'd heard it rained all the time, that it was constantly cold and the food was terrible. But at least Johnnie and Grace would be there soon, and for all she knew, despite her waiting and searching, she could simply have missed them. They could even be on their way back to England now. Yes, she decided, that must be it. That had to be the answer, the reason why she hadn't heard from her husband.

When she and Melody got home, Edward told them that he had managed, against all expectations, to get three passages back to England.

A crowd had formed by the gangplank. Ella moved as though in a trance as she tried to manoeuvre Toby's push-chair through the press of bodies, but it was hard with a suitcase in one hand and bags dangling from the handle of the pushchair. How could this be happening – leaving Singapore an evacuee as chaos reigned all around? It seemed like the end of everything and she tried to turn back, but Melody put a hand on her arm and shook her head.

'Think of Toby. You've got to put him first.'

Numb and hardly able to process what was happening, Ella took note of the long queue of people jostling each other on the other side of the gangplank.

'They're all trying to get a ticket at the last minute,' Melody said as she followed behind. 'Poor things, they won't have a cat in hell's chance.'

'Name?' a steward demanded of them as the queue they'd joined moved along.

'Anderson,' Edward said.

Melody looked at him, her forehead furrowed in a silent query. Really?

'They're boarding passengers alphabetically,' Edward whispered. 'I know it's an untruth, but so what?'

The steward gave his list a cursory glance. 'All right, join that line over there.' He pointed with his pen towards some people who were already boarding.

They shuffled along. The noise was unbearable. A baby was crying, people were shouting and chattering, and someone was playing a violin of all things. Nausea took hold, but then Ella heard a low humming overhead and a plane came into sight. A single sniper on a nearby roof started firing at it, but the plane dropped lower and sprayed machine-gun fire towards the waiting passengers who, almost as one, dropped to the ground as though it would help them avoid the bullets that mercifully missed them all.

'What the hell was that?'

'Bastards!'

'Can't they see there are women and children here?'

Voices from the crowd shouted up at the sky as the plane flew out of sight. Ella watched the trail of engine vapour disappear, then heard more gunshots. On the horizon she could see the black smoke of a building burning.

'Sorry, mate.' Another steward stepped in front of Edward. 'Women and children only.'

Melody froze. 'What?'

'Women and children only. I'm afraid, sir, you'll have to step aside.'

'No.' Melody shook her head, panic frozen on her face. 'You have to let him on.'

'It's all right,' Edward said. 'I'll do what he says.'

'No!' Melody's voice rose. 'I'm not going without you.'

'But, darling, you have to.' Edward wrapped his arms around her and kissed her cheek. 'If there's another way out, I'll find it.'

Melody started to cry in big sobs that came from deep within her chest. Ella felt helpless as she watched Edward hug her, then a moment later, he peeled himself away.

'I'm sure I'll get another passage.' He stroked his wife's hair. 'Another one will come up soon. But if not, I'll stay here and help. God only knows, they're going to need doctors.'

Before Melody had a chance to protest once more, he nudged her towards the steward collecting passports and tickets then turned to go. All too quickly, his figure was absorbed by the crowd.

'Come.' Ella touched Melody's arm, trying to process what had just happened. 'His mind's made up.'

Melody's shoulders were shaking as she wiped her eyes with a handkerchief and nodded. Toby was screaming and it was hard wheeling him through all the passengers, but at last they managed to get on deck.

'Where are our cabins?' Melody asked a steward. He looked at her and pointed at the lower deck where there were mattresses laid out in rows with pillows and blankets piled on them.

'You're not serious?' she said.

'Take it or leave it,' the man said curtly. 'There are plenty of others who would happily take your spot. Now, if you don't mind, get a move on, please.'

Stunned and still in shock, both Ella and Melody looked around them. The deck was getting busy but at last they found two empty mattresses near a lifeboat that was set slightly away from the bustle of people.

'At least we'll be the first ones aboard if we need it,' Melody said with a wry smile that Ella knew cost her dearly.

Ella flopped down on a mattress. How could this be happening? Despite having tried to convince herself that Johnnie and Grace had made it out to England already, she'd still clung desperately to the hope that they might somehow still appear at the quayside in the last hour. But as the minutes ticked away while she sat on the mattress clutching Toby, she knew the chances were decreasing rapidly.

Toby was still screaming and she tried to calm him by giving him a bottle of water. There were only a few inches between her mattress and Melody's and their belongings spilled onto each other's beds. Ella sat down as Toby drank and stared into the middle distance, tears pricking her eyes.

'I'm going to see if we can do better than this,' Melody said. 'I'll be back when I've sorted it out.'

While she was gone, panic seared through Ella. As she looked hazily around at her new surroundings, she watched more and more women and children piling onto the ship, hoping against all hope that she'd see one of them holding Grace's hand. Everyone was carrying suitcases and gazing around them in quiet disbelief and none of the young faces looked anything like her daughter's.

When Toby had finished drinking, she lay down with him on the mattress, curling herself around him to protect him. The mattress was damp and smelt mouldy, and she wondered how many bodies had lain on it before her and then decided not to think of it. She shut her eyes, trying to block out the sounds of everyone around her – the mothers calling to their children, babies crying, the hum of the engine and, in the distance, yet more gunfire. The ship's engine was idling. *Grace, Grace, Grace*, the rhythm of it seemed to say.

The minutes crawled past until Melody returned, flinging herself down on the neighbouring mattress.

'No bloody chance of anything better.'

Ella refocused. Melody was fuming, her face flushed and eyes filled with tears.

'It's not forever,' Ella snapped. 'And don't you think there are worse things to be worrying about?'

'But how on earth are we meant to sleep like this?' Melody looked genuinely shocked. 'Or to keep warm and dry? And where is the bathroom?'

'For Christ's sake, I don't know!' Ella's voice rose. 'And I don't bloody well care.' She couldn't bear it. All Melody cared about was own comfort, not even a second thought for Edward or the family Ella had left behind.

Ella looked at her friend with new eyes. Her face was red, the anger almost bouncing off her. In complete despair, Ella struggled to her feet. Having made a note of where they were, she stormed away. Passengers were still boarding, people milling about in all directions dragging cases or shouting to each other, children were screaming while stewards attempted to direct them to where they were meant to be as the ship's siren sounded and the gangplank was being lifted. She stumbled across the dining room, where long tables had been set up in rows with chairs squeezed in between, then to a communal toilet and washing area.

At last, she found a quiet spot and stood by the rail to look out at the harbour with Toby on her hip, feeling as though something was stopping her from breathing. The ship was pulling away from land and she found it impossible to stifle her sobs. She glanced back at the quay and at the plume of black smoke from the burning building she had noticed before. It had grown now and had been joined by several others dotted around the horizon.

How could this be happening? Regret and guilt roiled through her as she recalled her parting from Johnnie – a petty exchange of words over their passports that might well be the last memory she had of him. Her body seemed to buckle as though someone had kneed her in her solar plexus. She screamed, 'No!' But the cry was lost beneath the screams of the gulls following in the wake of the ship.

'Oh, Christ!' she sobbed. 'It's just us now, little fella.' She kissed Toby's head, her tears dripping onto his face. He lifted his fist and caught hold of the cross around her neck and pulled, trying to suck it, but the chain broke and he pulled it away from Ella's neck.

'Hey, no, don't do that.' She wiped her face with the back of her hand.

Her mother had given it to her when she had been confirmed and Ella had worn it every day since, but now as she looked out at Singapore burning, for the first time in her life she began to question not only her belief in God but her own existence. If there was a God, how could he possibly prise her family apart like this?

She took the broken chain and cross from her son and pushed them deep into her pocket.

Chapter Fifteen

At first, the journey had seemed impossible. Poisoned by guilt, Ella found it hard to get up off the mattress, let alone eat, but Toby couldn't fend for himself, and his cries forced her to rally. As the weeks dragged past, she found herself gaining strength, like a convalescent, and as she settled into a routine her grief started to become less raw.

Every morning, she would wake, wash and dress and have breakfast with Toby at one of the long tables in the dining room: porridge and egg, toast and marmalade or fruit, and bitter cups of tea with milk. After that, she joined the long queues to wash her clothes or Toby's nappies in buckets by the lavatories. Then she'd walk him around the deck in his pushchair, carving her away around mattresses or groups of women and children. When he'd fallen asleep, she rolled up her mattress and did some keep fit with Melody on the small patch of space they'd created for themselves. The other women stared at them at first. Ella wondered if it was because of the colour of her skin. Maybe they thought she was Melody's *amah* and Toby her child, and were trying to work Ella out. Eventually, though, they seemed to understand and even joined in the keep fit. After a time, there was a group of a dozen or so of them. Afterwards, they'd sit on someone's mattress in a huddle and exchange stories of life in Malaya, Singapore or even England, for those of them who had been. Ella found herself curious about the country she was going to and asked questions about the weather, the food, even about the King and Queen and the princesses. She'd learnt the King and Queen remained at Buckingham Palace while their daughters were living in greater safety at Windsor Castle. Occasionally, someone would have news from the wireless – another ship torpedoed in the Atlantic – or they'd listen together to a programme on the World Service.

One of the women in the group was a seamstress and she used to sew as they spoke. The other women began to bring items of clothing for her to repair or adapt to life in England. Occasionally they swapped books or magazines while their children chased balls or played games close by.

Melody became downcast in a way that Ella had never seen in her before. Whatever Ella did or said seemed to annoy her. But then, one day when the sun was shining over the sea, making the waves sparkle as though they were made from tiny pieces of crystal, she pulled out her paints and cartridge paper and started to sketch.

'It might help me,' she said, 'to stop thinking and to forget.'

And it seemed to do exactly that. Ella would sit near her, reading or sewing, while Melody painted, clearly glad to have something to focus on, to take her mind off the days that took so long to pass. Once or twice, Ella picked up one of Melody's sketch books, and when she had tired of sewing, tried to sketch the faces of other passengers: old women with years of living cobwebbed over their faces, children for whom every new day was an adventure. She began to look around with interest and see stories all around her. And despite the pain she carried, the art of observing fascinated her.

'You're getting to be quite good,' Melody told her. 'You should keep it up.'

'You're flattering me,' Ella said, but she was secretly pleased.

Time played tricks and it was difficult to remember which day of the week it was, but after a time they arrived in Bombay where the dying sun melted into the sea and turned the sky an orange-gold that was reflected over the low-lying hills silhouetted on the horizon.

As they passed the Gateway to India and the temples dotted along the water's edge, one of the passengers told Ella, 'We have to change ships here. I've heard the Red Cross will be there to help us. I'm worried that they aren't going to send us on to England. I've heard a rumour many of us will be sent to Australia.'

Ella was concerned by this news. All this time, she'd been banking on getting to England, but it turned out that the woman was only partially right.

'Have you got an onward address?' one of the Red Cross volunteers asked when they'd disembarked.

'Yes.' Ella handed her the piece of paper on which she'd written Edward's parents' address.

'That's good. It will help your case if you have relatives there. Do they know you're coming? If not, we can try to contact them for you.'

'Yes, they do, but I'd be grateful if you could confirm it.'

'And you have your passports with you?'

Ella handed them over. The woman examined Ella's. 'You're Malay?' she asked. 'Lucky that you have a British passport, then.'

'Half. My father was British, and my husband is, and so of course is my son.'

'Ah, I see. That explains why the baby has his own passport. Wasn't sure if you were his nanny or not. Well,' the woman snapped the passports closed and handed them back, 'in that case, we can try to get you another passage back to England, but I'm afraid it might take a while.'

Once they'd disembarked into the colour and chaos of Bombay's streets, the stalls selling cotton in every colour imaginable, they had to wait for two weeks in a small boarding house until another passage was found.

On the next ship, they were told to take blankets and warm clothing from a pile as they got on board. 'You'll be needing them,' they were told. Once again, they slept on mattresses on the deck and the days turned into weeks. At nighttime, they lay in complete darkness in case the lights on board announced their presence to the enemy. Ella had heard stories of ships that had been torpedoed and they all lived in constant fear of a similar fate.

Eventually, the weather changed and they sailed through fitful sun and storms until the air began to cool. In Gibraltar, the ship docked for a day, and she was surprised to find a mail bag had been delivered to the ship. There was an aerogramme from Johnnie's mother:

Dear Ella,

We were shocked to receive your letter, but of course you can come and stay with us for as long as you need. How awful for you – we can't imagine what you must be going through.

God willing, we will hear from Johnnie soon and you will all be reunited here.

I will try to meet you, but can you get yourself to Wood Eaton (train to Oxford then get a taxi) in case not?

We have all the details of your arrival,
Polly

As they inched through European waters, the passengers spent less time outside as the skies turned to grey, and Ella noticed the cold air starting to bite. She shivered constantly and walked around with a blanket wrapped around her, wondering what kind of world she was going to where the sky was leaden and her breath stretched ahead of her in feathery plumes. Then one day, twelve weeks after they had set off from Singapore, as she stamped her feet and rubbed her hands together for warmth under the blanket, the silhouette of a city loomed on the gloomy horizon.

'Liverpool,' Melody said. 'Welcome to England.'

Ella leant against the rail as fine misty rain soaked into her hair and clothes. She took in the scene materialising in front of her. Everywhere, there was debris and the shells of bombed-out buildings, though some still stood tall and proud.

So, this was England. No wonder her father had left and never wanted to return.

'I knew it had been bombed,' she said. 'But I hadn't realised the destruction was so terrible.'

Ella took in the scenes of demolition as the ship slowly came into the quay where it eventually docked. All around her there was movement, excited or tired voices, children shouting, babies crying, the grinding of machinery as hawsers and gangplanks fired into action. She looked at the dishevelled women she had travelled with: the faces that had lost their fullness over the past few weeks at sea, and the clothes hanging from their now-thin bodies. She realised that they were a grim reflection of how she, too, must look.

'I guess this is going to be it?' Melody hugged her as they prepared to disembark. Ella wanted to hold on to her forever, never to let go of the love and warmth that they had shared since they'd been young girls.

'When you get there, let me know, won't you?' Melody said, letting go of Ella and wiping away a tear.

'And you. Tell me when you reach London safely.'

Melody bent down and kissed Toby for one last time. He was sitting upright in his pushchair swathed in all the blankets that Ella could muster.

'Look after this little chap for me, won't you?'

'I promise.'

Passengers began to move, and the line of people soon started to filter off the gangplank and down onto the jetty where a crowd stood waiting to meet them. There were groups of Red Cross volunteers with tables stacked with blankets, coats and a variety of clothing. Others offered plates of sandwiches, big urns of tea. Behind the stands Ella spotted people holding up makeshift signs with names on them – 'Marjorie Greenwood' or 'The Bell Family'.

She shivered and rubbed her hands together, noticing how blue they were, but nothing seemed to take away the pain of the cold or the numbness in her toes. Inch by inch, people moved forward until she too reached the shore. Melody hugged her one more time and then turned her head away and was called forward, carried away by a sea of people.

Loneliness hung over Ella. Being parted was as painful as ripping off a plaster and exposed anew her lingering wounds. She pulled the blanket around her shoulders then continued to push Toby and their belongings towards the table where a woman was checking passengers' names and handing out supplies for their onward journey. The sky and the buildings here looked so bleak, washed with a flat dull colour that Ella hadn't known existed. Never had home seemed so far away.

'What's your name?' the voluntary worker asked. She was wearing a grey coat with a red cross sewn onto the sleeve.

Ella gave her their details and the woman wrote them down.

'You'll have to fill in some immigration details. It's just to check you've got the right rations registered – that type of thing.'

Ella's hands were shaking as she filled in the forms.

'Have a cuppa,' the woman said. 'There's a table over there with hot drinks, coats and some other bits. You'll have to rummage through. And if you go over there,' she pointed to another woman by yet another table, 'we can get you some money for your onward journey along with some sandwiches for you and the little one. Where are you off to?'

'Oxford.'

'Well, you can walk to the station. You'll need to get a ticket. After that, I'm afraid, you're on your own.'

Ella wasn't sure which way to go as she looked around at the devastated streets. She noted the pinched looks on people's faces, the lines of breath that they exhaled in the cold air and the way they constantly rubbed their hands to keep warm. She moved on and found herself a thick coat from the pile on the table, a hat and a pair of gloves. They were far too big for her, and briefly she wondered where they had come from, but the thought didn't last long; she was too grateful for the clothing to complain. She found some items for Toby – a hat, a coat and some mittens, collected some money in a brown envelope, sandwiches that were wrapped in greaseproof paper, and sipped a mug of steaming hot tea as she asked how she would find the station and how to buy a ticket.

She looked around desperately. She had no idea where to go and the unfamiliar streets seemed hostile and threatening, the cold wind chilling her to the bone. Everything was so bleak here in England, not at all the way she had imagined it, but there were colourful posters everywhere: a wholesome-looking man smoking a pipe and holding a basket of vegetables under the slogan *Dig for Victory!* Another portraying a man wearing a tin hat with a large 'W' printed on it, and blowing a whistle. Beneath the image was the message: *In a raid open your doors to passers-by – they need shelter too!*

Ella saw some women from the ship whom she guessed might be going to the station. She followed them, pulling her coat tight against the cold. How low the sky seemed – was there ever any sun in it? she wondered. And how dull the houses and shops were, crammed in next to each other along such busy streets.

At last, she got to the station and the train arrived. It was crowded with servicemen and a few of the women she recognised from the ship. She had been lucky to get on, but not lucky enough to find a seat.

As they travelled through the countryside, what she saw shocked her – buildings ripped apart revealing skeletal remains; rows of houses knocked down like dominoes; belongings smouldering in wreckage. She caught sight of what must once have been someone's home: an exterior wall was sliced off revealing a neatly made bed and a picture hanging on the wall. What had happened to the people who had lived there? she wondered.

They journeyed on, witnessing sandbagged streets with gaping holes like toothless mouths where people rushed about their business, heads down, or helmeted wardens sifting through rubble alongside shop girls and factory workers. She'd heard about it all, of course, in the paper and from the other passengers on the ship who'd listen to the wireless and relate the latest tales of destruction. She'd even heard bombers overhead at sea, but nothing had prepared her for the reality of what wartime England really looked like.

And it deepened her fear of what might be happening in Malaya. After a few stops, some passengers alighted, and Ella and Toby managed to sit in their empty seats. Toby was crying, tired and grubby from their journey. She unwrapped the sandwiches that she'd been given and broke them into tiny bits: it was bread and a strange pink spread that she thought tasted like fish. It wasn't very palatable, but she was starving.

After changing twice and what seemed liked days, her last train crawled into Oxford station. The sky was illuminated by the full moon, which cast a silvery light over everything she could see. She was completely exhausted, her nerves stretched to breaking as she wheeled the pushchair out of the station. The only time she had met her mother-in-law Polly was when she and James had visited Malaya for Johnnie and Ella's marriage. She hoped she'd remember what Polly looked like. She glanced around to see if anyone who looked familiar was waiting but was disappointed. She wasn't certain what to do next and thought about asking a queue of people who were standing waiting for a bus how she got to Wood Eaton.

'Ella!' She turned at the sound of her name. 'Ella!'

And there, thank God, was the most welcome sight in weeks. A woman she immediately knew was Polly came walking towards her. To Ella's surprise she was holding the hand of a young girl of around five with a boy of about seven in tow also.

'Polly?'

'Thank goodness!' Polly dropped the children's hands and clasped her arms around Ella. 'I know I said I might not be able to come, but it was only because I wasn't certain I'd get the petrol.'

The relief was too much, and Ella began to weep.

'Come on, you're shivering.' Polly's arm was around her comfortingly. 'I hardly recognise you, you've grown so thin. And this must be Toby?'

'Yes. I'm sorry for all this trouble, and for you meeting him the first time this way.'

'Don't talk nonsense. It must have been awful for you – the journey, everything. Of course, we'll do anything we can to help.'

Ella tried to calm herself and thank Polly, but could only nod.

'Let's get you both home and into the warm. Thankfully, I managed to get some petrol from a friend in exchange for sugar. We need to get some food in you, too, I can see.'

Polly led her to an ancient Jaguar that was parked a couple of streets away – the vehicle's cavernous interior was welcome after the claustrophobic train. The seats crackled as they sat down and smelt of leather. As they drove through darkened and unfamiliar streets, where not even a flicker of light escaped from the windows of the houses they passed, Polly started to chatter.

'These two are Jenny and Peter,' she explained. 'Evacuees from London.'

'Hello,' Ella said, turning to greet the two children who looked as frightened and diminished as she felt.

'Honestly, the house is full to the brim at the moment.' Polly sighed. 'We've had evacuees and soldiers billeted on us non-stop. You wouldn't believe it.'

Tiredness possessed Ella as she tried to listen to Polly's words. 'I can't put the headlights on full beam – even they have blackouts. Any chink of light and Gerry could find us. Luckily, though, Oxford's been clear so far.' Polly hunched over the steering wheel as she tried to make sense of the darkened streets with the dimmed-out headlights and only the brightness of the moon to show them where to go.

Ella's limbs and joints were aching with fatigue and this last part of the journey had a surreal quality to it. She fought hard to stay awake. Eventually, the car slowed and Polly pulled into a drive.

'This is us,' she said.

Ella could see the outline of a house at the bottom of a tree-lined drive. So, this was where they lived. To the left stood a smaller building, an old coach house, by which Polly drew the car to a halt.

She opened the boot and helped Ella lift their belongings out. Long furls of their breath were visible in the biting air. How strange it all was, to be here and thrust into a life, a world, she didn't know. Polly was doing her best to be welcoming, and Ella remembered her as being kind and caring from that visit to Malaya all those years ago. But right now,

Ella felt like a complete stranger, almost an imposter, arriving here without Johnnie and Grace.

Jenny and Peter, the evacuees, had already let themselves out and were stamping their feet in the cold. Ella tried to smile at them, but they looked away and she wondered if it was the first time they'd seen someone who was Asian. Once again, she felt so very much alone.

'Johnnie used to love playing here as a boy,' Polly chattered on. 'He used to bring his chums from school and camp in the attics.'

Ella followed her upward gaze. It was hard to imagine him as a boy, and it occurred to her for the first time that he'd had a life here long before she had ever known him – one that she didn't know about at all. His parents probably held onto a version of him that she had never experienced, and she in turn knew a different side to him. But, she realised, Johnnie was the one thing that connected them, although the thread seemed fragile as she stood looking at these unfamiliar surroundings. How much of him still lingered here, she wondered, like a ghost from the past?

'Come on.' Polly ushered Ella and Toby into the hall. The warmth hit them like a wall. The floor was wooden boards partly covered with a blue and red Persian rug, and ancient maps and landscapes hung on the walls at odd angles. A couple of the paintings had collected dust and cobwebs. Rows of dark coats in different sizes hung from hooks along the wall of the hallway along with a collection of gas masks. How cramped and stuffy it seemed compared to the spacious airy rooms she had known in Malaya.

'I'll show you up to your room later.' Polly took Ella's coat and hung it on one of the already bulging pegs. 'I've had to rearrange things a bit. I've put you in the room we used to use for the billeted servicemen. If any of them want to stay when they're on leave they'll have to rough it.' Polly's chattering was incessant, and Ella wondered if it was nervousness or merely wanting to make her feel welcome. 'But come into the study first. James will be back later – he's been in London, doing something for the War Office.'

Ella nodded. Carrying Toby, she opened the door that Polly indicated. It revealed a room where there was a coal fire smouldering behind a metal screen. As she stood in the doorway, Ella was struck by the fact that there was so much carpet everywhere and long curtains on top of the swathes of dark fabric, which Polly explained were called blackouts. More paintings lined the walls, while piles of dusty books were scattered across the floor. Ella's head was spinning from all the information Polly had given her about coupons and rations, air raids, gas masks and shelters, jumble sales where she might pick up some more winter clothes. All she wanted to do was to get warm and go to sleep, but she didn't want to seem ungrateful.

'Now, you settle yourself down here.' Polly indicated a chair next to the fire.

Ella sank down with Toby in her lap. His eyes were flickering, taking in his new surroundings.

Polly bustled into the kitchen from where the sound of the kettle being put on and china being placed on trays emerged. Ella and Toby watched as Jenny and Peter sat down on the carpet in front of the fire and opened a wooden box to take out a collection of toys: tin soldiers, a packet of cards, a doll that was missing an eye. Everything was damaged, and yet, as she watched them play, firelight illuminating their fresh and youthful faces, Ella felt that a new chapter of her life was beginning. Like these children, she knew that in order to survive, she needed to forget that everything else in her life was broken and cling on to this new source of hope.

Chapter Sixteen

Noor glanced up to see Naoki's frame filling the kitchen doorway.

'The emperor commands that all children must be educated,' he said, looking at Grace. 'They must learn to be good citizens of the empire and how to honour the emperor. Why isn't this child at school?'

Noor lifted her eyes from the chicken she was gutting and swung her gaze towards him, then to Grace, who was sitting on a low stool at her side.

'I'm sorry,' Noor said, wiping her bloodied hands on the kitchen cloth. She gave a bow and then another, as she now knew the soldiers expected her to do. 'I didn't know. I'll make sure he goes immediately.'

Naoki's black eyes seemed to bore into her, and she wondered for the hundredth time if he could see through the pretence of Grace's gender. But of course, she told herself, he couldn't; both she and the child would have been punished by now if he had. Naoki left the kitchen but his presence lingered, tainting the room with fear.

Noor dropped the cloth next to the chicken and looked at Grace. The child was still pining for her parents, and with the lack of good food and company, Noor thought she looked paler and more ill than she had done even yesterday. The more she thought about it, the more she realised that the kampong school would be a good thing for Grace, and for more than one reason. It would do her good to be out of the villa, away from the toxic presence of the soldiers, to mix with other children and to focus on more than her missing parents, but Grace leaving the villa and going daily to the kampong would also be the perfect way for Noor to pass and receive information from Omar. It was so obvious now – why she hadn't thought of it before?

'It will be nice to go to the kampong school, don't you think?' Noor said encouragingly. 'You will have friends to play with and you won't have to do so much here for these *babis*. I'm afraid you will have to keep it secret that you are a girl. Do you think you can do that?

'I don't know. Won't they be able to tell? And what happens when I need to go to the lavatory?'

'You're clever, you'll find a way to keep it from them. I'm more worried about someone working out who you are and giving you away. People will be eager to keep in with the soldiers. Do you think you can keep up our game? We could say you are a refugee.'

Grace said nothing, and Noor took that to mean yes.

The following morning, she packed Grace a lunch of leftover rice wrapped in banana leaves that she carried in a small canvas rucksack that had once belonged to Mr McCain. Somehow, it had ended up in her larder cupboard, probably after one of the picnics the McCains had liked to go on.

'It will be as if your father is here looking out for you,' she told the child and then wished she hadn't. Grace's eyes welled with tears and Noor wiped them away with her thumb as she handed her the rucksack. 'I'll walk down to the perimeter fence with you today, but you'll have to come home on your own. Do you think you can manage that?'

Grace nodded.

'See, here, I've wrapped you some lunch.' She opened the rucksack to show Grace the banana-leaf parcels. 'I popped a couple in there for Omar, too. Make sure you share them with him,' Noor said. 'I put some chilli in his. See, these two here. I know you don't like yours so spicy.'

Grace peered inside and nodded again. What Noor hadn't told her was that she'd hidden a note inside Omar's parcels asking if he had any more information about what was happening beyond the mine compound. She also hoped he might have some news about Mr McCain.

'Come on,' she said, taking hold of Grace's hand. 'You'll be all right. Don't say more than you need to and try not to get into any trouble.'

The two of them made their way to the exit gate, where a soldier grabbed the rucksack from Grace. Noor's nerves almost got the better of her as he took out the parcels and sniffed them, but they didn't seem to be to his liking as he thrust them back inside.

Noor stood to her side of the gate as Grace made her way through. The child turned and raised her hand, then Noor watched her make her way down the long drive to the kampong. It was pitiful to watch her slight form walking away along the dusty road. All Noor wanted to do was call her back, tell her not to go alone, but she knew she couldn't.

The day passed slowly. By mid-afternoon, Noor's nerves were frayed. Had Grace got to school all right? Surely the soldiers wouldn't hurt a child. Had Omar found the note inside his rice parcel? What would he do?

At last, she heard Grace's footsteps outside. She came into the kitchen looking weary.

'How was school?' Noor asked.

'It wasn't as bad as I thought it would be.'

'What did you do?'

'We had to learn the national anthem.'

'That can't have been hard, you already know it.'

'No. Not ours. The Japanese one.'

'Oh.' Noor was taken aback. Surely Omar wouldn't be teaching the children that lightly.

'Well, have you got any homework to do?' Noor took the canvas bag from Grace's shoulder. 'Did you give the rice parcels to Omar?' She looked inside the rucksack wondering if there might be a reply, but was disappointed to find only a notebook and a pencil.

Omar didn't communicate with her at all over the following days, but a week later, she found in a returned rice parcel a note folded carefully into the woven leaf. '*Make a secret hiding place in Grace's rucksack,*' he wrote. '*I will find it and pass on information.*'

Another week passed and he told her how the Japanese soldiers had occupied almost all the neighbouring towns; how when the planes from Japan had landed at Butterworth and Alor Setar aerodromes, scores of Japanese had arrived with bicycles to enable them to make their way easily through the country. She learnt how many villagers were being kept as prisoners by the soldiers in camps close to the mine, but there was no news of Mr McCain.

The more she read, the angrier Noor became. She hated the Japanese for the barbaric killings she read about, and found it harder and harder to serve them. Once again, she longed to run away with Grace and wrote to Omar asking him if he was certain he couldn't help her escape to the jungle, but her cousin told her he needed her to stay, that having her in the villa passing on information was an opportunity the MCP couldn't afford to lose.

And so she did what she could. She listened at doors, hoping to hear some vital piece of information. Whenever she heard blasts of gunpowder from the tin mine, she let Omar know that excavations were increasing. She told him the soldiers' routines, enabling the MCP to blow up recently laid track or to steal tools, all because of information Noor had provided. The more she told Omar, the more connected she felt to the outside world, and the stronger her resolve to undermine the Japanese became.

Sometimes, at night when the house was silent, she'd creep out to the yard and look up at the stars and then out towards the jungle canopy. She imagined Omar and his compatriots out there along with the British soldiers he said were still out there in hiding, possibly even in the caves he had told her about. She could almost picture them, huddling by a campfire, lean and tired, but watching and waiting. One of the British soldiers had been badly injured early on, Omar told her, and they'd had to get him out and back to England. She liked to think of their secret heroic adventures and exploits taking place, all of them concealed by the darkness, and wondered what acts of defiance they were planning next. The jungle was so dense that it was hard to see anything, but on occasion she wondered if she could see woodsmoke and hear the voices of those in hiding. Those poor men, if only there was a way she could help them. The only way she knew was to pass them food, but she had no way of knowing where to leave it, and besides there was little to spare.

Weeks passed and bit by bit, often delayed, she learnt of the fall of Singapore, and how Burma, Thailand and Indonesia had also succumbed to the Japanese stranglehold, but still, every day, she prayed for a miracle to happen, that somehow the British army would find a way to defeat the Japanese.

The days and the weeks blurred, and Noor found it hard to mark the passing of time other than from the notes that Omar managed to send to her. Sometimes, she wished she didn't know how the kampong elders had been beaten for not letting the soldiers have a cupful of rice; that most of the time all the villagers had to eat was rice or tapioca – she wanted to help them but there was nothing she could do. She cried when she heard how a local family with two young children had tried to run away to the safety of Thailand. They had been caught by the *kempeitai*, the police arm of the Japanese military, and tied in chains then left in the middle of the kampong for days before they died. Their corpses were left to rot where they fell as everyone had been too scared to bury them.

People disappeared on a regular basis, Omar told her. Neighbours turned on neighbours if they thought a piece of information might gain them a bowl of rice or a favour from the Japanese. *See nothing, hear nothing, say nothing* became the code of conduct for everyone as they were all fearful of betrayal.

But of all her troubles, it was Grace who worried Noor the most. Every night she had terrible nightmares: her body would shake violently and then she'd open her eyes and stare blankly ahead, her face bathed in perspiration.

'Shhh,' Noor soothed as the girl's limbs twitched. 'It's only a dream.'

But Grace would continue to cry in her sleep, asking again and again for her parents. Noor, unable to fathom the dark corridors that the girl's unconscious mind led her through, didn't know why these dreams had started, nor what she was supposed to do to help.

And then the child began to sleepwalk. She'd pace the kitchen floor, eyes wide open and wringing her hands, calling for her parents in English. *'It's me, Grace, where are you? Why have you left me here? Please, please, come home!'*

Noor was terrified the girl would wander around the house or that she'd go upstairs to where her old bedroom had been. What if she woke the soldiers and they discovered that she wasn't who she said she was? The game would be up for them both.

Noor tried everything – giving her ginger tea to drink before bedtime didn't work. Next, she tried adding banana blossom to a curry, but the child didn't like the taste and wouldn't eat it. Noor tried all the herbs and beans she knew of that aided sleep, but Grace's dreams and terrors were stronger than all of them.

One night, she woke to find the girl wasn't lying on her mat on the kitchen floor. Noor sat up. In the half-light, all kinds of thoughts raced around her head. Had one of the soldiers discovered the truth about Grace, or worse still had the girl run away to find her parents? She would surely be shot. But then Noor thought she could hear music. She sat up straighter and listened. Yes, someone was playing the piano. Noor stood and crept towards the kitchen door, opening it carefully. Across the corridor, she noticed that the drawing-room door was closed but a light shone through the crack at the top. Grace lay curled up on the floor at the foot of the door, completely absorbed in the music.

'What are you doing?' Noor half-hissed. 'Come back to bed before they find you.'

Grace turned to face Noor. Her eyes sparkled and there was a flush of pink in her cheeks.

'It's so beautiful,' she whispered. 'Please, just let me listen a while longer.'

Noor tiptoed to the closed door and knelt down next to Grace. The child was right, the music was magical, and they dared not move in case the spell was broken.

Chapter Seventeen

The music stopped. Before they could jump away, the door opened. It was Naoki.

They both bowed their heads, expecting to be beaten or dragged back to the kitchen by their hair, but Naoki continued to stare at them, and for a moment his expression softened.

'What were you doing?' he asked, his gaze falling on Grace. 'Were you listening to me playing?'

Noor lifted her eyes to see the girl nodding.

Naoki continued to stare, then he turned away sharply. Before either of them could speak, he'd clumped up the stairs.

'What were you thinking?' Noor hissed as she took Grace by the arm and led her back to the kitchen. 'You could have had us both punished – do you want them to find out who you really are?'

'But, auntie, it was so beautiful! I wish I could play like that. My father used to read from a music book, but Naoki, he seems to play from somewhere inside his head. How does he do it?'

'I have no idea.'

Noor lay on her mat and Grace settled next to her, humming the tune they had both just heard. Before long she quietened and Noor knew that she had fallen asleep. She braced herself for the nightmares to follow, but somehow the music had calmed the child and the dreams didn't come.

The following morning, Noor mulled over what had happened: the way that Grace had been completely entranced by the music, how instead of it upsetting her, it had calmed her. The more she thought about it, the more she wondered if music was the secret to ending Grace's terrible dreams, and keeping them both safe from the secrets they carried.

She went into the garden, sat down in the shade of a coconut tree and thought hard. She realised that there was no way she could arrange for Grace to play the piano, and she didn't dare let the child listen again for fear of Naoki's wrath or that he might discover she wasn't the boy she was pretending to be.

After a while Noor stood up, knowing that she had chores to do in the kitchen. The larder was almost empty – just rice and tapioca. There were still tamarinds and papayas growing in the garden, along with the occasional coconut. From time to time, the soldiers brought her meat or other supplies from the village as her trips there had been stopped, to her frustration, not long after Grace had started at school.

She closed the larder door and almost jumped out of her skin. Naoki was standing right behind her. Instinctively, she bowed as low as she could.

'*Sensei*,' she said, wondering if he had come to punish her for what had occurred the previous night. She felt a tremor run down her spine.

'What were you doing last night?' he demanded. 'You

shouldn't be out of the kitchen wandering around the house. It is forbidden.'

'I'm sorry.' Noor bowed.

'I don't want it to happen again. You hear?'

'It won't, *sensei*.' Noor bowed again, but this time she noticed that Naoki's arm was swollen just below the elbow. There was an angry red bump, and she couldn't take her eyes off it. She recognised that type of bite, it came from the leeches that populated the jungle. The bites weren't always bad if you left them alone. She'd grown up knowing that the best thing was to let the leech drop off when it had finished feasting, but if you ripped it off too soon, its teeth remained in place. Then, if you were unlucky, an infection would soon follow, making you seriously ill.

Naoki must have noticed her looking, because his eyes followed hers to the spot on his arm.

'That isn't good,' Noor said instinctively. 'I can help you. I can cut the teeth out and bathe the wound. Let's hope an infection hasn't started. Please will you permit me?'

He thought for a moment then gave a curt nod of the head.

'Come, sit down here.' Noor pulled out a stool for him to sit while she boiled water to sterilise a small kitchen knife. When the blade was ready, she placed her fingers over the site of the wound and spread out the flesh then dug deep. Blood and pus oozed out. As she pressed the blade deeper, she felt Naoki wince. For a moment, she thought of what she could do with the knife, how easily she could kill him, but pushed the thought away.

'There,' she said, using the flat edge of the blade to show

him the remnants of the tiny teeth. 'These jungle leeches are vicious, never pull one out. Use tobacco mixed in water and put it on you as a deterrent – it will protect you from them.'

Next, she cleaned the wound with salt water. When she had finished, Naoki thanked her.

'Will you come back later, *sensei*?' she asked. 'I want to check it has healed.'

She wasn't certain if he'd heard her, or if he'd return, because he left without speaking, but later he came back. The skin around the bite was angry and still livid; she bathed the site again, and this time placed a poultice of dried leaves, garlic and ginger on it, and told him to return in the morning.

The next day, the wound was healing nicely. As she put a fresh poultice on his arm, Naoki told her, 'My wife had a good knowledge of medicinal herbs, too. You know, you remind me a bit of her.'

Noor paused, noticing the softer expression on his face. *Had*, she thought. 'What happened to her?' she asked, knowing that her question could be seen as impertinent and that he could punish her.

To her relief, Naoki looked away from her and focused his eyes somewhere distant, as though his thoughts could take him back to a place he could never actually revisit. 'She died after my daughter was born. Both of them died, within hours.'

'I'm sorry to hear it. That must be very hard for you. Do you have any other family?'

'Yes.' He nodded. 'A son.'

Once more, she noticed how sad he seemed to be. 'You must miss him.'

Naoki nodded. 'More than anything. But I have my orders, our honour to maintain, so I must be here fighting for our emperor. For Japan.'

His honesty and vulnerability surprised her. Until now, she had only seen the Japanese as a ruthless enemy, not as individuals who suffered too. Naoki, for whatever reason, had let down his guard with her, and for a moment she had seen him not as the enemy but as an ordinary man.

'Tell me about your son,' she said, tidying away the remainder of the poultice.

'He is only seven, but he is very skilled at mathematics and martial arts.' Naoki smiled, and Noor saw for the first time that he was a handsome man when his face lit up. 'Now he is with his grandparents. He writes to me that he likes to play the piano like I do. I miss being able to teach him, to listen to him play.'

'It sounds as though he likes the piano as much as Jaza does.'

'Tell me, why does the child sit by the door listening? The sound of the piano must surely travel to all parts of the house.'

Noor swallowed. It wouldn't hurt to tell Naoki about the nightmares, surely?

He listened as she explained that unknown terrors possessed the child, how much it worried her, and that she was certain the music soothed Jaza. It was difficult for her to know what to do.

Naoki was silent for a moment. Then he said, 'You could have used that knife to harm me the other day – but you didn't. You were kind when you had no need to be, and so in return I will help you. The child,' he continued, 'for whatever reason, is troubled and music helps. I will teach him the piano. At home in Japan, the emperor commands that everyone should be cultured. I cannot teach my son right now, so perhaps I can teach Jaza instead. But there is a condition.'

Noor's heart raced, wondering what he might say.

'This piano is a good one, so the child must keep it clean with special oil I have and place a bowl of water inside to keep the wood from cracking. You understand? It must be done every day.'

'Thank you, master, thank you.' Noor bent low, relief flooding out of her like a balloon deflating, then she bowed again. 'Thank you.'

She couldn't wait to tell Grace, confident her nightmares and sleepwalking would cease, that from now on their secret would be safe.

Grace was a quick learner. Like Naoki, she was able to pick up a tune and play it by ear. After her lessons, Grace would move her fingers along the table as though she were still at the keyboard, a smile on her face, or fall asleep still humming a tune. Her nightmares faded and Noor began to relax.

Sometimes, after the lessons, Naoki would come into the kitchen. He would sit at the small kitchen table as Grace told Noor what she had learnt. Once or twice after she had expended her excitement and gone to finish her homework, he would stay a little longer. He'd ask Noor what she was cooking, and on one occasion helped her repair a saucepan handle. His kindness continued to surprise her – she knew that he was firm with the other soldiers, but unlike most of them, she had never seen him be cruel, and he didn't attend their drunken evenings spent in the kampongs with the 'comfort women'– those women or girls who were forced to satisfy the carnal needs of these enemy men so far away from home.

For this she respected him. He began to sit with her in the evenings when the men were out in the kampong, and their conversations shifted from pleasantries to confidences. She told him how she had grown up in the villa as Ella's companion, how she had shared her lessons and tried to educate herself. He told her he admired her for that, and that he was not surprised to learn she was good with numbers, reading and writing. After that, on occasion, Noor started to find the *Perak Times* on the kitchen table, but the news was always slanted favourably towards the Japanese, always showcasing their superiority. There was never any of the local news she craved.

One evening Naoki came into the kitchen and said, 'Noor, there is something I want you to do for me.'

A bitter taste flooded her mouth: she'd heard from Omar about the women other soldiers had taken as mistresses. She knew that they were only trying to support their families, but the thought of what they did disgusted her. How could they become consorts to the Japanese and parade their new status in the kampong? Was this what Naoki was thinking? No, she thought, he would never suggest it, he wasn't that type of man.

'I wonder if you can help me,' he continued, his voice gentle. 'You see, there is something I cannot do alone. I have important documents that need translating from Japanese into Malay. I will write them in English, but can you help me with the rest?'

Noor thought for a moment, then nodded – after all, what could be the harm?

And so, Naoki would sometimes arrive in the kitchen after Grace had gone to school. He didn't speak but left a document in English on the kitchen table. She hid it in the larder, then when no one was looking, she would painstakingly translate it.

In the afternoons, Grace would return from school, polish the piano with teak oil, refill the bowl of water to keep the wood from drying out, and if he were there, Naoki would teach her. But what neither he nor Grace knew was that in the child's rucksack Omar frequently hid notes for Noor, providing snippets of information from the kampong: how they'd intercepted an army transport vehicle driven by Japanese officers containing precious food they had stolen from the kampong, or about their attacks on the railway line, the wires they had cut along the perimeter fence and the workers they had managed to help escape.

As the weeks and then the months passed, Naoki showed both Noor and Grace courtesy and much kindness. Noor knew he missed his family and, despite herself, during the times she spent with him in gentle conversation, she found her feelings changing. Surely the Japanese weren't all bad? Sometimes, Naoki would leave a bag of wheat or some sugar in the kitchen. At first, she was reluctant to take these supplies, after what Omar had told her about the treatment of the locals in the kampong, but need forced her to turn a blind eye. Sometimes, she used these gifts to earn extra money: she baked bread that Grace would sell in the kampong on her way to school; at other times, she would sell small bags of rice. Noor hid the money she'd earnt in the larder – not the dollars she was used to, but the strange new notes the Japanese had imposed on Malaya that she learnt were called 'banana money' because of the pictures of banana trees on them.

As time passed, Naoki brought her more personal gifts: a pair of cream Western-style shoes waited for her in the kitchen one day. She picked them up, marvelling at the craftsmanship, but had no idea when she would wear them nor why he was favouring her so. A few weeks later, a pink and orange silk scarf followed, then a white, loose-fitting dress. He never said anything to her, and when she tried to thank him, he avoided her eyes.

Noor found that her feelings shifted. She also noticed that although the faces of the other officers in the villa changed, Naoki was the one who always stayed. More and more often, she found her thoughts turning to him. There was an air of loneliness and solitude about him, this kind, gentle man who really didn't want to be here, but his position and his honour forced him to stay. The only times his sadness seemed to disappear were when he played the piano, when he was teaching Grace, or when he talked to Noor in the kitchen. She could only guess at the feelings that lay hidden within him, but realised that he, like her, longed for company and for the outside world.

The time came that whenever he came into the kitchen, she imagined their eyes connecting, that he would tilt her chin with his hand before lowering his face to hers and then at last she would feel the softness of his lips on hers.

Her own feelings puzzled her. Again and again, she chided herself for wanting Naoki's attention, yet her longing turned from being a dream to a need. Her youth was slipping away and with it any hope of rising above her situation, of having a family – of finally being someone.

Then Noor discovered a small black velvet box containing a pair of diamond earrings in the kitchen. They were larger and glittered more brightly than the pair belonging to Ella that Noor still had hidden away. She opened the box and held them in her hand; surely Naoki's feelings were just as strong as hers? They were so beautiful and caught the light so perfectly, but both the gift and Naoki's behaviour mystified her, and with every day that he avoided her gaze, the ache within her deepened.

When an angry note arrived from Omar wondering why she didn't share any news with him anymore, she scrunched it up and threw it in the bin. Omar had got it wrong, she told herself, the Japanese weren't so bad – and did he really think being governed by them was any worse than being ruled by the British? She was done with telling tales, and Omar ought to think of how much better his life could be if he stopped being a troublemaker.

One morning, when she was making rice porridge in the

kitchen, Grace told her, 'Did you know that there are musical concerts where children play? The best players win prizes.'

'No, I didn't. How do you know?'

'Naoki told me. The emperor has decreed it. The children play the violin or the piano. He said that I am really good – that I only need to hear a piece of music to play it well. I told him I can even hear the music in my head to play it and he said that I must be a genius. I really wish I could go.'

Noor lifted her head from the stove. She'd been worrying about Grace for some time now: she was looking less like the boy she was supposed to be, and Noor wondered when her figure might start to fill out.

'And where exactly do these concerts take place?'

'Menglembu. Sometimes further away.'

Noor placed the spoon she was stirring with down on the counter. 'How would you get there?'

'I don't know. I thought you might be able to ask Naoki.'

Noor gazed out of the window. Perhaps this was the opportunity she had been waiting for to see a little more of the outside world, and if Grace really was as good as Naoki said she was, it would only be right for her to attend. But did she have the courage to ask Naoki to take them?

Later that evening, after the soldiers had eaten and he was playing the piano, Noor lingered in the kitchen, hoping to catch him before he made his way up to bed. At last he stopped playing and she heard his footsteps coming towards her. The door opened, but fear got the better of her and she turned away.

'Noor?' he said, his voice gentle.

She turned to face him, unable to read his expression or to articulate her request. He stepped closer. She drew in her breath and said the words she had been rehearsing a hundred times.

'Jaza says that there are concerts for the children – I wonder how we can attend?'

'Noor,' he said, taking a step closer. 'Do you think I don't know?'

'What?'

He lowered his face to her ear. 'Your secret.'

She pulled away, the intake of her breath deep and sharp. 'I don't know what you mean.'

'Of course you do. I know that Jaza isn't a boy, that she isn't yours.'

Cold settled in her legs, weakening them and making them tremble. So, he had known all along and never said a thing. She didn't know where to look, but at last she managed to ask, 'Do the others know?'

He shook his head. 'Of course not. Your secret is safe with me. Now, we should make some plans for how to get the girl up to standard.'

It was agreed that from time to time they would attend public competitions where Grace could perform. Naoki or one of the junior officers would take them there in his staff vehicle. Grace won most of the competitions, and her reputation as a pianist grew. She won many types of prizes – packs of pencils and notebooks mainly, items that were deemed educational but were desirable to local children who couldn't get hold of them, and so acted as currency.

On their journeys to the venues, Noor would sit in the front next to the driver. She wondered what people would be thinking when they saw her in her smart clothes and diamond earrings. Her feelings for Naoki deepened, but still he only spoke to her with great politeness and courtesy. She hoped that by seeing her wear his gifts in public, he had registered her appreciation.

One day, as they arrived outside the village hall in Menglembu, she spotted Omar's face in the crowd. Their eyes met but Noor quickly looked away and focused on her feet in their cream-coloured shoes.

I'm only doing what anyone would, she told herself as she climbed up the steps into the hall, *and none of it is wrong. Who wouldn't want to better themselves, to survive?*

But Omar's expression haunted her.

That night she dreamt that she was in the jungle during a tropical storm. There was strange music playing – she didn't know who it was or where it was coming from. As she searched, her clothes and hair drenched by the pounding rain, she came across Omar who was sitting in the mouth of a cave. Behind him were guns and the bodies of scores of murdered MCP members. He sat by a fire, and when he lifted his face to hers, his expression was as dark as thunder.

'Traitor!' He spat on the ground. 'Prostitute!'

'That's not fair, Omar. I'm not doing anything wrong.'

'Look behind you. See – the faces of these dead men! May their blood be on your hands forever.'

'Omar, please. Think of the child. Everything I do, I do for her!'

'Do you lie in his bed for the child?'

'How can you say such a thing, Omar?'

A flash of lightning lit up the sky, illuminating the faces of the dead men who lay behind him.

'Liar. Traitor. When was the last time you had anything useful to tell me, hey?' He brought his face close to hers – his teeth were stained with betel-nut juice, and the colour seemed to have bled into his eyes. He spat on the ground, but the spit didn't soak away. Instead, it bubbled like blood cascading from an open artery.

Chapter Eighteen

Sleep evaded Ella. She lay in a large mahogany bedstead in a draughty room as the unfamiliar noises of the house mingled with whispers from her past. The stew that Polly had cooked for dinner lay heavily on her stomach. She wondered if all English food was like this, sloppy and tasteless with overcooked vegetables, and then she felt bad for thinking that way.

Toby slept in a wooden cot at the foot of her bed; it was painted blue with a large white bunny rabbit on the headboard. She suspected it had been Johnnie's and the idea unsettled her. Her thoughts moved on, to the servicemen that Polly said had been billeted here. She tried to think of the faceless people who had slept in the bed and then it occurred to her that once this must have been Johnnie's room and his bed, and it unsettled her further to think that he should be there with her now, not thousands of miles away and goodness knew where.

She got out of bed and pulled on the navy towelling dressing-gown hanging on the back of the door. It was a little too big and from the aroma of soap and its scratchy surface, she assumed it had recently been washed. Had this been Johnnie's, too? she wondered. She pulled the collar up to her chin and inhaled, as though it could bring her closer to him, but couldn't detect the slightest trace of his scent. After all, it would have been years since he'd worn it.

She opened the door and listened. The landing and stair-case were in shadow, and she could see her chilled breath frosting in front of her as she looked about. To her left was the bathroom and a little further along from James and Polly's room she could hear snoring. James McCain had got back just after supper, but his welcome had been as cold as the English weather.

'Ah,' he had said, when she had stood to greet him as he came into the study. 'Ella.' Her memory of him from his visit to Malaya was of a tall man with dark hair. Now, his face along with his hair had whitened and he stooped a little. His gaze turned to Toby and lingered a beat too long. She guessed that her son must be reminding him of Johnnie as a child, and again, the sense of her betrayal in abandoning her husband and child surged through her. However hard it was for her, it must be just as hard for James, not knowing where his only son was. Eventually, Polly made Ella repeat all the details of her escape, then she insisted that James found an atlas and made him spread it on the coffee table to see where their route had taken them.

Now, as she listened to him snoring, Ella continued to look about and noticed that to the right the stairwell plunged into darkness. She pulled the dressing-gown tighter around her waist and followed the stairs down.

The smell of Polly's stew still hung in the hall, and the study door creaked as she opened it. Embers flickered like fireflies in the fireplace, casting a mellow glow over the room. She could see dents in the cushions, the impressions of those who had sat there acting like ghostly reminders of Grace and Johnnie's absence, and it choked her. She closed the door, deciding to explore the rest of the house.

Now, she was glad of the carpet as her feet padded along the hallway. The first door she opened revealed the dining room, where they had eaten. Moonlight illuminated a large mahogany table surrounded by eight perfectly aligned balloon-backed dining chairs, the highchair where Toby had sat propped up on cushions, a large dresser of a dark wood she didn't recognise containing plates and silver tureens. Polly had explained again that from time to time they had servicemen from RAF Benson to stay whenever they had leave and that sometimes their wives or children joined them and this was where meals were always served. Ella didn't like this room as much as the cosy table she had seen in the kitchen.

'We've all got to do our bit,' Polly had said. 'There probably isn't a single bedroom in Oxford that is vacant now.'

The hall clock struck the hour, the pendulum sending a vibrating shudder through the air. She closed the door and wandered further along the hallway and discovered another door. She paused, then turned the stiffened handle and pushed hard to open it. The smell of the room made her think of books that had been left too long unopened, of the beeswax and polish that the servants had used at home.

As the door swung open, a baby grand piano in the middle of the room captured her attention.

It was a little dusty, yet silver photograph frames glittered from its surface, reflecting the watchful moon. Silently she walked towards it, her heart pounding but her feet silent. She picked up a frame: Johnnie as a toddler, sitting in a pit of sand; Johnnie in his prep-school uniform – a crooked row of teeth visible as he grinned; Johnnie with his arm wrapped around a spaniel's neck, making her think of Apollo. Wondering what on earth had happened to him brought a stifled sob to her throat. With the tip of her finger, she followed the line of Johnnie's jaw and the angle of his nose on the photograph, then she returned it to the top of the piano. She sat down on the stool and lifted the long-untouched lid to reveal the ancient keyboard.

Her fingers lingered over the ivory as she traced the places she knew Johnnie's fingers must have touched. Each key had felt the impression of his skin, had been caressed as he swept his hands backwards and forwards over the expanse of black and white.

Tears trickled down her cheeks and she wiped her face with her sleeve as visions of Johnnie clustered around her. She could almost hear him humming a tune, feel him next to her. It was as though all she had to do was to turn her face, and she would see him looking at her and feel the force of their eyes meeting.

'Oh, my God.' Her shoulders heaved. The not knowing was making her go out of her mind. 'Whatever happens, I will find you both and we will all be together again,' she vowed.

Her hands hovered over the keyboard. She wanted to play but didn't want to wake the others. Stillness hung in all the corners of the room as though time had stopped here and didn't want to move, but she thought she felt something moving near her. Did she imagine it, or did she hear Johnnie whisper that he loved her, that Grace was safe? She resisted the desire to turn her head and look, for if she did, she knew that the sensation would disappear, and she wanted to cling to the whisper of hope forever.

It became her habit to wander down to the piano at night. When she thought all the house was sleeping, she would creep down the stairs and sit on the stool, running her fingers gently over the keyboard, quietly reproducing the tunes she had loved to hear him play and desperately hoping to recapture the presence she had felt that first time.

During the day, she and Polly scoured passenger lists and wrote to the Red Cross, hoping for news of Johnnie and Grace.

One morning, shortly after James had left for Oxford, fixing his bicycle clips to his trousers before heading off to discuss a paper he was writing with a colleague, Polly placed a pile of newspapers on the kitchen table.

'Time to start again,' she said.

'I know. Thank you.'

'See if you recognise any names on the passenger lists,' Polly said as she sat down and turned to the relevant pages. 'They might know what happened to Johnnie and Grace.'

Ella sat and chewed the end of her pen, scanning the names. She looked up. 'Yes, I do, actually. Edith Gibbins. Her husband was our doctor. And I think this one here might be Sarah Harris, she was someone I used to know in Ipoh, but it's years since I've seen her.'

'Well, you should write to the Red Cross and see if they can be contacted. Either of them might have news of Johnnie and Grace.'

Ella glanced up at Polly: there were dark shadows under her eyes. Last night, after she'd been sitting at the piano, Ella had heard Jenny crying then wandering along the corridor, calling for her mother, and Polly gently coaxing her back to bed, explaining that she'd see her mummy soon. Ella had frozen hearing Jenny's cries – it cut her to the quick as she remembered the nights she had comforted Grace from fevers that had taken hold. The poor child needed her mother, and here was Ella desperately wanting her own daughter. Where was the sense in any of it? As soon as she thought she could leave the piano, she had heard another creak on the landing and Polly's patient voice. 'Jenny – go back to bed.'

But Jenny hadn't, as Ella discovered when she crept back up the stairs and found the child standing on the landing in her nightie. Ella started, uncertain what to do as the girl looked at her with tear-filled eyes.

'Would you like a story?' she eventually asked.

Jenny nodded and Ella crept into the children's room and

sat on Jenny's bed reading two chapters of *The Secret Garden* to her before noticing that she had fallen asleep. Ella had been reluctant to leave then. She had stroked Jenny's blonde hair, thinking how unfair the world was. Perhaps someone was looking after Grace like this for her, but it was bitter comfort. Eventually, she had crept out of the room and finally got to sleep where her dreams of Grace had merged with Jenny's face.

'Shall I make us some tea?' Polly asked, forcing Ella to concentrate on her current task. Polly took off her reading spectacles and placed them on the table. 'I think I've still got some digestives if you'd like one.'

'Not for me.'

The biscuits, she'd discovered, were mealy and stuck in her throat. Ella longed for fresh papaya with lime or mango or spicy chai instead of the dark brown tea that Polly made. The cold damp house was making Ella's fingers and toes ache, and it didn't matter how many layers of Johnnie's pullovers or socks Polly retrieved from the attic for Ella to put on, keeping warm seemed impossible. She longed for the warmth of the tropical sun.

As Polly waited by the stove for the kettle to come to the boil, Ella looked out of the window. The glass was frosted still. Beyond it there was a bird she didn't recognise perched on the wall.

'What's that bird with the red breast?' she asked.

Polly lifted her head. 'Ah, that's a robin. I've got a bird book somewhere if you'd like to borrow it.'

'Thank you. That's kind.' Ella wondered if any of the

birds, other than this robin, were colourful in England. So far, they all appeared to be brown or black, not like the jewel-coloured ones she was used to in Malaya.

She watched Polly warm the teapot, hunched over the stove in a fashion that made her look much older than her fifty-five years. She spooned tea leaves from a tin, but then her body sagged. Ella put down her pen and crossed the floor, putting an arm around Polly's shoulder.

'Is there anything I can do to help?'

Polly took a handkerchief from her pocket and blew her nose before lifting her face to Ella's. The rims of her eyes were pink and her irises as watery-blue as the sea.

'Sometimes I think I'm a little too old for all of this.' Polly forced a smile. 'By the time you get to our age, you expect to be able to put your feet up. Now we've got the evacuees to look after, along with the servicemen who board here, and James, poor man, has hardly any time to do his own research with all the fire-watching obligations he's got and the work at Bletchley.'

'I'm sorry. The last thing you probably need is us here, too.'

'I didn't mean that.' Polly sniffed as she wiped her nose. 'We're glad to do what we can to help. You're family.'

'But you'll let me know, won't you, if it gets too much?'

Polly nodded. 'Now, this tea won't make itself. If you really want to help, how about you start on that washing up over there? We can have our tea when the kitchen is tidy.'

Ella slipped her arm away and turned to the sink: there

was a pile of plates soaking in the grey-greasy water. She'd never washed plates before and wondered where to start. She grimaced as she plunged her hands in to discover that the water was cold and revolting to the touch. She didn't know if she was supposed to use her hands to wipe the plates, but thankfully Polly handed her a strange-looking brush on a wooden handle and poured boiling water from the kettle into the sink. Still, Ella found it impossible to get the plates clean.

Spring arrived without news from the Red Cross, but the German bombers had launched a devastating attack on Malta. Meanwhile, Polly told her she could feel a hint of better weather coming. Ella wasn't convinced that England would ever be warm, but at least over the coming days the house didn't seem as freezing at it had when she first arrived. In the morning, after James had either gone to the university or caught a train to London, Ella and Polly would read and write letters in the warmth of the kitchen. It surprised Ella how quickly she had learnt to enjoy sitting in the small cosy room with layers of clothes on instead of at her desk in an airy room, listening to the birds singing in the trees outside the open window. While the women sat in the kitchen, the children played in the study. Jenny had taken a liking to Toby and enjoyed brushing his hair or trying to read to him. Now, when she woke at night, instead of disturbing Polly, Jenny would creep into Ella's room, bringing a book with her and a battered old teddy. Ella didn't have the heart to turn her away.

In the afternoons, Jenny and Peter would have what Polly called 'quiet time' in their rooms upstairs, and Ella and Polly would sit by the fire reading the newspapers while Toby slept on the sofa nearby. Ella would scour the papers for news of what was happening in Singapore or Malaya. She was shocked when the Philippines fell to the Japanese and delighted when she heard that the US had sent a fleet of B-25 bombers to carry out the first air attacks on Japan.

'There's still no mention of Johnnie and Grace on any passenger list.' Ella folded up the paper she'd been reading. 'I really don't know what else I can do.'

Toby woke and she picked him up.

'Let Mummy get you your drink,' she said, placing him on the study floor. In the kitchen, she warmed a bottle of milk, marvelling at the way she was now managing to juggle domestic chores and motherhood when in Malaya she had not been able to do the simplest of tasks. On her return she found that Toby, a competent crawler now at eight months, was moving around swiftly on the floor. She caught up with him just too late as he pulled himself up on one of the bookcases, managing to dislodge books from a shelf and scatter them everywhere.

Polly sighed then got up briskly and put the books back on the shelf, tension etched in her face.

Ella picked Toby up then returned to her chair and sat with him on her knee, trying to get him to drink from the bottle, but instead he grabbed a teaspoon from a nearby cup and saucer and started hitting it against the edge of a coffee table – *bang! bang! bang!* He looked up and smiled.

Ella took the spoon from him, but he wriggled on her lap and tried to snatch it back. She held it away and he started screaming.

'Can't you ever stop him screeching?' Polly snapped. 'I'm sorry.' Her hands started to shake. 'It's just that—'

But she didn't have to explain. Ella knew. Polly was exhausted. The events of the last few weeks were beginning to take their toll on them both.

Ella placed her free hand on her mother-in-law's. 'I'll take him upstairs.'

She went to her room and put Toby on the floor next to a pile of wooden alphabet bricks that Polly had found in the attic. Ella curled up in a ball under the eiderdown and hugged the pillow as she looked towards the window. She was used to being in control but now everything was wrong and jumbled, and she felt powerless to take charge of this alien situation she found herself in. Somewhere, miles and miles beyond, were Johnnie and Grace. She tried to conjure up their faces, but the harder she focused on their images, the more their features seemed to blur and the ache of not knowing where they were was like lead in her chest. Why had she left without them? Why had she not clung on to Johnnie and told him how much she loved him when she'd left home, instead of having that stupid row and petty words? And now all she had left of them both was a couple of small photographs in her handbag.

She sat up, an idea occurring. What if she were able to sketch their likenesses to keep their memories alive? In the chest of drawers, she still had the pencils and paper she'd used on the ship to sketch the other passengers. It didn't take her long to find them, then she propped herself up under the warmth of the eiderdown and started to draw. She began with Grace – her oval face, then her eyes, slightly close-set, and next her ears. Her nose was the hardest feature to draw but Ella just about captured it before she added the curling long strands of hair. No, it still wasn't quite right.

She let the pad fall and looked across at Toby, realising that he'd become very quiet. He'd crawled to her dressing table and managed to grab her makeup bag. Streaks of lipstick stained his face and hands, and he was now intently rubbing a red sticky mess on the carpet.

'Oh, for the love of God, Toby!'

She'd leapt out of bed and begun washing his hands in the bedroom sink, staining the white flannel a bloody pink, when there was a knock on the door.

'Can I come in?' Polly asked. 'It's only me.'

'Just a minute.'

She finished wiping Toby down then opened the door to Polly who was carrying a tray with two cups of tea on it.

'I'm sorry,' she said, putting the tray down on the dressing table. 'I shouldn't have snapped.' Then she noticed the mess Toby had made. 'Oh.'

'I'm sorry.'

Ella's heart sank.

Polly pinched her lips together then said, 'I might be able to get it out with white vinegar. I'll try later.'

She sat down on the bed and glanced up at Ella. 'But I suppose this brings me on nicely to what I've been thinking.'

Anxiety prickled Ella's skin as she waited. Was Polly going to tell her that they must leave?

'I don't need to tell you that it's getting a bit crowded in the house, and if I'm honest, I think it's hitting James rather hard.'

Ella swallowed. This was it. Polly was going to tell her to go.

'Before the war started,' she continued, 'James and I were going to convert the coach house in the courtyard into a property to rent out. Of course, that idea has gone by-the-by now. But what if you and I had a go? I thought we could clear it out ourselves, I mean. There would be plenty of space for you and Toby in there, if you wanted to use it.'

Ella's whole body relaxed in relief. 'I don't want to be a burden.'

'Nonsense.' Polly glanced at the carpet. 'But I think we have to face the fact that a household of this size is exhausting and that you might be here for a little longer than we first thought.'

Ella traced a swirl along the pattern of the eiderdown and nodded.

'I know. But I should pay you some rent.'

'No. We couldn't take that. But if you want to pay for the conversion, then that might be fair.'

'That wouldn't be a problem.'

'Fine. Then it's settled.'

Ella continued to trace the pattern with her fingers.

'What do you think has happened to them both?' she said, a tear trickling down her cheek.

'Honestly? I really don't know. But we can't give up hope, can we?' Polly put her arm around Ella and rested her head on her shoulder. 'I've spent most of my life hoping for something or other and it's usually come good. Right now, I hope more than anything that they're both alive and will get here in the end. We can't give up hoping, ever, don't you think?'

Ella nodded. But still she blamed herself and living with the guilt was almost too much to bear.

Chapter Nineteen

Polly and Ella emptied the coach house of the stored furniture. There were tea cases filled with books, school and university photographs, notebooks with Johnnie's writing scrawled across the title page, bundles of letters. They read them, sitting on broken chairs in the cold with their coats around their shoulders. Ella digested the contents with a mixture of curiosity and apprehension, trying to equate Johnnie's previous life with the one she knew in Malaya. Touching the pages brought him closer for a moment but also made him seem further away, and the guilt grew heavier within her. Wherever he was, she wondered if he reflected on these memories, if they were topics of conversation between him and Grace. She forced herself to imagine him telling their child about his own childhood and reassuring her that one day they'd all be reunited in England; that the strange stories he told her about his upbringing would one day be as familiar to her as the bananas and coconut trees.

One morning, a blue envelope with writing in a strange hand lay waiting for her on Polly's kitchen table.

'Aren't you going to open it?' Polly asked, watching from the corner of her eye as she boiled the kettle to make a fresh pot of tea.

Ella examined the postmark – Southampton. She hadn't heard of it and wondered where it was. She picked up a knife and slid it into the crease of the envelope to open it. She gasped as she read the letter.

'It's from Sarah Harris,' she said, unable to take her eyes off it. 'She says that there was a girl matching Grace's description who came out on their ship when she was evacuated from Singapore. She's included the address of where they've taken her.'

Polly put the kettle down with a bang on the stove and joined Ella.

'Let me see.' She took the page from Ella. 'She says she thinks the child's at Wellington Court . . . that must be where they're looking after unaccompanied children. You'll have to write to them and find out if it is really her.'

Ella wrote straight away, her hand shaking, and the days stretched endlessly as she waited for a reply from Wellington Court. When it arrived, she braced herself before opening the letter.

Dear Mrs McCain,

Thank you for your recent correspondence regarding the search for your missing daughter, Grace McCain, and the information from Mrs Harris who believes that she might have been brought to Wellington Court.

I'm very sorry to have to inform you that the little girl of whom she spoke is not your daughter. We have identified her, and she has already gone to live with relatives in Wiltshire. However,

please rest assured that if we have any information regarding
a child we believe might be your daughter, we will be in touch
with you immediately.

The words danced in front of Ella as she tried to re-read them. This didn't make sense. She lifted her head and through misted eyes looked towards Polly, unable to process the information. She didn't need to say anything. Polly had already guessed. She came to Ella and took the letter from her hand.

'It might not be her this time,' Polly said, folding the letter. 'But it could be the next. She's out there somewhere and someone will have the information that you need to find her. You can't just give up hope.'

But the disappointment was harder than Ella could bear. Although she pretended to Polly that she was fine, she was far from it. It was difficult to muster the strength to carry on with the day, let alone to start searching for her husband and daughter all over again, but she knew she had to. She'd picked herself up a hundred times before, and knew she might have to do it again and again, but it would be worth all the effort when she finally found Grace and Johnnie.

In the following days, the only way she could cope with her disappointment and heartache was by telling herself that she was creating a new home for Grace and Johnnie in the coach house for when they were reunited. She scoured jumble sales and junk shops for a kitchen table and some chairs and tried to patch up an old chesterfield that she'd found. She made some cushions too. Although she was proud of her handiwork, she had found it exhausting. Everything had been so easy at home in Malaya – whatever she wanted, she merely ordered, not thinking about how it was achieved or the effort involved. She tried not to think of all the beautiful dresses hanging in her wardrobe at home; the smaller versions that had been made for Grace. All those days of luxurious living meant nothing to her now. She'd exchange it all forever if she could only find Grace and Johnnie. Whenever she saw women with children the same age as her daughter, she struggled. Sometimes she caught herself thinking: how dare they have daughters when my own is lost miles away?

At night, she tossed and turned, wondering for the hundredth time what had happened to Johnnie and Grace, to the mine and the people who had worked for her – not just the mine workers and their families, but to Farid, Lian, Malik and especially Noor, to whom she had once been so close, almost like a sister. She'd do anything now to turn back the clock and be with them all once more.

Who was occupying her home now? What would have happened to all of their belongings – the photographs she loved of the children, their clothes and toys? And what about Johnnie's dog Apollo? Then there were all the other things that once she had cared about but which didn't seem to matter to her now – the silver, the beautiful silk cushions and inlaid Malacca tables. And, of course, Johnnie's piano. Would it be sitting in the window, bleached by the sun, or had someone closed the shutters to protect it? For a fleeting moment, she remembered the presents she'd bought for Christmas. They had seemed so important to her at the time – how could she have been so foolish as to care about material things when she should have been focusing on the danger that was threatening to divide them all? If only . . . If only . . .

Although Polly had given her a cookery book, Ella struggled to get to grips with English food. The shopkeepers looked at her with suspicion or amusement as she tried to come to grips with English cuts of meat or the names of vegetables and how to cook them, like cabbages and turnips. The rations she got baffled her and trying to produce a meal when she had never had to cook before overwhelmed her. Her hands became chafed and callused from housework and hand-washing clothes; her fingers bore the scars of accidents with kitchen knives as she did her best to cook.

'You've lost so much weight,' Polly said one morning as they drank tea in the kitchen. 'You were a bag of bones when you arrived, but I'd hoped we might have put some flesh on you by now.'

Ella shrugged. Between her anxiety and inability to cook, her appetite seemed to have disappeared.

'And you've got the darkest rings under your eyes that I've seen on anyone.'

'It's so hard—'

'I know.' Polly touched her arm. 'But you've got to think of Toby, apart from anything else.'

'And I feel so guilty just for being here.' Ella dropped her head in her hands and let out a deep sigh. 'And I know you're probably right, but how can I go on when every moment of my day I'm wondering where they are and how I can find them?'

'No one's telling you what you should do.' Polly paused.

'But you will find them. Meanwhile, you've got to get on with your life. I know it's miserable, but you must grin and bear it. There's nothing else you can do.'

Ella knew that Polly was right, but her words didn't take away the pain and longing. Nothing seemed to lighten the heaviness of her heart and there wasn't much that made her feel welcome in this strange and far-from-home land.

As the days became longer, she found herself spending more time with Polly and the evacuees. Jenny would curl up close on the sofa and ask to be read to. Ella was torn – she wanted to resist becoming fond of the girl, knowing that one day she'd return to her mother in London. Ella didn't know if she could cope with another loss, but it was hard not to offer comfort to the motherless child. She hoped someone would be doing the same for Grace, even though the softness of Jenny's breath on her cheek, the brush of her hair against Ella's hand, pained her more than she could say.

Every moment of every day, Ella's thoughts turned to Grace and Johnnie. When she pooled her rations with Polly, she wondered what Grace was eating for lunch. In the evenings when they cooked together, she pictured Grace at the villa eating her *roti* or drinking coconut milk flavoured with mango. When Toby fell asleep, she'd sit with Polly, listening to the wireless or reading, imagining that Grace was asleep upstairs and that all she had to do was go up and she'd find her underneath the woollen blankets, her black curls spilling over the pillow.

And every day the papers reported more air strikes against the Allied forces and how the Japanese seemed to be gaining political control in Indonesia, Burma and India. Ella absorbed the news, her breathing shallow, as the prospect of them all being reunited seemed to slip further and further away.

Then one day she received a letter from Melody:

Dear Ella,

I hope that you are well and have settled in England. I have at last found out that Edward didn't make it out of Singapore – my understanding is that he's in Changi. The Red Cross have tried to get notes to the prisoners, so if he's there, he might learn that we made it out safely.

I know it must be difficult for you, for as I remember, you'd had no news of Johnnie and Grace when we last wrote. Whilst I can't be certain that they are safe, I do hope that one day you, too, will receive some news. I know it doesn't help, but if Johnnie is in Changi, I am certain that he and Edward will be together, and we should let that be a comfort.

Meanwhile, I have been called up. I'm in the Fire Service. Every night there seems to be something to attend to. There's always another raid, people needing to be rescued from rubble and taken to hospital. I'm quite busy, but if you're in London, I would love to see you. My flat is near Sloane Square and very handy.

With love and best regards,
Melody x

Ella wrote back:

234

The Forgotten Promise

Dear Melody,

I am so sad to hear about Edward, but it is good to know that he is at least alive. It is good also to hear that you are well, and I am sure you are being kept very busy. I can't imagine what it must be like in London – I've seen the bombers going overhead, of course, and we've had our share of running to air-raid shelters in the middle of the night, but luckily we haven't been hit here in Oxford. I've seen such terrible photographs in the newspapers and in newsreels at the pictures.

Unfortunately, I still have no news of Grace and Johnnie. I think about them all the time and can't bear to picture what they must be experiencing in Malaya. I pray every day that I'll hear from them soon – that they're on a boat or a ship bound for England. Every knock at the door, I expect it to be them, and you can't imagine the heartbreak when it isn't. I've written repeatedly to the Red Cross and I'm permanently checking passenger listings, but nothing so far.

Meanwhile, James and Polly have kindly given me a small coach house to live in, which I have done up ready for when they do get here. It's not a palace, but if you ever find yourself needing a weekend out of London, I would love to see you.

Ella x

Tips of blossom began to appear on trees and at last the early-morning frost and mists gave way to warmth in the air. Ella found the change unexpectedly beautiful; the dramatically changing seasons weren't something she was familiar with after the constant climate of Malaya. She sat for hours looking out of the window, finding it hard not to imagine Grace playing amongst the apple trees with Johnnie and Toby, who was now coasting about but not yet walking.

'I thought you might like to help me,' said Polly, knocking on the coach-house door one morning. She was carrying a stack of small terracotta pots and wearing a pair of navy overalls that she called her siren suit. She made her way over to the kitchen table where she set down the pots. 'I've always liked to garden and last year we managed to grow a lot of potatoes, carrots, parsnips and sprouts for ourselves. Herr Hitler might be trying his best to starve us, but I for one can dig very well for victory. I kept a lot of seeds from last year and you can grow potatoes in almost anything.'

'I've never grown a thing.' Ella had just finished feeding Toby a bowl of eggs and milk, which she had got used to making with hot water and powder from a tin. 'I wouldn't know where to start.'

'Well, it's a bit early but we can begin with these – you've got a sunny window ledge and now that the warmer weather is on its way, it won't be long before you see the shoots appearing.'

Ella finished feeding Toby. Then, with Polly's guidance, the three of them began to fill pots and trays with soil, pricking out spaces for seeds. She helped Toby drop seeds into the holes and watched while Polly wrote on labels.

'You do know,' she said, putting down her pen and pursing her lips for a moment before she continued, 'that they might not come back?' Still she didn't look at Ella, but nevertheless was assessing her reaction.

'They will,' Ella said with force. 'I'm certain of it.'

Their eyes met across the table. 'Yes. But what if they don't? What if they have to spend the rest of the war in a POW camp or some such place? It's something you might have to face.'

'No. They will get here. I really need to believe it.'

Polly sighed and took hold of her hand. 'I'm not asking you to give up hope, but who knows when this damn war will end and how long you might have to wait? You can't spend all your days gazing out of the window waiting for them to return.' Ella felt Polly squeeze her hand. 'I find it hard to see you looking so sorrowful all the time.'

Ella shrugged. She wanted to say that it was easy for her to say that, it wasn't her daughter who was missing, but as soon as the thought formed, she knew it was wrong to think like that. Polly must be in knots too, wondering what had happened to Johnnie.

'I don't really know where to start. Everything I've tried has ended in failure, and –' she felt awkward saying it '– everything in England is still so strange.'

'I understand that, too. But you can help me in the garden. It might give you pleasure to see things grow.'

And so the days took on a new form. In the mornings, Ella helped Polly in the blooming garden while the evacuees and Toby played on the lawn. Sometimes they'd all walk by the river as the powder-blue light filtered through the leaves overhead or feed any crumbs of bread they could spare to the ducks.

Ella looked towards the water. Two swans were gliding a short distance away. They moved with such grace even though they had to paddle hard to keep moving. Life was like that, she realised, not just for her, but for everyone around her. The war affected everyone, and everyone was finding it hard to keep afloat.

'Thank you,' Ella said to Polly, watching the swans. 'I don't think I could have coped these past few weeks without you. Who'd have thought this time last year that all this would have happened?'

'I know. But I'm a great believer in trying to find the good in whatever situation we can.'

'And how do you see that working for me?'

'Try not to look back on things, to dwell too much. And try to think about all the things you've achieved, however small they might seem. Toby is a happy little boy. And you are learning to manage by yourself in a place you don't know or understand – I think Johnnie would be impressed by all that.'

Ella thought for a moment. It was difficult to express the sense of failure and guilt that followed her around like a shadow. But there was another layer now to her feelings, she realised. Instead of being someone who mattered, who could make a difference to others, she felt she had no purpose – essentially, she was no one. Would Polly understand this or view such thoughts as self-indulgence?

'But every day,' she sighed, focusing on what she thought Polly would sympathise with, 'I feel terrible, so guilty, for being here, for being alive.'

'Just because they're missing doesn't mean they can't be

in your thoughts every day or that you're disloyal for finding pleasure in your own life. You'll find a way to make sense of it all, I'm sure. But what that is will be for you to discover.'

High summer began to fade. Montbretia flamed in the garden while rosehips filled the hedgerows. There was more beauty in England than Ella had realised. Polly's words of encouragement lingered with her like the warmth of the sun, and it was while she was enjoying a walk by the river, with a by now tottering Toby, that she decided to make some small sketches and drawings of moments she had enjoyed, to show Grace when they were finally reunited. *These are blackberries*, she wrote on the back of a watercolour sketch. *Toby and I walked along the footpath to Oxford. We saw so many and picked a bowlful for our afternoon tea.* And on another day, she captured a moorhen gliding on the water. *There are lots of these birds on the riverbank, Gracie, I'm sure you'd like them, although Toby and I prefer feeding the ducks. They're so enthusiastic when we throw breadcrumbs into the water.* She added a small line drawing of Toby in his wellingtons scattering bread into the river and a duck dipping its head into the water to catch it.

One afternoon, eight months or so after arriving in England, Ella had just come back from a walk where she'd been picking hips and haws to display in jugs. For the first time in ages, she was feeling content after drinking in the mellow and comforting autumn colours. At last, after all the upheaval, her life was beginning to settle.

When she returned home, she found a letter for her postmarked from London. She ripped it open.

Dearest Ella,

I hope you don't mind, but I have a few days' holiday at the end of the month and I thought it would be lovely to visit you. I could get a train on Friday 16th if that suits you and stay for a few days. It would be so good to catch up again.

Melody x

Chapter Twenty

On the morning of Melody's arrival, Ella busied herself baking ginger cake and walnut bread from the recipe books that Polly had given to her. It took her a long time and was probably not up to Noor's standard of cookery, but when she had finished, she was proud of what she had achieved. As she washed up, her thoughts turned to how much Melody's life and her own had run in parallel. For a moment, her memories wandered back to the happier times they had shared: their voices ringing out in stifling hot school corridors; lying on beds as teenagers discussing makeup and boys; the day of Ella's wedding; Melody as Maid of Honour catching the bouquet of apricot-coloured orchids tossed with the full intention that she should catch it. How far away that life seemed now.

The past continued to hang over Ella as she collected apples from the store where Polly had wrapped them in newspaper and laid them in sand, and memories of servants and parties followed her as she returned from the butcher with a few meagre slices of ham and a couple of ounces of cheese.

Finally, she placed a vase of marigolds on the kitchen table and dusted the living room, where Melody was to sleep on the sofa, then stood back and admired her work as sunlight blazed through the gleaming windows. She tried to picture her old friend sitting on the sofa, her laughter rippling through the air just as it always had, although this time it would be through cold English air rather than while sipping sundowners on a warm verandah to the chirping of crickets.

When everything was ready, Ella realised she was a little late and cycled in a hurry to Oxford station along the riverside with Toby perched in the rear child seat. There were servicemen crowding around the entrance, noisy with their bulging kit bags and hot in their khaki, as well as a scattering of uniformed doctors and nurses. She leant her bicycle against a lamppost and was about to ask the conductor if the train from Paddington had come in, when she saw Melody waiting by the entrance with a small cream suitcase at her feet. Her head was down and she was reading a copy of *Woman's Own*.

'Ella!' Melody beamed. 'It's so good to see you.' She stepped towards her and kissed her on both cheeks. 'And look at Toby! He's walking!'

'I know. And it's wonderful to see you, too.' Ella kissed her back, a glow of happiness radiating through her.

'What a journey! The train was absolutely packed with servicemen, but luckily I got a seat.'

'You're here at last, I can hardly believe it,' Ella said. 'Are you all right walking?' She looked at Melody's feet. Burgundy court shoes, not suitable for the uneven path. 'I should have said really – I cycled here with Toby, and thought we could catch up on the walk back. I can balance your case on the front of my bike.'

'That would be lovely. After that journey, I could really do with some fresh air.'

Ella took the case – thankfully little heavier than an overnight bag – and led the way out of the station.

'It's glorious here.' Melody paused and looked around her then at the college spires in the distance. 'So peaceful and strangely undamaged after London – and the river is so pretty.'

'Yes. Oxford has been lucky; we seem to have been spared the bombing. You can even cycle for miles in both directions without having to worry about sirens going off and needing to find an air-raid shelter if there's a plane flying overhead.'

'Can you really?'

'We should take a ride out – what about a picnic? Polly would be happy to lend you her bike if you want.'

'That sounds like a dream. What about you, Toby, I bet you'd like that, wouldn't you?'

'Oh, he certainly will. He loves nature – especially the ducks.'

They walked a few steps further, then a grimace twisted Melody's features and she slowed.

'Stupid shoes. I knew they were impractical but I wanted to look nice. Do you mind if I sit down?' She nodded towards a bench facing the river.

Ella propped her bike against a tree. Toby pottered on the path picking up stones as Melody and Ella settled on a nearby bench.

Ella stared ahead of her at a pair of swans floating by and asked her friend, 'It's been ages. How have you been?'

'To be honest, it's been hard. I think about Edward every day, holed up in that damn prison. I'm glad I've got the Fire Service to take my mind off it, but what's happening in London is so dreadful.' Melody dabbed her eyes with a handkerchief, then took a packet of Pall Mall from her bag and lit a cigarette with her silver lighter. The flame sparked then settled down as the tobacco caught. 'I suppose it was a shock to start with. All the bombing, the flattened buildings and injured people. Often children.'

Ella winced.

'I'm sorry to talk about it, Ella, but it's dreadful. You've never seen anything like it. It's enough to drive anyone mad. Night after night of air raids, sleeping in the tube stations if you're in the wrong place when the raids begin.' Melody started to cry. 'And all the time I keep thinking, why am I here? I should be with Edward. What if he's no longer alive . . . if I never see him again? And sometimes I think I can't live the rest of my life, hoping and waiting in limbo like this.'

Ella nodded. How well she understood. She wasn't certain what to say but repeated the phrases Polly had used to soothe her. *We can't think like that. We can only look forward to better days – when all this is over, we'll be reunited.*

'But what if we never are, Ella?' There was fear and exasperation in Melody's voice. 'Isn't that something we have to consider? Just think,' Melody lowered her voice to a whisper, '*we* could be dead tomorrow – a bomb could drop on us and then we'd never have had the chance to say we were sorry for leaving them behind.'

Ella flinched as though punched; the weight of the prospect lodged in the pit of her stomach.

'I know how you feel – the helplessness is maddening. I've tried so hard to find out what happened to Grace and Johnnie. Once, someone wrote to me with a description of a child like her in a reception centre in Southampton. It wasn't her, of course. It's so dreadful not knowing.'

'They could be in Changi, Ella. So many people were taken there. Or if not there, another camp. Have you had any joy from the Red Cross?'

Ella shook her head and Melody placed a hand on her arm.

'I really can't imagine what it's like not knowing.'

'I have to hang on to the hope that someone might be able to tell me something – anything at all.'

A cloud covered the sun as silence fell between them.

'But that's not the only thing.' Ella picked at a piece of fluff on her skirt. 'Do you remember when I left home, those last words I had with Johnnie . . . how annoyed I was about the passports?'

'Yes.'

'I should have told him that I loved him.' She wiped away a tear that clung to her lashes. 'I don't want some cross and hastily said words to be the last memory he has of me.'

'Oh, Ella, he knows. We all say things we don't mean, but you know he knows that you adore him. Push that thought away right now or it will destroy you.'

Ella mulled it over for a moment. Melody was probably right, but it didn't make her feel any better about things.

'Come on,' Ella said eventually. 'We ought to get back home. You've come here for a break, and that's what we should be doing.' She stood up, glancing at the two swans swimming in tandem ahead of them, then took Toby's hand. 'This one will be getting tired and hungry.'

'You're right.' Melody thrust her handkerchief into her handbag, closing it with a loud snap. 'You and I, we've been through some things, haven't we? Thank goodness we have each other.' She joined Ella and they made their way along the tree-lined path back home, but something hung between them like a shadow.

'I love it,' Melody said as they approached the coach house. Her words were bright and breezy, if a little forced. 'It's so tucked away, and I can't believe you've got your own place.'

'There's a veg garden at the back.' Ella took the key out of her pocket and opened the door. 'I've become a bit of a gardener this year.'

The door swung open. The afternoon light was mellow and hit the inside of the coach house at just the right angle. Melody gasped.

'This is amazing!' she said. 'Did you do all this?'

'Yes. It was hard, though.'

Ella watched with pleasure as Melody ran her fingers over the old chesterfield and the polished table.

'I'm glad you like it.'

Ella placed the suitcase on the floor by the sofa. Melody picked Toby up and her face glowed. Ella filled the kettle and put it on the stove, then she warmed the teapot, slowly swooshing the water around the base before filling it with leaves, watching them unfurl in the warmth. Melody's visit, she realised, was bittersweet. Her friend's presence was making Ella's wounds feel raw again and that was going to make it harder to push her own feelings to one side and try to enjoy their time together. And it was difficult not to think about their life in Malaya, the escape from Singapore and that awful journey back on the ship. If only she could cope with the wave of feelings, perhaps she could find a way of being happy, as Melody was trying to do, without every moment being haunted by her loss.

Melody stifled a yawn. Her face was flushed from the walk.

'Would you like some ginger cake?' Ella asked. 'I thought we could eat dinner after I've put Toby to bed. About seven-thirty, if that's all right?'

'Fabulous.' Melody flopped down onto a chair with Toby next to her. 'What do you think, Toby, shall we have some ginger cake?'

He nodded. Ella cut thick slices and spread a thin layer of butter over them. The cake was moist and sticky, just the way she liked it. She passed a plate with cut-up slices to Melody, who picked at it between feeding small pieces to Toby. When he'd finished eating, he clambered from the sofa and played with his blocks and a wooden train set. Ella and Melody chatted until the clock struck five.

'I'd better give Toby his bath.' Ella pushed back her chair. 'Why don't you put your feet up – there are some books by the sofa. I've even managed to find a few magazines.'

'I've got this.' Melody pulled her copy of *Woman's Own* out of her bag. 'Not much chance of buying any of this lot now that clothing is rationed,' she said, flicking through the pages. 'Look at that dress, will you? Duchess satin. Imagine.'

'It won't last forever.' Ella lifted Toby from the floor. 'I guess we all have to *make do and mend*, as they say.'

Melody yawned again.

'Why don't you make yourself more comfortable? Lie on my bed until I've sorted Toby out.'

'I'll be fine here, but shouldn't I help you clear away first?'

'No need. But thank you for offering.'

As Ella mixed powdered milk with water for Toby's bottle, she glanced up at Melody. The milk mixture boiled in a pan and she stirred it. However hard it was going to be, she was determined to enjoy her friend's company without allowing the ghosts of the past to intrude.

When Toby was finally asleep and she got back to Melody, she said, 'I've got some sloe gin somewhere, if you fancy it? Homemade. My mother-in-law made it last year.'

Melody nodded. 'You know, that would be really nice.'

While they drank, Ella sliced the walnut bread, which she thought would go well with the apples, put slices of ham on a plate and tomatoes in a bowl, then boiled the new potatoes she had dug from the garden that morning. Her folder of drawings was propped up by the sofa and she tried not to let her eyes wander towards it as she prepared the food.

'Apart from a ride along the river, what would you like to do while you're here?' she asked. 'We *could* do a tour of Oxford – although it's still a university holiday and there won't be many students, especially with all the men away. The cathedral will be open. And the Pitt Rivers Museum. Toby loves the artefacts there. We could even go to the pictures, later, if you like, providing Polly can look after Toby.'

'Maybe. Let's see tomorrow. Come on. Let's sit outside with our dinner and enjoy the summer evening. I know it's a bit cold, but we can take our coats and a blanket. It's so nice to be away from London. You can show me that garden of yours if you like.'

Ella placed everything she'd prepared on a tray and together, armed with coats and a blanket, they took their food outside. Melody placed the blanket on a patch of grass under an apple tree and they ate listening to the blackbirds singing while rooks traced their route home through the air.

After they had eaten, Ella showed Melody the vegetable garden. The sunlight was mellow, and bees and butterflies flitted between the flowers and vegetable heads. It was one of those lovely endings to a glorious day, made drowsier still by the effects of the sloe gin. Almost perfect. It was the type of moment she wanted to capture and hold onto forever.

But she couldn't help thinking: what if this war dragged on for years? Or worse still, what if Johnnie and Grace never came back? Melody had planted a niggling seed in her mind, and like the plants that had germinated in the garden, she wondered how much worse her loneliness would become, and whether it could ever possibly grow into something good.

'We ought to get back in,' she said, as the last remnants of sunlight flooded the garden, casting long shadows from the trees. 'Once the sun's in, it will be cold. Five, ten minutes at the most.'

They were a little tipsy when they returned to the house; the gin was much stronger than she had realised. Melody tripped up, almost knocking Ella's folder flying from the table, and they giggled like the schoolgirls they once were.

'Don't worry about it,' Ella said, dabbing at her laugher tears with a hankie. 'But are you sure you'll be all right sleeping in here on the sofa – you can share the bed with me if you like?'

'I'll be fine sleeping here,' Melody said. 'I'll only keep you awake. I think I've started to snore.'

They laughed again. And for a moment, it was like old times, when they were young and didn't have any worries. Ella hugged Melody, so very glad that she had come to stay.

Chapter Twenty-One

'How about going into Oxford?' Melody asked the following morning.

'We could take a picnic, if you like. It looks like it might stay sunny today.'

'Great!' Melody grinned. One of those smiles that lit up the whole of her face and which it was impossible not to give in to. It was a smile that Ella had missed, and one she loved so much. 'What shall we take?'

'Let me see.' Ella ran through in her mind what they could pack. 'I've got some walnut bread left over – we could take some cheese, apples and tomatoes, too.' She thought of the elaborate picnics she'd had in Malaya. Noor would spend the morning making curries, coconut rice and spicy chilli *sambal*, *roti canai*, plantains cooked in batter, all packed in tin containers with lids that kept the food warm until they wanted it. Sometimes they'd drink fresh mango juice or eat soursops or rambutans – she suddenly longed to peel away the red spiny skins and reveal the glistening fruit beneath.

Her mind was still far away as she cut slices of bread and cheese and wrapped them in greaseproof paper. It took her back to that day when she and Johnnie had visited Lake Peyang. She'd worn her favourite teal-coloured dress, the one that set off her delicate complexion and the colour of her hair. Johnnie had carried the picnic basket from his car while she carried a blanket. When they'd finished the curries he'd brought with him in a stack of steel containers, they'd eaten a small selection of the sweet *kuih* Noor had made, and then out of the blue he got down on one knee and asked Ella to marry him.

'*Yes! Oh, my God, yes! Absolutely!*' She'd been unable to prevent her instant acceptance from fizzing out of her. They'd drunk a bottle of champagne that somehow he'd managed to keep hidden and chilled, and then he'd given her a ring, which sparkled like the iridescent wings of a kingfisher flashing across the water.

Now, as she turned the ring on her finger, she longed for the innocent glow of that afternoon, along with the thrill and promise of their future life together.

'How about taking something to drink?' Melody's voice broke into her reverie.

'Good idea.' She nodded. 'There are a couple of bottles of ginger ale in there.' She indicated the cupboard.

Melody fetched the bottles and put them in the wicker basket that Ella had placed on the table.

'What about a blanket?' Ella asked. 'To sit on?'

Melody shrugged. 'No harm, I suppose.'

Ella collected her cardigan, a lightweight blanket from her bedroom along with a pullover for Toby and a hat. From the window she noticed low, long wisps of cloud in the sky that hinted at possible rain.

When she and Melody were ready, Ella picked up the

picnic basket, hitched Toby to her hip, and they made their way outside. The scent of roses hung in the air and gentle sunlight warmed their skin.

'Here we go.' Ella put Toby in the rear seat and Melody borrowed Polly's bike, then they cycled along the bank of the Thames. The Oxford spires grew closer, and Ella glanced at the sky once more. The clouds were lower, slightly threatening now, and she wondered if they'd made a mistake. Still, they didn't need to go for long, she decided, an hour or so would be enough. They cycled beside the river to the point where the Cherwell and the Isis merged and then on into the town.

They pushed their laden bicycles through the covered market and into Broad Street. There were RAF personnel in uniform mingling with nurses and academics in black gowns. As they walked past college gates, they glimpsed the tents temporarily erected there to house the medical and military personnel who Ella explained to Melody now occupied most of the buildings.

'James says Oxford is busier than ever. There might not be as many students, but the military and medical staff have requisitioned most of the grounds. They've even grown vegetables in the fellows' gardens.'

Melody admired it all, comparing it to the devastation in London, and saying how lucky they were, despite the bombers overhead and servicemen filling the streets, to have so far avoided the full onslaught of the war. After viewing the centre of town, they made their way through Christ Church, where Melody admired the vast quadrangle, before heading back to the river. Boats were tied up by the riverbank, and

Ella and Melody got off their bikes and leant them against a tree before unloading the picnic basket and blanket.

Ella shook out the blanket on a patch of ground under a tree where they faced the river, then took Toby out of his seat. He seemed happy and his cheeks were rosy as he tottered about in the grass.

Melody took the small packages of food that Ella had wrapped in brown paper and placed them on the blanket. With the birds singing overhead and the sun glancing off the water, she couldn't think of a more perfect place to share a picnic. They ate, picking at the open parcels of food, sipping ginger beer from the bottle, and watching the river go by as though there wasn't anything to worry about, least of all German forces trampling over Czechoslovakia and Tobruk falling into enemy hands.

Toby, tired from the fresh air and activity, soon fell asleep. Ella lay down with her head on her rolled-up cardigan and watched the white clouds drifting overhead. 'You know, I feel so much better after our conversation last night. I think you're right. Johnnie must have left Menglembu and reached Singapore with Grace. The more I think about it, they must have missed the last ships home and then, of course, the Japanese would have taken them to Changi. It doesn't make any sense for him not to have done otherwise.'

Melody lay down next to her. 'I know. I certainly think that's the only explanation. But try not to picture them there too much. I find it helps, you know, to remember Edward in happier times, otherwise I think I'd go a little mad.'

Ella shut her eyes. She focused on the image of Johnnie on the doorstep the last time she had seen him, the blue of his eyes and the golden light in his hair. She could almost smell the sandalwood soap and the sun on his skin. She pictured Grace next to him, her soft curls falling to her shoulders, her long dark lashes, the touch of her fingers against Ella's. Melody was right. However hard it was not to focus on that stupid parting exchange with Johnnie, she found it comforted her to think of them all at home. She told herself it was as though she had gone on holiday for a while, and they were waiting for her, and how happy they would all be when they were reunited on the steps of the villa once again – it was futile to focus on anything else.

She began to doze as she dreamt of them, half-listening to the hum of a bumblebee inspecting nearby flower heads and lulled by the lapping rhythm of the water. Melody turned on her side. A plane flew overhead, and a gentle warm breeze fanned their cheeks. Time drifted by idyllically for Ella as she lay wrapped in the comfort of her thoughts.

'Melody?' A man's voice with an American accent broke into her dreams. 'Is that you?'

Melody shifted, then sat up. Ella opened her eyes, and then she, too, sat up. Standing a few feet away was a tall man of around forty, dressed in a pair of light trousers and a linen jacket. He had dark hair, visible beneath a Panama hat, and a Leica slung casually over his right shoulder. His skin was slightly tanned and his eyes were a dark brown, almost black. They looked deep and penetrating, as his gaze fell upon them both, and utterly alive.

'Andrew!' Melody's voice seemed full of surprise. 'Fancy meeting you here!'

'I'm based in Oxford, didn't you know?' He stood with his hands in his pockets and head to one side.

'No, I didn't. What an absolutely wonderful coincidence.'

'Having a picnic?'

'We are indeed.'

'Well, it's a lovely day for it.'

Melody's laughter rippled over the water. 'Ella, this is my friend Andrew Howard. Andrew, this is my best friend, Ella McCain.'

Andrew lifted his hat from his head. His eyes sparkled as he said, 'How do you do?'

'Pleased to meet you,' Ella replied. She raised her hand to her blouse, where her fingers pinched the top button as she took him in. He looked steadily back at her, and it made her feel as though she were the most charming person in the world.

'So, what are you doing?' Melody asked. She was sitting completely upright, one hand to her forehead, shielding her eyes from the sun. 'Shouldn't you be working?'

Ella took in Andrew's civilian clothes and the cut of his jacket and wondered if he was one of the personnel from RAF Benson.

'Or are you on leave?' Melody continued.

'Sort of. I live here now.' He smiled again. 'I've been doing some photo-reconnaissance work over at Mount Farm – it's a temporary RAF base, do you know it?'

'No.'

'I'm just having a bit of time to myself today.'

'Andrew's really a photo-journalist.' Melody lowered her

hand and turned to Ella. 'He's always on the lookout for some big story.'

'Well, I'm a bit of a failure at the moment. Everyone who is everyone in journalism seems to be beating me.' He touched the edge of his hat with his right hand. 'Enjoy the rest of your day. It's been nice to meet you, Ella McCain.'

'Oh, don't go.' Melody stood up. 'We'd love you to stay for a bit, wouldn't we, Ella?'

'Well, if it's what you want.' Ella nodded. She glanced at Toby, who was still sleeping, and it looked as though he was out for the count. 'I don't think we're going anywhere any time soon.'

Andrew hesitated. 'I really don't want to gate-crash. '

He sat down on the edge of the blanket and took off his hat. Melody handed him a bottle of ginger beer. He snapped the cap off with his thumb and forefinger then sipped, looking at Ella through half-closed eyes. She could feel him watching her.

'So, what brings you two ladies here to Oxford, eating a picnic on the banks of the river?'

'Oh, I'm on leave from the Fire Service in London,' Melody said. 'Ella lives here and as yet hasn't been called up.'

'Really.' His gaze swung towards her and Toby.

'I'm not originally from here,' Ella said.

'Ah, I see. Are you from Malaya, too?'

'Yes.'

They sat for a moment without speaking as fractals of sunlight skipped across the surface of the river, radiating light. Andrew lit a cigar. The rich scent drifted on the air.

'Tell me something about yourself, Ella,' he asked. His voice echoed the soothing rhythm of the water.

'Me?' Her hand found her top button again. 'What do you want to know?'

'Well, you've already told me you are from Malaya – where were you born?

'Menglembu. Near Ipoh.'

A flicker of recognition drifted across his face.

'Do you know it?' she asked.

'A little. I used to travel a lot.' He waved his hand vaguely in the air.

'Andrew visited us once when I was at school,' Melody joined in. 'Our parents were friends.'

Andrew's eyes turned to Melody than back to Ella before he took another sip from his bottle.

'As well as being a photographer, Andrew's a bit of an art dealer. He's sold a couple of paintings of mine in the past.'

'It's more of a hobby, really.'

'Actually, Ella paints, too,' Melody continued.

Ella flashed her a warning look.

'I'm hardly a painter,' she interrupted. 'Just a few small things I've done for myself.'

'That's not true!' Melody smiled. 'She's very talented. You should see them, Andrew. I'm sure you'd love them.'

Ella looked up at him. His eyes were on her, as though waiting for her to say something. Her face burnt with a sensation like prickly heat. 'No,' she said breathlessly. 'I really don't think so.'

'Fair enough.' He finished the contents of his bottle and placed it on the ground.

They chatted for a while. Melody talked about a raid she'd been stranded in; Andrew about his time taking news photographs during the Blitz. Ella sat with her arms around her knees, listening, watching the line of his jaw, the way his Adam's apple moved as he spoke. His voice was as soothing as the rhythm of the water and lightness took hold of her, as though she were a cork floating on the water.

'I ought to be getting on now.' He looked at his watch and stood up. 'Thank you. It's been a pleasure. I hope we meet again.' He placed his Panama back on his head and left.

Ella watched him disappear along the path towards the centre of town. A frog jumped from the bank onto a lily pad, ducks scattered across their path to hide in the rushes. She turned to Melody.

'Now, you,' she teased. 'Tell me again how you know someone like him?'

Melody grinned. 'Like I said, our parents were friends. His father was interested in art and Andrew inherited that from him. When I started painting, as an old friend, he sold a few of my paintings for me.'

A gentle breeze ruffled the leaves of the trees around them, followed by a drop of rain, then another. Ella looked up at the sky: a dark cloud had covered the sun. She listened to the pattering sounds all around them.

'Quick!' she said, gathering up their belongings and waking Toby. 'Let's shelter over there until it passes.' She indicated a bridge they could stand beneath.

The rain grew heavier and continued for half an hour, soaking their feet as they sheltered. In the end, the clouds broke and the downpour eased off, though stray drops still formed glittering rings on the surface of the river. They decided to head back to Wood Eaton, laughing as they cycled, dodging the puddles on the tow path in a desperate bid to get home before another downpour started.

As Ella opened the coach-house door, thunder clattered above and lightning burst across the sky, illuminating the interior with an intense electric light.

'Thank goodness we're home, if a little soaked,' Melody said, placing the picnic basket on the table. 'Shall I put the kettle on?'

'That would be nice.' Ella sat Toby on a chair and took off his jacket, shaking droplets of water all over the floor.

It was then that she noticed a letter on the table. Polly must have placed it there when they were out.

'I hope you enjoyed that,' Melody said as she filled the kettle from the tap. Her skin had been kissed by the sun earlier and freckles were forming like the markings of a butterfly across her nose and cheeks.

'Yes,' Ella said. 'I really think I did.' She paused, fingering the letter on the table and wondering who it was from. Could it possibly contain some information about Johnnie and Grace?

The women changed into dry clothes, then Melody filled the teapot and brought two cups and saucers along with the teapot and some milk to the table. They sat down.

'It's a bit like old times, don't you think?' she asked. 'You and me getting into the occasional scrape?'

'Perhaps.' Ella smiled, glancing at the envelope once more.

Melody stirred the leaves in the pot, waiting for the tea to brew, and nodded absently at the letter Ella was still toying with. 'Well, aren't you going to open it then?'

Ella took a knife from the table and ran it crisply across the envelope. A letter, handwritten in blue ink, lay inside. She unfolded the sheet of paper, which crackled like a log fire spitting. She gave a small gasp, and her hand flew to her mouth.

'What is it?' Melody asked. 'Whatever is the matter?'

'It's from Edith Gibbins. She was our doctor's wife in Ipoh. I saw her name in a passenger list and wrote to her via the Red Cross weeks and weeks ago. She says she's in Witney. And, oh, my goodness, she's invited me for tea at her house a week on Wednesday.' Ella lifted her head and looked at her friend. 'She says she might have some news about Johnnie and Grace.'

Chapter Twenty-Two

The night before her visit to Edith, Ella woke long before the birds were singing, and the first rays of sun had crept through the gaps in the curtain. She sat by the window, waiting, and watching the sun rise, with a massive knot in her stomach.

'Take as long as you like,' Polly told her as she picked at her breakfast. 'Toby will be fine with me. And when Jenny and Peter are home from school, they can help me entertain him.'

Ella nodded and got ready. She left the house clutching her bag and walked along the street to catch a bus to the station. The train journey was painfully slow, and her nerves were jangled and frayed long before she reached the semi-detached house where Edith had said she was staying.

The address was easy to find, and on Ella's arrival, Edith was keen to settle her by the fire. The weather had changed: it was much cooler, and Ella had started shivering with anticipation as soon as she'd entered the house.

A tea tray had already been set out on a low table: finger sandwiches, a Victoria sponge. The thought of eating anything made Ella feel sick. She sank onto the sofa as Edith indicated she should.

'I'm so glad you wrote to me – it's a miracle that you found me, really. Thank goodness for the Red Cross!'

'Yes, I'm glad I did.' Ella picked at her thumb, ripping at a tag of skin, desperate to get the polite conversation out of the way. She just wanted to shout – *so what do you know?* But part of her was fearful of what the woman might say.

'Well,' Edith smoothed her mint-green linen skirt as she sat down in a high-backed chair, 'as I wrote to you, I think I have some news of your family.'

Suddenly, Ella's shoulders shook and she wiped the corners of her eyes with her handkerchief.

'My God, Edith. Please tell me.'

'When we got to the docks in Singapore, they wouldn't let Bernard board the ship. Women and children only, they said, and now he's in that ghastly gaol . . .'

'I'm sorry. That's terrible. It was the same for us too, with Edward. But—' Ella hesitated, not wanting to seem insensitive but desperate for more information. 'Do you know anything about Johnnie? Do you know if he made it out of Malaya, and did he have Grace with him?'

Edith concentrated on Ella. 'Ah, yes. Johnnie. That's why I asked you here. I do go off at a tangent sometimes.' Ella waited, her heart pounding like galloping hooves.

'There was all kinds of chaos when we left. Everyone was in such a panic once Ipoh was bombed. Bernard had been to Menglembu to take our money and my jewellery out of the bank when he met your husband. Bernard thought Johnnie was doing the same, you know, so he could make his way to Singapore with everyone else. But it turned out that he was taking out money to pay the mine workers and said that after that he was on his way to join you in Singapore. Our husbands made plans to meet up outside Menglembu so we could all travel on together – safety in numbers and all that. But then, Bernard said, Johnnie had to sit down – he was shaking and covered in perspiration.' Edith paused. 'Now then . . . did Bernard say he'd actually got diphtheria or was he just worried that he had? Or was that your daughter . . . Honestly, my memory! Not as sharp as it used to be. Anyway, the long and the short of it was that Johnnie can't have been at all well as he didn't arrive at the meeting point. We waited and waited, but he never came. In the end, we simply had to leave.'

'I see.' Ella absorbed the information that Edith had just given her.

'There's something else.' Edith gazed towards the window. 'When we got to Singapore, we heard that the Japanese had taken many of the British still left in Malaya prisoners.' Edith reached across to Ella and took her hand. 'I know nothing is definite, but if your husband isn't in Changi, which doesn't seem likely, then he's in a POW camp somewhere else. I suspect the same will be the case for Grace, too, but I can't imagine that they've been kept together.' Edith's voice faltered, as though she knew she had said too much.

The news was not what Ella had been hoping for and she spent the rest of her visit dizzy with anxiety. When she finally got the train back home, which was late and horribly crowded, nausea seeped through her. She gazed out of the window, pressing her face against the glass, going over in her mind again and again what Edith had said. Rain lashed against the pane, and she watched the drops slither and slide like headless worms until they pooled at the bottom of the frame where they disappeared and the whole process started again. Why had Johnnie broken his promise to join the others on their way to Singapore? How could he not have put the safety of Grace above everything else? Edith implied he'd been ill, and now Ella recalled the last two telephone conversations she'd had with Johnnie. He'd clearly been a lot worse than she'd realised. Diphtheria – after all he'd done to protect everyone. The thought was almost too much for her to bear. Her fragile heart seemed frozen, and she wondered if her blood would ever thaw, or if her heart would shatter from the strain. There was simply no way of knowing what had happened to her husband or to Grace. She closed her eyes, trying to shut out the images of them in a POW camp. But all she could picture was her precious Grace and hope against hope that there was a woman there, a mother perhaps, who might take care of her daughter.

She brushed away a tear with the back of her hand and then was jolted by the train stopping. They had just pulled into Oxford station. Somehow she managed to heave herself from the seat and get out. Her feet moved automatically along the pavement. It was raining heavily, but she didn't feel the cold or the rain soaking through her coat, nor the way it pooled on the rim of her hat before dripping down onto her face. She walked on oblivious to the details of her surroundings, wondering whether she would ever feel joy or happiness again.

The rain kept pouring as she walked towards the bus stop, digging into her face like vicious nails. There was a long queue, and as she made her way to the end, she tripped against a loose paving stone, stumbled and just caught herself from falling. But the heel had twisted away from the body of her shoe like a wobbly tooth.

'Damn it!'

'Can I help you?' a voice asked.

She glanced round, seeing a man wearing a raincoat with the collar turned up and the dome of a black umbrella spread above his head. It was Melody's friend Andrew whom she had met by the river recently.

'Ella?'

She said nothing.

'Are you hurt?'

'I'm fine.' She hobbled on.

'These damn pavements,' he said. 'Full of pot-holes and goodness knows what.'

She nodded and looked beyond him to the bus stop. He was saying something, and she turned back to face him.

'I'm sorry,' she said. 'I'm in a hurry to catch my bus.'

'I doubt there will be one for ages,' he said. 'They're always delayed at this time of night.' He paused. 'And with that shoe, it won't be very comfortable walking home. I could fix it for you if you like.'

'No.' She shook her head. 'I wouldn't dream of it. I'll wait for the bus.'

'I insist. Look at the rain and you're wet through as it is. I live just around the corner. It won't take long. Please.'

He held his umbrella over her. Realising that she had no choice, she nodded and walked lopsidedly beside him.

'So,' he asked. 'Been anywhere nice?'

She dug her hands into her pockets and clenched her fists, not wanting to tell him her devastating news. 'I . . . I was visiting someone I knew from Malaya. You?'

'I had business in London.'

They walked on, the only sound the splash of their footsteps on the waterlogged pavements.

'I really can get a bus,' she said.

'We're almost here now.'

They turned a corner to where a row of Georgian cottages stood a small garden's length away from the pavement. Once, there had been railings, but she could see the stumps like amputated fingers where the iron had been cut down for war use. Andrew took a key from his pocket and led her to a blue front door, which he unlocked and held open.

'After you.'

She stepped in and he led her along a corridor to the back of the house. Ella was surprised to find that she wasn't in a dark hall like James and Polly's, but in a vast room that in fine weather would be bathed in light.

'Goodness!'

'I had the walls taken down and glass put in where the back of the house used to be,' he said. 'It's a bloody nightmare now with the blackouts.'

'But on a sunny day, the light must be so pure and strong.'

'That's the best kind of light.'

He took his coat off, shook it and hung it on a hook then

asked, 'Would you like a cup of tea and a chance to dry out before I take you home?'

'No.' She shook her head, trying to think of a polite excuse. 'I must get back to Toby, and I shouldn't keep you either.'

'Right-o. Give me that shoe and I'll see what I can do.'

She looked around her. The room was not at all what she'd expected. Photographs and paintings covered all the solid walls: there were black-and-white photographic portraits, life drawings, landscapes and still-lifes in vivid colours, all hung in interesting arrangements on the wall. It was quite a collection, she realised, and it must have taken him years to build. Under normal circumstances, she'd want to linger here and explore. Most of the houses she'd seen in England were cramped, dull and usually painted brown, but he'd used the space cleverly and placed each piece of furniture as though it were a work of art. A Persian rug lay on the floor, bringing the whole room to life with its reds, blues and greens. Despite the sadness in her heart, she could take pleasure from the way he had decorated his house.

She didn't hear him returning. It wasn't until he spoke that she knew he was there.

'You look so sad,' he said. He was holding a tiny hammer and a box of small nails.

'I—'

Caught off guard, her shoulders shook and it was as though a door had opened inside her, allowing all the words she was bottling up to come out in one long confused flow. He guided her to a chair, placed a glass of brandy in her hand, and encouraged her to tell him what was wrong.

He sat near her, listening attentively, as she told him all the things Edith had said.

'It must be incredibly hard,' he said, topping up her brandy. 'But if I might say something: she's only speculating, you don't know anything for certain.'

'Where else can they be?' she said, clutching her glass. 'It's either that, or—' She couldn't bring herself to say the words.

'You can't think like that,' Andrew said. 'It will eat away at your soul. It must be awful, but you'll find out the truth one day. We all do, one way or another.'

She lifted her face to his, wondering what he meant, but he was concentrating on her shoe, moving the heel back into place.

'There,' he said, and handed it back. 'Nothing is ever as bad as it seems.'

She finished her brandy and stood to leave.

'Thank you,' she said as he fetched her coat. She held out her arms and he slipped it on for her, then to her surprise he put his own back on.

'No, honestly, you don't have to come with me.'

'Nonsense. I'm not letting you walk back alone. Apart from anything else, you might break that heel again.'

The rain had stopped when they left the house.

'Thank you,' she said as the bus eventually came into view. 'For listening. I feel a little better for it, truth be told, but I'm dreading telling my mother-in-law the news.'

'Remember, you don't know anything for certain. But I'm glad if my listening has been a help.'

The bus stopped and she got on, then found a seat by the

window, but when she looked out to raise her hand in thank you, he'd already gone.

Silence hung in the hall when she got back to Wood Eaton. She pushed open the study door to find Polly and James both asleep in chairs on either side of the fireplace like a pair of bookends. Ella guessed that Toby would be in bed upstairs on a put-you-up in Jenny and Peter's bedroom.

She closed the study door quietly. In the hall, her hand lingered on the stair newel and she looked up. The hall clock ticked loudly, echoing the hammering of her heart as she walked along the corridor towards the piano. She sat down, opened the lid and ran her fingers along the keyboard.

'Where are you both?' she whispered.

It had been a while since she had sat here. Now her fingers struggled to remember the tune Johnnie had written for Grace when she was born. *The Cuckoo Dance*. A fun, light piece that had brought tears to her eyes the first time Ella had heard it. She was pleased to discover she could recall some of the tune when her fingers connected with the keys. As she played, a light breeze came from nowhere and ruffled her hair. She turned, expecting to see an open window, but it was firmly closed. She returned to the keyboard and the breeze started again, touching her neck and chin, gently wafting her hair. Ella stopped playing. It was as though someone were stroking her face and hair. But then, almost as quickly as it had started, the sensation diminished, as though whoever had been responsible was stepping further and further away, until finally they completely disappeared.

Chapter Twenty-Three

Time passed. Ella's spirits were lifted then dashed again by the occasional piece of news filtering through of civilians who had escaped from Malaya or Burma. They told of the horrors of POW camps around Padang, Lombok and Banka Island where, if disease and lack of food didn't get you, the cruelty of the Japanese soldiers would. There were also harrowing tales of slave labour on what they described as 'the death railway' in Burma, men dropping down in their tracks or being beaten until they died if they couldn't haul the building materials the Japanese commanded them to move; of civilians being shipped off to Japan and interrogated under unbearable conditions. Then hundreds of Australian civilians being moved to Bangkok for internment by the Japanese were drowned like trapped rats when an American submarine sank the ship off the coast of Singapore.

Ella sometimes avoided reading the newspapers or going to the cinema to watch the news bulletins, but another part of her craved information, wondering if she might glean another piece of the puzzle to fill the empty gaps. Although her life in Malaya was distant in reality, it was still a constant presence in her mind, and sometimes she woke at night and fingered the cold sheets next to her or the untouched pillow by her head. As the days passed, she could see Grace in Toby – the way he held his head on one side when she spoke to him, how his hair had darkened and curled, falling in spirals over his forehead.

And as the weeks and months passed and the seasons changed, her heart hardened like a fossil, keeping within it only the impression of what had once been there.

As Toby turned two, the German army surrendered in North Africa, the Italians and Germans were forced from Sicily, Russian troops moved into Rúmania. Then the Allies landed in Normandy. Paris was liberated as Toby approached his fourth year. Ella read about it all in the newspapers or watched the news at the cinema, taking it in, hoping that the Japanese army would be defeated soon. She settled into a life where growing vegetables with Polly, sketching or volunteering at a WVS café in Oxford twice a week became her routine while Polly looked after Toby for her. That was, until the day the government conscription officer called.

'All women who are able to must help the war effort, Mrs McCain,' the woman explained. 'Now that your son is old enough, perhaps you can leave him with your mother-in-law? What skills do you have?'

They were sitting at the kitchen table where Polly had taken them, a pot of tea and some cups on the table between them.

'I used to keep the accounts for my business in Malaya.'

'Well, I'm not sure that will help, but you have a clear

speaking voice.' The woman made a note in a large black notebook. 'Anything else?'

'No. I don't think so.'

A fortnight later, she was called up to become a telephone operator for the Ambulance Service working two days a week at a wage of two pounds and five shillings. Once again, Polly offered to look after Toby. The hours were long, the other girls seemed confused by her foreignness and were a little distant. Once again, Ella's feelings of being alien and insignificant haunted her. She wondered if she would ever truly fit in, in England. Most of the women she worked with were young and unmarried and their interests centred on which dance or picture house they would go to that evening, would they ever get a pair of nylons or be able to buy mascara ever again? They continued to avoid her, suspicious of her different looks and ways. Once she overheard them saying, 'Her Majesty won't be coming' while they spoke about a dance she hadn't been invited to, but to which they were all clearly going, over at one of the local RAF camps.

Spring came, bringing with it swallows and swifts. Snowdrops gave way to daffodils and the cherry blossom dropped its blooms, covering the streets in candy-coloured petals. Ella had been almost too busy to notice them, but as she and Toby headed away from the Children's Shoe Exchange in Oxford, where they had just chosen some not too-worn brown shoes with a strap and buckle, she was pleased to note the changing world.

'Mummy, I'm hungry,' he said as he walked beside her. 'And also, I need a poo-poo.'

'Oh, Toby! Why didn't you say before we left the Exchange?' She glanced around. The covered market was across the street and she remembered a café in one of the alleys. 'Let's try over here.'

He skipped beside her as she wove through shoppers queuing at vegetable shops or at the butcher's, hoping for a scrag end. She'd noticed how the market stalls were getting emptier by the day and people's clothes more patched and worn. Eventually she reached the café. She knew she had a few ration points left, but hoped she'd manage to get to the lavatory without having to use them by buying a drink or an iced bun. She pushed open the door and headed to the cubicle with Toby.

No one seemed to notice them as they wove through the tables. It always surprised her that people still had the time and money to eat out. Most of the customers were men – elderly dons, she assumed, or their wives, people who, like James and Polly, probably only had their dwindling savings and fixed habits to get them through the war. She sorted Toby out then led him back through the café. Her handbag brushed against the shoulder of a man wearing tortoiseshell glasses and reading a newspaper. The aroma of his cigar seemed vaguely familiar.

'I'm sorry,' she said.

He looked up. His hair was greyer and his face thinner.

'Andrew?'

He stared at her then slowly took off his spectacles. A look of pleasure spread across his features, lighting up his face.

'Ella?'

Her heart fluttered, like leaves rippling in the wind.

'Have you just arrived?' he asked. 'Don't say you're leaving already?'

She looked around as the urge to stay took hold, but the café was now full with hardly a free seat at any of the tables.

'Well, we were on our way out.'

'Oh, I see.' He paused for a moment then said, 'Why don't you join me for a cup of tea and perhaps a cake? It would be good to catch up.'

'Of course. I'd be delighted, thank you.'

He pulled out a couple of chairs and they sat down.

'It's been a while,' he said, folding his paper and finishing his cigar. 'How have you been?'

'Oh,' she said sitting down, 'we're surviving. How about you?'

'So-so.'

They chatted about the weather, and how hard it was to get fresh vegetables and meat. She ordered a pot of tea and a toasted teacake for Toby, cutting it into small pieces when it arrived. Toby sucked on a piece then plopped another into his tea.

'Toby, no!'

He picked it out with his fingers, then smeared the mush on the table.

'That's very naughty.' Ella wiped him clean with her handkerchief. 'I swear he's trying me today.'

'The terrible twos?'

'He's almost four.'

'Goodness. Where has all the time gone?'

Indeed. She studied Andrew's face. The last time she'd seen him was the day she'd been to Edith's. She'd called a couple of times to thank him, but he was never there, and in the end she guessed that the house was shut up and that he must have gone away. After a while, she'd stopped trying.

'Have you had time to paint?' he asked, taking a sip of his tea. 'I seem to remember Melody thought you were good, although you were rather shy about showing anyone.'

'Fancy you remembering.' Ella smiled. 'Not really. I'm far too busy. I got called up. I'm working as a telephone operator for the ambulance service as well as helping at a WVS café. Polly looks after Toby for me, which is very kind of her, and by the time I get back she's exhausted, so I often cook for her. Even if I had the time, I can't get hold of any paper. And besides, even if I could, you've seen Toby with that tea-cake. Can you imagine what he'd do if I left paints around?

'Well, you do have a point there.' Andrew's expression turned serious. 'And what about your husband and daughter? Have you had any news of them?'

Ella slowly stirred the tea in her cup and shook her head. 'No. I think I've come to a dead end there.'

'I'm sorry. You will find out in the end, I'm certain.'

She didn't reply, fixing her gaze on her cup instead.

'You must miss Malaya very much,' he said, leaning back in his chair. 'Before the war, I'd been out there a few times. Such a beautiful country.'

'Yes. It is.'

There wasn't a day she hadn't thought about it. How many times had she wondered what had happened to everyone at home: the people who had worked at the mine, Malik and Lian? And of course Noor – and how she'd never had the chance to say goodbye to her. Her mind often replayed the day they had all parted; she hoped that they had survived and wondered how she'd ever find out.

'Are we going home now?' Toby interrupted. He had finished his teacake and was swinging his legs back and forth against the chair – *thud, thud, thud!* 'I'm bored.'

'That's a bit rude, Toby.' Ella frowned at him. 'I'm sorry, I ought to take him back.'

But she stayed a little longer, enjoying Andrew's company, until her son began to howl.

'I'm sorry. He needs a run about.' She hesitated a moment before asking, 'I don't suppose you'd like to join us, would you? A walk along the riverbank?'

'Well.' Andrew looked at his watch. 'I am meant to be meeting someone in half an hour. But I'm sure I could manage twenty minutes or so.'

He insisted on paying for their refreshments and using up some of his own points. They made their way to Christ Church Meadows and the banks of the river. A man was throwing breadcrumbs into the water and several ducks were diving into the river or catching pieces as they fell. Ella sat down on a nearby bench with Andrew and Toby and they watched.

'Three, four, five little ducks.' Toby pointed towards the water and squealed. 'Sing it, Mummy.'

'"Five little ducks went swimming one day,"' Ella sang while Andrew sat next to her. Butterflies flittered in front of them and bright sun shimmered on the water. Something splashed on the bank, and she wondered if it was a frog.

'I haven't been here for ages,' Andrew said. 'Perhaps I should come more often.'

'You know, I called on you once or twice,' Ella said, watching the man on the bank throw more bread to the ducks, 'to thank you for taking me home and mending my shoe that day.'

'There was no need.'

'Perhaps not. I wondered if you might have been away.'

He was silent for a moment then told her, 'Yes, I've been in Europe. On the Western Front.'

She was about to press him for more details when a clock chimed from the bell tower behind them. A group of women appeared from one of the boathouses nearby, shouting and joking as they hauled a racing skiff down to the water along with several sets of oars. Ella waited for Andrew to continue, but his face was turned away from her, watching the rowers, by now in the boat and moving down the river like a giant water-boatman.

'It's good to see that life still goes on,' he said, watching their progress. 'Oxford is such a bubble. Sitting here, it's hard to take in what's happening everywhere else in the world.'

'Apart from the planes overhead, the sirens, the bombing in the distance, you mean? We've been lucky, I suppose. Hitler has his eye on Oxford for his capital, they say, if he ever gets to England.' A fly had landed on her skirt and Ella batted it away. 'I pray he never does.'

'He won't.' Andrew looked straight ahead of him. 'At

least, I think the tide is turning. The Allied Forces are making progress on the Western Front. Mark my words, all of this will be over soon, although things may never return to how they were.' He indicated the river with a nod of his head. Ella took him to mean Oxford, the absence of its men, but then realised his comment had a wider significance.

She stole a glance at him. His mind seemed elsewhere, far away from Oxford and the riverbank. What was he thinking? What did he know? He was difficult to read. He was a stranger to her really, but there was something about his company that she was beginning to enjoy. Sitting with him here in the sunlight seemed so comfortable. Easy.

She sighed and Andrew looked at his watch. 'I suppose I ought to be getting back,' he said. 'It's time for my meeting. It's been lovely to see you both.' He got to his feet. 'I'm in Oxford for a while now that I'm back from the front. If you're passing, please, do call in.'

'Thank you.' She helped Toby to the ground and stood up. 'I will.'

She watched Andrew walking away towards the town. Light filtering through the trees speckled the back of his raincoat and seemed to cast a golden aura around his head.

Chapter Twenty-Four

As Toby grew older, he became more restless and needed to expend more energy than he could burn off in the coach house or on walks along the riverside. He needed to climb and to swing, to play with other children, and Ella often took him on trips to the park, riding there on her bicycle with her ever-growing son in the child seat at the back. There, she would watch the other mothers with their large broods of children, and on the occasions she caught fleeting glimpses of girls like Grace, she had learnt to harden her heart.

One afternoon at the park Toby fell off the swing and scraped his knee. He howled and howled. All the other mothers in the park stopped and stared, even when Ella had picked him up and sat him on a bench where she patted the blood pouring from the wound with her handkerchief. She wished that someone would look past the colour of her skin and see for once that she was a woman just like them and one who needed help.

The cut was deep and wouldn't stop bleeding. She pursed her lips. Did he need stitches? She didn't know and wasn't sure where the hospital was in any case. The other mothers were still watching her but didn't offer any advice or assistance. She'd learnt from work that these silent stares were based on suspicion of her as a foreigner; that people often seemed surprised she spoke English just as well as, if not better than, them.

With her handkerchief tied firmly around Toby's knee, she put him in the bicycle-seat and decided to see if she could make her way to the hospital.

As she pushed him out of the park, Toby's sobbing quietened.

'Is it still hurting?' she asked.

'Yes.' He wiped away a tear with the back of his hand.

'I'm not really sure how to get to the hospital,' she said. 'But I think it's this way.'

She turned left at the corner of the street and passed a row of houses, realising that this was the street where Andrew lived. She paused. Would it be too forward of her to ask for his help once again? Wouldn't he think she was accident-prone if every time she came to the house it was because of a broken shoe or an injured child? But if Toby's injury wasn't too serious, she didn't want to waste time waiting at the hospital, or have to deal with the brusqueness of an overworked nurse, so it might be better to call on a friend, after all.

She propped her bike against the wall, then lifted the lion's-head-shaped knocker on the blue front door. The sound thundered along the street, and she was certain that anyone passing by would be able to hear her heart thumping. She waited. Footsteps. The door opened.

'Ella!' Andrew was wearing an open-necked shirt and wiping his hands on a cloth mottled with paint. The smell of turpentine or white spirit hung in the air. 'What a lovely surprise. Do come in.' He stepped back to allow her past and the light flooding the room made her blink.

'I'm so sorry to disturb you, but we were in the park close by and Toby fell off the swing. And, well, he's cut himself badly. I don't suppose you can help?'

Andrew lowered his eyes to inspect Toby's knee. 'That looks nasty, little soldier. Please, come this way. I've got a first-aid kit somewhere.'

Everything was as she remembered it. She sat down on a chair and he left the room. In the distance, she could hear him moving something, and while she waited for him to return, she gazed about. There were magazines piled on a coffee table; three unframed paintings stacked against the wall; a bookshelf packed with books about artists along with exhibition catalogues: *Picasso*, *Klee*, *Rothko*. Footsteps fell along the wooden floor and then Andrew returned with a first-aid box and handed it to Ella.

'I would offer, but I think you'd do it better.'

She opened the box and found a ball of cotton wool and bottle of iodine, which she opened and poured onto the cotton wool before dabbing Toby's knee. It really didn't look too bad now and she was glad she had made the decision not to go to the hospital.

'Ouch!' Toby squirmed. 'That hurt.'

'I know, but it will make it better. Here.' She rummaged around in the box and found a sheet of sticking plaster and a pair of scissors. 'Let me stick this over it and it will soon stop bleeding. Better?'

Toby whimpered. Ella ran her thumb under his bottom lashes to wipe away his tears and kissed him on the forehead.

'How about this, young man?' Andrew held out a small square from a Hershey bar. Toby's eyes widened and he held out his hand, his expression incredulous.

'You must have had that hidden away for years.' Ella grinned. 'Thank you.'

'Army rations. From when I was out in Europe. Cup of tea or something stronger?'

'Actually, I'd really love a cup of tea.'

'Why don't you come through to the front of the house? It's a bit cosier. I've got a photograph that I've been framing, and I need to make sure it's aligned properly before the glue sets.'

She followed him through to a smaller room, which was just as bright as the first.

'See here, what do you think?' Andrew asked. She saw six small frames laid out on a table. They revealed black-and-white studies of soldiers in uniform, the lines of their faces darkened by worry and dirt. They were dramatic and startling. She didn't think she had the words to express the emotions they evoked in her.

Then he turned over some canvases to show her. 'I have a client in London whose house was damaged, along with these frames, which I've been restoring. They're beautiful, aren't they?'

'They're extraordinary.' Ella moved from one painting to another. 'And the frames are lovely, too, but do people still have time and money to spend on paintings and frames?'

'Of course. But to be truthful, people don't buy many paintings nowadays, which is fine, I have so much work to do at the moment with the photo-journalism. Do you mind, I'll only be a few minutes, but I've got something developing?' He indicated another room, door closed and a red light glowing outside.

She sat down and waited. The walls here were painted white and densely hung with paintings. A Utility armchair, an Art Deco lowboy and a low coffee table were carefully grouped together, and on the table a spiral of pebbles had been arranged, each clearly carefully chosen and placed in order of size. There was also a tin box on the table, embossed with an image of King George V and *Christmas 1914* on the top. She ran her fingers over it and lifted the lid – it held a handful of cigarettes. Her gaze wandered to a framed display above the door: a row of medals lined up with military precision on a black silk background. They glinted in the clear light of the room, as though not wanting to be overlooked.

'Won't be long now.' Andrew looked in on her when he'd left the darkroom. 'I'll make that tea.'

She lifted a book from a shelf and flipped through the pages, half-listening to a kettle boiling, the clatter of plates. After a while, he brought it in on a tray – two cups and saucers and a white porcelain mug for Toby. He poured milk up to halfway in the mug then added tea.

'I guess this is right?'

'Thank you.' She took the mug and held it while her son sipped.

Andrew settled down into the Utility chair that was made

from metal and thin strips of leather. He seemed to fill it and as he leant back, it moved and moulded itself to his shape. His tortoiseshell glasses were perched on top of his head.

'I can't believe how many paintings you have here, and such beautiful objects,' Ella said. Everywhere she looked there was something exquisite on view: blue glass the colour of lapis lazuli, a cloisonné vase, an ivory figure of a horse.

'Every piece tells a story,' he said. 'I like photographs, but I like objects, too.'

She sat back in her armchair and told Toby to sit on the floor. He made his way straight to the coffee table and started to play with the pile of pebbles.

'Toby, don't!' She leant forward to stop him.

'It doesn't matter – let him. I'll enjoy rearranging them later.'

'Your home is so lovely.' She watched Andrew sipping from his cup. 'It must have taken you years to collect all of this.'

He replaced his cup on the saucer. Unlike Polly's rose-patterned china, Andrew's was as plain and as white as the walls around them.

'Yes,' he said. 'Between the wars I travelled a little and did some collecting. I suppose I'm lucky – the house was left to me along with some of the art. My father was an American who loved Europe and my mother was what you call an English rose. They were interested in artwork of all types – they lived in Paris for a while, too. Most of this is what they acquired. My father was an architect by profession – a little visionary perhaps but very interested in light. After his time

in France, he couldn't stand what he felt were claustrophobic English interiors.'

'I like it. All the space and light. It makes me think of
Malaya. Houses are open there and full of light, too. We used
to have whole exterior walls that were shutters really. You
could open them out and fold them back, bringing the outside world in.'

Andrew tilted his head, observing her. 'You think about
it all the time, don't you? Not just Malaya. About what your
husband and daughter might be enduring.'

'Of course. It's hard to keep something like that out of
your mind.'

'Yes. I know.' His voice had a depth of feeling in it.

'Ah,' she said, glancing at the medals on the wall, the cigarette tin on the table. 'The Great War?'

'Yes.' He nodded. 'Again, as a photographer, but I came
in right at the end. Since then, I've struggled to make sense
of it. We all hoped it wouldn't happen again. I think that's
why I used to travel – in Asia and the Americas. I wanted to
forget what had happened in Europe and find a meaning to
life again.'

She was surprised by his honesty. The men she knew
weren't so open about their feelings – even Polly had to be
prodded to say what was really going on in her mind.

'I'd love to go to the Americas. I've never been anywhere
apart from Southeast Asia. My father promised me a trip to
Europe, but he died before he could take me.'

'I think you'd like it. You never know, you might find
yourself going one day. Life is full of surprises.'

She placed her teacup on the coffee table. 'I suppose we'd better go. Thank you for helping me patch Toby up, and I'm sorry about the intrusion.'

'You don't need to apologise. I'm happy that you called.'

'You're very kind.' Ella picked Toby up from the floor. 'Come on, sweetheart, time to go home.'

She glanced around the room one last time, at the paintings, on the walls, the sculptures and rugs displayed to show them off at their best. It was a lovely home, full of life and meaning, and she wished she could create a haven like this for herself.

A week later, Ella was scrubbing potatoes in the kitchen for their evening meal when she heard a knock on the door. She lifted her head. She wasn't expecting anyone and rarely received visitors. Toby was sitting on the rug playing with a toy truck that Polly had borrowed from a friend whose own grandchildren had outgrown it.

Ella wiped her hands on her apron, then went to open the door. It was Andrew.

'Hello,' he said. He was wearing a navy striped shirt, pale cotton trousers and maroon sweater. The colour suited him, the grey around his temples, the olive tones of his skin. 'I hope I'm not disturbing you.'

'Of course you're not. Please, come in.'

'I decided to go for a walk along the river,' he explained. 'Where you took me the other day. I thought I'd take a chance and see if you were in.'

He handed her a paper bag. 'You don't have to open it now,' he said.

'My goodness. Thank you.' She put his gift on the table. 'Can I make you some tea?'

'Please.' He stood with his hands in his pockets while she put the kettle on to boil then opened the bag, revealing tubes of oil paint and brushes.

'Oh, Andrew. That's so kind.' She glanced up at him. 'But you really needn't have.'

'You said you couldn't get hold of materials. Now you have no excuse.'

'Well, apart from Toby,' she laughed. 'And not having enough time. But these are so lovely, thank you.' Warmth radiated through her, like a hot drink on a cold day. It was only a small gift, but the thought behind it ran deep.

The kettle started to boil. She was about to make tea but Andrew said, 'Do you mind if we have something a bit stronger?' He pulled a small silver flask from his back pocket. 'I've a little whisky if you'd like it?'

'Or I have some of my mother-in-law's sloe gin?'

She took off her apron and found the bottle and a couple of glasses, indicating that Andrew should sit on the sofa close to where Toby was playing.

'I really ought to be teaching him to read,' Ella said. 'He's starting school in September. He's a little young, but Polly knows the head teacher and managed to persuade him to let Toby join. I must say, it would be wonderful to have some more time to myself.'

'You could start painting regularly again.'

'Oh, I don't know about that.' She poured sloe gin into the glasses. 'I'm a bit short of ideas.'

She handed Andrew a glass.

'Actually,' he said, turning it in his hand, 'there is another reason I called.'

'Really?' She lifted her face to his.

'I've been thinking that there might be a way I could find out a little more about Johnnie and Grace.'

'What?' She examined his features to see if he was teasing, but his expression was serious. 'Go on.'

'As you know, I'm a photo-journalist. Well, I know quite a few people who owe me a favour. Over at Mount Farm they undertake reconnaissance missions – mainly in Europe, but also further afield.' He ran his hand through his hair. 'There are British spies everywhere including Malaya. They've been there for years, hiding in the jungle. Sometimes they manage to send radio messages back to England. What if I called in those favours to see if there's any information that can be gleaned on the ground about your mine and plantation?' He lowered his voice. 'And if there's any sign of Grace and Johnnie, they'll be sure to know that, too.'

Ella picked up one of Toby's toys from the floor – a wooden train engine that he loved. She didn't know if she could go through all the anxiety and disappointment again. Every time she had thought she'd been on the verge of finding something out, it had been snatched away from her. She mulled it over, then looked Andrew straight in the eye. 'But do you really think there could be a chance of finding something out?'

He shrugged. 'Isn't it worth a try?

And suddenly it was as though she could feel Grace and Johnnie in the room again: Johnnie just behind her, almost touching her shoulder, and Grace sitting on the floor next to Toby. Wasn't this what she'd been waiting for?

'Think about it.' Andrew placed his glass down on the table in front of him. 'Knowing something has got to be better than knowing nothing at all. But for now, I'll leave you to think about what I've said.'

Chapter Twenty-Five

Ella's sleep was haunted by images of Johnnie and Grace and peppered by vivid dreams of being back in Malaya. In her dream, she saw them walking on the opposite side of a river from her. However hard she tried to attract their attention, they couldn't hear so she had to stand and watch helplessly as they moved further and further away.

The following morning, Ella stood in her dressing gown sipping her morning tea while she fingered the tubes of oils that Andrew had given her; it was kind of him to suggest she should start painting again, but really, she didn't have the time or the motivation. However, she sat down at the break-fast table and wrote to him, accepting his offer to contact the undercover services. She promised herself that she wouldn't tell Polly about this; there would be no point in both of them waiting day upon day for news that might never come.

In the following weeks, she tried to keep busy. Every time she heard footsteps outside her door, she thought it might be Andrew returning with some news. She spent extra time helping at the WVS café, forcing herself to be bright and breezy with the servicemen who came in for a cup of tea and a chat. On other days, when Polly still needed help in the garden, she joined in, digging her trowel in the deep soil, her mind miles away and taking her to the other side of the world. There were occasional visits from servicemen who stayed at the house as paying guests. Ella helped Polly prepare meals and sometimes would serve breakfast.

Chores became easier, though, as Polly now had help: a few weeks earlier, an Austrian woman had knocked on the door asking if they needed any cleaning done. She was wearing a man's overcoat that was much too big for her, a headscarf and a pair of stout walking boots.

'My name is Lena. I am victim of Nazi oppression,' she introduced herself. 'Do you have any work – cleaning, washing?'

'Please, come in,' Polly had said. 'You poor thing. Have you been wandering the streets of Oxford looking for work?'

Polly had given her a hot meal and taken her on immediately, so now they were quite a household. In quiet moments, Lena told Ella how she had left Austria when Herr Hitler's Nazi policy began to oppress both the Jews and the Catholics. 'I am Catholic,' she explained. 'The Nazis hated us as much as the Jews.' She described Vienna; how it had turned from the most beautiful place to live in, to a place of horror. 'Since I left, I look for work in many houses – then I come here,' she explained. 'I hope the Allies will defeat Hitler, then I can return once more to my home.'

'Do you have children?' Ella asked.

'I had a son,' she said. 'He was killed when I left Vienna. My husband, he died years ago.'

Ella placed her hand on Lena's. 'I'm so sorry. You and I seem to have a lot in common.'

Then she explained her own story, starting with the Japanese invasion of Malaya, her journey to Singapore and the final evacuation by ship, watching the smoke and planes bombing the city as they pulled away from the harbour. Her voice choked as she related how she had tried in vain to discover news of Johnnie and Grace.

'This war,' Lena said, her gaze far away, 'has brought nothing good for anyone. I pray every day for it all to end.'

Ella drew some comfort from her presence. It was a relief to have someone who understood her position, unlike her work colleagues, who had no idea what it was like to be a refugee and a foreigner in an unforgiving land, along with the loss of absolutely everything that she held dear.

Meanwhile at the back of her mind was Andrew's plan to call in the favours owed to him and see if anyone undercover knew what might have happened around the mine, though she was starting to think it was another wild goose chase.

But one evening, just after she had kicked off her work shoes and was settling down on the sofa in the coach house, Ella heard a knock on the door. She ignored it, tired from her day at the call centre, and undid the clips in her hair, allowing it to fall loose around her shoulders, hoping that whoever it was would go away. The knocking was repeated.

She heaved herself up and reluctantly opened the door.

It was Andrew.

'Hello,' he said. 'You don't mind my calling again, do you?'

'No.' Ella hesitated. 'Why don't you come in?' She glanced

at Toby who was playing with his toy farm animals on the carpet.

Andrew followed her and said hello to her son, who lifted his head for a moment from the cow he was holding in his hand before returning to his game.

'Tea?' she asked. 'Or gin.'

'Nothing, thank you.'

Ella watched from the corner of her eye as Andrew sat down on the sofa. She tried to read his expression, but he gave nothing away.

'I wanted to give you an update. My friend at the base has agreed to help us as much as he can. As soon as there is any news, I'll let you know.'

'Seriously?'

'Yes.' He smiled at her as her hands flew to her face, covering her mouth in astonishment. 'All we have to do now is to wait.'

As the days passed, Ella couldn't sleep and found it hard to concentrate at work. On one occasion at the café, she was so jittery she dropped a pot of steaming tea, scalding her hand and her arm. Whenever the post arrived, she ripped it open immediately, hoping against hope that there was an update from Andrew.

Then, her heart almost stopped when she received word from him in a note that he had something to tell her, and could she possibly arrange for a babysitter on Friday evening after work?

She told Lena she was meeting some friends at the pictures, and Lena seemed delighted to be asked to help. Time crawled by until Friday evening. Lena arrived early to look after Toby, while Ella was still deciding what to wear. Lena settled down on the sofa with a bag of darning to finish. 'I do when Master Toby goes to sleep,' she said.

Ella decided to wear some slacks and a loose shirt, then cycled over to Andrew's, focusing hard on the rhythm of the pedals to calm herself. When she arrived, the street was quiet and the sky still a cloudless bright summer blue. She rested her bicycle against a nearby tree. A little nervously, she knocked on the door and waited to hear his footfall. There was the turn of the latch and the slight squeak of the hinges as the door opened.

'Hello,' she said, her words as faint as her breathing. 'Please, I can't wait a minute longer . . . tell me, do you have news?'

'Come on in,' Andrew said, taking her by the arm. He led her to the small room she'd sat in on her earlier visit with Toby. He made her sit down on the chair next to the coffee table that was covered now with papers, books and a dog-eared manilla envelope.

'I do indeed have some news,' Andrew began. 'Someone knows a chap who might be of interest to us – he was part of reconnaissance and undercover operations in Malaya at the beginning of the Occupation but was injured and evacuated out. I think we should try and pursue it as a lead. Strictly off the record, of course, why don't you have a look at this?'

He handed Ella a letter. She frowned as she read it.

'He was brought back at the beginning of '42, injured, it says. Would he really know anything?'

'Worth a shot, don't you think? Can I get you something to drink? Brandy? You've gone awfully pale.'

She nodded, and he poured her one.

'Do you think you could get away to meet him if I fixed something up?'

'Yes. I suppose.'

'Great. I'll see what I can do. And if you have any photographs of your husband and daughter, that might help.'

Silence hung between them, and she wondered if he could hear her heart pounding as she sat with her hand clasped around the glass of brandy, worried that it would all lead nowhere once again.

A week later, Andrew told her that he'd managed to arrange a trip to London to meet his friend's contact, a man called Percy Williams.

'Why don't you make some plans to come too?' he suggested. 'Maybe stay over with Melody?'

And so, after much thought, Ella agreed and wrote to ask if she could stay.

I'm afraid it will be yet another wild goose chase, just like when I saw Edith Gibbins, and then that false lead from Sarah Harris about Grace possibly being in a children's centre in Southampton. I pinned my hopes on that – I don't know if I can bear having them dashed all over again. I suppose it really can't do any harm – it's so draining, though. Still, it would be lovely to see you. We haven't met in ages.

*

But the more Ella thought about her decision, the more she started to think it might be a mistake.

'What should I do?' she asked Lena one morning when they were cleaning up after breakfast. 'I don't think I can go. What if it's bad news?'

'You never know if you don't go,' Lena said, as she rinsed a plate at the sink, then picked up a dishcloth to wipe the worktop. 'You must go.'

'I'll have to take Toby with me.' She hadn't thought of that. 'I shouldn't have agreed to it.'

'Of course I look after Toby for you,' Lena said. She rinsed the dishcloth under the tap and wrung it out. 'I love have him. And if I have a problem, I ask Mrs McCain help me.'

'Thank you,' Ella said. 'It will only be for one night. I don't see how anything could go wrong.'

Chapter Twenty-Six

Ella's nerves tensed like a piece of tightly sewn cotton as she got ready to go to London.

'I fine with Toby,' Lena reassured her. He was sitting on the kitchen floor pushing a wooden car backwards and forwards. 'Please. I am happy to help. You are all so good to me. Now I return the favour. Please go.' Ella hugged Toby one more time then left the coach house and cycled to the station.

The train was crammed and she couldn't find a seat, so had to make do with the aisle where she sat on her case getting hotter by the minute. When she got to Paddington, her dress was soaked with perspiration and her discomfort grew as she wandered out onto Eastbourne Terrace, bewildered by where she should look for the number twenty-three bus that Melody had instructed her to catch.

When she finally found the right one, Ella stared out of the bus window at the ruined streets and the caved-in buildings still spilling their contents like entrails. There were so many taped-up windows, people carrying gas masks, piles of rubble on the street. Once again she reflected on images she had seen at the pictures of Singapore, the bullet-riddled buildings and the Japanese in control, and wondered what was happening back home.

Polly had lent her a *London A–Z*, so Ella followed the passing street names on the map with her finger to confirm where to get off the bus. She pulled the cord at what she thought was the right place, but when she alighted, she was too early and had to lug her case two more stops. Heat throbbed from the pavement and thirst made her long for a cold drink while the handle of her case became slippery and difficult to grasp. She noticed her shadow quivering in the heat and was thankful when at last she arrived at Melody's flat.

The interior was blissfully shaded and cooled by a marble floor. Ella admired the wooden trim around the interior doorways – it gave the building an air of solidity, like being inside a church or a library. She called the lift, which was brightly lit and lined with mirrors.

She reached the third floor and made her way to flat eight. The door was as glossy as a chestnut. She knocked and waited, then heard footsteps on the other side. Melody appeared, looking cool and elegant in a loosely fitting red floral tea dress; it set off the blonde hair that flowed in soft curls to her shoulders.

'Oh, Ella!' Melody leant forward and hugged her. 'Please, come in. What a day to travel! The hottest of the year.'

'I know. I feel as sticky as Toby's hands when he's been holding a sweet.'

Ella stepped into a large room that served as both hall and living room. The interior was light and airy with sheer curtains blowing at the open windows.

'This is so nice,' she said. 'Even more so after the heat outside.'

'I'll get you a drink, shall I? Water, lemonade, tea?'

'Water, thank you.'

'Take a seat and I'll bring it out.'

Ella sank into a sofa that faced an open window, cooling her face in the breeze.

Melody returned and handed her a glass.

She sat down on a chair opposite Ella. 'What time do you have to be there?'

'Seven.'

'You must be feeling nervous.'

'It's like waiting to find out the results of some dreadful exam.'

'Do you want me to come with you?'

Ella shook her head. 'I'll be fine. Honestly.'

'Silly me,' Melody said. 'I was so excited to see you, but I should have asked – do you want to freshen up?' She led Ella to the bedroom, explaining, 'I hope you don't mind, but we're going to have to share.'

The double bed had a pink and green floral eiderdown with crisp white linen just visible underneath. A Victorian-style inlaid dressing table stood against one wall, while a pink-upholstered chair had been placed by another open window. Although the room was on the opposite side of the building from the main road, she could still hear the hum of traffic. Next to the bedroom there was a bathroom with a large white bath, marble floor, white towels, soap from Yardley and some Epsom salts. Ella flopped down on the bed, perspiration beading on her neck, and yawned.

Melody yawned, too, as she sank onto the pink chair. 'I'm so tired.'

'It's the heat. It's exhausting.'

'I'll open this window a bit more.' As she pushed it, her dress fell softly over the mound of her stomach. Ella brought herself up to sitting as she looked at Melody's figure and noted how her complexion glowed and that there was a fullness to her face she hadn't noticed before.

'Melody?' she asked, unable to keep the shock out of her voice. 'Are you pregnant?'

Melody's face flushed pink. 'Oh, Ella.' She wiped at her eyes. 'I don't know what to do. London's such a lonely place at times, and I wasn't expecting it to happen.'

'Oh, my God, Melody, what on earth . . . ?'

Melody dabbed her eyes with a handkerchief, then took a packet of Pall Mall from her bag and lit a cigarette with a silver lighter. The flame sparked then settled as the tobacco caught.

'Where do I begin?' She exhaled sharply.

'I suppose you know whose it is?'

Melody nodded. 'Laurence.' Her voice was low. 'I've been seeing him for some time now.'

'Oh, Melody.'

'Don't judge me, Ella.'

'But what about Edward?' she asked as gently as she could. 'When this is over, won't he mind?' And she didn't just mean about the baby.

Melody started to cry. 'Oh, Ella. It's all such a mess. I don't know what to do. I love Laurence and I've wanted a child for years, but I can't possibly keep this baby.'

'But . . . surely you're not thinking of giving it away?'

'What else can I do? And please don't lecture me. I'm not a saint. Just a woman who is lonely and trying to make the best of her life. What else do you suggest I do?'

'It's not for me to say. But it's your child. You can't simply give it away. Think how you'd feel if you abandoned your baby?'

'You're a fine one to talk about *abandoning* your child,' Melody snapped, flicking cigarette ash out of the window.

'What did you say?' Melody's words ripped open the painful wounds that Ella carried around with her every day.

'I said, you're a fine one to talk.'

'How could you even think such a thing?'

Melody got up, banging the bedroom door behind her. Ella sank back on the bed as rage boiled within her. She pressed her nails deep into her palms, then with the pain still stinging, picked up a pillow and hurled it at the wall, knocking over a bottle of perfume as the cushion hit the dressing table.

From deep within her, a howl released itself. It was primal and terrifying, shaking her to the core. It was as though all the bottled-up emotions she'd been holding onto for the past few years had been unleashed. Of all the people in the world, Melody knew the truth of what had happened, but that wasn't what hurt Ella the most; it was her own guilt combined with the acknowledgement that there was an element of truth in what Melody had said: had she really abandoned Grace, and that being the case, how could her daughter ever forgive her?

A white haze of anger took hold of her as she went through to the sitting room. 'How dare you . . . how bloody dare you?' she shouted at Melody who was sitting on the sofa. 'You know damn well that I didn't abandon Grace.'

Melody looked shocked and remorseful. 'I'm sorry. It came out all wrong. I didn't mean it like that.'

But Ella couldn't be pacified so easily. She shook as she spoke. 'You were there, you know what happened. How could you be so cruel? You don't know the guilt I live with every day, wondering how I can ever forgive myself, wondering if my child is still alive.'

'I know.' Melody was ashamed to meet her eyes. 'I'm not blaming you, Ella. It came out wrong – my emotions are all over the place. This war – it's forced us to make such diffi-cult, no, destructive decisions. But that doesn't give you the right to judge me, all right?'

'I wasn't. I was just taken by surprise, that's all.' Ella could hear the traffic noise and a pigeon cooing outside on the window ledge. She waited, trying to calm herself, Mel-ody's words still stinging.

'Ella, can't you see, I'm in a mess?' Melody turned her face to Ella's so that the light from the window fell on her features; dark shadows were visible under her eyes.

'That's no excuse for what you said.'

'I know, Ella. It was from anger with myself more than with you. But try and see this situation from my point of view.'

Ella fought to calm herself. When she was ready, she sat down next to Melody and picked up her hand. 'I know you

303

spoke in the heat of the moment. But it was the worst thing that you could possibly say. I don't know if I can forget it right now, but I will try.'

'Thank you.'

'Now,' said Ella, summoning all her strength, 'why don't you tell me if there is anything I can do to help you?'

'I don't know yet. Laurence is coming here later. I'm going to talk it through with him.'

'I see.' Ella tried to keep any hint of judgement out of her voice. Melody clearly had no idea how much having this baby and then giving it away was going to hurt her.

'No, you don't, Ella. You don't *see* anything. Laurence is a good man. In a different world, I'd marry him and keep this child.' She started to cry again. Ella put her arm around her friend's shoulders. 'And the thing is, I don't even know if Edward is still alive, or what kind of a person he'll be if he ever comes back.'

'Shhh. Don't rush into anything. I'm sure in the end you'll make the right decision. Look, why don't I run you a cool bath? You're worn out.'

In the bathroom, she ran the water and added a good quantity of Epsom salts. While the bath filled, she found she could no longer stem the tears she'd been holding back and hoped that the sound of the running water would drown out her crying. She caught sight of herself in the mirror – her face was crumpled and blotchy, eyelashes spiky with tears.

She thumped the side of the bath with her curled fist, feeling that something was tearing apart in her chest. No one knew how many times she'd wished she could turn back the clock and return to Menglembu; how much she blamed herself and how hard it had been for her to leave Johnnie and Grace behind in the peninsula. She'd come to terms with it by telling herself there had been no other choice and had focused endlessly on their reconciliation.

The bath was full, but as she sat on the edge, staring into the water, her stomach turned. Eventually, she stood up. While Melody was occupied bathing, Ella decided to go outside and walk off her mood.

The waves of guilt roiled through her once again. Had she really abandoned Grace, and was that what her daughter thought too? All this time, she'd been thinking Grace would welcome her back with open arms, and that they could pick up where they had left off, but what if that weren't the case? What if Grace didn't, or couldn't, forgive her?

And then Ella's thoughts turned to Melody. Here was a friend in need, someone who was here with her, someone she could actually help. Did she want to lose the one person who had been there almost all her life, the friend who knew and understood her better than anyone else in the world? How could any of them ever recover from the whole bloody mess of this war? As she pounded the streets, she decided that nothing good would come from holding onto her anger, and that she had to deal with the situation at hand. Her daughter was miles away, and the time would come when Ella could be with her again, a time when they would have to learn to live with each other again, but right now, Melody needed her. If only Ella were able to forgive and forget what had been said.

An hour later, she returned to the flat. Melody was at the

dressing table, pinning her hair so that it was swept up a little at the front while falling gently to her neckline at the back.

'I'm sorry.' Ella tried to sound untroubled by their earlier conversation. 'Did you have a nice bath?'

'Yes, thank you.' There was a hint of remorse in Melody's voice.

A little apprehensively, Ella snapped open her case, took out her sponge bag and a fresh dress.

'I'm sorry, too,' Melody said. 'What I said was unforgivable.'

'It was really – it was the worst thing you could possibly have said. But I know things are sometimes done in the heat of the moment. Melody, I care about you, and I more than anyone know what it's like to lose a child. What if you change your mind about giving up your child, or do so and spend the rest of your life wondering if you've done the right thing?'

'I know.' Melody gave her a wry smile. 'But really, that's my problem.'

'Of course. I was only trying to help. I'll always be there for you, you know that, don't you?'

'I know. Now, can we both forgive and forget?'

Ella nodded slowly. 'Let's try.'

'Would you like me to do your hair and makeup?'

'All right, but let me have a freshen up first.'

'Of course.' Melody nodded. 'When you're done, come and sit here. Let me put that brave face back on you.'

When she'd washed, Ella sat on the stool in front of the dressing table and Melody brushed her hair.

'Up or loose?'

'I don't know. You decide.'

Melody took some bobby pins from Ella's makeup bag and swept her hair up into a French pleat. 'It's a bit easier if it's damp,' she explained, with pins in her mouth. Then she opened her makeup bag and took out a well-used powder compact. 'Turn around,' she said. Ella obliged and Melody patted the puff on her face, then opened a small bottle of red liquid, and poured a few drops onto her finger to rub into Ella's cheeks instead of rouge.

'What is that?' Ella asked.

'Beetroot juice, of all things, but it does the trick. And it can be used as lipstick, too.' She dabbed a little on Ella's mouth as she spoke.

'Got any mascara?'

'No. I've been using black shoe polish.'

'Me, too.'

Melody took a tin from the table and a tiny mascara brush that she tapped into the polish before carefully coating Ella's lashes.

'There. Simple but elegant.'

Ella examined herself in the mirror, turning to left and right. 'I don't know how you do it,' she said.

Melody stood back and admired her handiwork. 'How do you feel?'

'Nervous. But, like you said, there's nothing like putting on a brave face.'

In the mirror's reflection, they smiled at each other. Then Melody opened her dressing-table drawer and placed a string of pearls around Ella's neck.

'You can borrow this for tonight,' Melody said, adjusting the clasp.

'That's so kind, I left all of my jewellery in Malaya,' Ella said, running her fingers over the strand. The light caught the pearl's pink lustre and the dainty diamond clasp.

'It's like the old days,' Ella said. But deep down, she knew that something between them had permanently changed.

Chapter Twenty-Seven

The pavement still radiated heat as Andrew and Ella approached the street where Percy Williams lived. The front garden had neat rows of lettuces lined up and a tabby cat lay lazily on the wall. It lifted its head to look at them while Andrew checked that they had the right house, then they walked up the path to a pristine green front door with a highly polished brass knocker.

'You're sure you want to do this?' he asked.

'Yes.'

Ella smoothed down her dress as Andrew lifted the knocker. The sound ricocheted around them and into the street. As she waited for Percy to open the door, she felt eyes watching them from other houses and her stomach rippled nervously.

Percy was in his late twenties, she guessed when he opened the door, and the right half of his face was strikingly handsome. The left side was pink and disfigured, bringing melting wax to mind, while an eyepatch covered his left eye, the strap partly concealing the bald, shiny skin on his head. He supported himself on a pair of crutches and she noticed that his right trouser leg was sewn up just below where his knee should have been.

'Percy Williams? Andrew Howard and Ella McCain.'

'Right. Yes. Come in. Good, you're on time. Follow me.' Percy's voice was breezy with a clipped tone, and he turned skilfully on his crutches. 'Wife's out, I'm afraid. Gone to her mother's with the little one for the evening. It'll be just me. Cup of tea or something stronger?'

'That's very kind of you. Whisky if it's no trouble.'

'No trouble at all.'

'And for you?' Andrew glanced at Ella. Her nerves were in shreds so she merely nodded.

Percy led them to the front sitting room where a floral-covered sofa and two armchairs with scatter cushions were set around a low table. As she sat down, Ella noticed a blue and white jug of multi-coloured sweet peas on the table, and a picture of the King in ceremonial uniform over the fireplace. Next to the sweet peas there were piles of letters and a copy of the *Evening Standard*.

'Water with the whisky?' Percy stood at a sideboard that was dominated by a highly polished wireless and rows of gleaming bottles and glasses.

'None for me, thanks.' Andrew glanced across at Ella.

'Nor me.'

Andrew took the glasses from Percy after he'd poured and then they all sat down. The windows were open. Despite the warmth of the day the room was airy and the scent of sweet peas made it feel homely and welcoming. Ella began to relax.

'Well,' Percy began. 'No point in beating about the bush, is there? Now, I trust none of this will go any further? I shouldn't really be talking to you at all, but a favour is a favour.'

'Of course,' Andrew and Ella said in unison.

Percy examined both faces and, seemingly convinced, continued. 'Right then. I was stationed out near Singapore when the Japs invaded, then sent out for reconnaissance work up along the east coast. A couple of weeks in, I was dropped by parachute into the jungle – partly to keep an eye on things, partly to extend an olive branch to the MCP. Turns out,' he glanced towards Ella, 'I was dropped near your neck of the woods. Menglembu. The Wosterholme tin mine, that's right, isn't it?'

'Yes, that's right.' Ella clutched her glass and inched forward to the edge of her seat, wondering if they could both hear how hard her heart was beating. She focused on Percy's face as he continued speaking, not wanting to miss a word.

'Yes, I was there before that bloody grenade got me. Lucky that the boys and the MCP managed to get me out and back home.'

'Goodness. I'm so glad that they did.'

'There's a fair few of our boys still in the jungle around there. The Japs have taken control of everything – your mine included.'

'And you, have you been there?' Andrew prompted.

'Not exactly.'

Ella's heart sank. She knew this was a mistake.

'But close enough to see what was going on with a pair of binocs.'

'So, what did you see?' Ella tried to keep the impatience out of her voice. She needed not only to know if Grace was still alive, but to be sure that her daughter didn't believe she'd been abandoned. It was unbearable to think that her child might have perished and never known how hard Ella had tried to find her or how much she loved her.

'Well, it's a while ago now, but the tin mine was still in full operation when I was observing it. The Japs had started to build a railway with POW labour. Malays, mainly. No Chinese. Certainly no Brits. The big house . . . I guess that was where you lived . . . is occupied by their officers.'

Ella felt the blood drain from her head. She opened her handbag and took out the photographs she had of Grace and Johnnie and slid them across the table to Percy. 'Did you see my husband or my daughter, either at the mine or at the villa?'

He leant forward and picked them up, examining them for what seemed like hours.

'I'm sorry.' He shook his head. 'Most likely thing is that your husband would have been taken to one of the camps in Japan. Either that or Burma.'

'What about my daughter?' she pressed.

Percy picked up the photograph again and stared at it a bit longer. 'You know, there wasn't a girl, but there was a boy. For a moment, I thought that perhaps there was something similar about them. I could have been mistaken, but your photograph was taken when your daughter was much younger and it was a while ago that I was in Malaya. I'm sorry, I can't be sure. No, I don't think the boy could have been her, but it's hard to tell from a glimpse through binoculars and an old photograph.'

'Was there anyone else about?' Ella asked. 'There used to be servants, a cook, a houseboy, a driver, even a dog?'

'Dogs would all have been shot, sorry. I know that's not what you want to hear. There was a woman, about your age and colouring. Eurasian probably. She seemed to be a cook or housekeeper at the villa.'

'Noor,' Ella whispered her name. 'I wonder if it was her. We used to have a cook and Noor was her daughter, a childhood friend I've known all my life, really. She was more like a sister to me when we were children.'

Her thoughts briefly flickered back to Noor, standing with her in the hall as Grace was taken to hospital, the gentle, reassuring touch she had given Ella as her daughter was taken away in the ambulance. And Ella had merely shrugged it off – what wouldn't she give now to be able to thank Noor, to try and rebuild their lost childhood friendship, to sit in the kitchen drinking chai with her, for old times' sake.

'Well, there you are,' Percy said, interrupting her thoughts. 'That's all I can tell you, I'm afraid. Like I said, strictly off the record. Some of our chaps are still out there and if any of this got out it would put them in real danger.'

By the time they left Percy's house and were back in the tree-lined street, through the open windows Ella could hear families sitting down to their evening meal and wirelesses broadcasting the news followed by music. A group of children played on the street, kicking a football, and a couple walked along eating fish and chips out of newspaper. It all seemed so normal, as though nothing was out of place in their world while Ella's felt completely topsy-turvy.

'Was that helpful?' Andrew asked.

'I don't know. Yes, I guess.' But the meeting had shaken

her more than she realised. 'I can't help thinking about what Percy said. That must be Noor he was talking about. And the child . . . there wasn't ever a boy at home. Do you think it could be Grace?'

'It's too hard to tell.'

Ella stopped abruptly in the middle of the pavement.

'It seems too much of a coincidence, doesn't it?' Her hands were shaking but she was beginning to feel hopeful. 'I'm convinced it's them, but what about Johnnie?' She shuddered. 'I can't bear to think of him in a POW camp.'

'Come on, let's get something to eat. You've had a shock and we can discuss this better off the street.'

Ella agreed, although she wasn't sure she could eat anything. What a day it was turning out to be.

'We could get some fish and chips,' Andrew said, his gaze following the couple who were now walking off into the distance. 'And there's a place I know, Bailey's, where we could get a drink.'

'All right,' she said. 'Why not?'

The evening was still warm and it felt surreal to be walking along the pavement together, eating their supper. Ella only picked at hers while her mind churned over the news Percy had given them.

'It's going to be a clear night,' Andrew said, when he'd finished eating. He gazed up at the sky as he scrunched up newspaper wrappings.

'Is that a bad thing?' Ella looked up too.

'No.' He continued to scrutinise the sky. 'But it's the longest night of the year and if I were an enemy pilot—'

She followed his gaze. There was nothing to see for miles, not even a cloud. She weighed up the probability of a raid but decided to dismiss what he was implying.

At Bailey's, the waiter sat them at a table at the front, a little way away from the band.

'It's busy tonight,' he said. 'We've got Pearl Prince and her Rhumba Band on, so it's this or nothing. Now, what can I get you to drink?'

'How about a couple of Martinis?' Andrew asked.

Ella nodded. She really would have preferred a quiet table away from the dance floor, but she would kill for a drink.

She looked at the other couples on the floor, bodies held close and moving together as one. The pulse of the music and the rhythm of the beat vibrated through her. It felt foolish, absurd even, for her to be here.

'Perhaps we should go home?' she said, but then their cocktails arrived and Andrew persuaded her to stay, then one drink turned into another, and her head began to spin from the alcohol, the music and the heat in the room. She struggled to make sense of everything – Melody, Percy, the spinning sensation.

'That poor man,' she said. 'Putting such a brave face on things.'

'Percy?'

'Yes. This bloody war, it destroys everyone and everything.' The alcohol was making her both melancholic and talkative. 'I should be grateful for what I've got – that Toby and I are alive – but somewhere thousands of miles from here, in my real home, the rest of my family are not even aware of whether Toby and I made it home or not. It's all too much for me sometimes. Do you think I abandoned them?'

Tears filled her eyes.

'No, of course not. Why on earth are you saying that?'

'Something Melody said. We had a bit of a falling out.'

The waiter passed their table and, before Ella could stop him, Andrew ordered a couple more Martinis.

'Knowing you, there's no way in the world you'd abandon your daughter. Ever since I've known you, all you've done is pursue every opportunity to find out their fate. I don't understand why Melody would say something like that.'

Ella wanted to explain, but knew she'd be betraying her friend further. Instead, she shrugged and took another sip of her drink. The alcohol numbed her, and she was glad of it. Somehow or other, Andrew ordered another round, and before she knew it, she was feeling a bit sick.

She glanced at her watch. 'It's almost eleven, time for me to be getting home. Do you think I can get a taxi from here?'

'I'll walk you back,' he said, 'if you like.'

'That would be lovely, thank you.'

Ella picked up her bag then dropped it. Andrew retrieved it for her. She wobbled on her feet, so he put his arm through hers to guide her. Outside, the sky had darkened. Although it was cooler than in the day, the air still retained the warmth of summer.

'You don't have to walk me,' Ella said. 'I could always find a bus.'

'No.' He looked at his feet and shook his head. 'Not like this. I'd rather see you to the door.'

Stars flickered and a church clock chimed half-past the hour as they walked along the pavement. There was no moon visible, but the night had a clarity to it that she hadn't expected. As they walked, her eyes became more accustomed to the dark, but the music still throbbed in her ears and she wished she weren't drunk.

'You know, I really appreciate all your help,' she said. 'And I know I've had more to drink than I ought to, but I suppose it's just a way of letting it all out.'

'I know. I'm not going to judge you for it.'

They walked on for a few minutes without saying much until they passed a small patch of grass where there was a bench. A wave of nausea washed over Ella. She needed to sit down.

'My feet are killing me,' she said. 'Do you mind if we rest for a bit?'

They sat down and he looked up at the sky. 'Just a few stars. You never get such a clear view of them in London as you do in Oxford.'

'No.' She took off her shoes and rubbed her toes. 'I don't suppose you do.'

'Now, that's Pegasus, and I think that's Cassiopeia.'

'What's that one over there?'

'A meteor shower, I think.'

'It's very beautiful.'

'That's the one good thing about the blackout – you get to see more stars.'

It was nice sitting next to him. Despite the lateness of the hour and her spinning head, Ella could smell his aftershave and the scent of sandalwood. It reminded her of Johnnie and that in itself both comforted her and made her want to cry because this man wasn't her husband. She looked up at the sky and wiped away a tear that was forming.

'What's that star over there?' she asked. 'The one that's moving?'

Andrew glanced up. 'I don't know.' He looked again and squinted. 'Unless of course—' A frown crossed his face. 'I think it's a plane.' He grabbed her by the hand. 'Quick!'

Before she had a chance to think, he was pulling her in her bare feet along the street. They hadn't got very far when the light from the plane was directly over them and Ella could hear its droning engine. Andrew pushed her into a doorway and stood against her with his back to the street.

Almost immediately, a high-pitched wailing broke through the air as the air-raid siren burst into life.

'We ought to find a shelter,' she said.

'There isn't time. If there are any more planes, they'll see us running along the street.'

As he finished speaking, a sharp *ack-ack-ack* sound pierced the air. She held her hands over her ears and could feel the pressure from another plane's passage close overhead pushing her backwards. The door she was leaning against vibrated as the plane zoomed past.

'Christ!' Ella leant into him. They stood together and waited, not daring even to breathe, then the sky lit up with searchlights scanning for enemy planes. She gripped her bag as aircraft fire was launched and immediately one of the planes trailed fire across the sky. Her breathing was shallow as she followed its progress, expecting to hear the boom of an explosion as it crashed, but it carried on flashing through the sky like a meteor, then just as quickly as it had arrived, it had gone.

They stood in silence, watching and waiting, not speaking until, after what seemed like a lifetime, the All Clear sounded.

The plane had flown so close it had almost grazed them. It reminded her of the time the Japanese had passed overhead while she was in Malaya, and all the other memories she'd been suppressing came flooding back: Johnnie's final farewell to her on the doorstep of the villa; Grace being taken off to hospital in the ambulance; Malik placing the Lagonda's keys and the gun in her hand, then walking forever out of her life along with Lian.

Fear paralysed her as she scoured the horizon, looking to see where the plane might have gone or if there were others on the way.

'Ella, are you all right?' Andrew asked, concern on his face.

She looked up at him, still shaking.

'Ella?'

'That was terrifying.'

'Enemy Messerschmitts. Yes. I think that's what they were.'

'Do you think they will come back?'

Andrew shrugged. 'Who can tell? But I'm sure it's over for now. We should hurry back.'

A shiver of fear slithered down her back as she imagined the plane returning. *No*, she thought. *I can't move. I'm safe here. What if the plane returns – or worse?* Now, with the sound of its engine still throbbing in her ears, the need to be with someone who cared, to be comforted and protected, pulsed through Ella, along with the fear that the next moment could be her last.

'Look at you,' said Andrew. 'You're shaking.'

'Oh . . . am I?'

She leant into him, trying to calm herself; seeing that plane so close – it was just like glimpsing death flying past.

'Andrew?'

'Yes?'

He lowered his head to hers and, fuelled by alcohol and fear, the memory of and her need for Johnnie, Ella locked her arms around his neck, and slowly, with her heart fluttering like a butterfly's wings, kissed him.

Chapter Twenty-Eight

His hands touched hers and gently released them.

'Ella, don't, please.'

She froze. 'I'm sorry. I—'

'Oh, Ella.' He shook his head. He let go of her hands and stood looking down at her, as though saying, *'Don't you see, we can't?'*

'I'm sorry,' she repeated. Her cheeks burnt with mortification, and she wished for the ground to swallow her up.

'Come on,' he said, his gaze still fixed on her. 'Let me get you home.'

She nodded. Her shoes were still in her hand and she slipped them back on, grateful for something to do other than meeting Andrew's eyes.

They walked back in agonising silence until they reached Melody's flat. Ella took the key from under the mat where her friend had told her she would leave it. They stood awkwardly by the door, neither of them knowing quite what to say.

'I suppose I'll see you in Oxford?' she asked eventually.

His gaze was distant as he shook his head. 'I don't know how to tell you this, but I'm going away very soon. I'm waiting for a call.'

'What?' Her voice was soft, almost a whisper. 'I don't understand.' How could this day be getting any worse?

'We all know the war will end soon. The hydrogen bombs the Americans are designing are so powerful and destructive that they'll use them on the Japanese if they refuse to surrender. When this happens, there will be chaos.' He fixed his eyes on her. 'What I'm trying to say is that this bomb – if I can get the story in the bag, it might just make my name worldwide. I'm going to join up with Homer Bigart. Hopefully we'll get the scoop before anyone else does.'

'Goodness.' Ella's hand touched her throat as she tried to take it all in. 'He's one of the biggest names in war reporting, isn't he?'

Andrew nodded. 'So, I'll be off any day. But I'll write to you when I can. And if there's anything else I can do to help, you know you only need ask.' He held out his hand and she took it. 'And please, forget about just now. It was one of those things. All forgotten.'

'I suppose,' she whispered. 'Look, thank you for everything.'

He gave a final nod and, before she knew it, he was walking away. She watched him retreating until she was alone and feeling ridiculously stupid outside Melody's door with the key clutched in her hand.

Inside the blackout blinds were closed and a single lamp was shining on one of the side tables. Gin glasses and bottles stood where they had been left, evidence of Laurence's visit, she supposed. Ella looked at the soiled ashtrays and glasses rimmed with lipstick then sank down in a chair.

Her hair was beginning to come loose, and she noticed that she'd caught her hem on something. Her head was truly throbbing.

There was so much to absorb along with her hope and shame. It felt like sitting on a seesaw over which she had no control. She sat for ages in the dimly lit room trying to regain her equilibrium.

When she finally decided to turn in, Melody was fast asleep. Ella collapsed onto the blankets, fully dressed, and stared into the darkness before falling into a fitful sleep.

When she woke, her head was pounding, and she was surprised to find that Melody had already left for work. Ella sat up. Her mouth had a woolly feel to it. In the kitchen, she made herself some tea, still wearing her crumpled dress, then ran a bath, noting her smeared makeup before she slid off her clothes and lay in the water. The events of the previous day flickered through her mind with horrifying clarity.

Melody was pregnant. Andrew was leaving. She had come to London to find out about Grace and Johnnie and had discovered more than she had bargained for. And then she remembered trying to kiss Andrew and groaned with embarrassment.

Eventually, she got out of the bath and tidied up the clothes she had borrowed from Melody before packing her case. Then she wrote her friend a note, explaining that she had decided to go home earlier than arranged. Although she didn't agree with Melody's decision about the baby, she wanted their friendship to continue, so she repeated that things had been said in the heat of the moment only, she knew she must appreciate what other people were going through, and could they please both try and put everything in the past?

'I'll support you in whatever you decide to do,' she wrote. 'You're my best friend and you've made me realise more about myself and other people than I ever have before. I'm sorry for speaking too hastily.'

When she had done that, Ella let herself out and made her way back to Paddington station.

Later that evening, when Toby had fallen asleep, she sat down and tried to write to Andrew to apologise. Nothing came out right, no matter how long she played with the order of her words or rearranged the clauses. In the end, she scrunched up the writing paper and threw it on the floor, poured herself another glass of Polly's sloe gin and slumped on the sofa clutching a cushion to her as the chill of the room settled over her like a ghostly breath.

The following day slipped away like an icicle slowly thawing.

The next morning for breakfast she made scrambled eggs with powder from a tin, then when they'd finished eating, dressed herself and Toby for an outing.

'Would you like to go for a walk along the river with Mummy this morning?'

There was a gentle breeze and a nip to the air as they walked along the bankside. Toby pottered along, picking up a stone, then a paperclip.

'Mummy, can you carry it?' He held out his hand and

placed the clip in hers. She wrapped her hands around his and kissed them.

'Come along, sausage.' She put the paperclip in her pocket along with the stone. For an hour, they walked along the bank while Toby chattered, pointing at the flowers, the swans and the occasional passer-by. Leaves danced ahead of them as they approached Andrew's house. She knocked, but there was no answer. She knocked again and glanced up to the window where she thought she saw a shadow moving, but still there was no reply.

'I don't think he can be there,' Ella said.

Toby pointed to the upstairs window. 'Mummy, I think I can see him.'

'I don't think so.' Ella took the boy's hand. 'Shall we go to the park instead?'

Toby made a beeline for the swing.

'Make Toby go as high as the sky,' he said as she settled him in the seat and pushed. While she did, she watched other mothers trundling prams and an old man with a walking stick ambling by. A couple walked past: the man was in RAF uniform and the woman wore a summer jacket that had been cut down and tailored, while on her head she sported a jaunty saucer-shaped hat. Their arms were linked, and Ella caught hints of perfume and laughter as they passed. Loneliness and shame cut through her.

She gently pushed Toby on the swing; he shrieked and his cheeks flushed with joy. Clocks chimed from distant spires. Ella looked up at the sky – grey clouds were interlaced with golden sunshine.

'Shall we go, Toby?'

He leapt off the swing and took her hand. They walked along the street towards the bus stop as the rising wind tugged at her coat and drops of rain began to fall, catching in her hair like lace before dripping away.

Over the following days, she wondered about riding over to see if Andrew was at home but decided there was nothing to be gained by it. A week later, she changed her mind and made up an excuse to go that way. She left her bicycle in the park, securing it to a bench, then walked to his house again, noting the half-drawn curtains in the upstairs windows. She sat a few doors down on a step, hoping no one would notice her.

She waited, convinced that if she stayed there long enough, Andrew would return. It would be enough just to catch a glimpse of him. A man turned into the street. His coat collar was turned up and his face carried at an angle, the brim of his hat shadowing it. He carried a leather suitcase in his right hand. Her heart began to race as she watched him search for the key in his pocket. Ella shrunk back closer into the shelter of a doorway as she watched him walk closer to Andrew's front door.

But then he passed it and looked towards her, and she saw immediately that it wasn't him.

Andrew had surely left. A woman turned down the street next, pulling a shopping bag on wheels – she looked at Ella with suspicion. Ella got to her feet, deciding she had to leave. As she collected her bicycle from the park, she wondered if she'd ever see Andrew again. She decided that she couldn't ·

let him go out of her life without making one final effort to contact him.

Dear Andrew,

I wanted to say goodbye before you left but now I wonder if you have gone already. I called a few times to say farewell – just to wish you luck as, who knows? I might have left for Malaya by the time you get back.

Best wishes,
Ella x

She sealed the envelope, but couldn't face going to his house again, so she walked to the post box. Once she had posted the envelope, she stood still for a moment then walked back home with her hands pushed deep into her pockets. Now was the time to move forward, to put all the bad things that had happened well and truly in the past. All she could do was focus on the longed-for end of the war and her eventual return to Malaya, even though there would be much in England she would be sad to leave behind.

The following morning, while she was cutting slices of bread for breakfast, there was a light knock at the door. The knocking was repeated. She tightened the belt on her dressing gown, then answered the summons.

It was Polly.

'Hello,' she said. 'May I come in?'

'Of course. I'm just getting breakfast – would you like some tea or toast?'

Polly shook her head, but sat down at the table and smiled at Toby who was sipping milky tea from a mug.

'Morning, young man. Are you drinking hot milk?'

'No, Gran'ma, I'm drinking tea.'

Ella continued cutting slices of bread and spread them with a thin layer of butter, and blackberry jam that they had made after collecting the berries from hedgerows in the autumn.

Polly picked up a teaspoon and turned it in her hand.

'The evacuees are leaving next week.'

'Are they?' Ella didn't look up but cut the bread into tiny slices before putting them on a plate and handing it to Toby who was playing on the floor. So much was in flux. It was as though once the changes began, an unstoppable momentum would carry them all quickly to the end of the war.

'Yes.' The teaspoon glinted in the morning light as Polly carried on turning it.

Ella looked up to find her mother-in-law's eyes fixed on her. 'Oh, Polly, you'll miss them, won't you? And what about Lena, will she be leaving too?'

Polly shook her head. 'I don't think so.'

Ella sighed. Toby was playing with a selection of wooden spoons and saucepans on the floor by the range, and there was a pile of sock puppets that he'd made with his grandmother: a frog, a snake, a pig, a horse, all put together from items they had found in second-hand shops, charity or jumble sales.

'I'll make some fresh tea.' Ella swilled out the pot with boiling water then added two large spoonfuls of leaves.

Polly sat on a kitchen chair close to Toby, who was now energetically banging the pans.

'Toby, shhh!' she said.

'He's fine.' Ella brought the teapot to the table and sat down and her mother-in-law burst into tears.

'Oh, Polly.' Ella placed a hand on hers and squeezed. 'It's not going to be easy for any of us, is it?'

'I know. You think all you want is an end to the war, but when it comes it brings nothing but uncertainty.'

'Why don't we take Toby for a walk? There's so much to think about – we could all do with a breath of air.'

They took the path along the river.

Polly stopped walking and scuffed a stone with her shoe. 'I'm scared, Ella. I know I've never said it before, but this war . . . it's taken so much but it's given me things I never had before. I don't think it's going to be easy returning to my old way of life. And then, you'll be gone. And Toby.'

Ella placed her hand on Polly's arm. 'You know, I've been thinking exactly the same things.'

'Oh, Ella. It's a mixed bag, isn't it?'

She nodded. 'But you'll manage. We all will.'

'Sometimes, I wonder if I can. It's as though I've forgotten how to lead a normal life, how to stop worrying – but I expect we'll get used to whatever fate throws at us next.'

'I suppose we will.'

Toby bent down, picked up a handful of stones and threw them into the water.

'I'll teach you how to skim.' Ella leant over him and flicked a pebble towards the water, where it bounced along the surface. 'One, two, three!'

Toby clapped his hands. 'Again, again, again!'

She picked up another pebble and tossed it.

'Toby do it!' He picked up a small stone, which plopped straight into the water.

'Never mind, Toby. It takes practice. We'll try again, shall we?'

He nodded, and on his fifth attempt, the pebble skimmed across the water.

'Clever boy!' Ella and Polly clapped. 'You did it.'

'It's like everything else, I suppose,' Polly said. 'The unknown is hard to comprehend, but in order to let go, you have to pin all your hopes on the future. All you need is a little practice and patience and then hopefully it will all land right.'

Chapter Twenty-Nine

Noor became the keeper of secrets. By day, she'd translate documents for Naoki, by night, she'd pass that information on to Omar by any means she could. But at least, she told herself, although she felt like a traitor to them both, for now the secret of Grace's identity was maintained, she was keeping her promise to Mr McCain – and the child's safety was what mattered most.

Sometimes, this information led to railway lines being blown up, or attacks on convoys of lorries taking minerals to the airports on their way to Japan, or at other times there were guerrilla attacks on military patrols in lonely parts of the jungle. Recently, the monsoon had brought destruction with it, causing landslides and rendering the jungle roads impassable, but that hadn't stopped the MCP from causing as much additional disruption as they could.

The damage they inflicted worsened the Japanese soldiers' temper. Their anger filtered everywhere, filling the villa with a mood that was as black as the monsoon clouds.

Today, she crept into the drawing room as the sound of dynamite blasted through the hills, anxious to see if she could discover some news on the wireless. She knew if she were caught the punishment would be severe, but Omar had reported rumours that the war might soon end in Europe, and that coupled with what she had read about in the *Penang Tribune*, the newspaper the soldiers had left lying about, made her feel that the risk of finding out what was really going on was justified.

She stood by the piano and turned the dial until the radio crackled into life, then tuned the wireless, waited and listened.

It took a while for her to find a station that wasn't broadcasting in Japanese, longer still to find one that reported the news. Her breathing was long and shallow as she discovered that the rumours were true: Hitler had committed suicide in Berlin and an unconditional surrender by German forces was expected any day.

She switched off the wireless, checked everything in the room was as it should be then returned to the kitchen where she sank down onto a kitchen stool and wondered what to do next. The more she thought about the implications of what she'd heard, the more she needed to discuss it with someone right away. And that person was Omar.

There were many risks that she'd need to take to get to his home, and she decided that if she were stopped at the perimeter fence, she'd tell them Naoki had given her permission to go out on urgent business. As he was their superior officer, she doubted the soldiers would challenge her. She scribbled a note asking Omar if there was any way they might be able to meet, then scooped out the flesh from a coconut and pushed the note inside, checking carefully to see if anything untoward was visible.

Wind rustled through the palms as she hurried along the jungle tracks. In the distance, she could hear the workings of the mine: another blast of dynamite, the sound of the dredging belt moving. A monkey swung through the branches and bared its teeth at her, while ahead of her she could see threads of woodsmoke rising from the kampong houses. To her surprise, there were no sentries at the gate and she made her way through unchallenged. She scurried to her cousin's house, hugging her basket with the coconut in it close to her chest, hardly daring to lift her eyes from the ground in case someone stopped or questioned her, causing unnecessary delay.

When she'd placed the coconut inside Omar's door she hurried back, anxious that the sentries might have returned, but they were still nowhere in sight.

She waited and waited as anxiety seared through her. Darkness came and her restlessness increased. Had Omar found the note?

The monkeys howled in the trees, the wind blew, but the heat of the day lingered inside the villa. When it was time to sleep, she rolled out their mats on the floor and lay down next to Grace, who fell asleep quickly. Noor's thoughts churned. The war would be ending soon and that brought with it the hope that the Japanese might surrender. Her thoughts turned to the gifts she'd received from Naoki, the days out to the concerts where everyone had stared at her as though she were his mistress. If the Japanese surrendered, what would that mean for the likes of her?

A clock struck midnight. She thought she heard something scratching at the door. A rat, no doubt. The noise continued.

She sat up and listened, uncertain, then got up and opened the door.

It was Omar.

'Shhh!' He put his finger to his lips. 'Follow me.'

She glanced back into the kitchen. In the shadows, she could see Grace's recumbent form. As quietly as she could, she closed the door and followed Omar, who moved like a panther familiar with his territory through the darkened jungle until they arrived in a small clearing.

There were two men there, both British soldiers, as thin as skeletons with scruffy beards and dirty clothes.

'I don't understand.' Her eyes swung between Omar and the men. 'What is going on?'

'I got your note,' he said. 'These men are British spies – some of the many who have been hiding in the jungle throughout the Occupation. As you know, the war in Europe is ending. One day soon, the Japanese too will surrender. When that time comes, we need to act swiftly to retake the kampongs and stop the communists taking complete control.'

'What?' said Noor. 'You will betray the communists who have supported you?'

'Not really,' her cousin continued. 'But the resistance members and the British don't want the communists to gain complete control here. That would be almost as bad as living under the Japanese. All we are waiting for is the Japanese surrender. Then we'll come out of hiding and take back control.'

'What's all this got to do with me?' She looked from one man to the other, hardly able to distinguish their features in the dark.

'What we need you to do,' one of the soldiers explained, 'is send us a signal the moment the emperor has surrendered, then we'll come out of hiding.'

'What kind of signal, and how will *I* know?'

'You'll know,' he said. 'You'll see the panic on the soldiers' faces.'

'What would be a good signal?'

'A fire, perhaps?' the other soldier joined in.

'It would have to be a big one,' the first man said.

'But nothing too out of control. We can't let the flames spread to the jungle, but the blaze needs to be big enough to be seen up here.'

The months moved slowly by as Noor waited. Although the war in Europe was over, the emperor hadn't surrendered and it seemed as though the Japanese were unlikely ever to release their grip on Asia. Life continued very much as usual: Noor's days were spent housekeeping, interspersed with conversations with Naoki, while Grace continued to practise the piano and excel at the concerts Naoki arranged for her to attend. Could Omar and his spies possibly have got it wrong? All she noticed was that the prisoners working in the mine worked harder, and the soldiers' tempers grew shorter, and their food came in smaller supplies. When he wasn't in it, Naoki now kept his study door locked and Noor noticed how objects around the house had slowly started to disappear, including her old wireless.

Then, just as suddenly as the monsoon rains came, the behaviour of the soldiers changed. They started shouting, burning piles of paper on the drive. The sound of vehicle engines revving, along with the smell of petrol fumes, filtered through the air. She hung back, nervous of what was happening, and then just as quickly as it had all begun, there was silence. They had gone.

It was hard to process what was happening, but her thoughts turned first to the new freedom she would have now that the Occupation was over, and then to Naoki. He hadn't said goodbye. Surely he wouldn't leave without saying something to her? She decided she would search the villa for him.

She tried the study first, but the door was still locked.

'Naoki! Naoki!' she called. She leant her face close to the door, wondering if he were on the other side, but as she waited, she heard a moan from the drawing room across the hallway.

Noor wasn't certain what she was expecting when she entered the room, but she saw Naoki sitting in an armchair by the window.

'You're here! I knew you wouldn't leave without saying goodbye to me.'

She walked towards him, but then she noticed how his right hand was hanging at his side. Blood trickled from a wound in his head and his eyes were open as though looking at something far away beyond the window.

'Naoki!' Her hands flew to her face and she knelt by his side. She took his hand in hers; it was still warm and she could just detect his shallow breathing.

'Naoki! No!' Tears fell as she pressed his hand to her face. 'Why?'

There was an almost indistinguishable pressure from his hand, then for the last time his face turned slowly towards her and their eyes connected. His gaze lingered on her face long after his last smile had formed on his lips. Long after she heard his final breath, she felt his hand relax within hers.

Flies had begun to settle on Naoki's face by the time Noor placed a sheet over his body. Earlier, she had closed his eyes and wiped away the blood staining his face, the shock of what he had done still reverberating through her. *Why?* she asked herself over and over again. *We could have gone somewhere far from here, been together, been happy.* But as she thought it, she knew that this would never have been possible. Their situation would always have been difficult – freedom or Naoki? An impossible choice. Now that she thought about it, she knew she couldn't have had both. Had Naoki known? Was that why he'd made the choice for her?

She didn't know and never would. Besides, her relief that the Occupation was over, that Malaya was free again, was complicated by the loss of the man she'd loved. And now, her own situation might be precarious if she didn't do what Omar had asked of her, for she knew this was the moment he and the soldiers had been anticipating.

She didn't want to leave him, but she had to.

Noor stood in the doorway and looked back at him, then wiped her eyes with the back of her hand before making her way to the kitchen. Her body was achingly tired as she collected matches from the kitchen and left the villa, moving as quickly as she could to the soldiers' empty quarters in the old servants' wing. She dragged mattresses and furniture into a pile, her breathing fast and desperate, then rolled up shirts and sheets that had been left by the retreating men and added them to the centre of the pile before lighting it. She watched as the flames licked and curled, then caught the tinder-dry furniture.

She coughed as smoke filled the room, causing her eyes to smart. There, she had done what she had been instructed to do, but her thoughts kept returning to Naoki and it was only then that they shifted to Grace.

The child was at school, but Noor needed to tell her what had happened. She made her way to the perimeter fence unchallenged, then on to the kampong via the jungle paths, panting as she picked up speed, listening to the rhythm of her breath and the pounding of her feet on the ground. The kampong was filled with people chattering – so the news had already spread. There was a flickering of eyes towards her, but no one greeted her.

The children were already outside the school, standing in huddles and pointing at the hillside. She knew that they were watching the smoke rising. Passers-by stopped and joined them; a tall thin man wearing a sarong wrapped around his waist, a woman in a faded *abaya*, both pointing at the smoke while their voices filled with excitement and fear. Suddenly, a massive explosion erupted from the direction of the mine, making the ground shudder beneath their feet.

'*Waaa!*' a man shouted. Other people came out onto the street and a small crowd formed. Some had their hands raised to their eyes, while others stood silently in shock taking in the unfolding scene.

And it was then that the first of the now-free prisoners began to emerge from the jungle: Tamil followed Malay followed Tamil as the men poured out of the trees and onto the village street. Cheers and clapping erupted from all around while more and more people left their houses to join the swelling crowd on the street.

All the while, Noor stood alone on the side-lines with tears pouring down her cheeks.

Chapter Thirty

Buds began to fill the trees then flowered as German soldiers surrendered on the Eastern Front. Melody had her baby in a convent in Warwickshire and Ella visited her, promising herself in advance that she wouldn't judge her friend for allowing the child to be adopted. She decided, though, that meeting Laurence was one step too far.

Time passed, and rumours filled the air along with the scent of cherry blossom. The war could be ending soon, though Ella scarcely dared believe it. When she read about the liberation of Auschwitz by Russian soldiers, she was shocked, and her heart was filled with fear when she wondered if the Japanese had treated their prisoners as badly. Like dominoes falling, Mussolini was executed, then Hitler committed suicide followed by the surrender of German forces in Italy and Berlin. Every day the news revealed a new capitulation – Bavaria, Central Europe, Göring making his way to the US lines in the hope of surrendering but being taken into custody, until at last, Churchill announced the unconditional German surrender signed by General Jodl in Reims.

Ella could hardly take it in when she heard the announcement on the wireless. Polly leapt up and hugged her, tears streaming down her face, and Ella was dizzy with the joy of it.

'Listen,' Polly said. 'Can you hear?' She opened the front door; there were church bells ringing everywhere. There was more noise than Ella had heard for months: chatter, children's voices, dogs barking, sirens blazing, and people shouting, 'God Save the King!'

'It's really over! I can't believe it.'

'Yes!' Polly hugged her once again. 'Yes. It truly is.'

Ella's hands were shaking. 'After all these years.'

'Come,' said her mother-in-law. 'We must celebrate – I've a bottle of champagne in the cellar.' She disappeared to return a few moments later.

'Shouldn't we wait for James?' Ella watched as Polly filled the sink with cold water and ice.

She shook her head. 'I've been waiting years for this day – I can't hold out a minute longer.'

While they waited for the champagne to chill, they sat in the garden laughing while they listened to the fireworks and rockets being let off. In the distance, they could see that bonfires had been lit: huge beacons of celebration and jubilation. As they sipped the champagne, something within Ella finally relaxed and she breathed out, releasing all her worry.

In the days that followed, one by one the German units ceased fire and surrendered, but whenever Ella listened to the wireless there was no indication that the Japanese in Malaya were about to do the same. She was let go from the telephone exchange: 'You're demobbed,' they told her, 'the men will need the jobs, love, now that our boys are all coming home.' The other telephonists invited her out for a farewell drink.

and she found herself unexpectedly sad to think she wouldn't see them again.

'Always the way,' Polly said when Ella told her. 'Women are the backbone of the country, but as soon as they don't need us anymore, we're thrown away like dirty water.'

In the coming days, James spent more time in Oxford, his work at Bletchley at an end. He told them that the military tents had already been taken down in the colleges and medical staff had mainly returned home. It was the most incredible and unbelievable feeling to see the mechanisms of war being dismantled, and then to Ella's joy she received a letter from Andrew.

I can't tell you exactly where I've been, so I've asked a chum of mine to post this for me. I was right about that new bomb the Americans were making – they're going to use it in Japan any day.

It was no secret now about the H-bomb; she had heard much speculation about when, not if, it would be dropped. Everyone seemed to think that if the Japanese wouldn't surrender, then they damn well deserved it.

I have a very bad feeling about what might be coming. If you need me for any reason, you can get hold of me poste restante at the following address . . .

It was just a series of numbers. Ella clutched the letter, grateful to have heard from him at last, and wondered if he had ever received the one she had written to him. He might be in

Japan by now, for all she knew. It occurred to her that, like the girls she had worked with, she might never see him again, and was glad that she'd tried to make her own peace with him after the thwarted attempt to kiss him.

After three and a half years of being in England, although the war might be officially over, when August came, rationing and hardship were still their constant companions. One afternoon, as Ella sat in the study listening to the wireless while darning the holes in Toby's socks, the newsreader's voice crackled to life.

'*President Truman announced yesterday that the first atomic bomb had been dropped by American aircraft on Hiroshima. The bomb was more powerful than 20,000 tons of TNT and more than 2,000 times the blast of any bomb used up to now. An impenetrable cloud of dust has covered the target area making an accurate report of the damage impossible . . .*'

Ella listened, needle suspended in mid-air. Despite the warmth in the room, cold rippled down her back. The size of the bomb and the damage it had done were incomprehensible. She wondered if that was where Andrew was and hoped that he was safe. Slowly, she put down her needle and jabbed it into the sock, then stood and fiddled with the wireless controls, trying to find another report, but there was nothing.

Polly knocked on the door.

'Have you heard?' she asked, her voice trembling.

'Yes. It's terrible, but do you think it means that at last the Japanese will surrender?'

'I don't know. We'll have to wait and see.'

For the next couple of days, Polly and Ella listened to the

wireless and scoured all the papers. Destruction on a scale never before imagined was described and depicted; horrific images of Hiroshima revealed that ninety per cent of the buildings had been wiped away, with reports estimating that eighty thousand people had been killed.

'Eighty thousand. It's incomprehensible,' Polly said, her face pale as she put the paper down. 'Those poor children and their families. Far, far worse than Coventry or Dresden.'

'I only hope they didn't suffer too much or for too long. Surely the emperor will surrender now?'

But he didn't, and then the Americans dropped another bomb, this time on Nagasaki.

'There's hardly anything left,' Polly said, looking at the photographs in the newspaper that revealed wasteland with just the occasional façade of a building standing, bewildered people staring at the incinerated remains of what once had been their homes.

Ella wondered if any of the images she had seen could have been photographs that Andrew had taken. He might be ambitious and seeking a scoop, but she couldn't bear to think that he'd witnessed people being killed like that. It must be even more shocking viewed from the ground.

Three days later, the announcement they had all been longing for came.

'"*To our good and loyal people . . .*",' Ella read aloud a translation of Hirohito's surrender. '"*We have ordered our Government to communicate to the Governments of the United States, Great Britain, China and the Soviet Union that our empire accepts the provisions of their joint declaration . . . the enemy has begun to employ a new and most cruel bomb . . . Should we continue to fight, it would not only result in an ultimate collapse and obliteration of the Japanese nation, but also it would lead to the total extinction of human civilisation . . ." '*

'That's it then,' Polly said. 'Singapore must surely surrender next, then Malaya will follow.'

Ella and Polly waited nervously as August gave way to September. And then, just as they thought it would never happen, it was announced that the Japanese had finally surrendered. A slow trickle of British soldiers who, just as Percy said, had been hiding in the jungle, had re-emerged and taken various villages in Malaya including Kota Bharu. Singapore followed and Ella stared at the photographs in the paper, unable to believe what was happening, even when Mountbatten stood on the steps of the Municipal Building there after the surrender ceremony. She scoured the images of the watching crowds, hoping against all hope that she'd see Johnnie or Grace.

'Look.' She passed Polly a copy of *The Times*. 'Prisoners have been released from Changi – they're just skin and bone.'

Polly took the paper. 'And they're the lucky ones.' She placed it in her lap. 'You know, we should write to the Red Cross again, see if they have anyone new on their lists matching Johnnie's description.'

Ella didn't need to be told twice, she wrote immediately,

but several days later did not receive the news she was hoping for.

Dear Mrs McCain,

Thank you for your letter. To date, we do not have any information matching a person of your husband's description.

As you may know from your previous enquiry, the names of military personnel will be listed, and their information posted in the Gazette. *As for civilians, we currently don't have full records of everyone incarcerated. This will take time. However, do not give up hope, as the Japanese kept extensive details of their prisoners: camp, name, nationality, place of capture, father's name. We do hope that with the release of so many POWs currently we will have some information soon. Rest assured, when we do, we will contact you.*

Ella folded the letter once, then twice. All around there was joy and celebration, but for her it was as though smelted iron had seeped into her heart and was setting hard. The one thing she had been hoping for was still beyond her grasp and her mood darkened as she struggled with another dead end.

In search of information, she decided to write to Noor. It was the wildest of long shots, but if Percy had been right, then Noor could still be at the villa and now that the Japanese had left there was a chance she might get the letter, even though Ella knew it would take months to reach Malaya. She sat down at the kitchen table, wondering where to begin. In the end, she decided to keep it simple.

Dear Noor,

I hope that you are well and that Grace is with you. I am in England, but as soon as I can, I will be returning to Malaya, back to the mine. Please, if you are still there, or if you know where Johnnie is, can you write to me at the above address? If you have news of my family, I will get to you as soon as is humanly possible.

A couple of days later, she had a letter from Melody telling her that she'd had some wonderful news. Edward had been found by the Red Cross in Changi and was now on his way home on HMS *Sussex*. He'd be docking in Liverpool, then shortly after a debriefing and medical, he'd be on his way to London.

'I'm meeting him at St Pancras Station next Wednesday,' she wrote. 'The Red Cross have done everything – even bought his train ticket home. But you'll come with me, won't you, Ella? I don't think I can cope if he's not on the train. It's simply the most wonderful news!'

Of course it was, Ella wrote back, and said she would be there if her friend really wanted her. But as she wrote, she wondered what Melody would do about Laurence now that her husband was coming home.

The following Wednesday, Ella caught the train to Paddington, where Melody met her before they took the bus to

St Pancras. Melody chattered nervously as she clutched the rail of the seat in front of her, while Ella listened and nodded, keeping an eye out all the time for their stop.

'Here we are,' she said as they arrived at the station, 'are you ready? It's time to get off.'

'Oh, Ella,' Melody said. 'Now that I'm here, I'm terrified. Promise me, won't you, that you'll never mention a thing to Edward about Laurence and what happened?'

Melody wrung her hands, which looked hot and sweaty in their cotton gloves. Beneath the fabric there was the bulge of her engagement ring. She turned it occasionally as though it were a talisman.

'Of course I won't. But you'll take good care of him, won't you? It's going to be hard for you both, having been apart for so long. Be as patient and gentle as you can with him.'

On the platform, they waited and waited and eventually the train pulled into the station. Doors opened and slammed and suddenly the platform was a sea of people in uniform with the odd civilian distinguishable between them. Ella and Melody scanned the descending passengers for Edward.

'Oh, Ella,' Melody said, taking a deep breath. 'I think that's him.'

'I'll wait until you're certain, then I'll leave you, shall I? I'll call you next week.'

But Melody had already stepped forward to greet a man. Ella stared at the figure, trying to recognise the remnants of the person she used to know. Edward had always been so tall, so proud, but the man she saw now was stooped and painfully thin. She watched for a little longer as Melody and

Edward stood still and took each other in while the crowd surged around them.

Edward lifted a hand to his wife's face and ran his fingers over her features as though he could hardly believe she was there. His other hand he kept in his pocket. After a time, he used the hand he had been touching her face with to take something from his other pocket. He held out a small box, which he gave to Melody with an air of awkwardness. Ella didn't wait to see her open it but turned away, the sight of them reunited once more blurred by the tears filming her eyes.

The following week, Ella returned to London to visit them both.

As she walked along the street towards their apartment, all she could think about was Grace and Johnnie. Where was the letter she had written Noor? Would anyone ever receive it? She kept picturing Johnnie as he had been the last time she saw him, standing on the steps waving to her, sunlight in his hair, the blue of his shirt reflecting in his eyes. He had been so strong and full of vigour. He wouldn't look like that now, she knew, he would have aged like Edward. He too would probably be skin and bone.

Ella had to knock twice before Melody answered the door. She was full of smiles, but dark shadows circled her eyes.

'Thank you for coming,' she said with an air of shyness Ella was surprised to see. 'Please come in.'

Ella followed her to the living room and there, sitting on a sofa, was a dozing Edward. Words stuck like fish bones in

Ella's throat. It was sad to see him so broken. Something must have alerted him to her presence because he lifted his head.

'Ella?'

Slowly, he struggled to his feet but immediately slumped down again.

'He's still very weak,' Melody said.

Ella's eyes fixed on Edward: his hair was the same colour, a little thinner perhaps with a hint of grey at the temples. And his eyes, once the colour of sapphires, had faded to a grey-blue. His cheeks were hollow and his skin sallow. As she took him in, she could see how much his muscles had wasted away; beneath the line of his shirt, she could see his ribs, and his trousers hung loose from his waist. His shoulder blades protruded beneath his shirt. But the worst thing of all, the thing she hadn't been expecting, was his hand – his right arm seemed wasted and the hand twisted.

'Edward,' she said as she stepped towards him to give him a hug. He flinched at her approach. 'Oh, Edward. It's so good to see you.' She took his good hand and held it in her own; his skin felt hard and callused.

'Can't tell you how good it is to be home,' he said. 'Although Melody's been fussing non-stop, baking and cleaning, making constant cups of tea.'

'Of course I have.' Melody kissed his forehead. 'Nothing's too good for him now that he's home. Now then, how about some tea and cake?'

'Please,' Ella said. 'I'm never going to pass up the option of cake if it's available.'

Melody returned to the kitchen and Ella listened to

plates clattering before following her. She leant against the doorframe.

'How's he doing?' she asked.

Melody's shoulders sank. She turned and faced her friend.

'To be honest, it's been hard, though I'm so glad to have him home.'

'What happened to his hand?'

'I don't really know,' Melody replied. 'A punishment. I think the Japanese crushed it between two stones, but he breaks out in a sweat every time I raise the question.' She hesitated before continuing, 'To be honest, he starts to shake at almost anything. One minute he's fine, the next—'

'Poor Edward. I'm sure it will get better.'

Melody lowered her voice. 'Sometimes I wonder if he'll ever be the same again. I have to mash his food and spoon it for him like a baby. And as for the sores on his skin – they're so painful, he can hardly lie on them even though I keep applying a soothing cream. And I can't tell you about the lice . . . We were so lucky, you know, getting away when the Japanese invaded. However hard things might have seemed here, we really had no idea what it was like to be left behind.'

Ella gave a wry smile as Melody turned to the kettle and made the tea. She watched as the pot was warmed and leaves spooned out, her thoughts on the plight of the returning prisoners. If only Grace and Johnnie were among them.

She noted that there was sugar in a bowl, as well as milk, proper milk, not the powdered stuff Ella used in her tea. It was clear that Melody was doing everything she could to help her husband. If only Ella could have that chance herself.

'Ready?' Melody picked up the tray, but when they got back Edward was fast asleep on the sofa. Melody set the tray down on the table and then placed a hand on her husband's shoulder.

'Do you want me to help you to bed or to close the curtains?' Melody asked him. 'Then you can sleep properly.'

'No, thank you.' He pulled himself up, wincing. Melody sat down on the sofa next to him; there were tears on his cheeks and she wiped his face with her hand as though she were comforting an injured child.

But then his tears turned to sobs and she put her arms around him.

'Shhh. You don't need to think about it now. Rest. Take your time. We can take each day as it comes.' Melody's voice was soothing. It pained Ella to watch the tenderness and love she was giving to Edward.

Ella didn't stay long. She told her friend she'd visit again in a couple of weeks when Edward was feeling stronger.

When she got back to Oxford, Polly was sitting in the kitchen, folding washing.

'You look done in,' she said, placing a towel on the pile. 'How were they both?'

'Oh, it was so pitiful to see him.' Ella sank down into one of the chairs. 'To think that he used to be such a strong man. Now Melody has to mash all his food into a pulp so he can swallow it – after all those years of not eating anything other than rice he can't manage very much.'

Polly came to her and slid one arm around her shoulders. 'It's dreadful, and I know what you're thinking, but there's no point in trying to picture yourself and Johnnie in this situation. What will be, will be. Now the fate of those left behind rests in God's hands.'

Ella started to cry. Slowly at first, then wild sobbing. When finally it ceased, she pulled away from Polly, pain and exhaustion rippling through her body.

'Oh, Polly, I don't know if I can take it anymore. I thought that once the war ended, I'd get an answer, but I don't feel any closer to it today than I did when I first arrived here. What else can I possibly do?'

Her mother-in-law shook her head. 'You're doing everything you can. I know it's hard, but you have to wait.'

'I can't.' Ella's thoughts turned to Melody and Edward – she needed what they had *so* much. 'There's only one thing for it. I need to go back to Malaya. It's the only way I will ever find out what has happened to them.'

'I think you're right,' Polly soothed her. 'And you know I'll do all I can to help you. And if you do go back, I will look after Toby for you. The house is empty now without all the visiting servicemen and evacuees. It would be a pleasure to have him. Why don't I make you some Ovaltine and then you can get to bed? When I've cleared all this away, I'll bring it to you, and we can talk things over again.'

Ella nodded. 'Thank you. But you're right, I'm exhausted. I think it would be better if I went straight to sleep.'

In the days that followed, Ella wrote to everyone she thought could help, to see how she might get back to Malaya. No one was cleared for return yet, she was told, it wasn't safe for British nationals. There were no commercial flights, and a voyage, even if she could find a passage, wouldn't be safe yet and would take forever. She'd have to think again.

She wrote to the Red Cross one more time, not expecting an answer, but a reply came back almost by return.

Thank you for your letter, Mrs McCain. We suggest you contact anyone you know in Malaya – you could try the government offices, in Singapore, Ipoh or KL – but I hope you appreciate that our offices here are inundated and any help we can offer is limited and would take several months to complete. It would be better at his stage for you to start your own enquiries but be advised that any return to Malaya at this time is unwise.

'Honestly,' she finished reading the letter aloud to Polly who was sitting in the coach house with Toby on her knee, 'I don't know what to do next – it will take me months to write to all the Malayan government offices and receive replies. I'm at my wits' end.'

Polly placed her hand on Ella's. 'I know it doesn't seem like it now, but I'm certain it will sort itself out.'

Chapter Thirty-One

Naoki was buried in a secluded part of the jungle. In the following days, Noor focused on cleaning and tidying every room in the villa.

'But won't my parents be coming back now?' Grace asked one late-September afternoon as she watched Noor place dust sheets over the furniture.

It was a question she had asked herself many times since the surrender, and one to which she still didn't know the answer. She had been waiting and wondering about it for days.

'They will come eventually,' she said. 'And when they do, everything will be ready for their return.'

But her thoughts kept turning to what *she* should do. She couldn't stay here without money or purpose forever; in reality, it could be years before the McCains came back – if at all. She had made a promise to Mr McCain to look after Grace, come what may, and she would honour that vow until he returned. And then there was Naoki. She couldn't help thinking, over and over again, that he had done what he had for her sake. There must be a way that she could honour him, but she was at a loss to know how.

She was cooking rice parcels stuffed with chicken when

her thoughts crystallised. Her mind had been focused on Grace, helping her wrap the parcels in palm leaves. Now as they cooked gently on the edge of the pan, giving off a tempting aroma, she knew that she must go to Ipoh to find a fresh start. She could make something of herself there, be the woman she knew, in other circumstances, Naoki would have been proud to have at his side.

'You have been asking me about when your parents come back,' Noor said. 'Well, I've decided that while we wait for them, we'll go to Ipoh.'

Grace lifted her face to Noor's.

'Why?'

'For a change of scene, but only for a bit,' she said, not meeting the girl's eyes. 'If we go, you won't need to pretend to be a boy anymore, either. You can be yourself again. Don't you want that?'

The girl nodded.

She didn't want to tell Grace how the villagers here ignored her whenever she went to the kampong to buy food. Why, only the other day, her old friend Suyin had refused to sell her vegetables in the market. Then she'd started to hear that horrible rumours about her were spreading. Omar eventually told her that people didn't trust her as they thought she had collaborated with the Japanese soldiers. They said she'd been Naoki's mistress, living in comfort, and had turned her back on her old friends. He'd tried to defend her, of course, telling them that she was acting as a spy for him, but they didn't believe him.

And it was more than that, she realised, as she turned the

parcels in the pan. As a child born half-caste, she had been neither completely British nor Malaysian. She had been the odd one out who received favours from her master's family, without any of their security or privilege, while the other servants had treated her with suspicion, and she had never quite been one of them either. People would always judge her, she knew that now – they would always think of her as a conspirator one way or another, if not for the Japanese, then for the British. There was a real fear in the country that Britain would step in and take complete control of Malaya again, and no one wanted that. If the McCains did return, she feared the villa would soon come under attack from the communists and then they could be forced out of the area. Only the other day she had heard on her wireless how Ching Peng, the new MCP leader, was more determined than ever to take back control for the nationalist party – meaning that anyone mixed-race like her would need to watch out.

It was a curse on her, being Eurasian. Her thoughts ebbed and flowed like a wave, and she muttered under her breath, hoping Grace couldn't hear, 'We can't stay here. This place is full of ghosts.'

Two weeks later, the house was clean and covered in dust sheets and Noor and Grace's belongings were tied in sarongs on the hall floor. Noor sat at Ella's desk. Omar would be arriving in half an hour or so with the truck he was borrowing to take her to Ipoh. Before she left, she had one last thing she needed to do: write a letter for Mr and Mrs McCain in case they returned. She picked up a pen.

Dear Mr and Mrs McCain,

I very much hope that you return to Malaya and the villa. For now, Grace and I have gone to Ipoh. I have looked after her the best I could during the Occupation, and she has flourished. I will continue to care for her until your return. When I have a new address, I will send it to you here at the villa, but in the meanwhile, you can always ask my cousin Omar where to find me.

Yours,
Noor

When she was satisfied, she sealed the letter and placed it on the hall table, then walked through to the drawing room. Everything had either been packed away or covered up, apart from the piano, which Grace was polishing for the last time. A shutter was partially open, allowing a shaft of light to illuminate the instrument.

As she looked about the room, Noor reflected. She was glad to be leaving this place where so many bad memories clung like cobwebs. At the same time, she was fearful of moving away to a place where she didn't belong. But it was necessary, she thought, as she picked up a bundle from the floor, for both of them. Grace was almost twelve and growing, although the years of not eating enough had left her looking younger. It was such a relief for Noor no longer to be hiding the fact that she was a girl; a charade she had long wished she had never started as the months had turned to years and she lived with constant fear that Grace's delicate features and form would give her away.

She held her bundle of precious possessions close as she listened for the sound of Omar's vehicle approaching. Of course she was nervous, who wouldn't be? She wondered if she would ever return here, and realised that although she was apprehensive about the future there was no longer anything to hold her here. Unlike Grace, she didn't belong.

Her thoughts turned to Omar and how she would miss him. As usual, he had helped her more than she could have expected. He had a contact in Ipoh, someone who could put Noor up in a shared house. He had even found her work as a cook in one of the hotels in the Old Town in Ipoh. She wasn't happy about that, but told herself that at least it was a start.

It was then she realised she had forgotten to collect the photograph of her mother she had hidden in the kitchen. She'd better hurry and pick it up before Omar arrived – it was far too precious to leave behind.

She ran to the kitchen to fetch it, just as she heard the chugging of the truck swinging into the drive. A moment later, she heard Omar and a friend of his entering the villa by the front door.

'*Salam,*' Noor said as she returned from the kitchen, clutching the photograph to her chest.

The men collected the bundles of belongings and she went to the window to close the shutter.

'Are you ready, Grace?'

'What about the piano?' The girl looked crestfallen as she

ran her hand over the shining wood veneer. 'How can I play if I don't have one to practise on?'

'It will be here for when you get back.'

'But who will look after it when I'm away? It needs polishing and to be kept out of the sun.'

'We'll put a sheet on it, and the shutter will keep out the sun.'

'But the humidity – the wood might crack.'

'I can look after it, if you like,' Omar said. 'I can take it to the school, then the children can use it. We can bring it back when you need it again.'

Eventually, Grace nodded, but Noor knew how much leaving the piano behind would hurt; not only had it been her salvation, it was also part of her soul.

'Right, that's everything in,' Omar said.

Noor picked up her last bundle. She hadn't had time to put the photograph inside and was trying to undo the knot and slip it in while she made her way to the truck. But as she reached the doorway, she tripped and the photograph frame fell and landed with a loud crack on the floor. She looked on in horror as the glass shattered into tiny pieces.

'Oh, no!'

She bent down to examine the damage. The glass was completely ruined, and the frame had landed on one corner so that the sides were now out of alignment. She examined it then undid the back to take out the photograph before straightening the crooked edges of the frame.

As she did so, a thin piece of folded blue paper fell out. How curious, she thought, as she opened the letter.

'Come on, hurry up, Noor!' Omar shouted. 'We haven't got all day.'

But there was something familiar about the handwriting, so she ignored him and read the letter, hunched over the fractured frame and glass. What she read was the last thing she had been expecting to see and the words had the effect of a tsunami on her, sweeping away everything that had seemed fixed and certain in her world. And like a tsunami, the shockwaves and undercurrents were powerful and irreversible.

Chapter Thirty-Two

Noor hadn't travelled further than Menglembu before, but as the truck puttered over the bumpy roads winding through the hills, she couldn't focus on the passing scenery as the words of the letter reverberated in her mind, making her stomach churn.

My dear Noor,

I write this because it grieves me that I can never put things right for you, although I had always hoped that one day perhaps I could.

Your mother, you see, was a beautiful woman and I loved her, perhaps more than I should have allowed myself to, and if I'm honest, I wronged her. You see, the result of this love was you. I was so ashamed of the way I treated your mother, and really should have tried before to make amends to you as best I could.

You might recall how you used to play with Ella, sharing games and even going to school together?

I am such a coward – I don't even know if you'll ever receive this letter, but I am going to hide it in a place where I hope one day you will find it, behind the frame of the only photograph I ever had of your mother, which I am now giving to you.

You are my daughter, Noor, and I am ashamed of myself for not publicly acknowledging it – ashamed of the way I treated your mother and, therefore, you.

And so, I hope you will find this letter because, if you do, I need you to know that my will has been written with this in mind – I have left my estate 'to my heirs and successors', who have specifically not been named. So you see how much of a coward I really am. I am too weak to name you as mine even in my last will and testament, although I hope one day you will receive a share of what is rightfully yours by using this letter to prove your parentage.

Your loving father,
Graham Ferguson

It sickened her. All of it. But she didn't know which part of the revelation was worse: the fact that he had used her mother, while never acknowledging her, or that her mother had been dishonest with her, too. She tried not to picture them together, bile rising in her throat as they wove along the hillside away from the villa and the mine.

The truth about her parentage was still very difficult for Noor to comprehend. She turned to Omar, desperate to ask him to stop, to show him the letter and talk it through. But as she stared beyond the windscreen, she realised that there would be ramifications to this news, not just for herself, but also for Grace.

'You're looking pale,' he said. 'Feeling travel sick?'

She clutched the edge of the dashboard, unable to speak. 'Omar,' she whispered, desperate to tell him, but Grace was sitting next to her so all Noor could do was nod and say, 'Yes, I think so.'

The journey took hours and all she could think of was the terrible secret she had uncovered. The more she thought about it, the more it sickened her. Was that the reason why her mother had daily taken baskets of food to Mr Ferguson at the mine? How long had it been going on? Did he look after her financially? Did Mrs Ferguson ever know?

Hours later they arrived in a crowded part of Ipoh. Grace stared out of the window at the buildings lining both sides of the street and washing hanging from poles sticking out of upper-floor windows. Noor could smell garlic and chicken cooking but did not feel hungry after the long journey, her emotions still too raw and bruised. Hiding her feelings had been terrible and had exhausted her, but she had finally resolved that she wouldn't tell Grace; there was already too much for the child to deal with as it was. As for Omar – discovering that his cousin was the daughter of an Englishman, and more so of old Mr Ferguson, might drive a wedge between them. Noor decided that the secret was hers and no one else's.

The apartment he had found them was small and on the ground floor of a house. There was one room that would be used for living, sleeping and cooking. Outside there was an area where they could wash plates and pans – a cold tap with a single bucket provided for pots and pans, clothes and personal hygiene. A curtain hung from the ceiling to divide the living area into two: one part to sleep in and the other in which to cook and eat.

Noor tried to hide her disappointment; it swelled like rice in her stomach and made her whole body ache. *This is the fresh start I wanted*, she told herself, *and I will do all in my power to make it work.*

When Omar left, they unpacked and tried to make themselves at home. Noor couldn't help looking at Grace and for the first time thought she could see something of herself within the child's features. Her hair perhaps, the curve of her chin and nose? When she caught sight of her own reflection in a mirror as they were unpacking, she examined the lines of her face with fresh eyes – she had never noticed it before, but yes, she wasn't imagining it, the shape of her face resembled both Ella's and Mr Ferguson's. She was stupid not to have seen it all before, she thought as she reflected on the moonlight walks her mother had taken or the early-morning returns across the lawn when she'd arrive back with dew clinging to the edge of her *abaya*. Noor saw these things from a different perspective now.

All the safety and protection of the villa, her only real home to date, was permanently tainted for her. And if she was indeed entitled to share in it, as her father's letter said, she didn't care. She didn't want it. Her place there was founded on a lie, soiled by deceit and disappointment. Besides, if Ella and Mr McCain never returned, in Noor's eyes the place belonged to Grace. She vowed to herself that, whatever happened, she wouldn't tell Grace the truth until she was an adult. Until then, Noor would look after her like her own child and make the best life possible for them.

When everything had been unpacked and put away, she picked up the photograph of her mother in its damaged frame. She ought to find a place to display it, she knew, but she hesitated, then pushed it beneath a pile of clothes.

Noor began work in the hotel the very next morning. The hours were long and the work frantic; it wasn't the same as cooking for a family where she could see the pleasure in everyone's eyes as they ate the food she had prepared. Here, she never saw the diners, and the head cook often shouted when meals were delayed or the customers impatient. On the other hand, sometimes there was leftover food she could bring home, which compensated for the meagre wages she earnt.

The family who owned the house she lived in inhabited the upper floors, and Noor would take them small gifts of bread or sweet cakes she had made. Soon the landlady, a woman of about her own age, and she became friends. They would talk as they shared cake and tea, and once or twice played a game of mah-jong.

Grace, now no longer disguised as a boy, enrolled in one of the local schools and because the hours Noor worked didn't match the hours that the girl was home from school, the woman upstairs, whom by now they called auntie, offered to look after her in exchange for a regular supply of sweet treats from the hotel, the occasional chicken or bag of rice, along with a few extra cents that Noor would drop into her hands.

But this wasn't the life she had imagined she would find for them both. While ambition spurred her on, her secrets haunted her. Although she didn't miss the villa, she longed to hear the cacophony of birds in the jungle canopy, the monkeys chattering, the gentle breezes of the monsoon, the sound of its heavy downpour on the leaves. She missed the sight of the orange-gold sun that rose in the mornings from below the distant hills. For her, the innocence of this paradise was lost forever – there was simply no way of retrieving it and she must fight on.

The days turned into weeks, and then the weeks into months and their circumstances didn't improve. Noor noticed in the mirror that her face had developed a darkness to it, as though a shadow had fallen across her and seeped deep within. It was like a bruised pineapple, she thought; the blemish looked skin-deep, but the damage had crept right through to her core, and she didn't know what to do about it. Grace, too, seemed to be suffering. She would return home from school despondent and quiet, and her bad dreams had returned.

One morning, Noor didn't have to be at the hotel to cook, so although she and Grace had woken up at the usual time, they lingered before the girl headed off to school.

'What do you want for breakfast?' Noor asked. '*Roti*?'

They were both lying on their mats as sunlight filtered through the windows across the bare floor. Over the past few days Grace had become increasingly subdued, and

Noor had been trying to tease out of her what was ailing her. Of course, she'd be missing home, wondering if her parents were on the way back, as well as missing Naoki and playing the piano. Noor had done all she could to reassure her that her parents knew where Grace was and would find the letter Noor had left for them when they returned, and that when they did, her old life, including playing the piano, would resume.

'You need to stop worrying, my love.' Noor kissed the child on her forehead and smoothed back the hair from her face. 'I know it's hard coming to a new place, but things will get better soon. I'm trying as hard as I can to make that happen.'

'I know,' Grace said. 'But it's not that so much. You know, I really miss the piano – it helped me so much. And I was good at it – not like some of the things I have to learn at school here.'

'Ah.' Noor let out a sigh. 'Is that what it is?'

'Yes.' Grace propped herself up on one elbow. 'It used to make me happy when I played. I could forget everything and be where the music took me. I wish I could have a piano here or take lessons.'

'I'm sorry, there is no way we can afford piano lessons, even if I knew where to get them.' Noor patted Grace's hand. 'Now come on, hurry up and tell me what you want for breakfast. I have to be in the hotel later, but I thought I could make us something nice to eat before auntie comes to take you to school.'

Grace sat up without enthusiasm and they took it in turns

to wash at the outside tap and to dress in the bedroom with their backs turned to each other.

'Now,' Noor said when they were both in the kitchen. Grace sat on a stool as Noor brushed her hair, dividing it in the middle to form two short plaits, 'I might have to work late today, so auntie will collect you from school and she'll look after you until I get back.'

Grace scrunched up her face at these words.

'And why not?' Noor tugged a ribbon tightly around one of the plait ends.

Grace pursed her lips then said, 'It's Halim. I don't like him.'

Noor sighed. How many times had she heard Grace complain about auntie's son? Halim was just a couple of years older than Noor. His name meant 'gentle', but it was definitely the wrong choice for him. Noor wished that there was a way of stopping him from teasing Grace and using her as the butt for his bullying nature, but unless there was a radical change in their lives, she didn't see how it could be managed.

'Don't be silly.' She kissed Grace on the top of her head in an attempt to be reassuring. 'Boys are just different from girls. Let's eat some breakfast. We still have time for *roti*.'

Noor poured tea from the pot into a large glass containing milk. Then she made some *roti* and they sat together, eating it with the spicy *sambal* she had brought back from the hotel kitchen.

Just before they had finished, there was a knock on the door and auntie came in. She was wearing an old loose grey dress with a pattern of orange flowers, and her black hijab was bleached grey by the sun.

'*Selamat pagi!*' she called. 'Good morning. Are you ready for school?'

Grace nodded, then slipped off her chair, still chewing the last mouthful of her breakfast. Halim was loitering outside, kicking up dust with his shoe.

Noor watched them leave then turned and looked at the plates on the table. However hard she tried, everything in the room looked tired and shabby. She sat down and drummed her fingers on the table.

After a time, she heaved herself up and cleared away, putting the plates in a bowl and taking them to the outside table where she washed them, then returned to the kitchen where she laid them on a drying cloth before casting her eye over the room.

All morning, her thoughts troubled her and when her shift ended, she stood outside the hotel on the street to which the heat of the day still clung. There was a European woman talking to a friend and a girl about a year older than Grace. Both women wore well-cut if slightly old-fashioned dresses: one blue, the other green, nipped in at the waist. They wore pearls at their throats, and hats that had been dyed to match their dresses were perched on their heads. One woman wore a heart-shaped diamond brooch and held a creamy-white bag on her arm. The girl was wearing a white school uniform; the delicate gold cross around her neck glinted in the sun.

Although she was used to seeing such women, what marked them out for Noor was how these two stood and spoke with more than the usual confidence. She paused and listened. The women revealed in conversation that they had recently returned from England. This didn't surprise Noor as she had noticed a steady trickle of Europeans arriving at the hotel. Their presence in the country was steadily growing, so that now some of the British Military Administration officers had been joined by their wives who, despite the damage that war and the Occupation had dealt the peninsula, seemed determined to live as though nothing much in life had changed now that they were 'back home'.

The woman in the green dress had a pinched face. She leant closer to her friend and confided, 'I couldn't possibly send Moira to school in England. I know I should, but we've only just arrived back. I'd rather she was here with us for now, even if it means the Main Convent School.'

'Well, it is a good one,' the woman in blue said. 'But can you be certain it offers everything Moira will need?'

'Certainly. It's always been one of the best. No reason to think it won't be again very soon.'

'And what do you particularly like to study?' The woman in blue smiled encouragingly at Moira.

'Well, I like drawing and handicrafts, but I suppose I like playing the piano best of all.'

Noor fixed her attention on the group. It had never occurred to her that piano lessons could be had at school. She listened intently, but the conversation turned and the group were saying their farewells as they caught sight of Noor and gave her dismissive looks.

She watched them leaving, wanting to call out and ask

them about this school, but the woman in the blue dress was going in one direction, and the woman in green, with her daughter in school uniform beside her, in another. Noor knew that, in any case, they would never speak to someone like her.

She asked auntie about the school and whether Grace might be able to go. Auntie looked at her as though she were mad, but told her where the school was. That was all the information Noor needed for now, so she decided not to probe further. Although her days were so busy and her time so limited, when she finally had a half day free, she set out after Grace had left for school and made her way to where she had learnt the convent school was located. It was a long, white Dutch-style colonial building with a red tiled roof. She looked at the windows and thought of all the girls who were sitting behind them – sewing, reading, writing, painting, playing the piano. Wasn't this where Grace belonged?

Noor took a deep breath and straightened her *abaya* then walked along the path to a large door that stood open. She stepped inside, crossing from one world to another, finding herself in a hushed corridor where polished panels with lists of girls' names written in gold hung on the walls.

Chapter Thirty-Three

As she stood beneath the fans in the wide, echoing hallway, Noor could imagine girls arriving here for school in the morning, the ring of their shoes on the tiled floors and their lively chatter as they headed off to their classrooms. Hanging on a far wall there were portraits of people she didn't recognise, and she looked again at the rows of varnished teak boards with the names of head girls and prefects written in gold.

Footsteps fell and she lifted her face to see a woman watching her. She was dressed in a nun's habit and her voice was gentle.

'May I help you?'

Noor swallowed. 'Yes. Please.'

The woman, a nun and one of the teachers it turned out, showed Noor around the school and explained the entrance requirements. For the rest of the morning, she clung onto the information like a precious jewel that she would present to Grace later that evening.

When she got home after work, Grace was sleeping on her mat with her face turned away to the wall. Noor couldn't see her features, but she could hear her gentle breathing. As she lay down on her own mat, she was disappointed that the girl wasn't awake for her to hand over the gift.

For a moment, Grace's eyes flickered open. Noor kissed the top of her head. Grace wriggled closer, bringing with her the scent of jasmine flowers and coconut. Sleep evaded Noor as her mind whirred, exploring new possibilities. It surprised her to find that she had fallen asleep when sunlight glided across the floor, waking them both. Grace stirred and Noor propped herself up and turned to look at her face.

'Grace?'

'Mmm?'

'I think I have found a way for you to have piano lessons.'

The child sat up slowly, still shaking off sleep. Noor looked into the dark pool of her eyes.

'Really?'

'Yes. I have discovered that there is a good school here and, if you are clever enough, you can attend without paying. They have things called scholarships, including one that would allow you to learn to play the piano. Would you like to visit?'

Grace sat up and hugged her arms around her knees. Noor waited for what seemed like minutes as she watched the changing expressions on the girl's face, attempting to ascertain what she was thinking.

At last, she said, 'Yes. I would like that very much.'

Noor and Grace stood outside the sugar-white school building. Grace was wearing a white school uniform that auntie had borrowed from a friend; it was a little tight across the chest and an inch too high above her knee, but Noor didn't think it mattered. Earlier, she had styled Grace's hair in plaits that reached to just above her collar. Grace kept flipping them backwards and forwards, the green ribboned bunches jumping like frogs.

Noor had modelled herself on the women she had seen outside the hotel the other day. She wore one of the dresses Naoki had bought for her; the green silk with buttons that ran all the way up the skirt and bodice. She had fastened a string of pearls around her neck and was pleased to see how they sat above the neckline of her dress. Then she slipped on the creamy-white shoes he had given her and slung a matching bag over her arm. She fixed her hair in a chignon, the way she had seen the smart women who used to visit the villa do.

'I'm scared,' Grace said.

Noor squeezed her hand. 'Try not to be. Be yourself. But tell them about your love for playing the piano, how you used to win all the prizes at the concerts you attended, as well as showing them how clever you are.'

Grace nodded, although Noor sensed how deeply the child was drawing on all her will-power to keep calm.

'Good morning,' Noor said to a woman sitting in the reception area of the school. 'We've come for a meeting with the principal. For my niece, Grace McCain.'

The secretary indicated that they should sit and wait while she knocked on the principal's office door.

After five minutes or so, they were called in to the office. A tall woman with eyes the colour of a gas flame greeted them.

'Please, sit down and make yourself comfortable.' The woman indicated a pair of rattan chairs with plain white cushions. Grace sat on the edge of one, her feet dangling, while Noor sat tall and upright, projecting what she hoped was a genteel air.

The principal sat down and read some notes. After a few moments, she lifted her head and placed her hands one over the other on the desk before her.

'I see that you have recently arrived in Ipoh,' she began.

'Yes,' Noor said. 'From Menglembu. We suffered at the hands of the Japanese and have come here in search of a better future.'

'Indeed. We have all suffered greatly in this country and must all trust in God to help us recover. Now,' the woman glanced towards Grace, 'about your niece. I see you are twelve, which would make you a year late in starting here, but I don't see that it matters much, given that we're all starting life anew. Regarding the entry examinations, we ask our students to sit a set of papers – in mathematics, comprehension and composition – prior to admission. It is late to be applying but given that we are still building up our classes owing to the recent reopening of the school, I thought that perhaps you might leave Grace here with us for a short while so that she can take the tests.'

'Of course.' Noor nodded. 'You'll be all right with that, won't you, Grace?'

Her eyes were as big as saucers when she nodded her agreement.

'But first,' the principal continued, 'why don't you tell us a little about yourself, Grace? I understand from the letter your aunt wrote,' she glanced up at Noor then back to her notes, 'that you're an unusually good piano player.'

'Yes. I love to play the piano. I used to win all the competitions I entered during the Occupation.'

'Indeed? Have you had many lessons?'

'Well,' Grace inched forward on her chair, 'a friend helped me a little to start with. He said I had a natural ear.'

The principal smiled as she jotted down something in her notes. 'That's good because you do need to be of an exceptionally high standard in something to get a scholarship here.'

'Music is part of me. It's in here.' Grace placed her hands on her chest. 'And here.' She moved them to her head.

The principal tilted her own head to one side and looked at her with a quizzical expression. 'What do you mean, my dear?'

'The music. It's like a *need*.'

'A *need*?'

'Yes. The need to play. Sometimes, I have a dream. There's a man playing the piano and a woman standing near him. I can't see what they look like, but she is helping him by turning the pages of sheet music as he plays. I can hear the man humming the tune as well. When I wake, I can still hear that beautiful music in my head and I have to play it before I forget it.'

The principal leant forward. 'So you hear music and you have to play it?'

'Yes. But it's not only the music from my head. I can play most of the things I hear.'

'That's quite something. I'm looking forward to hearing you playing later.'

Noor looked at Grace's face. For the first time that day, she seemed relaxed.

The principal turned to Noor. 'Perhaps you can come back in two hours or so?'

She left Grace at the school and walked away, wondering what she could do to occupy herself until it was time to return. She wandered into the smarter part of town where the Europeans lived and there were fewer signs of the Occupation. There were wide, tree-lined avenues and large sleepy-looking white houses set well back from the road, ones that she knew had been requestioned and lived in by senior Japanese personnel. She walked along the palm-shaded pavement until she found a small tea shop on the corner of the residential area and a wider avenue where shops and businesses, that now bore no evidence of the recent Japanese administration, met between the bougainvillaea and plane trees.

She went inside the tea shop and was shown to one of the white linen-covered tables where silver cutlery sparkled beneath a swirling fan. She drank some Ipoh white tea, which arrived served in a silver teapot along with a tiny porcelain cup and saucer and a dainty jug of condensed milk. As she sipped her tea, she observed the other customers: a woman in a cream dress with a black hat set at an angle on her head, who reminded her of one of the women she had seen outside the hotel the other day. The woman looked at Noor then smiled at her.

Noor glanced one more time around the room: at the pearly orchids on the tables, the pink and white cushions on the chairs, the ornate cakes displayed on a trolley in the corner. She knew in that moment what it was she wanted, and that if she worked hard, it would soon be within her reach.

She turned to face the European woman. Drawing herself to her full height, Noor smiled back at her.

There were celebrations all round when Grace was offered a full scholarship to the school. Auntie cooked *laksa* for them and even Halim seemed to be on his best behaviour when they shared a meal together on the night before Grace started.

Noor took the day off work and walked her to the school, promising to collect her when the day ended. Once again, Noor wore her best dress and shoes and made her way to the Old Town where she spent the morning walking through the business quarter, soaking up the buzz and rush of people making their way to work: there were men in military uniform; businessmen in smart suits along with secretaries in tailored dresses and neat hats. On the periphery of it all, she sat on a bench outside a dress shop and enjoyed studying the bustle of city life.

Later, she made her way back to the tea shop she had visited when Grace had taken her scholarship exams. Once again, she settled down in the window, reading the free newspapers they provided, flicking idly through the pages.

As she drank her tea, an advertisement in the classifieds section caught her eye:

Wanted. General office work for the BMA offices in Ipoh –
Malay and English language essential.

Noor re-read the advertisement, her mind revisiting those scenes of men and women going to work in smart offices, and how much she had loved seeing the busy spectacle. She glanced quickly at the other people in the café, then tore the advertisement from the paper, leaving an ugly gap in the page, before folding it in half and placing it in her purse.

When Grace had gone to bed that night, Noor pulled out the advertisement, spread it on the table and smoothed out the creases with her hand. She could read and write Malay, and had done plenty of translating for Naoki, but wasn't certain what general office work might entail. Answering the telephone? She could do that. Writing letters? She could learn. Filing? Again, she could learn.

She sat down and wrote out a letter applying for the job, ensuring that her writing was its neatest and that she hadn't made any spelling mistakes, and then decided it was time to sign herself Noor McCain.

She wasn't expecting a reply to her letter, but a week later one arrived inviting her for an interview.

That morning, after Grace had gone to school, Noor dressed once more in her best dress and pearls then made her way to Rangoon Street, where the BMA offices were housed. The building was in the Old Town, in another old-style Dutch colonial building with a grand wooden door that had been left wide open to let the breeze in. Noor stepped inside the building and was confused by the number of office doors, noticeboards and people bustling backwards and forwards across the entrance floor. A man wearing khaki uniform walked down the stairs towards her.

'Excuse me, please. Can you point me in the right direction for Max Jeffries?' She spoke as politely as she could, attempting to copy the clipped accents of the women she had often listened to in the tea shop

'Of course,' the man said, pointing up the stairs. 'First office on the right.'

Noor thanked him and ascended. All around her she could hear the zip of typewriters behind closed office doors and fans whirring from ceilings along the corridor. There was the scent of jasmine through open windows, along with polished wood and incense, and the smell of someone cooking curry; spices mingling with garlic from somewhere below the open windows drifted up to her.

When she reached the top of the stairs, she paused and looked about. Another corridor opened out in front of her with yellowing notices tacked to corkboards along the walls. Her footsteps echoed as she made her way to the first office on the right. A polished teak door with an opaque glass panel was closed, but a brass plate bore Max Jeffries's name.

She knocked and waited. There were heavy footsteps and then the door opened to reveal a tall British man in his early forties. He too wore khaki uniform, his hair cut short and his face neatly shaved.

'Hello,' she said, holding out her hand. 'I'm Noor McCain.'

'Ah. Yes,' he said stiffly, looking at a clock on the wall. 'Come in.'

He held the door open and indicated that she should sit on a red leather seat opposite his desk, which was piled with toppling stacks of files and paperwork. Two telephones sat side by side next to a desk lamp that blazed angrily onto the cluttered desk. The window was open and the breeze from it, along with the overhead fan, gently stirred the top pages in a gentle rhythm.

Max picked up her letter of application. 'So, you can read and write in both English and Malay?'

Noor smoothed her dress as she looked at the wall behind Max's head. There was a picture of King George VI in ceremonial uniform. Queen Elizabeth stood at his side wearing a tiara and strands of long pearls over a beautiful embroidered dress. Hanging next to the picture there was a group photograph of army officers sitting in rows with their arms folded all looking at the camera, then finally a framed map of Malaya.

Yes,' she said.

'And can you type?'

'No.' Noor glanced at the black typewriter on the desk next to Max and wondered how hard it could be. 'But I'd be happy to learn.'

Max nodded. 'Well, typing is almost a prerequisite.' He sighed, picked up his pen and tapped it against the desk. 'You know, the work we do can be highly sensitive. The BMA acts on behalf of the British government here, mainly instilling law and order, but we also look after the interests of British nationals, particularly those who need to pursue property claims. One of our main tasks is to track down insurgent behaviour, that type of thing. Do you have any connection with groups or parties that might conflict with British authority here?'

Well, there was Omar, but surely Max had no way of finding out that there was any connection to him, especially now that she had changed her name.

'No.'

'Well.' Max paused. 'To be honest, you're not really qualified for this work, but we haven't had anyone else come forward who can do translating, and as you say you can read and write both Malay and English, I'd be prepared to offer you a job subject to a month's trial. If at the end of that time you aren't suited to the work, I'll have to let you go. As for typing . . .' He let out a sigh. 'I'm a two-finger typist myself and I'm struggling. If you can do better than me, that would certainly help, but you would need to learn, mind, as quickly as you can.'

And Noor did.

Determination and ambition grew within her like a seed that had been planted and watered. It swelled, then having pushed its way through the dirt, reached for the light and blossomed. Through auntie, she found someone to teach her to type. At first, she found it hard pushing down the heavy keys that punched the paper, or she hit the wrong key, making a nonsense of the words. But soon they seemed to form themselves at the tips of her fingers, and any mistakes she made, she corrected as neatly as she could. She learnt how to frame letters, how to space the paragraphs and prepare the pages for signature.

And when the tasks seemed too daunting, she pictured Grace heading off to school, her neat plaits, tied with green ribbon bouncing off her shoulders.

As the end of her trial period approached, Max told her she could stay. It was with a glow of happiness that Noor decided she could soon save enough money for them to put down a deposit on an apartment in the New Town.

And so, at last, she was truly independent, and could leave the past behind her and be the woman Naoki would have been proud of. She could look after Grace in the way that she deserved, she'd be keeping the promise she had made to Mr McCain, and through Grace's accomplishment at playing the piano, she, Noor, would be honouring them both.

Yes, she told herself. Everything had worked out nicely, and everything was going to be all right.

Chapter Thirty-Four

The last person Ella had expected to receive help from was Laurence. It had been during one of her visits to Edward that Melody had made the suggestion that he might well be able to.

'I don't know what to do,' Ella had said as they talked in the kitchen. 'I want to go back to Malaya but there seems absolutely no way of getting there.'

'Hmm.' Melody pursed her lips as she dried her hands on a tea towel. 'Do you think that's wise, going all that way by yourself? It must still be dangerous.'

The look on her face suggested that she was thinking, *And what if something terrible has happened to Johnnie and Grace? I'd hate to think of you being all alone.*

But it was all Ella could think of doing: like hunger gnawing in her stomach, the ache wouldn't go away.

'Well, if you're really determined,' Melody said, 'I think I might be able to help. I owe you so much already – what with the baby and keeping mum about Laurence. Meet me next Friday at Lyons' Corner House in Coventry Street and I'll see what I can do.'

When Ella arrived, Melody was already there wearing a pink and white tea dress and a matching hat. Sitting next to her was a man in grey trousers, a blue-striped shirt, jacket and a military tie. He stood up when Ella approached. Immediately, she guessed this was Laurence and her heart sank.

'How do you do?' he said, holding out his hand.

He was in his early thirties with thick wavy hair and dark brown eyes. Although she wanted to dislike him, Ella couldn't. She could see why Melody liked him; he had lovely manners and his voice was confident but in a quiet and understated way.

He held out a chair for her. Ella sat down. A teapot and some iced buns were on the table already and Melody's cup was half full.

Laurence didn't beat about the bush.

'Melody's filled me in. I must say, it's pretty brave of you, wanting to go out to Malaya so soon. I gather you've had no joy from the Red Cross?'

'None whatsoever.'

'Well, I do have a suggestion. A chum of mine, Charles Atwell, has recently gone out to KL as our High Commissioner. If you give me some photographs, I can get them to him to circulate, maybe that will help to track Grace down. Now, as for getting you there, have you thought of accompanying the diplomatic bag?'

'The what?'

'The Foreign Office is always looking for someone reliable to accompany important documents to our commissions overseas. I'm sure that if I had a word in Charles's ear, I could fix something up to get you assigned to Malaya. You'd need

to be screened and it could take some time. Might be dangerous flying, too, but what do you say?'

Ella leant forward. 'That sounds wonderful. Do you really
think you could arrange it?'

'I don't know. But it's worth a shot.'

The days dragged, and her optimism faded as Laurence's
suggestion didn't bear fruit until the following spring. Then,
suddenly, she had a call and was told to be ready in less than
two weeks.

Ella was so excited at the prospect of going to Malaya and
flying – actually flying. When she told Polly, she could see
the disbelief and excitement in her mother-in-law's face, too.

'But, Ella, I don't like to think of you going all that way
alone.'

And the truth was, neither did she, but she had no alterna-
tive. She wondered again if Andrew had meant what he said
when he wrote to her all those months ago. She had heard
nothing of him for ages, and didn't know where he was in
the world now.

That night, she wrote to him via the poste restante address
he'd given her and asked him if he meant what he said, and
could he possibly meet her in Singapore? She told him the
date she was flying out. The rest, she decided, was in the
hands of fate.

It wasn't easy but, eventually, Grace settled into her new
school. At the beginning, Noor had noticed how much
smaller than the other girls she was and very quiet, but after
a time, the raw edges smoothed and she found a friend of the

same age, a girl called Lia, who started to wait for her in the mornings outside the school's front door.

Noor, too, found it a mixed bag getting used to her new job. Although she got the hang of the paperwork and filing, the other secretaries kept her on the side-lines. She took to going out alone during her lunch breaks and sometimes after work. She would walk along the avenues in the Old Town, admiring the beautiful houses and the vast lawns and gardens that caught her eye. From time to time, she returned to the tea shop and always seated herself by the window where she could watch the world go by behind the glass.

Despite the recent Occupation, many of the British had returned bringing wives and their European fashions with them. Noor admired them and made mental notes of the cut of their dresses. While she read a complimentary copy of the *Malay Tribune* that the tea shop provided, she would eavesdrop on other women's conversations and in this way her knowledge of local matters and etiquette grew. She copied the way the women held their cups with the saucers at chest height; how when they left the table for a moment, they would leave their napkins on their chairs, not on the table; how they crossed their legs at the ankle or greeted each other by kissing the air next to each other's cheeks. The more she learnt, the easier it was to emulate their manners, and the more she copied their behaviour, the more restless she grew.

Spring turned to summer, and Noor noticed a change within Grace. She was blossoming; her skin and hair were shining and her body filling out. Noor felt a swelling of pride that it was because of her and all her efforts that her charge was thriving.

And, much against her own expectations, Noor was doing well at the office, too.

'I didn't think you were cut out for it, if I'm honest,' Max said. 'But now you're here, I find you're indispensable. I'm giving you a rise. It isn't much, but it should make a bit of a difference.'

With the extra income, they were able to move away from their old ground-floor apartment and into another – a small two-bedroomed flat closer to the Old Town, for school and the office. When Noor got the key, she wandered around the interior with a lump in her throat. A room each, imagine it, and a large living-dining area with a small kitchen and a bathroom at the end of the corridor. It was perfect, especially for Grace; she was spending more time after school practising the piano or going to Lia's house to work on their homework together, and now she had somewhere she could return the favour. Noor made sure she wrote to Ella again at the villa, letting her know of their change of address.

Meanwhile, the BMA office was increasingly busy. There were enquiries from people in England or returning to Malaya trying to find missing relatives; claims for land to be returned or compensation for businesses lost owing to being confiscated by the Japanese. There were so many letters that needed typing and filing, along with disputes that needed settling. Noor read the letters and absorbed a knowledge of bureaucracy that she had never known before. She kept her head and earnt a reputation for being calm and reliable. Eventually, the other secretaries began to ask her for help with work when they got behind and to invite her to join them at their lunch or coffee breaks.

At one lunch break, they started to discuss a case in Singapore that was now in all the papers about a girl called Martha Hollande, the daughter of a Dutch national who had been adopted by a Malay family during the Occupation. The girl had been made a Ward of Court and been extradited from Malaya and taken to Singapore. The women had mixed views on what should happen to her now and Noor listened to the details of how she had been separated from the family in Malaya who had lovingly tended her for these past few years. A parallel between the girl and Grace's situation was apparent and this troubled Noor.

Her anxiety grew. What if what had happened to Martha happened to Grace? Although Noor had tried writing to Ella there had been no reply. When no one else was in the office, she had attempted to telephone the villa but the line was dead.

Martha's fate unsettled her, and she knew she had to do something to keep Grace safe. Until her parents returned, she decided it was in Grace's best interest if Noor formally adopted her. When she was eighteen, Noor would tell the girl about her parents and how she and Noor were related also. She worried about the mine too – what if the government repossessed it? Until she could prove that Mr and Mrs McCain were still alive, she had no documents whatsoever to prove that the property belonged to Grace or Toby, and if any dispute went to court, the little money they had would soon be used up in legal fees. But if Noor, as her aunt, became the child's legal guardian, the property would surely remain safe with them.

She had thought of asking Max for his advice. After much hesitation, she decided she couldn't risk it, so went instead to a Chinese lawyer. In order to protect Grace's financial future, he created paperwork to show Noor had legally adopted Grace at the suggestion of the girl's father, and that in the event of her parents' deaths the Wosterholme tin mine belonged to the girl.

For a while, everything was smooth as the water on a windless lake, but Noor knew that settled weather always changes. All her life, she'd watched for signs of the monsoon, but even with a trained eye, sometimes it was impossible to know just when the storm would blow in.

'Guess what?' Grace had come home with her face beaming and her cheeks rosy. 'I've been asked to perform at the school prize-giving. Just me! A piano solo. It will be in front of all the distinguished guests,' she continued. 'I must admit, I'm feeling awfully nervous.'

Noor smiled as she listened to the child chatter.

'There are going to be prizes, too – oh, and a special guest.'

'Do you know who it is?'

'No. But I know that he's just arrived in Ipoh from England. What are you going to wear? I think everyone gets dressed up, and there's a tea or something after.'

Noor thought of all the mothers dressed in fine clothing, wearing hats and gloves and proud smiles. She had been wondering for a while now about buying a camera. She'd long admired the one that Ella had owned, and it occurred to her that she could take snaps of the occasion, and of other important events in Grace's life, to show Ella and Mr McCain when they returned.

When the day came, Noor arrived early at the school hall with her box brownie. She was wearing a new pale blue dress and hat. The hall had the atmosphere she associated with churches and there were rows of chairs set up for all the parents and guests. Despite the fans turning overhead and the doors that stood open wide, it was already warm and stuffy. Noor would have preferred to sit next to an open window but chose a seat close to the front and roughly in the middle, where she would have a good view of the piano and could take a snap of Grace. On the stage there was a wooden podium, a table full of books, which must be prizes, and a dozen chairs arranged in a half-moon shape, waiting like a smile for the important visitors to arrive.

Noor fanned herself with a programme and waited as the room filled with noisy conversation. A woman sat next to her and nodded in greeting but didn't speak. The room grew warmer and warmer, but at last the principal walked in and asked them all to rise. A hush fell over them as a few teachers, an elderly man in a linen suit and a younger man in military uniform walked in.

The principal introduced the guests and announced that prizes were going to be given out to their star pupils. 'To those girls who have excelled in music, art or mathematics,' she said with a smile, 'prizes will be given by Charles Atwell, the new British High Commissioner, who has recently returned from England.'

Noor sat up a little taller and focused on the man's features. He was imposing – handsome in a conventional way, with grey eyes that scanned the room. He didn't smile but pressed his lips together as he gazed out at the audience.

The principal then gave a speech, explaining how remarkable it was that only a few short few months after the Japanese had left, the school had managed to re-establish itself and was able to welcome so many talented girls back into education.

'I must thank you all for your hard work,' she said, casting a glance over the audience, 'and I promise you that we will go from strength to strength.'

Speech followed short speech, then a procession of students received their prizes and at last Grace came out and sat down at the piano. Noor's body tensed as she watched the girl focus and compose herself.

Then Grace raised her hands and a hush fell over the audience. Noor hardly dared breathe as she waited, then it was as though magic was being made as she listened to Grace's fingers dance across the keys. The music was light yet powerful, layered with emotion and sensitivity. When Grace finished, clapping erupted around the room. Noor stood and clapped the loudest as her heart swelled. Grace bowed to them. Everyone was clapping or standing now, and Noor noticed Charles Atwell looking attentively at the soloist as he applauded.

After the prize-giving had finished, Noor joined the other parents and pupils outside where cups of tea, sandwiches and sweet cakes were being handed out from a large table. The important guests had started to mingle with the parents of the head girl and prefects, but Noor caught sight of the High Commissioner looking at Grace once more.

He placed the teacup he was holding on a table and walked towards them. Noor nudged Grace, whose face paled as such an important visitor approached her. Noor's stomach tensed as she noticed one of the mothers turn her head as the High Commissioner held out his hand to Noor.

'Good afternoon. And this clever young lady must be your daughter?'

'Oh, no. Not my daughter. I am Grace's guardian. She is my niece.'

'Well, you're a very talented girl, Grace. There aren't many people your age who can play the piano as well as you can. I've done a few prize-givings in my time and, I have to say, you stand out.'

Noor's heart fluttered as he spoke, aware of how heads turned to watch her conversing with such an important visitor. 'We have recently come to Ipoh, though,' she explained nervously. 'We lived out in the country before, near Menglembu. Our home and tin mine were occupied by the Japanese. We moved here when they had left.'

'That's very interesting.' The High Commissioner gave an absent-looking nod, his gaze still fixed on her. 'Well, it's been an absolute pleasure meeting you, young lady. I do so hope nothing gets in the way of your piano-playing.'

Chapter Thirty-Five

Ella tensed her hands into fists when the plane came in to land. The sun was at its highest. Out of the window, she could see miles and miles of jungle – the fronds of palm trees like an undulating green sea – and then small islands came into view. This was her home, yet although her memories were all anchored here, she felt like a stranger, as though she didn't belong in Malaya, just as she didn't belong in England.

For a moment, she took in the panorama of the peninsula and outlying islands, scattered like emeralds in the glinting sea. She tried to shake off her unease before the plane descended further and previously tiny buildings grew larger and the barracks and red tiled roofs of Seletar aerodrome drew closer.

Anxiety knotted and settled in her stomach at what lay ahead. Even though Andrew had finally responded to her letters and written, '*I'm out East and, as luck would have it, on my way to Singapore,*' she was nervous of discovering what had happened to Grace and Johnnie.

And now, after a journey of almost sixty hours with two stops, the fact that Andrew was actually going to be there in Singapore when she landed, that together they would visit the mine and the villa, possibly find out the truth, was almost too much for Ella to bear.

Humidity punched her like a physical blow as the door opened at Seletar. She'd forgotten what the climate here was like. Already she could feel sweat dripping down her spine as she clutched to her the bag of documents she was carrying. She collected her suitcase from the hold, then looked out for the BMA driver to whom she had been told to hand the bag. Walking across the landing strip to the hut where an official was waiting to check her passport, she looked about her.

A parrot screeched from a nearby palm tree and instinctively she jumped. Toby would love it, she thought, he'd find it incredible. And it was a miracle, she realised, for her to be here again, for the war to be over, and for Andrew to be waiting for her in a car outside.

Once she'd had her passport checked, she continued to look for someone to give the documents to and was relieved to see a smart-looking official black car waiting. The door opened as she approached it.

'Ella McCain?'

'Yes.'

There was a brief exchange with the driver as she showed him her passport, then some form-filling before she handed over the documents. And that was it. She was here, in Singapore, with free time stretching ahead of her, allowing her to begin her search. She took a deep breath and looked around.

Andrew was waiting for her beneath a palm tree. He was very tanned, wearing light trousers, a navy polo shirt and sunglasses. As she made her way towards him, he took off the glasses and grinned at her.

'So,' he asked, 'how do you like flying?'

'Well, I have to admit it's much faster than sailing, but that's probably all that's good about it. I shan't tell you how queasy I feel. But I can't believe you are actually here in Singapore and can't tell you how grateful I am to have your support.'

He took her suitcase and walked beside her. 'Lucky I was here reporting. Besides, I couldn't let you do this alone.'

'Oh, Andrew – that's so kind of you, really. Now, tell me. What on earth *have* you been doing out here?'

'Jesus, I've been all over the place! Japan to start with. This is us.' He indicated a battered open-topped scout-vehicle parked beneath a tree. 'I managed to buy it off a savvy local. Used to belong to the Japanese and, my guess, the Brits before that.'

'Were you in Hiroshima? Was it awful?'

'I'd rather not talk about it if you don't mind. But, yeah, Hiroshima then Singapore. I've been into Malaya a couple of times. And Burma.'

He put her case in the back where she noticed several jerry cans of petrol, canteens of water and his camera equipment, then indicated she should slide into the passenger space next to him. The leather was burning and stung her legs, and a haze of heat lifted from the bonnet as Andrew started the engine. She wished she had a pair of sunglasses and a hat. It was stupid of her not to have remembered how blinding the sun could be, but it hadn't occurred to her that they would be travelling in an open-topped vehicle.

'I thought we should head straight to Johore, if that's all right with you?' Andrew asked, handing her a canteen of water. 'I don't think there's much to be gained from hanging around in Singapore.'

Ella had been hoping for a rest before they headed off, a wash and a change of clothes. Instead, she took the canteen and nodded. She drank as he drove.

'It's hard to believe,' she said, 'that only a short while ago the Japanese were here driving along these roads. Do you know what's happened to them all?'

'Goodness.' Andrew ruffled his hair with his hand. 'I think many of them have been taken to the islands – Rempang, Galang – ready to be repatriated.'

'There must be thousands of them.'

'As well as all the Japanese civilians who were here. I understand that many of them had been living in Malaya for years before the war, acting as informants. Is that true?'

'I suppose so. There was a Japanese couple who lived near our village. They were rather sweet. I'd hate to think that they were informers, but they probably were.'

They drove past a river with a small rickety bridge crossing over it. There were so many bridges like this in Malaya, she recalled. Unstable and flimsy, a couple of men could destroy one in no time. With such poor defences, no wonder Singapore and Malaya fell so swiftly to the Japanese.

'Tell me,' she said, watching a mother with a baby slung in a sarong around her back, fetching water from the river, 'what was it like when you arrived in Singapore? The people here, they don't seem at all interested in us as we drive by.'

'Well, then people were lining the streets, waving flags and clapping on the quaysides. I don't think the locals have ever been so glad to see the British.' His hands slackened on the steering wheel. 'But like everywhere else I've been lately, there's so much destruction – it's hard to take it all in.'

Of course, she was expecting it. She'd seen all the photographs of the London Blitz – Oxford Street with the store fronts blown out and debris covering the street; the liberation of Bergen-Belsen and the piles of corpses and dying people; finally, the atomic destruction in Hiroshima and Nagasaki. Really, was there anything else left that could shock her?

'But I have to warn you,' Andrew was saying, 'things aren't that great in Malaya.'

As they drove, she listened to everything he told her, trying to picture it all, but her stomach was tense and a wave of sickness took hold as she worried about discovering the truth of what had happened to Johnnie and Grace.

'When Singapore was reoccupied, there were truckloads of soldiers driving through the streets,' Andrew said. 'As for Changi, well, there the Japanese had just upped sticks and left the poor blighters in gaol with instructions not to move. The Union Jack and Australian flag were hoisted high, and Mosquito planes flew like insects against the jungle, dropping canisters of food and medical supplies. I watched it myself from high ground. The air was thick with planes.'

She refocused. Changi.

'You know Melody's husband was there? Do you think there's any chance Johnnie could have been too?'

Andrew shook his head. 'They're all out now and the Red Cross know the names of everyone who was incarcerated.'

Her mood sank.

They crossed the causeway into Johore. Ella had got so used to the buildings and streets in England that seeing her homeland with fresh eyes made her want to cry. The small streets of terraced houses in her adoptive country were now replaced by narrow thoroughfares where shop-houses kept their windows shuttered against the sun and chik blinds were used to make temporary awnings, to shade the produce sold out on the pavement from the sun. Bamboo poles holding washing had been set out of every upper window, and all about her she could hear birds singing. Unease fell upon her as people stared at them, and Ella wished then that they had a covered car that would shield her from these curious gazes as well as the heat.

'Don't worry about it,' Andrew reminded her. 'Half of them haven't yet accepted that the Occupation is over.'

Ella tried not to stare back at them, but it was hard for her to see the marks of pain and suffering in their emaciated faces.

'We should try to pick up some supplies in a bit, or at least get something to eat. I've got water, some dried army rations and tins as well as a camping stove in the back, plus rice. We'll need to see if we can get fresh food as we travel on. Everything is in such short supply.'

He passed her the canteen of water again. 'How are you doing? Do you want to stop? I was hoping to get to Malacca tonight and maybe push on to Negeri?'

'The roads should be pretty good up to there. It's once you get into the tea plantations and the tin mines further north that it gets really tricky.'

They drove on. The warmth was making her feel drowsy and she fought sleep, but as they progressed further north it surprised her to see a shift in the way that the locals were behaving. Children ran beside the car waving. On street corners, people cheered at them; once when they stopped behind a bullock cart, a group of men sitting on the side of the road started clapping. A young man riding a bicycle stopped and gave them a thumbs up sign.

'Goodness,' Ella said as they passed under an archway made from palm leaves that straddled the road. 'It's overwhelming. They make me feel as though I'm personally responsible for their liberation.'

They stopped in Malacca. A Malay man standing on a street corner watched them park then walked across the street towards them with a determined look on his face. Ella tensed as he drew close, but the man bowed then took Andrew's hand and started shaking it before he bowed again. He started to speak, his words rapid.

'What's he saying?' Andrew asked, nodding and bowing back.

'*Berterima kasih*. Thank you. I'm thankful.' The man had tears in his eyes, and although his sarong was worn and his ribs clearly visible through his skin, he indicated that Andrew and Ella should follow him. He invited them to sit down on a frayed rug and join him in eating a bowl of rice.

In Negeri, they stopped again when they saw a group of

men knocking down a Japanese monument. Andrew parked the car in the shade of a large fern tree, then jumped out to photograph them. Afterwards, the group pulled him by the arm along to the river, where they all sat down. The men took turns to tell him how the past few years had been for them – a nightmare.

One man, who was much taller than the others, started speaking. 'When the Japanese arrived,' Ella translated, 'we were surprised. We had always thought the war would stay in China. My father was an accountant, which the Japanese valued. I was lucky. The Japanese allowed me to go to school and my family had food and rations. Others were not so lucky. One day one of the village aunties was killed because she wouldn't give the soldiers her chickens. To think, being bludgeoned to death for protecting what was hers.' He shook his head sadly.

Another man piped up, 'I was only small when they arrived, but they killed my mother right in front of me. She stood there, shielding me, but I could still feel their blows.'

It was the same story in every village or town where they stopped. Everywhere there were tales of brutality, people being rounded up and shot; the remains of discarded 'banana money', the currency the Japanese had forced on them; tales of how people would betray others to the Japanese for a bowl of rice and how families were rounded up and shot, then buried in a hole dug by their neighbours, or simply disappeared without trace. It shocked Ella to hear these accounts. How would these people take her tales of living as an evacuee in England and her discomfiture on returning home? They would view her concerns as trivial, her time spent in England as a luxury. Listening to their stories of suffering, a desire to help her compatriots restore their lives and dignity formed within Ella – if only she could think of a way to do it.

At Slim River, Andrew stopped to take photographs of the bullet holes riddling the bridge.

'This was meant to be one of the British strong defence lines,' Ella said as she stood by his side. She'd seen photographs of the ill-prepared British soldiers sitting in groups under parasols, waiting for the enemy with guns facing across the river towards the jungle, but had heard how the Japanese had surprised the artillery regiments by ploughing down the road in tanks instead. The British and Hyderabad regiments had fought well, some of the British even escaping into the jungle for weeks, but it had been a massacre. 'Everyone underestimates the jungle,' she muttered.

'Hmm . . . What's that?' Andrew was concentrating on taking a photograph.

'The jungle. It hides everything – it always has. You never know what's lurking beneath the foliage or waiting for you around the next tree.'

Andrew lifted his head and glanced across the river at the jungle canopy. 'Well, the Japanese used it to their advantage, didn't they?'

'As did the KMM before them. And I shouldn't think they'll be the last.'

The tone of the journey was a little sombre after that. As they got closer to Ipoh and the north there was chaos everywhere: abandoned lorries; banana money fluttering in the breeze; artillery cases dumped on the ground. Andrew made her turn away when they passed a tree with a decomposed body hanging from it, but she saw it anyway, along with the sign around the corpse's neck. She guessed it had been a Japanese soldier. At one point, they passed a mound of freshly turned earth – a hastily dug grave.

As they travelled on what she saw angered and sickened her. This was her homeland, and all the people here had suffered more than she could have imagined. Guilt and anxiety seeped through her. It terrified her to think what they might find when they reached the tin mine.

She asked herself again and again, could either of them possibly have survived?

Chapter Thirty-Six

Darkness wrapped itself around them as they reached Menglembu.

'I don't think we should go on tonight,' Andrew said. 'Do you think you can wait until the morning? It will be safer then.'

Although Ella was disappointed, she knew the jungle was dangerous after dark. Besides, she was exhausted. 'There used to be a hotel here,' she said. 'The Green Cow Tavern. It was run by a woman called Frances Stevens. We might find a couple of rooms.'

The doors and shutters to the hotel were closed and they couldn't see any lights on. Andrew parked the car and knocked on the door. They waited, then knocked again. After a time, they heard footsteps and a British accent calling, 'All right, I'm coming, hold your horses!'

The door opened to reveal a woman in her sixties with grey hair in a long plait. She was wearing a long *abaya* and smoking a black cigarette in a long gold holder from which she flicked ash as she said, 'Yes?'

'We were wondering if you had a couple of rooms for the night?' Ella asked.

'You'll be lucky! Bloody Japanese have stripped this place

bare. Hang on a minute, aren't you Ella McCain from Wosterholme? I thought you'd run off to England.'

The words stung.

'Yes, I am. Please, do you have a couple of rooms?'

Mrs Stevens dropped her cigarette on the floor where she stubbed it out with her foot.

'Well, I could probably put you up if you don't mind sleeping on a mattress on the floor.'

She stepped aside and Ella entered the tavern. There were a few chairs in a dining room, a couple of armchairs, but the place looked dilapidated and sad.

'Bedrooms are almost devoid of furniture,' the woman said.

'It's fine,' Ella said. 'We'll take what you've got.'

Later, they sat outside with Mrs Stevens. 'Call me Frances,' she said. She'd made them a pot of tea to which she added a shot of brandy. After that she sat cross-legged on the floor and fired questions at them: *How had Ella got back? Had they been to Wosterholme? Yes, better to wait until the morning, God knows if there'd be any escaped soldiers or communists hiding in the jungle.* She was full of information and advice, telling Ella that she would need to go to the police station or the BMA offices, at some stage, to register her claim to her property. Damn load of crooks that the BMA were, they'd try to claim it for the British government if she didn't get it back quick.

Ella struggled to keep her eyes open, but Andrew questioned Frances back.

'When did you get back to Menglembu?' he asked. 'How did you know it was safe?'

'It's my home, of course I wanted to come back, although

the bloody administration wanted me to go to the Cameron Highlands. Said it wasn't safe out here for a lady.' She sniffed and lit another cigarette, half-closing her eyes as if she were tasting something bitter. 'Bloody fools.'

'You don't seem to think much of the BMA.'

She leant forward, pointing her cigarette at him. 'No. Not really. This might surprise you but, for all that happened here, the Japanese did try to look after Malaya. But the BMA really are a load of small-time administrators sent out by the British government to run this place for the benefit of the Motherland. They want to line their own pockets while they're at it, too. You mark my words, if you don't take good care of your own property, some greedy bureaucrat will try to take it.'

'Really?' Ella said, her eyelids fluttering with tiredness. 'Can they do that?'

'Of course they can. They're trying to establish their power here again, show everyone who's boss.' She lowered her voice. 'They think they're our saviours, but both the Chinese and Malays think it was the locals who were ultimately responsible for pushing the Japanese out, not the Brits. You mark my words, there's going to be a struggle here of a different kind before too long.'

'That's interesting,' Andrew said. 'But also worrying.'

Frances shrugged. 'Let's wait and see, shall we? But if I were you, I'd get all your papers in order. Your tin mine will be very valuable to anyone who decides to claim it.'

The following morning, the sun had barely risen in the sky and the air had a fresh bite to it as they climbed the Kledang

Hills. Ella's dreams had been punctuated by vivid images of Grace's toy rabbit hanging in a noose from a tree. As it swung it swivelled around and the rabbit's face was replaced by Grace's, eyes partially open and tongue hanging to one side.

The broken night had drained Ella, but as they climbed higher and wound through the jungle, she clutched the edges of her seat with renewed energy and leant forward, straining to see the roof tiles of the villa that she knew wasn't very far away. She prayed and prayed that Grace would be there with Johnnie.

At first, everything was as she remembered, but of course she knew that everything had changed. It wasn't just the half-built railway track cutting into the countryside like a raw white scar, nor the unfamiliar train engine shunted and abandoned in a cut-out in the mountainside. Not even the high fence that ran all the way around the perimeter of her property. It was the silence – like a mournful presence that hung over the estate.

The vehicle lurched over the uneven surface of the road, scattering dust that drifted into her eyes. She blinked the small particles away and then, at last, they drove through a gap in the fence and around a corner. Apprehension filled her as she saw weeds growing along the steps to the front door and lining the edge of the verandah. The shutters were mainly closed, but one dangled from its hinges, as though someone had forced it open. Monkeys sat on the window ledges. As the car approached, they screeched and ran back to the safety of the jungle.

The house was a ghost of its previous splendour and there

were no signs of life. Had she really been expecting to find Grace and Johnnie here on the drive, or Farid the houseboy sitting on the verandah; Johnnie's car parked outside the front door; Malik sitting in a chair to the side of the house chatting with Lian? And Noor – dear, dear Noor. Ella could almost picture Apollo rushing out to greet them, his tail wagging as he barked with excitement. She held up her hand to Andrew, wanting him to stop the car so that she could hold on to this moment and preserve the images of her past life before they were shattered forever.

He waited. Then she inhaled, a deep long breath, and nodded for him to carry on.

For years she had longed for this moment – imagined Johnnie standing on the steps to welcome her home, Grace running down to join them, but the whole place was deserted, and the disappointment was drowning her like a wave.

'I'm scared,' she whispered. 'They're not here. No one is.'

'Don't be. Remember, you don't have to go in, if you don't want to. But whatever you choose, I'm right behind you. If you've changed your mind, you just have to say the word.'

She hesitated. 'No. I have to. Whatever has happened to them, I must find out.'

They both got out of the car. Although it was still early, the sun seared her skin and the metal doorknocker burnt her hand as she touched it. Ella held her breath and pushed.

Of course, there was no Apollo, no Lian, no Farid, no Malik and no Noor waiting to greet her in the hall, but still she recalled how many times she had walked into the villa on returning from a day out, calling out to the houseboy to collect her shopping or to Noor for a glass of lemonade on the verandah. All these memories were in the fabric of the building; it was as though everyone she remembered here was standing in another room, just out of sight. All she had to do was call them and it would be just as it was before.

She turned to look at Andrew. He said nothing, but his expression was patient and encouraging.

'I wasn't sure what to expect.' Ella stepped into the hall, noticing that the rugs were rolled up and someone had placed dust sheets over the paintings on the walls.

She pushed open the door to the drawing room. Sunlight was flooding into the room from the broken shutter, illuminating dancing motes of dust that fell like fairy dust over the armchairs and sofas. It surprised her to see that these too had been covered in sheets.

'Goodness. It's as though we've just returned from holiday.' She lifted the dust sheet from one of the sofas. 'I remember buying this fabric in Ipoh. It was the monsoon, and I thought it was so jazzy – just the thing to cheer us all up.' Amazed that they were still intact, she ran her hand over the green-and-yellow chintz of the chairs.

'There used to be a piano,' she added. 'Just there. Johnnie liked the shutters closed against the sun in case it damaged the wood.' Her heels ricocheted around the room as she walked across the tiles.

In silence, she made her way upstairs. The mahogany banister was dusty and she could hear Andrew following just a few steps behind her as she walked into the master bedroom. Here, the bed was neatly covered with a sheet and the shutters closed. The chandeliers were also covered in dust sheets, but it pained her to see that a bevelled wall mirror that had belonged to her mother had a crack in it.

She lingered by the bed recalling precious moments: her wedding night, their first Christmas, the birth of Grace then Toby. If she closed her eyes, she could hear the familiar sounds of the wind rustling the leaves, macaws calling to each other from the branches of the banana tree.

In Grace's room, the furniture had been carefully protected in a similar fashion to the rest of the house. Ella gazed about the room, then went to the window and looked at the jungle beneath the window. Someone had cared for the villa, making sure it was ready for reoccupation. Was it Noor? But there were no clues as to where she had gone, nor what had happened to Johnnie or Grace. Ella wandered from room to room searching.

In the kitchen, someone had tried to light a fire on the floor to cook instead of using the stove. She picked out several half-burnt pieces of envelopes from the ashes and could just make out what looked like her name, but the letters inside were too badly damaged for her to read.

'Looks like all the mail's been used for firelighters,' Andrew said as he stood next to her.

'I know. But who's been in here?' She glanced about at the old table in the middle of the floor, and the saucepans and plates neatly stacked by the sink. Andrew ran his finger over the plates, which came away almost clean. 'Looks like they've recently been used.'

An opened bag of rice had spilt across the larder floor and a rat scurried beneath the shelves, making her jump.

'It's all so strange.'

'I know.'

'We should go to see the servants' quarters and the mine offices. There could be someone there.'

She opened the back door and Andrew followed her.

'My God.' Ella's hand flew to her mouth. 'They've all been burnt down.'

Andrew hung back while she walked between the ruins. Here had been Lian's room and here Malik and Noor used to live. She pictured them sitting out together in the evening or the early morning, enjoying a game of mah-jong or playing cards.

And Grace . . . she used to play in the garden close to the frangipani trees – Ella could almost picture her riding her tricycle under Lian's watchful eye while the macaques chattered in the trees nearby.

'Let's go to the estate offices,' she said, shaken. 'There's clearly no one here.'

They drove on up to the tin mine, past the gravel pits and dredgers, the tramways and carts used for transporting minerals for roasting and purification. Her dress was sticky in the heat and her mouth dry with fear.

'It's so odd to find it so silent,' she said. 'The last time I was here it was bursting with activity. I wonder where everyone has gone.'

It was a relief to see the offices still standing, although there was an abandoned bicycle with flat tyres propped up against one wall of the building.

'This used to be Johnnie's office,' she said, pushing open the door.

The air was stale and smelt of sweat but the room was furnished almost entirely as she recalled. Johnnie's desk stood facing them, his leather chair pushed back as though he had merely got up and stepped away. It caught her off guard, seeing the impression of where his head had once rested, and she pressed her hand to the surface.

On the desk, there was a pile of money. She picked up a dollar, examining the image of a banana tree, then dropped it to the floor and picked up a medicine bottle with Japanese writing on it. She opened a drawer to discover a gun and a handful of bullet cartridges. Account books were open and piled across the desk and samples stood in small dishes on the shelves. She recognised these as bismuth, copper, quartz, fluorspar and topaz. The door to the safe was open but the metal door to the explosives cupboard was firmly locked.

'It looks like they left in a hurry.' Andrew picked up a chair that lay on its side. The back was cracked, as though it had been pushed violently to the ground.

'Yes.' She shuddered. Not so long ago the Japanese had stood here where Johnnie should have been. Could they have known how to run the mine without him? She remembered what one of the men encountered on their journey had said about his father having been an accountant, and how the Japanese had needed his expertise. Was it possible they had needed Johnnie and that his knowledge of mining had saved his life? She needed more clues – any detail at all might help.

'You know,' she said, lifting piles of paper covered with

413

writing she didn't recognise, 'I've got a good feeling about all this. Johnnie must have been useful to the Japanese. When they left, he could have legged it into the jungle to hide. All the men must have done. And those plates in the kitchen . . . it could have been him coming back to the house to forage. I can't see any other explanation, can you?'

'I don't know. Could be. But wouldn't he have slept there too?'

'Not if he was worried the soldiers might come back.' Ella dropped a pile of paper onto the desk and flopped into the chair. A chit-chat scurried across the walls to the rafters. Exhaustion hit her; the heat was unbearable in this room. She wondered if there was any electricity or if the fan worked, but when she tried, the fan and the lights were dead.

'There used to be a generator up on the hill,' she said. 'I guess it doesn't work anymore. But I wonder if it's worth trying the fuses? There's a box up there, can you reach it?'

Andrew pushed the broken chair over to the fuse box. As he stood on it and ran his hand along the top of the box, looking for the catch, a notebook fell down. It was red, the type that Ella recognised as a school notebook.

'My goodness,' she said as it fluttered down, scattering dust. She picked it up and flicked through the pages. 'It's Johnnie's writing. I can't really see what it is . . . a list of some sort.'

She moved to the light and started to read. 'It's a list of all the workers who used to work here, dated when they arrived or left and signed by Johnnie. The last date is December 1941. And he's scribbled something at the bottom here.'

She scrunched her eyes up to get a better look. She lifted her head slowly from the pages, feeling a chill despite the heat all around.

'I can't read that last sentence but he hasn't added anything since '41.'

Andrew took the dusty notebook from her and peered at it. 'It doesn't mean anything, Ella,' he said. 'Johnnie could have written that any time and forgotten about it. What if he's here, like you said, hiding in the jungle, waiting until it's safe to emerge?'

She closed the notebook and put it in her bag, then took out a handkerchief, wiped her eyes and blew her nose.

'We can't stop looking,' she said, as they left the office and closed the door. 'I know they're not here, but however long it takes me, I will find them.'

Later, they walked around the mine, checking for signs of habitation or life. As she walked through the tramways and the conveyor belts, past the tips and trucks, Ella started to sense that someone was watching them, but whenever she turned, she saw nothing. She told herself she was only imagining it, that this blessed place was full of nothing but ghosts.

Chapter Thirty-Seven

Ella continued to sense that someone was watching her, but every time she glanced up there was no one.

'Can't you feel them?' she asked Andrew.

He lifted his head and looked about. 'No.'

It was probably her imagination – long shadows from the jungle had the habit of making you see things that weren't there, she remembered. But then she heard the crack of a stick and froze. There was definitely something moving close by. It could be a snake or a monkey creeping along the ground. But as she scanned the foliage, she was startled to see the face of a child staring back at her.

'Hello,' she called. '*Selamat tengah hari.*'

The child, a girl, hung back.

'Can I help you?' Ella asked.

The girl stared for a moment longer, then turned and was swallowed up by the foliage.

'Andrew,' Ella called, 'did you see?'

'What?'

'There was a girl in the undergrowth. When I called after her, she ran away.'

'She's probably come from one of the kampongs. I suppose

as far as she's concerned, there's no one living here and there might be something worth taking.'

'Do you think we should look to see if we can find her? She might be alone or in need of help.'

'Up to you.' Andrew joined her and followed the direction of her gaze.

Ella narrowed her eyes as she peered into the jungle. 'I think we should.'

'I'll grab some water then,' he said. 'And a stick.'

'I'm not really sure where to start,' Ella said as they pushed through the bamboo canes and undergrowth. 'The jungle is so overgrown now, but I think she headed in that direction.'

'Look,' he said. 'There's some kind of path.'

He was right. It was well-worn and must have been there for some time.

'I think someone is living here,' she whispered.

He nodded. 'It could be anyone. We should be careful.' Andrew pushed aside the branches that were trailing across the path. Ella followed, sweat soaking her dress despite the shade of the jungle canopy.

Ahead of them, rising through the foliage, she saw a thin wisp of woodsmoke.

'Andrew,' she whispered again. 'Look.'

He nodded and put his index finger to his lips, indicating that she should be silent.

Their footsteps were light as they crept forward. Blood rushed to her head, pounding like a drum; they could encounter escaped soldiers, rebels, men with guns. She could see now that there was a small clearing and a pot stood over the fire where a meal cooked slowly. A shelter had been made of palm branches – she'd seen in the past how the women could swiftly weave them into large panels and had always thought it a kind of magic, the way they used them to build huts that appeared from nowhere in the jungle in a very short time. Next to the hut, washing had been laid to dry on the banana trees.

Something rustled. The girl had appeared from the hut and was staring at them. Ella wondered how old she was: five or six perhaps. She wore an *abaya*. Although it looked clean the colour had faded to a mix of grey and brown, and her hair hung in a long dark plait down her back. A female voice called out the child's name, and the girl returned to the hut. A moment later, a woman appeared. When she saw Ella fear filled her face. Ella studied her closely and almost simultaneously the woman's expression changed.

'Lian?' Ella asked.

Her hands flew to her face. 'Madam? Is that really you?'

'My God, Lian!' Ella rushed to her and hugged her. 'I can't believe it's you!'

She was so thin; Ella was worried she'd break her as they embraced.

'Oh, madam, I am so happy to see you.'

'Oh, Lian, and me you.'

'I can't believe you came back, madam.' Lian wiped her eyes with her sleeve. 'All this time, I didn't know if you or Mr McCain were alive or dead.'

'I made it to England. But Johnnie and Grace didn't. That's

why I'm here with my friend, Andrew. I'm looking for them. I don't suppose you've seen them?' Ella gushed. 'And how about you? Did you get to your family? Are they all safe? Please, tell me everything that happened.'

Lian shook her head. 'The Japanese killed so many of my family. I came here with my brother and his daughter. We are lucky to live. We have been hiding in the jungle since the Japanese killed everyone in my home. We spent many days on foot running away and hiding.'

'I'm very sorry to hear this.'

Lian indicated that Ella and Andrew should sit on the ground by the fire, and then she continued with her story.

'After the Japanese left, I had nowhere to go so I hid in the jungle. Many, many people hid here for a long time when the Japanese were here, always moving and hiding. I wondered if maybe you and Mr McCain might come back so I decide to stay and wait.'

'I'm glad you did, Lian.'

'But then I found everything in the house was covered up and didn't know what to do.'

'But you survived.' Ella put an arm around her. 'And I'm so glad.' She paused then continued, 'Mr McCain is missing. I have no idea where he is. I don't suppose you know anything about him, or that you've heard anything about the whereabouts of Grace and possibly Noor?'

Lian shook her head. 'No. I'm sorry, madam.' She got up and stirred the pot cooking on the fire. As she did so, a man came out of the jungle towards them. Ella tensed.

'Don't worry, madam,' Lian said. 'This my brother.'

Lian called across to him, explaining who Ella was. He came forward and sat down on the ground near them. There was a look of defiance in his eyes; one that told Ella he had suffered much and was proud, but also that if you got on the wrong side of him there might be trouble.

'Ask her how long they have been here,' Andrew said. 'And if she knows what happened to the other people who hid hereabouts? Someone took the trouble to tidy before they left the house.' Andrew dug at the ground with a stick. 'And we know that someone has been using the kitchen probably since then.'

'Has there been anyone else around here?' Ella asked. 'Someone used the kitchen in the house.'

'Everyone is scared that the Japanese might come back, so they're hiding in the jungle,' Lian explained. 'Anyone could have broken in looking for food.'

'You should try to keep the house secure,' Andrew told Ella. 'Why don't you ask Lian and her brother to move in and caretake? That way it will be occupied until you have decided what you want to do with it.'

Lian relayed the message to her brother. Ella noticed the flash in his eyes, the way his chest expanded as he spoke and the tone of his voice, which was fast and angry.

Their conversation went backwards and forwards until at last the man nodded reluctantly.

'Perhaps we should go back to the villa,' Andrew suggested, 'and help Lian and her brother move their belongings there?'

'Yes,' Lian said. 'But first we must eat. Will you have some yam and rice curry?'

Lian spooned the curry onto banana leaves and they all sat around the fire eating with their fingers. After that, they spent the rest of the day moving the family. Lian and Ella set about tidying up the kitchen, sweeping away the broken bag of rice and dusting out the cupboards, while Andrew and Lian's brother walked about the villa checking on doors and windows, then on to the mine office, to secure it.

By the time Andrew had returned, Ella was exhausted, and they decided to head off back to Menglembu before returning to the villa the following day.

That evening, Ella sat puzzling over what had happened to Noor, Grace and Johnnie. She had been expecting the villa to answer all her questions, but she was still in the dark. She sat outside in the hotel courtyard, making lists of all the things she could do and the places she might look, but the task seemed even more impossible than it had before.

The following morning, while they sat outside eating rice porridge for breakfast, they discussed her plans.

'We should go to the district offices first,' Andrew said. 'They ought to have some kind of register where you can record missing persons. And you've got those photographs of Grace and Johnnie, haven't you? Someone might recognise them.'

'And then we should go to a lawyer,' Ella said. 'We need to sort out a legal agreement for Lian and her brother if they're living at the property, but I doubt anything will be open yet.'

The streets were busier than she had been expecting and

they made their way through the bustling crowds to where Frances had told them they'd find the district offices.

People stared at them, but Ella was getting used to it now: the curiosity, the waves, the thank-yous. When they entered the building, the sound of her footsteps seemed lost in the echoing corridors where ceiling fans turned above. It was a gentle reminder of the timeless nature of government, she thought, as though nothing had changed in Malaya and it would soon return to being a well-oiled British bureaucracy. There were rows of seats with people sitting on them, and a desk behind which a watchful officer sat. All eyes turned to them as Ella and Andrew made their way over.

'I wonder, can anyone help me?' she asked. 'I used to live here, up in the Kledang Hills. I lost my husband and my daughter during the Occupation and want to find out what happened to them.' She paused then added, 'As well as what happened to the people who worked at the mine.' She pulled the notebook from her handbag and placed it on the man's desk. 'This is a record of all the people who used to work at Wosterholme. I want to know where they are.'

The man picked up the notebook and flicked through the pages. Then, carefully, he closed the book, handed it back to her, and told her she'd have to take a seat and wait her turn.

An hour passed before they were called through to an office where they were greeted by a British man dressed in shabby regulation army khaki.

'How do you do?' he said, holding out a warm, bony hand. 'I'm Rupert Canning, BMA district officer here. How may I help you?'

Ella explained again that she was looking for Johnnie and Grace. She took out the notebook and placed it on the table along with their photographs. 'I'm looking for the servants, too, who used to live there. In particular, a cook called Noor.'

'Well,' Canning sighed, 'as you can imagine, there are many people looking for families and lost friends. We're rather overwhelmed, to be honest.'

'Would you have any records of local residents? They might tell me if any of these people are alive and still reside in the area.'

'There are some records the Japanese made,' he replied. 'But it would take some time to go through everything I have here. I'll do what I can, but we're looking at about three weeks, I'm afraid.'

Disappointment seared through her. She heard him ask, 'Now, can you tell me where you are staying? Just in case something crops up and I need to contact you.'

'The Green Cow Tavern,' Ella replied.

In her heart of hearts, she was beginning to lose hope.

Chapter Thirty-Eight

'Surely, we'd be better searching ourselves?' Ella frowned as they walked back out onto the streets.

'How?'

'I don't know – if Grace is here in Menglembu, we could go to the schools and see if any of the children match her description, or even know her or Noor.' She thought about it some more and then exclaimed, 'Omar!'

'What?'

'How stupid of me. I should have thought of it much sooner. There's a small primary school near the villa,' Ella explained. 'My father founded it as part of his plan to support education for the locals. Noor's cousin Omar was the headmaster. If he's still there, he's bound to know where she is.'

It was lunchtime when they arrived. Pupils were playing on a large piece of dry ground close to the building. Ella could see the boys kicking a ball to each other and a group of girls sitting plaiting each other's hair. There was a man sitting beneath the shade of a banana tree keeping watch on them.

'Hello!' Ella raised her hand to her eyes as she spoke. 'Omar?'

The man raised his head and examined her, then slowly stood up.

'Mrs McCain?'

'My goodness, Omar, it is you!'

She explained that she was looking for Grace and Noor. 'Have you seen them? Do you know where they might be?'

Omar smiled and indicated that they should sit in the shade with him.

'Yes,' he explained. 'Grace and Noor lived at the villa during the Occupation but they left a while ago. I'm not completely certain where they are now.'

Ella's heart raced. This was the first time anyone had confirmed to her that Grace was alive! She could hardly dare to believe it and Omar's words buzzed around in her head like a swarm of flies.

'The villa was occupied by Japanese soldiers,' Omar continued. 'Grace did come to the school here for a while, but after the Japanese left . . .' He lifted his hands with the palms facing the sky, and shrugged.

'But are you sure you don't have any idea where they are?' Ella examined his face, feeling there must something else he could say, but his features revealed nothing.

'I'm sorry.'

'Oh.' Ella looked at the ground, then raised her head. 'And do you know anything about Johnnie?'

She waited, hardly daring to breathe as she waited for Omar's response.

He swallowed and she watched his Adam's apple rise

and fall, then he pursed his lips and tilted his head slightly to one side.

'The Japanese took many people as prisoners. I think your husband was one of them, but not all of them have returned.'

Ella placed her head in her hands and pressed her eyes with her fingertips. This whole situation was like an awful game of Snakes and Ladders: one minute you seemed to be winning, then luck would knock you right back down to square one and you had to start all over again.

She dropped her hands into her lap and exhaled. A wave of tiredness came out of nowhere and threatened to overwhelm her.

'Thank you,' she said. 'It's so good to see you. It must have been awful, the Occupation.'

They talked for a while. Omar told them of the terrible things that had happened in the kampong, and how the British had kept spies in the jungle for years. He smiled as he told them about the MCP and guerrilla attacks against the Japanese. They both listened to his accounts then exchanged tales of their own experiences over the past few years until it was time for them to leave.

'Thank you, Omar. If you do hear anything, please will you let us know? We're staying at the Green Cow Tavern.'

'Of course.' He smiled. 'I most certainly will.'

As they drove away, Ella leant back in her seat, allowing the hot, dusty air to sweep over her.

'You know, I'm not sure I completely believe he doesn't know where Noor is. From what he said, she was instrumental in starting the warning fire that destroyed the servants' quarters. She wouldn't simply disappear out of his life after all they'd been through in the Occupation. Why would he lie to us?'

'I don't know. He must be protecting her.' Andrew shrugged. 'But we can't be certain of anything.'

Ella's fingers tapped the side of the open window as she thought, then she said, 'What do you think we should do next?'

'We should try to touch base with Laurence back in England, if we can, let him know what information we have and see if there is any further news of returning POWs.'

Ella looked at the passing scenery – how long had she known these hills? It was as though they had always been there like a good friend, but right now, even though they were beautiful, layered with varying hues of green and blue, she wondered how something so familiar and reassuring could keep so many secrets from her.

They spent the rest of the afternoon trying to send a telegram to Melody and Laurence but discovered that the only way to do it was by going back to the BMA office and handing five dollars to one of the clerks.

Everything goes full circle, Ella thought. *We're back right back where we started.*

The following morning, she opened the shutters and watched as the sun rose into the pink-and-orange sky, touching the rooftops with its rosy light. At least she knew that Grace was alive and that was wonderful. For all she knew, her daughter could be close by; it thrilled her to imagine that her child could be in one of the houses within her sight, and her thoughts turned to ways in which to find her.

Ella dressed in a clean blue cotton dress, pulled her hair into a loose ponytail and wandered downstairs to the courtyard garden where she settled into one of the rattan chairs, going over what she knew. She chewed the skin around her index finger as she thought of Johnnie, hoping that Laurence had received their telegram and that he would have some updated information about returning POWs.

As she thought, she could hear Frances talking to the houseboy, who came a moment later into the courtyard, carrying a tray with a glass of freshly squeezed mango juice. Next to the glass, there was a letter addressed to Ella.

'Madam said this was left for you last night,' he explained.

Ella took the glass and the letter, then ripped the envelope open and read:

Dear Mrs McCain,

Since your visit, the most extraordinary thing has come to my attention. I wonder if you could call at the BMA offices first thing tomorrow and I can explain.

Yours sincerely,
Rupert Canning

Ella didn't wait for Andrew. She didn't even look at her watch. Instead, she placed her drink untouched back on the tray and, clutching the letter, headed out towards the BMA offices.

There were clerks opening the front door and switching on fans; others were unlocking office doors. Ella sat down in one of the cane chairs, then immediately stood up. She noticed a table with a jug of water and some glasses on it. She poured herself a glass but was unable to drink. Her forehead and face prickled with heat and she dabbed at her skin with her handkerchief. She could hear her watch ticking like a metronome, beating out the minutes in an agonising rhythm as she waited.

She paced the floor until at last she heard the squeak of rubber heels across the floor. It was Rupert Canning. His face was flushed and although his features gave nothing away, she could sense he had something important to tell her.

'Mrs McCain, would you come this way?'

The windows to his office were open and sunlight blinded her temporarily as she sat down in the chair he had pulled out for her. She couldn't hold back her questions any longer.

'Have you news of Grace?' she asked. Her hands were in her lap. She couldn't help rubbing her thumbs against her index fingers and digging the nails deep into her flesh.

Rupert sat down behind his desk. The slowness of his reply was agonising.

'Well,' he said, 'yes and no. It's all rather strange, to be honest. I had a phone call yesterday from BMA officers in Ipoh.'

'Saying what?'

Rupert looked at her with new respect.

'It would seem that you have friends in high places, Mrs McCain. Your friend Laurence Napier has been in touch with the High Commissioner regarding your daughter. He has been looking into her case since his recent arrival in KL, I believe.'

'Yes, I know. We sent a telegram yesterday asking him if he had any further information. Was this why you wanted to see me?' Ella sighed.

'Don't be downcast, Mrs McCain. I have what I hope might be good news. The Commissioner recently visited a school in Ipoh and, while he was there, discovered a child he thought might be your daughter. He has notified the BMA in Ipoh – the matter is in the hands of a man called Max Jeffries.'

'Really? But that's marvellous.' Ella leant forward, sitting on the edge of her seat as she listened. 'But I'm not sure I understand it all.'

'You see, the Commissioner was asked to hand out prizes at a school – there was an extremely talented pianist who looked very similar to the photographs he'd been given by Mr Napier. He spoke to the girl and her guardian, and not only does the description match, but also the girl's name.'

Blood pounded in Ella's temples. She could barely believe she was hearing this.

'But now there's a bit of a problem because when Jeffries questioned the woman, who claimed to be the girl's aunt, she was able to produce some documentation. I'm afraid this is where there's bad news – it seems your husband gave her guardianship of the child.'

'No. That's not right. He can't have done.'

'She has documentation proving it to be the case.' Rupert scratched his head. 'It is all very strange, I must admit. I'm not certain what to think. My advice to you is to head on over to Ipoh, go to the BMA offices there and speak to Max Jeffries. If it is the case that she is Grace's legal guardian, I'm not sure how you can best move forward. I'm afraid it looks like you might have a battle on your hands to get her back.'

Ella telephoned Andrew at the hotel and he met her for a walk by the river.

'Honestly!' She kicked a stone, sending it spinning into the water. 'Whatever next? Can you believe this?'

'I'm sure it's just a misunderstanding, you know what these bureaucrats are like. And the good news is, at least you know now that Grace is in Ipoh.' Andrew took his camera out and focused on a group of women nearby, taking a photograph. Ella heard the shutter snap and listened to him turning the spool to wind on the film. Did he have to do that now?

'Have you any water left in that canteen of yours?' she asked. She had a headache forming.

Andrew shook his head.

'I wonder if there's anywhere we can get a drink near here then.' She stood with her hands on her hips, looking about. There was a small shop on the corner of the street with a makeshift awning of bamboo leaves casting a patch of welcome shade. 'Do you think they might have anything in there?'

They made their way to the shop where an old man in a sarong welcomed them. He found a couple of stools and indicated that they should sit on the pavement under the bamboo shade while he made them some tea, pouring the liquid high from the teapot to make the milk foam, just the way Ella remembered Noor's mother doing it for her when she was a child.

They sipped their frothy tea, watching the activity on the street. There were men on bicycles, trishaws, bull-carts, carrying pineapples, papayas and coconuts. A group of street urchins hung around on the road near them, smiling and giving shy waves.

Ella waved back and they crept forward, their dark eyes filled with curiosity, until Andrew tried to take photographs of them and they slipped away, just like Ella's hope of finally claiming her daughter.

Chapter Thirty-Nine

Noor felt sick to the bottom of her stomach. It had been terrible the way Max had abruptly told her about Charles Atwell recognising Grace at the school prize-giving. The way her boss then quizzed her, as though she were lying, hurt her more than she could say.

Afterwards, all she could think about was that poor girl whose case had been in the papers – Martha Hollande – and how she'd been taken away from her adoptive family. Noor couldn't bear it if no one believed her and Grace was sent away from her. She'd come back to their flat to collect the adoption certificate and a letter the Chinese lawyer had created, citing the words Mr McCain had told her the very last time she'd seen him with Grace: *You must do whatever it takes to keep her safe. I'll remember it forever. Remember that – you must do anything, anything at all, to protect her.*

When she had shown it to Max, he had spent a long time examining the documents but eventually had seemed to believe her.

Overnight she had tossed and turned. In the darkness her thoughts grew tangled and disturbed, logic twisting around, and her uncertainty about what to do mounted. Now, as she lay in bed having decided not to go into work, her head hurting from lack of sleep, she heard a knock on the door. She was fearful it was Max or someone from the BMA offices, or worse still the police, so she ignored it.

There was another more persistent knock followed by a female voice calling, 'Noor, I have a letter for you from Omar.'

Omar? That was the last person she was expecting to hear from. Surprised, she swung her feet off the mattress and opened the door to find a woman she had never seen before. The woman handed her an envelope with Omar's writing on it. Noor took it and tipped her a few cents, then she sat down in a cane chair next to the open window, turning the letter to the light to get a better look at it.

My dear Noor,

I thought you ought to know that Ella McCain is in Meng-lembu and is looking for you. She came here asking about you and Grace – perhaps you should return to Menglembu to speak to her?

Noor's hand shook as she refolded the letter.

So, at last, Ella had returned to Malaya. Noor knew that she'd be looking for Grace, wanting her daughter back, and although this was what she had long expected and planned for, now that the time had finally arrived, she knew that her heart would break if she had to give the girl back. Much as she loved Ella and knew that Grace couldn't wait to be reunited with her, the truth was that Noor felt more like the girl's mother now, as she in essence had been for the past few years.

And there was another issue – the matter of her father's letter to Noor. It wouldn't be easy saying goodbye to Grace in the knowledge that she was truly her aunt. Ella might take her away, back to England, and then Noor would never see her again.

No, she couldn't give Grace back so easily, hand her over as though these past years, everything she had striven so hard for, meant nothing. But Ella was Grace's mother and Noor knew she loved her child.

Noor really didn't know what to do. It seemed the only way she could ensure a place in Grace's life for herself would be by telling Ella the truth about their family relationship and showing her their father's letter. It would be better if she could arrange to meet her in private and explain everything, try to negotiate a continuing place in Grace's life as a blood relation.

Omar was right – there was only one thing for it. She'd go to Menglembu immediately. She set about packing for both herself and Grace, placed sheets on the furniture to keep them clean, and locked the shutters on the windows. When the girl came home, Noor told her, 'We have to go away for a few days. I have a relative, Omar . . . you remember . . . who is not well. We need to go to Menglembu and help him straight away.'

And although the girl protested and complained, arguing that she could stay with Lia or even auntie, Noor wouldn't be swayed. They caught the evening bus with only five minutes to spare.

*

It was late morning when Noor finally reached the villa. She had left Grace at one of the hotels playing cards with the proprietor, a woman she vaguely knew, explaining that she had a delicate matter to attend to, and would it be possible to leave the child here for a few hours? The hotelier had helped her find a driver to take her to the villa.

As they drove there, flashes of memories from the past came flooding back and Noor realised how much she loved this place, even though it held terrible memories also. As the car pulled up on the drive, she couldn't but help think of Naoki on that last day and didn't know if she could go back into the villa.

She took a moment then pulled herself together. She had to do this for Grace. She left the car and made her way to the front door, surprised to see that it was open. She could hear someone singing inside – could it be that Ella was here already? She smoothed out her dress and drew herself tall as she called out, 'Hello!'

It wasn't Ella who came walking along the corridor to meet her, but Lian.

'Lian, is that you?' asked Noor, stepping into the hall.

'Noor? Oh, my goodness, I can't believe it!'

'Is it really you?'

The two women embraced. After their surprise and laughter subsided, Lian took her to the kitchen where she sat Noor down at the old table and insisted on making a pot of tea.

Noor glanced around the room. How many months, no, years, had she spent here in this place that was simultaneously familiar but now so distant from her? She ran her hand along the surface of the table, trying to push back memories and think only of the future.

She stayed for an hour. Lian told her everything she knew: yes, Mrs McCain had been here but had now gone to Ipoh. Was there any chance Noor could telephone someone to let her know they were now in Menglembu? Why hadn't she left word of how to find her? Oh, she had. No, there hadn't been any letters here, but the villa had been broken into and letters destroyed.

Noor listened, irritated that she'd spent all this time and effort, not to mention the money, coming back to Menglembu when Ella was now in Ipoh. But it had been lovely to see Lian again. When it was time to leave, she hugged her friend once again, promising that she would be in touch soon.

'But,' she said, 'please don't tell Mrs McCain I have been here. There is something delicate I need to tell her in person, and I don't want to worry her. If she has gone to Ipoh, I expect she'll return here soon. I think I'll wait in Menglembu until she does. I really don't want to miss her again.'

There wasn't a cloud in the sky and the heat of the day still pulsed as she re-joined the driver who was waiting for her. Noor mulled over her misfortune and what to do next. Now she was here, she decided to visit Omar.

Smoke drifted lazily from the chimney of his house and Noor could smell a wood fire burning. As she alighted from the car, she could see that the door stood open. She called out a greeting then stepped inside to see him sitting on the floor, pounding coconut flesh in a ceramic bowl to release the creamy milk with which she suspected he would flavour curry. As she approached, a twig snapped beneath her feet and he lifted his head, frowning until he realised who she was.

'Noor!' He stood slowly, wiping his hand on the plain brown sarong he wore wrapped around his waist. He gestured that she should come in. 'Well, now, I see you got my letter. Come on in. Would you like some tea?'

She shook her head. 'No, thank you.'

They sat down cross-legged on a mat made of woven palm leaves and Omar took a small pouch from his pocket and selected a betel-nut, which he put in his mouth and chewed.

Noor sat down on the mat opposite him with her legs tucked to one side, adjusting her skirt over her knees. It was all so familiar and homely in this house. It wasn't until now that she realised how much she had missed Omar and this house that had for a short time been her home. She should have confided everything in her cousin, she saw. He had always been close to her, her strength really, more like a brother.

'I went to the villa but there was no one there,' she began.

'Ah.' Omar paused then carried on chewing, his lips turning red from the juice of the betel-nut.

'But now that I'm here, I'd really like to ask for your advice.'

'I see. What about?'

Noor took old Mr Ferguson's letter from her bag and handed it to him. 'I think you should read this.'

He put on a pair of glasses, took the envelope from her and began to read.

Noor watched attentively. It seemed like hours that she waited, wondering what he was thinking. The suspense was almost too much but then his gaze swung away from the letter to her face.

'Well?' she asked.

'I wondered when you would find out.'

'So you knew?'

'Let's just say, I always had my suspicions.'

'But this alters everything, doesn't it?'

'Actually, it changes nothing because you are still the person you always were. Look at you, in your European clothes and fancy shoes. You've done well, Noor, you've survived the Occupation and risen above being a cook – all by yourself, and not because of who your father might or might not have been. The question is whether you want to be part of Grace's life forever, which I think you do. I'd say you also need to decide how much you care about Ella, whether you could do such a terrible thing as to keep her daughter from her when you could be mending bridges?'

Noor sighed. 'But she abandoned her own daughter, Omar. What kind of a mother does that? No. I can't give up Grace. She's like a daughter to me. It would break my heart.'

'This may all be true. And, yes, that is what you have been to her these past few years. You've more than kept the promise you made to Mr McCain. But isn't it time to let Grace and Ella be reunited? Don't punish a woman for a mistake she made in an impossible situation. Concentrate on continuing this new life you have made for yourself.'

'I used to think that. But now I'm back, I feel that I belong here, that this is my home. And you're right. I don't want to go back to being just a cook. I'm Ella's sister, and isn't that something she should know?'

'Listen to me, Noor. None of what has happened is really her fault, is it? You told me that you used to be good friends as children but her mother put an end to it. How you could never forgive her or Ella for it. Are you punishing Ella for something that was beyond her control? If you love Grace, then you shouldn't hold on to her as a means of punishing Ella. Don't you think it is time to do the right thing and to make up for all the bad feelings from the past?'

'Honestly, Omar, it's all so confusing. I don't know what to do.'

'Well . . .' Despite the dimness in the room, his eyes sparkled. 'I can't see any of this being easy. If you want my advice, I'll give it to you, but before I do, I have a secret of my own to tell you. Are you ready?'

She nodded as she leant forward, her breathing shallow as she listened to his whispered words.

The Excelsior in Ipoh brought back mixed memories. As Ella climbed the steps, she imagined Malik waiting for her with the Lagonda and the bags of Christmas shopping he had stowed in the boot. Then there was the missed meeting with Melody and the journey home, bumping along the jungle roads and swerving to avoid an army truck full of soldiers.

Inside the hotel, the furnishings were just the same, but the paint on the walls and ceilings was starting to peel. At least they had two rooms free.

She flopped down on the bed and watched the ceiling fan turn above her, overwhelmed by the complications involved in finding Grace. She couldn't understand why Noor had left for Ipoh without saying where she was going. Surely it would have been better to stay and wait for Ella and Johnnie to return rather than move miles away to this city. A knife-like pain stabbed Ella's chest as she realised that Noor had probably thought neither of them would return. It was difficult to calm these troubled thoughts, so Ella decided to go for walk.

There were still plenty of people about. A hawker was selling coffee on a street corner; she bought some and cupped her hands around the warm and comforting drink. As she sat on a stool on the pavement, she examined the faces of passers-by, saw the pain and suffering that was still etched there, and it made her wonder how the world would ever regain its equilibrium.

She had to let go, stop dwelling on things that she couldn't alter. When she had finished her drink, she left the hawker stand and paced along the streets, but they were full of ghosts and shadows and letting go was harder than she'd thought. At the music shop, she was haunted by an image of the old man and wondered what had happened to him. Had he fled back to England or never made it home? And then, when she returned to the place where she and Johnnie had first met, she sat down and remembered it. If she could turn back time, conjure him up before her, what would she say to him?

In the distance, she could hear the hoopoes calling and the macaques rustling in the branches. She was losing track of time. She knew she ought to go back, but it was hard because, for the hundredth time, she was wondering if Grace would recognise her when they met. But what might be worse was if she simply didn't care.

The following morning, Ella met Andrew in the lobby at nine to go to the BMA office. They walked through the waking streets. Many of the buildings' upper windows were still shuttered, but traders had set up stalls selling mangoes, bananas, eggs, mixed in among bric-a-brac, bicycle parts and old newspaper. Toothless men lifted their browned faces to her, and she noted how the whites of their eyes were reddened by years of betel-nut chewing.

Eventually, they reached a white domed building: the BMA headquarters. There were tall royal palms either side of the entrance, and bougainvillaea grew along the paths leading to the high-arched entrance. Ella's stomach tightened as Andrew asked for directions to Max Jeffries's office and their heels clicked across Malacca tiles as they climbed the stairs. Ella grabbed onto the handrail, beads of sweat forming along her upper lip. The overhead fans did little to make her more comfortable. When Andrew knocked on Max Jeffries's door, she thought she might faint.

'Hello,' she said nervously as it was opened. 'I'm Ella McCain.'

'Ah. Come in.' Jeffries held the door open and they stepped inside.

'Can I get you a drink? Some tea or water, perhaps?'

'Water, please.'

Max then got straight to the point and explained everything. How Charles Atwell had spotted a girl at the Convent School recently who had looked very similar to the photograph Laurence Napier had given him. How he'd questioned Noor, who as it happened worked for him here. She claimed to be the child's aunt and legal guardian. Later, Charles had passed this information on to Max who had questioned Noor himself. He had asked for documentation to prove her relationship with Grace, and said he thought that everything looked genuine.

'So where is Noor now?' Ella asked. 'Can't she come here and explain everything herself? I'm sure that as soon we meet, we can sort all this out and then Grace will be able to come home with me.'

'Well . . .' Max glanced down at his desk and moved a piece of paper. 'I have tried to contact her, but I'm afraid she's gone away.'

'What? And taken Grace?'

'I'm really sorry, but no one knows. As for the child, I suppose you could try contacting the school, but they might not be at liberty to tell you anything about her.'

'But I'm her mother,' Ella groaned.

Max leant back in his chair and looked at her for a moment before speaking.

'You should seek legal advice. If Noor really believes she has adopted your daughter, then you'll need to take this issue to court to prove otherwise.'

'Well, that will be easy enough.'

Max picked up his pen and looked at the top, examining it.

'Normally, I'd agree. But when we spoke to her, she claimed that you abandoned Grace when you fled to England, and that your husband was forced to give her custody of the child in your absence once the Japanese were taking over the district. Unless your husband returns, you might well have a problem proving otherwise.'

Ella's breathing was shallow as she listened to him.

'I can't take this all in,' she said. 'I simply don't understand. My husband would never give our daughter away. And did Noor say anything about where Johnnie has gone?'

'I'm sorry,' Max said. 'Everyone's guess is that he was taken to a POW camp. Until his whereabouts are confirmed, it's a tricky situation.'

Ella's body shook and the tears came then, heaving sobs that she couldn't contain. She didn't care if they were looking at her – all she wanted was for this nightmare to end.

Andrew's arm was around her, and she didn't push it away. When the tears stopped, she wiped her face with the handkerchief he held out then dabbed at her nose with shaking hands. 'You're right,' she said, determination returning. 'We need to find a good lawyer. We've got to do anything we can to fight this.'

They spent the rest of the morning back at the hotel. After they'd contacted a few lawyers, they selected one called Freddie Hill, who told them to come to his office that afternoon.

It was in an old-style bungalow set back a hundred yards from the road near the railway station. Until he could see them, they waited in a cheerful reception room where caged green budgerigars sang. When they entered his office, they

444

saw it was brightly decorated, full of leather-bound books and rosewood furniture. He clasped Ella's hand firmly in his own, before inviting them to sit down on a yellow-and-green chintz-covered sofa in front of his desk.

'Right. Fill me in on all the details.' Freddie pulled a pair of glasses out of his jacket pocket and opened the large notebook on his desk.

Ella explained everything she knew. When she'd reached the end, she watched while he finished writing his notes, trying to read his expression. Facts and plans were then discussed at length. Ella was exhausted by the time they left his office.

'This is ridiculous! I'm Grace's mother, I should be able to go and collect her whenever I want.' And the more she thought about it, the more she wondered why she hadn't done so before. 'It can't be that hard to find the Convent School.'

It didn't take them long.

'I'm Ella McCain, Grace McCain's mother.' Ella recounted her story as soon as the principal would see her. She explained the entire situation, twisting her fingers nervously as she waited for the woman to reply.

'I'm very sorry, Mrs McCain. Grace hasn't been at school for the past few days. She was due to play in one of our concerts and has been absent for some time. When her class teacher made enquiries, it seemed that both Grace and her guardian had left the area for good.'

Chapter Forty

Ella wanted to shout, to punch her fist against a wall. This was awful: the closer she came to finding Grace, the harder it became. What on earth was Noor playing at? Anger and frustration fizzed within her like a rocket. She lost her step and cursed.

As children, she had thought they would be friends for ever. They were more like sisters, really – the shared secrets and futures planned, their hopes and dreams capped with the promise of eternal friendship. How simple life had been back then: playing in the rose garden; chasing peacocks and dancing like shadows across dewy lawns; watching the morning mists rising about the jungle canopy like delicate lace; the clouds bleeding with apricot and indigo light.

It had been more than fate that had divided them, she knew, not just circumstances beyond their control. Ella should have fought for their friendship more when her mother had separated them, and the longer she had failed to stand up for it, the wider the distance had become. Was Noor punishing her for letting their friendship drift by holding hostage the one thing that was the most precious to Ella?

Exhaustion took hold and time blurred as she threw all her energy into visiting Freddie Hill, sending telegrams to

Laurence, bribing the police in Ipoh to encourage them to track down Noor and Grace.

One morning, while she was reading documents in the hotel lounge, Andrew approached hesitantly. She looked up. 'What is it?'

He shifted his feet and said, 'I've been thinking about what I could do to help and it occurred to me that I could get in touch with some journalist friends in England. Or I could go down to the *Malay Tribune* and see if anyone there might run a feature for us.'

An unwanted thought dawned on her then. Andrew had been nothing but supportive and helpful, but what if there was another reason why he was doing this.

'You're not doing all this for another scoop, are you?'

'Of course not, I . . .'

'So why are you?'

'Well.' Awkward silence fell between them. He sat down, then pressed his hands together and formed a steeple with them. 'I know what it's like to lose people you love . . . And I couldn't let you do all this on your own.'

Hairs prickled on the back of her neck as she waited for him to continue. 'Go on.' Her voice was as soft and gentle as she could make it.

A frown formed and his eyes looked distant.

'When I was in my early twenties, I was engaged to be married,' he said in a faraway voice. 'A childhood sweetheart. Eleanor.' His eyes flickered towards Ella. 'She was killed in a train accident – there had been a landslide and the carriage careered into an embankment. Everyone in her carriage died.

Fifteen people in all.' He was talking slowly, and Ella could see how much it pained him to do so. She waited for him to carry on.

'It took me a long time to get over it. The pain of losing someone you love,' he glanced up at her then back to the floor, 'is unbearable. After some years I met another woman, someone who, despite myself, I couldn't help loving. It was just before the war broke out. Maddie was a nurse – very different from Eleanor, really. It took me so long to give myself to her, to let myself love someone again. And then,' he pinched the bridge of his nose and took a deep breath and continued, 'I heard she'd been killed in action.'

'Andrew, that's so awful.'

He lifted his face to Ella's and their eyes met.

'So, you see, I really had to help.'

She touched his hand gently. 'I'm so sorry, Andrew. I had no idea. And you've been carrying all of this around with you. You're so kind. I wish there was something I could do to take the pain away.'

'You know,' he glanced away, 'that you might not get all the answers you were expecting, don't you?'

'You don't think Johnnie's coming back, do you?'

'I didn't say that.'

'But it's what you meant.'

He shook his head. 'We shouldn't leave any stone unturned. I can use my contacts to try and track him down, but you should be prepared, that's all, for everything not going the way you are hoping.'

Ella drew her hand away. 'I can't ever give up hope.'

'None of us ever does, Ella, but that doesn't change the way things really are.'

His gaze lingered on her a moment too long, then he stood up and left. She watched him, her thoughts flickering back to all the acts of kindness he had done for her: the oil paints he had somehow found for her; the letters he'd written to Percy; staying longer than was necessary in Malaya, supporting her while all the time he was nursing his own broken heart.

In the following days, there was a shift between them. It showed in the way Andrew hung back when she spoke to Freddie; how he no longer offered an opinion but only gave one when asked; in how he would read quietly for hours while she copied photographs and only stuck them up on every surface available when she specifically asked him. The more distanced he became, the more she realised how much she had grown to rely on his support. The only time his old spark returned was when she decided to encourage him to head to the offices of the *Malay Tribune*. He returned with the hint of whisky on his breath, a spring in his step, and some good news.

The paper had agreed to run a feature on Johnnie and Grace along with reproducing the photographs Ella had given to Andrew. At the end of the article, there was a box number where anyone with information could contact Freddie Hill.

Ella waited, doubtful that they'd make any progress, but after a few days, Freddie asked them to come to his office at their earliest convenience. At long last, it turned out, Noor had seen the article and contacted the local BMA office in Menglembu. She wanted to meet Ella there.

For the first time in months, it was as though all the colours in the world had been switched back on. In the morning, they left Ipoh for Menglembu. Ella had woken early, watching the rose-and-apricot light of dawn reflected from the sugar-white buildings. She had listened to the birds and marvelled at the brightness of their plumage: the emerald-and-orange bee-eaters, the flash of scarlet as trogons darted between rain trees; the pink of hibiscus flowers, and grey storks standing fishing in the river that reflected the rainbow of colour dusting the early-morning streets.

They decided to stay at the villa, and the following morning, the day of the meeting, Ella woke early and watched the sun lifting over the jungle canopy. She took it as a good sign that there was a peacock standing on the lawn, fanning its tail feathers just as it had done so many times before. She believed now that Noor would never let her down. And besides, she was going to see her daughter.

They arrived far too early in Menglembu, and to pass the time, she showed Andrew her old haunts. They dodged bullock carts and bought peanuts from a hawker standing beside a frangipani tree, then drank chai that a street vendor made. Ella's hands were shaking from all the pent-up emotions. Later, they ate *roti* held in their hands, the taste bursting like the memory of a thousand summer days in her mouth. Andrew took pictures of everything: the crumbling buildings, the light on the water, people going about their daily lives.

'What will you do with all your photographs when you get home?' she asked.

'I don't know. So much will have changed when I get back. Part of me thinks it's time to look for something else to do.'

She gave a slight nod in agreement. He was right, nothing would be the same, but as he walked beside her, she couldn't help thinking how much she would miss him.

Noor decided to wear her best navy dress and a new crocodile handbag swung from her arm as she stood outside the BMA building in Menglembu. She glanced ahead of her, her face shielded by her hat but her heart thudding as she made her way towards the entrance.

In a few moments, she'd be facing Ella. Part of her wanted to turn around and walk right back the way she had come. It would be so easy just to move to a different part of Malaya with Grace and forget all about Ella, the mine, the letter she carried in her pocket. But then there were all the wise words Omar had said to her, along with the news he had given her.

It was strange, she thought, how so many things could lead, in their own particular way, to a certain moment. And this meeting, which she hoped would be a time of reconciliation and improvement, was no different. Her thoughts turned once again to memories of when she and Ella were children playing innocently amongst the banana trees. Images of them both flickered as though someone was turning the pages of a picture book, until it reached this moment, where she stood here outside this building, wondering what would happen next.

Noor hesitated for a moment, then she drew in a deep breath and held her head high, walked up the steps and pushed open the door.

Ella hadn't changed. She was a little thinner, a little more lined, but still had that air of authority and purpose; Noor would have known her anywhere. Despite the exhaustion shadowing her features, she smiled at Noor, then stood as though about to embrace her.

Noor was about to hug her back and ask her a million questions – *when had she got back to Malaya? Had she been back to the villa?* – but a man, tall with dark hair and gently tanned skin, sitting beside Ella, touched her arm, forcing her to stop. Noor had never seen him before and wondered if he was a lawyer or merely a friend.

A man whom she *had* met before reintroduced himself as Rupert Canning and asked them all to sit down. Ella and she faced each other from opposite ends of the table. Noor clutched her handbag. Silence filled the room. She waited, holding her breath, as she wondered what was going to happen next.

On the table was a manilla folder and a jug of water with a set of tumblers on a small bamboo tray. A ceiling fan gently stirred her hat but apart from that, little moved and the atmosphere in the room was strange. She studied Ella's features as Rupert Canning spoke.

'First of all, I'd like to thank you for coming here this morning. I know that we're keen to get this matter resolved as amicably as possible. We want to avoid getting lawyers involved or dragging it through the courts.' He faced Ella, whose mouth tightened, then turned to Noor. 'So, the facts of the matter are that Mrs McCain is back now. We all know that she was forced to flee Malaya at the onset of the Occupation without her daughter. During this time, Mr McCain disappeared, leaving Grace in your care.' He nodded to Noor.

'So, the questions we want resolved today are, where is Mr McCain and what proof do you have that you are now Grace's legal guardian? Would you care to explain?'

All faces turned to Noor. She looked at her bag, thinking through what she would say, then lifted her gaze and fixed it on the folder on the table as she spoke.

'The day the Japanese came, Mr McCain asked me to look after Grace. To do whatever I could to keep her safe. Of course, I said yes, despite not then being able to escape and save myself. We made an agreement and Mr McCain was taken away. I never saw him again.'

Frown lines formed on Ella's forehead. 'Do you know where they took him, where he could possibly be now?'

Noor thought of what Omar had told her and chose her words with care. 'The soldiers loaded everyone into a truck. Later, I learnt that they were taken to a camp.' She looked down at her lap. 'I did what I was asked. If Mr McCain were able to, I know he'd be right back at the mine just as soon as he could be.'

She didn't look up to see Ella's reaction but heard her gasp.

Rupert Canning skimmed past this comment and continued, 'And you have evidence, do you, that Mr McCain gave you custody of Grace in case of his non-return? But I should ask first: why did he assume that Mrs McCain wouldn't return for her daughter? Didn't that strike you as strange?'

'Maybe he thought she might never be able to. It was dangerous getting to England. He knew he had to do what was best for his daughter.' Noor lifted her face and stared into Ella's eyes. 'I'm sorry, Mrs McCain, but that's the truth of it.'

'But I'm here now.' Ella's voice was strained, as though she were trying to hold back a whole mixture of emotions. The man next to her placed his hand on her arm and offered her a glass of water, which she turned down. 'And I'm so very, very grateful to you for looking after Grace. It can't have been easy for you, any of it.'

Noor nodded.

'But now,' Ella continued, 'I've come home for my daughter.'

Canning coughed and they all turned to face him.

'Before all of this can be settled, Noor has some information she's brought with her that puts a rather awkward spin on all of this.'

'I really can't see what the problem can be. The facts are perfectly simple. I'm Grace's mother.'

'Indeed. But, as you know, Noor claims that she has adopted Grace and that she is her aunt. She has evidence to back this up.'

All eyes turned to Noor. She could feel them burning into her as she opened her bag and slid the adoption certificate onto the table.

Ella took the certificate. Noor watched her read it slowly, pausing over the words, and saw the colour drain from her face.

'This isn't possible.' She lowered the sheet of paper.

'Like I said, maybe Mr McCain thought that you might not be able to come back.'

'I would never do that to my children.' There was anger and indignation in Ella's voice. She looked as though she was about to faint but managed to glance at Rupert Canning then at the man next to her. The only sound was the movement of the fan.

Noor turned over in her head the words she was about to say. They were well rehearsed, thanks to Omar, and it was with great deliberation that she announced, 'I do have a possible solution, though.'

Ella cocked her head – staring at her with such intensity that Noor braced herself, knowing the information she must divulge would hurt her.

Once more, she reached into her crocodile bag and this time took out the letter from her father. She slid it towards Rupert Canning, who, after reading it, lifted an eyebrow. Ella was on the edge of her seat, her mouth slightly open as she waited for him to relay the contents. He coughed then said, rather awkwardly, 'This will definitely need verifying.'

'What?' Ella said, her tone anxious and impatient.

Slowly, Rupert passed her the letter and Noor watched her read it. The effect on Ella was tangible, as if the letter were a living presence. Noor waited for her to react. After a few moments, her half-sister slowly lifted her head.

Chapter Forty-One

Ella returned to the villa and collapsed into bed. However hard she tried to sleep, her mind wouldn't move from the conversation at the BMA office. Then in the early hours, memories of the past came into focus for her, like reflections settling on a pool.

Her thoughts led her back to the pale moonlight illuminating a jungle path while a woman left dewy footprints across the lawn. In her arms she carried a basket. She disappeared like magic into the undergrowth, walking towards the sleeping mine. Ella's mind moved on, and she saw herself reflected in a car window with a younger child, a smaller version of herself, by her side. She recalled a man's kindness to a single mother, and later her own mother's hostility to a motherless child. How could she have been so stupid; how could she not have seen it all before? It was easy now to understand how her cast-off dresses always made their way to Noor, whose little shadow skipped behind her across the grass or to the rose garden, chasing after peacock feathers and holding hands as though they would always be together.

She pushed back the sheets, opened the shutters and looked out. Wisps of cloud trailed across the full moon and the crickets thrummed. Somewhere, the same moon shone down on Grace and Noor, and she wondered if both of them were sleeping and what they might be thinking if they weren't.

Again and again, she wondered what she could do to make it all right, how she could build a bridge so that she and Noor's relationship could heal, how she could find a way to ensure that the mine and this house weren't places of division and separation, loss and suffering. Her thoughts flickered back to people she had met on her journey from Singapore to Malaya, the stories that had made her wish she could do something to help them. She had to think of a way for them all to heal and move towards a happier future.

In England, she had felt like a stranger; although she had forged a relationship with Polly and James, it was still a place where she didn't completely belong, but now she was back in Malaya, all that had once anchored her here had evaporated like the morning mist. Her sense of belonging, of being valuable and valued, needed to be reformed.

As she looked out, it was as though she could see shadows dancing across the lawn, just like two little girls chasing butterflies and peacocks, and at long last Ella knew what she must do. She'd made up her mind. She would start first thing by going to the BMA office in Menglembu.

'Are you certain?' Rupert Canning asked.

Ella folded her hands in her lap and looked him in the eye.

'Yes. I'm absolutely positive.'

It was just past nine o'clock in the morning and she had

been waiting on the steps outside the office for half an hour before he arrived.

'Well, you'll need to get a lawyer to draw it all up.' Rupert scratched his head. 'But if you want me to speak to Noor first, I'm happy to do so.'

'I think that would be best. And perhaps you could do it soon? Once she knows the situation, and everything has been settled, I would really like to see my daughter.'

Ella shook Rupert's hand firmly and left. As she drove along the dusty tracks from Menglembu to home, she reflected on her plan to give half of the mine and estate to Noor. Not only would it honour their father's last wishes, but it would also return things to how they should always have been – Ella and Noor, two sisters sharing their life together in the Kledang Hills.

And as for Grace, well, Noor was indeed her aunt. Clearly, she had loved and cared for the girl, sacrificing any hope of her own escape when the Japanese invaded in order to safe-guard Grace. What greater love was there than that, and what greater gift of thanks could Ella bestow?

As she drove, she thought of a conversation she and Malik had shared years ago before the possibility of a Japanese inva-sion in Malaya had been considered seriously.

'The British defences are very strong, but the local people also will do everything they can to save our people from attack.'

'They're my people, too, Malik.'

'Yes, madam, I know. But you have a foot in two places. One with your husband, the other here, in Malaya. But if the time ever comes for you to choose, I think perhaps you'd better not stay here.'

'I couldn't leave my home, Malik.'

Ella knew that the fact of the Occupation couldn't be changed, and there was a part of her that felt guilty for not having been here when her country was suffering, but just as she knew that she must heal her relationship with Noor, she wanted to find a way of making amends for all the years her family had benefited from the mine and plantation, making themselves rich and living charmed lives instead of investing in the local people and the future of the country. It was only through believing that she had lost something precious that she realised how much she treasured it – not only Grace, and Noor's friendship, but her belief in and love for Malaya. The images that she and Andrew had witnessed as they had driven north from Singapore still stuck in her mind – the cruelty of the Japanese and their lack of respect for human life had horrified her. If there was one thing she could do now with her wealth and privilege, it was to share them. As she drove plans crystallised in her head and she knew that she could easily make them a reality. Hopefully they'd go some way towards enabling her friends here to shake off the shackles of colonialism.

When she pulled into the long dusty drive, Ella paused and drank in the panorama. It was glorious to be here, and she was filled with certainty that although she could never forget the past, a new chapter in her life was just beginning.

She found Andrew on the verandah, back bent and head bowed as he examined the broken shutter. He looked up at her approach.

'You've been out early,' he said.

'Yes.'

'Anywhere in particular?' He took a penknife from his pocket and tightened the screws in the shutter's bracket, then tested it to see if it held.

She watched him focus as he gently swung it.

'I've got something to tell you. Why don't you come and sit down?'

He snapped the penknife closed and joined her as she sat on a step overlooking the drive. The sun warmed her legs as she stretched them out. He placed an old planter's hat on his head as they both stared ahead. A dog barked in the distance and a parakeet flew in front of them.

'I've been to Menglembu, to see Rupert Canning.' Ella paused for a moment. 'I've decided to make over half the property to Noor.'

Andrew didn't raise his head. She watched him draw long circles with his index finger on the step. After a moment, he said, 'Have you spoken to her about this?'

'Rupert is going to, but I believe it's what she wants.' She could feel him studying her. 'But that's not all. Not only do I think it is correct that she should be recognised as my father's daughter, I also want her recognised as Grace's aunt.'

'That seems a very generous thing to do.'

'And there's something else. On my drive back, I started to wonder what I could do to make things better for the people here, how they could start to govern themselves without foreign intervention, so I've decided to put more money from the mine profits into the school here. Education here is rudimentary. I believe that its children are the future of Malaya, and that this is the answer to the country gaining its independence.'

Finally, Andrew lifted his face to hers. 'I think that's admirable in the extreme. You'll be busy here. You know, I'll miss seeing what you'll make of the place.'

'Oh, Andrew,' she sighed. 'You'll always be welcome here. And if you want to stay, I'm sure we can find you work.'

'I don't know. So much is still undecided, isn't it?'

'Yes. And we're only just beginning to work towards answers.' She pinched the bridge of her nose. 'I'm so desperate to find out what has happened to Johnnie, but part of me is terrified of doing so – and then there are all those other people listed in the notebook. Someone, somewhere must know the truth.'

Omar was sitting outside his house overlooking a small courtyard garden when Noor found him. He lay on a pile of cushions underneath a durian tree, dozing with a dribble of betel-nut juice staining his lips. In a rattan basket lay a mango and a papaya that she had plucked from the trees on her way back from the BMA office, along with six hen's eggs from the market. Rupert Canning's words were still at the forefront of her mind.

She settled the basket down on the dusty earth and prodded Omar with her hand. He opened his eyes, revealing their red rims, then yawned and slowly sat up.

'I've brought you something,' Noor said, indicating the basket with a nod.

Omar's gaze turned towards her gift then back to her face. He yawned again.

'I also have some news.' Noor pulled one of the cushions from where he had been sleeping and sat down, his residual warmth radiating through her dress.

Omar's eyes narrowed as she settled. He waited for her to speak.

'Ella has decided that I'm to own half the mine and she'll recognise me as her sister and Grace's aunt.' Omar gave a slight nod to show he had heard. She continued, 'I've also learnt that she has plans for a better school and for the workers at the mine to be paid a bigger share of the profits. But there's something else—'

Her heart raced as she explained that soon Ella would be returning to England, to tie up her affairs and bring Toby back to Malaya. In the meanwhile, Noor would stay in Ipoh with Grace, who would continue at her school as a day girl until she was old enough to board. Then Noor would return to the Kledang Hills where she would be the new school's administrator.

'You will be able to continue as head teacher, but you must do something for me now, Omar. You guided me to this resolution, but I negotiated it and it has worked out well for all of us. Now you must keep your part of the bargain and tell Ella your secret – that you know what happened to her husband.'

She watched him wipe away the betel-nut juice with the back of his hand, then very slowly he stood. He made his way to the basket where he picked up the mango then examined each one of the eggs. Noor hated it when she didn't know what he was thinking, but experience had taught her that Omar would do what Omar wanted, and only when he was good and ready. A moment later, he went inside and the minutes stretched like evening shadows until he came back out wearing his best *songkok* on his head.

Together they made their way to the BMA office, where Omar insisted on speaking with Rupert Canning immediately.

When the sun was almost at its highest point in the sky, Noor, Omar and Rupert travelled in silence in a black government car to the Wosterholme mine. Noor's stomach twisted as they lurched along the bumpy tracks up the hill. All too soon, the villa came into sight, and she could see Ella sitting on the verandah.

As they pulled into the driveway, Noor watched her stand, smooth down her skirt and make her way to the car with a puzzled expression on her face.

The weight of the knowledge she carried made it hard for Noor to speak. Rupert opened the door for her and they made their way with Ella to the drawing room where a large ceiling fan stirred the oppressive air. She barely noticed where she sat down, but clutched her hands together and examined the rug at her feet.

Rupert spoke, his voice sombre yet self-assured. He introduced Omar, explaining that he was one of the MCP leaders and informers and had contacts throughout the peninsula, but more importantly, he had something he needed to tell Ella. Something that he, Canning, had spent some time verifying this morning. Noor's heart quickened as her cousin began to speak. She was listening to Ella's breathing, anticipating the bitter blow that was about to fall.

'Many men from Malaya were sent to Burma, to work on the railway there – you might have heard it referred to as the death railway?' Omar began.

Ella had and told them so.

'Many prisoners were taken there, and many men died from malaria and malnutrition. MCP spies have told me that your husband was taken to Kinsaiyok, then later to the construction camps in the north.'

Noor heard Ella gasp but couldn't meet her eyes. She dug her nails into her palms as Rupert intervened.

'Do you understand what we are saying, Mrs McCain?'

'I think so.' Ella's voice was distant.

'Many of these men died from maltreatment and starvation. We will need to investigate properly, but we know all the survivors from the camps in Burma have come home.' His voice lowered and softened. 'I'm so sorry, there really is little chance that your husband has survived.'

Noor could hear gentle sobbing. And still she couldn't look at Ella. A monkey screeched outside the window, drowning out the sounds of her sister's grief, but Noor could see nothing through her own misted eyes.

Chapter Forty-Two

Rupert had arranged for Ella to meet Grace at the Green Cow Tavern. Noor had gone out for the day and Ella was glad of it, knowing how hard the meeting would be for both of them. Having a third person present would only complicate matters.

Grace was taller than Ella was expecting and thinner. Almost thirteen now, her body still held the lean lines of a child. Her dark curls were plaited and reached to just above her shoulders. Ella couldn't stop looking at her daughter's face: her eyes were the same shade of blue as Johnnie's and her nose showed the same straight line.

Ella's knees trembled as her daughter walked towards her. She tried to calm the double-beat of her heart. 'Hello,' she said.

'Hello.' Grace's voice was light, like a feather floating on the breeze.

Ella wanted to hold her, to crush her daughter to her chest. How long had she waited for this moment? But now that Grace stood in front of her in the lounge of the hotel, Ella hesitated, uncertain what to do next.

'Would you like to sit down?' she asked, indicating an armchair. 'Or perhaps a drink of water?' Her words came out stiff and formal-sounding, not at all the way she had wanted them to be.

All she could focus on was her daughter: the way she sat down on the edge of the seat, how she held her hands together in her lap and nervously turned her fingers, so long and so much like Johnnie's. Her skin was pale, as though the sun had failed to colour it, her cheeks flushed a delicate pink. There was so much Ella wanted to say, but the words seem to stick in her throat. At last, she managed, 'How are you?'

'I—'

Tears flooded into Ella's eyes as Grace struggled to speak. She wanted to clutch her daughter's hand, tell her not to be nervous, that she should take her time, but instead she waited, tense and alert to every movement that her daughter made.

'It's all right. I know this must be a shock for you.'

'Yes.' Grace's forehead creased, then she started speaking again. 'I'm happy to see you, but it is hard for me as I don't really remember much about you or my father. Everything is a blur . . . very jumbled.'

'I understand.' Ella hardly dared to breathe. 'But you do remember us?'

Grace gave a shy smile. 'I used to have a dream about you both. There would be a man and a woman at a piano in front of an open window. I could never see their faces. The woman always had her back to me as she turned the pages of the music while the man played. I knew it was you and Daddy.'

'That must have been difficult for you,' Ella said. 'And then, not knowing if we'd come back.'

'I always believed that you would. But as for Daddy – Noor has told me what happened. I'm so, so sorry.' Grace's voice trembled, but then she jerked her gaze back to Ella and asked, 'But I have a brother. Toby. He was just a baby when you left. I can't remember much about him. Is he here?'

'No. He's in England. He's nearly six now. I have a photograph of him if you'd like to see?'

Grace nodded and Ella opened her bag. She took out a photograph of Toby and handed it to her. 'He looks a little like you, don't you think?'

Grace stared at the picture then handed it back.

'Please. Keep it,' Ella urged.

'Thank you.' Grace sat with the image in her lap, gently stroking the edge.

'Tell me about my father, please. I remember him as being kind. That he used to love playing the piano.'

'Oh!' Ella sighed. 'He was such a wonderful man and I know he'd have been proud of you – of how brave you must have been all these years. He was tall and kind, with a lovely laugh and a good sense of humour. And blue eyes, just like yours. He'd do anything for anyone. He adored reading you stories, but what he liked to do most of all was to play the piano. Did you know that he composed a tune for you when you were born?'

Grace shook her head. 'I wish I'd known that. I would have liked to hear him play it.'

'He would have liked that, too. More than anything.' The thought of it almost choked Ella. 'But why don't you tell me about yourself? There's so much I want to hear, and you do know, don't you, that I'm very sorry I left you here?'

Their eyes met. Ella wondered what Grace was thinking, whether she had felt abandoned or betrayed, whether she would forgive her mother and whether Ella would ever be able to take her daughter's hurt away.

'I don't remember much. It's such a blur.'

'How did you live?' Ella prompted as she inched closer. 'Did you stay at the villa? Were the Japanese there the whole time?'

'Yes.' Grace shifted on her seat. 'Noor cooked for the Japanese officers as well as doing the housekeeping. I went to the village school. When I wasn't there, I had to help her – washing up, peeling vegetables, waiting at the table.'

'I see.' Ella didn't know what else to say. It was hard to picture her daughter as a servant. 'That can't have been very nice.'

'It wasn't all horrible.' Grace looked up at her and smiled; an expression that brightened up her whole face. 'At school I had fun climbing coconut trees and collecting the ripe husks. I used to shake the branches to watch them fall, then break the shells open. I would drink the milk before scooping out the sweet flesh with a spoon. I had friends there, too. At the villa, we had banana trees, papayas and pineapples growing in the garden and herbs to favour Noor's cooking. Not that we got to eat them that much.'

Grace paused.

'Go on.'

Grace frowned, and her features set in concentration.

'Noor's food always smelt delicious: fresh garlic and chilli, tamarind and tapioca pudding. But we didn't get to eat much of it. The Japanese always ate first – until supplies started to run out, that was, then most of the time we ate rice or tapioca.'

'Were you often hungry?'

'Yes. I used to scrape the pots when Noor had finished cooking or eat bits from the plates if the officers left any food.'

'What were the soldiers like – were they unkind to you?'

'Not all of them. I used to hide in cupboards, as much as I could, if I heard them coming. Once or twice, I saw them beat Noor with a bamboo stick if there was something she hadn't done quite right.'

'That must have frightened you.'

'Yes.' She paused. 'But there was one officer, Naoki, who was kinder than all the rest. He didn't beat Noor. In the evenings, sometimes he would sit and play the piano in the drawing room. I'd listen from the hallway. It was like magic to listen to. I wish I could play like that.'

Johnnie's piano. It was almost too much to bear.

'Do you really?' Ella asked. 'I'm sure I could arrange for you to have lessons if you like.'

Grace's features lit up. 'Naoki taught me – he said I was really good, a natural. I play at school now, in all their concerts.'

Ella waited, wondering what Grace would say next. Her own thoughts and emotions were all over the place. Naoki had shown her daughter kindness and for that she was grateful. Perhaps he'd had a son or daughter that he'd missed back home in Japan. And how much Grace had put up with over the years; she'd been far braver than Ella could have foreseen, but still, she should have been there for her daughter all these years.

'Your father's piano is missing. I wonder what happened to it.'

Grace's eyes sparkled. 'I know where it is! When the Japanese left, Noor packed up as many things as we possibly could from the villa and sent them to Omar. He kept it safe at the school.'

'Really?' Ella couldn't keep the surprise out of her voice. 'But that's wonderful.'

'Yes.' Grace paused then offered, 'Perhaps one day I can play it for you. Would you like that?'

'Oh, yes.' Ella smiled. 'There's nothing I'd like more in all the world.'

Rain battered the windows and wind rattled the shutters all night, but Ella didn't mind, because in the morning Grace would be coming home at last. After their meeting at the hotel there had been lengthy negotiations, but finally everything had been set in motion. Noor now owned half the mine and Ella had set up a trust for the expansion of the school.

As for Andrew, he had been nothing less than a tower of strength, driving her here and there, helping Lian and her brother obtain supplies for the villa. He had agreed to stay and oversee the repairs to the estate until a permanent manager could be found. She'd also entrusted him with establishing the fate of the Chinese mine workers who were still missing.

'If you find out what has happened to them, I think this is one story you must publish. Try and track down their families. It won't be easy, but they have as much right to know what has happened to their loved ones as I do about Johnnie.'

And as for Johnnie – much as his spirit was interwoven into the fabric of Menglembu and the mine, if she were honest, deep-down Ella had sometimes feared she would never see him again, but had held on to that kernel of hope that he'd be here on her return. If only they could have picked up where they'd left off, with him standing on the steps of the villa, as she always remembered him, taking her hand and leading her inside the house, embracing her with a passion that made up for all the missed years. It would be so very hard not sharing the experience of their children growing up, or the future they could all have shared, but she knew it was time for her to start to let go – impossible as it might seem.

When she woke, the rain had lifted and sunlight filtered through the jungle canopy, dappling the ground. Droplets of water clung to the foliage, sparkling like rainbow-filled diamonds. The rain had started to evaporate and veils of mist cobwebbed the coconut palms. As she watched, she saw a man walking along the snaking grass walkways weaving through the rose terrace that were all covered in morning mist. For a moment, she thought it was Johnnie and leant forward, about to call out, 'Lovely weather for ducks!' But the man lifted his head and she saw that it was Andrew. She continued watching, noting how content he seemed to be here. A new kind of longing grew within her, one that she now dared to hope might blossom between them; one that she believed Johnnie would want for her, if only she had ever been able to ask.

Later, as she prepared Grace's bedroom herself, placing freshly laundered sheets on the bed and smoothing them down with the greatest care, her thoughts turned once more to Andrew: the way she sometimes caught his surreptitious glances at her, how he had travelled all this way to support her. As she polished the chest of drawers and placed roses from the garden in a cut-crystal vase that Lian had salvaged from the hidden cupboard in the kitchen larder, she knew that her feelings for Andrew couldn't possibly be wrong.

At ten, Ella watched from the verandah as a black government car appeared in the distance. It crawled along the drive, a cloud of dust following in its wake. Slowly, it turned into the drive and parked. Suddenly Grace was here, along with Rupert and Noor.

Ella took a deep breath and stepped forward to welcome her daughter home at long last.

She wasn't sure who was the most nervous. The house was beginning to return to its former state, but Ella was mindful of the last time Noor and Grace had been here. She'd heard about Naoki's suicide and had decided that the best place for them to sit would be on the verandah overlooking the roses. Lian had made *kuih* and a pot of tea, for which Ella was grateful. She poured out the tea and added sweet, thick condensed milk – Malay-style.

While monkeys chattered in the branches and honey birds flitted along with bright green bee-eaters, Ella studied her daughter's face. So much had changed between them, and so much ground had still to be made up. Sometimes, she didn't know where to begin. But she knew that later she would walk around the gardens with Grace, away from Noor and Andrew, then later still she would head towards the rose garden with Grace, where she would explain to Grace that she hadn't abandoned her and why she had been unable to return to collect her from the fever hospital when she was a child. She knew she would always wonder if her daughter would forgive her, and that even after all her promises never to do so again, soon Ella would have to return to England.

But for now, she glanced from Grace, who was biting into one of the cakes, to Rupert, busy talking to Andrew. A cloud of cigarette smoke hung over them as they chatted. Andrew caught her eye and smiled at her before returning to his conversation. Her gaze turned to Noor, quietly observing the men, and finally, when Ella had taken in all she needed to see to understand how the future might go, she looked back at Grace.

Time, like life, was limited, she knew. One day all this pain would recede and the rest of their lives would follow their destined paths. She sensed that this moment was pivotal and that the past would in due course be buried. But for now, she was more than content to sit here listening to her daughter's chatter mixing with the birdsong in the whispering trees.

The next few days passed happily until it was time for Grace to return to school and Ella to England. It was agreed that Grace shouldn't come with Andrew and Ella to the station but return with Noor to Ipoh, a day earlier than Ella's departure, to restart school. Although it was hard to say farewell, Ella told her to consider this the beginning of a new phase, and that when Ella returned, she'd be back for good – and this time with Toby.

On the morning of her departure, just before the purple hues of sunrise touched the mountains, they left the Kledang Hills. As the car snaked through the jungle and on through the layers of hillside terraces towards Ipoh, Ella's thoughts began to turn once more to England and the news she must take to Polly and James.

Finally, they arrived at the place where the jungle gave way to peanut and groundnut plantations, and on to lower ground where they passed through the final roadblock before Ipoh and its Old Town. Ella's stomach grew heavier as they reached the colonial district, knowing that soon she would be boarding the train and leaving Grace, Noor and Andrew behind. The last leg of their journey went all too quickly until the white walls of the city hall came into sight, followed by the domed Moorish roof of the station.

As she walked through the bustling station towards her train, she realised that there was one thing left for her to say before her long journey back to England.

'Andrew?' she said, as she clutched her first-class ticket tightly in one hand.

'Yes?'

She lifted her face and their eyes met. 'Thank you.'

'You don't need to thank me.'

'But I'm grateful to you for everything. You know that, don't you?'

'Yes. But I've told you before, I will do all that I can to help. I can't let you do all this alone.'

'I know.'

Her train pulled in and the passengers started to alight, but Ella lingered, uncertain.

'You'd better hurry,' he said.

Still she didn't move.

'I don't want to leave you,' she said again.

'I don't want you to, either.'

He reached for her hand. She squeezed his, realising in that moment something had changed between them both. Something that was irreversible and permanent. Something for which she was very glad.

For a moment, they stood holding hands, their eyes unwavering, then slowly Ella put her arms around his neck and kissed him; a kiss that felt so right and perfect. She waited, hoping that this time he would kiss her back.

Chapter Forty-Three

James got up from his chair when Ella had told him the news about Johnnie, then left the house, banging the door behind him. He was gone for almost five hours and when he returned there was whisky on his breath. Polly locked herself in her bedroom and wouldn't come out for the rest of the day. Ella took her some soup along with some cheese and slices of the walnut bread she had made. She sat on the bed and tried to coax her mother-in-law to eat, but Polly stared out of the window with a vacant and dazed look on her face.

Eventually, Ella succeeded in getting her downstairs and into the garden. Polly's eyes were dull and her skin had lost its lustre. However hard Ella tried to make her talk, she failed.

The fact of Johnnie's death seemed more brutal here, faced with the grey British weather and her in-laws' grief. Ella wanted to tell them that they weren't the only ones who were suffering, but she knew that bereavement took everyone in a different way. Polly thawed first, slowly fixing her attention on Toby. After a few days, they all walked along beside the river, Polly wrapped in a scarf and her grief.

Ella learnt to judge just how much time her mother-in-law

needed with Toby before exhaustion and a bout of crying gripped her. Toby seemed to sense his grandmother's need and snuggled into her, sat on her lap or asked her to read him stories. James was more distant, cocooning himself in his study, only coming down for meals and to collect the paper until he returned to the safe routine of academia.

The conflict between their grief and her needs troubled Ella. She decided that only when the time was right would she make plans to leave. Before that, hard as it would be, she would visit Melody and Edward one last time. Prompted by the need to keep busy, she began to sort through her belongings in the coach house and stumbled across the oil paints that Andrew had given her, remembering how painting had helped her heal in the early days of her evacuation to England.

The tubes of paint lay on the table for a whole day, catching the light, their silver-foiled bodies glinting and embedding themselves in her subconscious. If only there was something she could do with them, she thought, a way of capturing the memory of Johnnie for them all before his image faded from memory. And as she thought about it an idea formed. She would create a portrait of him, a painting like no other – one that would keep his memory alive.

It was much harder than she'd realised. Sometimes she grew frustrated after not having painted for so long. She remembered the artwork and catalogues that she had seen in Andrew's house and borrowed books from the library to help her understand different painting techniques. Then her ideas came together thick and fast. She sketched, teasing them out – experimenting with different media, any-thing she could use to bring her design to life. She scoured shops and jumble sales for inspiration, taking Toby with her, finding textures and materials, anything that grabbed her interest.

Polly grew curious about what she was doing and kept asking for a look.

'I'd rather you waited,' Ella said. 'Until it's finished.'

She couldn't stop. She worked in every free moment. Each brushstroke and layer of paint seemed to bring her closer to Johnnie. She worked feverishly, sketching and re-sketching until her design was right.

'I've made you a sandwich,' Polly called from the court-yard with Toby at her side. It was so kind of her, and Ella realised that Polly was herself taking a step forward in her grieving. She no longer spent hours staring out of the window, but had started cooking again, and was tidying or cleaning almost non-stop.

'Thank you.' Ella wiped her hands on a tea towel and took the plate: cheese and pickle along with a slice of fruit cake.

'You're very good to me, Polly. You know that, don't you?'

'Nonsense,' she said. 'Now eat.'

Polly looked exhausted. She glanced over at the canvas, which was turned away. 'Can I see what you're doing?' she asked again.

'Not yet. I want it to be completely ready before I let anyone see.'

Polly hesitated, showing her disappointment, then turned and made her way back to the house.

When she had gone, Ella stepped back and watched the light glide across her creation. She examined it from every angle. There was gold in her painting – it shimmered and brought the work to life.

The next day she told Polly, 'I want to show you both the painting now. Why don't you come around for tea at about four?'

Polly lifted her head.

'The painting. Is it of Johnnie?'

'You'll have to wait and see.'

Ella bought biscuits from the bakery, and after lunch she and Toby spent the afternoon making finger sandwiches and a sponge cake. When everything was ready, she changed into her floral tea dress then lit the candles that she'd placed in glass jars around the main room of the coach house and waited for Polly and James to arrive.

Shortly after four o clock, she heard Polly knock on the door and James muttering at her side.

'I've brought some wine.' Polly placed the bottle on the table.

'Thank you,' Ella said. She poured it into glasses and handed them round.

'Well,' she stood by the canvas that was still covered by a sheet, 'I expect you're wondering what I've got hiding under here. So, I'm going to explain.' She looked nervously at their faces – their expressions were interested but also a little apprehensive.

'I wanted to create a memorial to Johnnie, something that embodies him. Not simply his work, but his essence. As you know, he loved to play the piano. It had been his dream to be a composer but he never achieved that – other than writing two compositions when the children were born. So, I've created something that I think encapsulates him, and I've called it *The Cuckoo Dance*. It's the title of the piece he wrote for Grace when she was born.'

Ella stood to one side and tugged the sheet away. 'What do you think?'

She watched them looking at the canvas intently. Her breath seemed to have turned to lead in her chest. Excitement mingled with unease as she waited for them to speak.

'Goodness!' Polly said eventually.

James stepped forward a little and scrunched up his eyes. 'Can you explain it?'

'Of course. All of the texturing – the shadows, areas like that – are made up from tiny musical notes. I created the shadows on his face from staves. You can just see them if you step forward, hundreds and hundreds of them layered one on top of the other. And here,' she indicated Johnnie's hair, 'I've interwoven them into the darker shading.'

Polly raised her hand to her chin and looked to where she had pointed. Ella could see her examining the texture of the image.

'How did you make it three-dimensional?'

'Papier mâché – from old newspaper.'

'Well . . .' Her mother-in-law exhaled. 'It's certainly different.'

Toby tugged at Ella's dress but she didn't look down at him, trying to read Polly's expression. A nerve ticked in her cheek.

'Well?' Ella asked at last. 'Do you like it?'

Polly turned to her as James dug his hands into his pockets. At last, a grin broke across his face.

'I've never seen anything like it before.'

'And is that good?'

Ella glanced back at her mother-in-law. Polly was nodding.

'It's stunning,' she said. 'You've captured everything about him exquisitely – the shape of his face, the expression in his eyes – but best of all you seem to have caught the very essence of him.'

James took another step towards the painting. He lifted his hand and touched the canvas. 'But this is what I find the most impressive.' His fingers hovered over the tiny black notes she had painted. 'Each note made up from small dots, from the smallest starting here on his chin, to the largest ones that form his hair. And there's movement here also,' James said. 'The piece seems vibrant – so alive.'

'That's the best part,' Polly said. 'I don't know how you achieved it.'

'It's the gold paint – I mixed it with powdered egg white to give a variety of textures and depth. Each fleck that you see has been applied with a single brush stroke, then it has been allowed to dry. It's created a mosaic effect, and when the light falls in the right way, it creates the illusion of flickering and dancing.'

'I like it, too,' Toby said. 'But when are we going to eat the cake?'

Ella picked him up. 'You've been such a good boy, Toby. Would you like to cut it?'

'With the big knife?'

'Yes, but Mummy will have to help you.'

As he stood on a chair and sliced into the cake, Ella could hear James and Polly chatting. For the first time in days, the tone of James's voice was positive and encouraging, and it had been good to see the smile on Polly's face. It was going to be a long journey for them to recover from Johnnie's death, she realised, and telling them she was leaving was going to be difficult, but today was as good a day as any.

'How about we have a glass of my wine?' Polly said.

'That would be fabulous.' Ella nodded. 'A real celebration of Johnnie's life.'

'Here, James, you open it.' Polly passed him the bottle, which he uncorked and poured into their glasses.

He raised his. 'Here's to Johnnie!'

When it came to the announcement that she was returning to Malaya, Polly told Ella that she'd been expecting it. 'You can't stay here forever. It's time for you to go back home.'

It was difficult, all the same, packing up her belongings, placing her paintings in large crates to be sent on after her, explaining to Toby that they were going on a voyage, and that he was going to meet his sister at long last. Part of her wanted to stay in England, to bring Grace here and leave the ugly past behind, but Malaya was her country and in her blood. However hard returning would be, living there without Johnnie, she knew that it was what she really wanted. And that it was right.

'You must take the painting of Johnnie,' Polly said to her as she was packing up.

'But I made it for you.'

'I know,' Polly said. 'But I think that you should have it. It belongs in Malaya, along with Johnnie's soul – that's where I want to think of it. Keep it as a memorial to him there. And won't the gold look magnificent with the sun on it?'

Ella agreed that indeed it would.

When she had almost finished her preparations, she made her final visit to Melody and Edward.

'He's much better,' Melody said when she opened the door to the flat. 'But I don't think he'll ever be the same.'

'I'm sorry.' Ella came into the hall and Melody closed the door behind her with a gentle click.

'He's got a position at St Thomas's, though, which I'm certain will do him good.'

'And what about you? And Laurence?'

Melody hesitated then said, 'I'm going to make some tea. Why don't you come with me?'

Ella followed. Melody put the kettle to boil on the stove and turned to face Ella, leaning against the worktop as she spoke.

'I love Laurence,' she said, 'and I know he loves me, but I can't do this to Edward anymore. What happened to Johnnie, well, it's unbelievably sad. It's made me realise that sometimes what you've got is worth holding on to.'

Ella stepped forward and put her arms around her friend.

'I'm glad,' she said. 'I know it's been hard for you, especially with the baby. This war – I don't think it's left anyone unscathed.'

Melody nodded, then the kettle started to whistle.

'I'll bring this through,' she said. 'Why don't you go and talk to Edward?'

Although it had been hard saying goodbye to them both, Ella was glad that she'd been that one last time. She knew that Melody and Edward were unlikely ever to return to Malaya. For now, like so many people, they needed to rebuild the remnants of their lives, and it made her happy to think that at least theirs was a relatively happy story.

The last days were a flurry of activity. Although Ella tried to persuade Polly and James not to accompany her to Southampton, they insisted.

They said farewell in the biting wind, surrounded by their suitcases and other passengers ready to board the *Queen Mary*. Ella noticed a man and a woman standing next to them who were also saying their farewells. The man seemed impatient to get on board, but the woman was talking to an older one, her mother Ella guessed, who was giving her gift – a beautiful maroon writing case. Ella watched them from the corner of her eye, registering the meaning of the scene as Toby

pulled away from Polly, who was wrapping a scarf she had
knitted around his neck.

'I'll let you know when we arrive,' Ella said. And thinking
of the beautiful leather case she had seen the woman holding moments earlier, she added, 'I promise I won't forget to
write.'

Chapter Forty-Four

One year later

Sunlight filtered through the jungle, casting speckled shadows. Early-morning mist rose from the canopy like a veil lifting. The roses were in full bloom again, and Ella could capture their scent from her bedroom window. She inhaled: the scent of tea roses – the perfume was delicious and intoxicating.

This room had always been her favourite, with its pastel pink and green silks, and the wispy white voile floating at the windows that softened the blazing morning light flooding the room. It was more suited to her now and she had reclaimed it and used it as her own. Noor now slept in Ella and Johnnie's old room further along the corridor. She also had a private study there, where she could conduct business when she wasn't overseeing the expansion of the school. Ella couldn't sleep there now anyway, the memories of Johnnie lingered, and she and Andrew preferred this room, overlooking the garden. They'd lie in bed, arms around each other, watching through the open window the rosy pink- and peach-streaked sky.

From the window she saw Naseem, the new houseboy, watering the roses with the can Farid had always used. How strange that of all the things that had gone missing during her absence, it had been one of the few things she had still recognised. He walked backwards and forwards, draining the can carefully around the base of a bush, then walked off to refill it before returning. When the monsoon came, the blooms would be smashed, but for now they lingered. She enjoyed their transient beauty and the headiness of the scent. They seemed to confirm for her that returning to Malaya and the mine had been the right thing to do.

In the distance, she could hear the workings of the mine: the warning siren, then the blast of dynamite ripping through the jungle. The window frame shook a little, then the tremor passed. There were still only twenty workers, but their numbers were growing steadily, lured by the promise of partnership in the enterprise and places for their children at the new school. Andrew had said that there were more miners being trained up to the task every day. It would be a while until they were at full capacity, but everything in Malaya, she knew, would take time to return to normal, to grow and to flourish.

She stepped away from the window and onto the upper landing. Although it was only just after her breakfast of *roti* and dhal, the aroma of chillies and garlic cooking drifted up from the kitchen where Mei Ling, the new cook, was preparing lunch. Beef *rendang* or *laksa* she thought, for there were still plenty of tamarinds in the garden.

As she made her way along the corridor, she caught sight of Lian, who was in Toby's room folding his clothes: shorts and T-shirts, ankle socks and striped pyjamas were stacked in neat piles ready to be placed in his chest of drawers. Lian lifted her head and smiled and Ella returned it, before making her way to Grace's room where the bed was already neatly made and the mosquito net tied to the wall. Ella ran her hand over the bedcover and her fingers grazed the toys lined up on the bed – Grace's old plush rabbit took pride of place. The window and shutters were open, and a gentle breeze teased the sheer drapes hanging like gossamer from the rail above. Ella walked over to the window and looked across the jungle, at the palm fronds gently swaying.

When she went downstairs, Artemis lay in her basket in the hall. The spaniel lifted her head at Ella's arrival. She bent down and stroked the dog's head before passing the drawing-room door that for now was closed. From behind it, she could hear Grace practising her scales on the piano Omar had long-since returned, to the gentle coaxing of her teacher's voice: Angela Bishop, the young wife of one of the local planters who'd recently returned from England, was proving to be quite a success.

And then Ella walked into Johnnie's former study, now her own. On the desk were piles of letters along with a report compiled by the BMA with help from Andrew. She knew it by heart: Johnnie's death in Burma was being treated as a war crime along with the deaths of their Chinese mine workers; she now knew they had been executed the day the Japanese arrived, on the hilltop overlooking the mine, and their remains only discovered after extensive searches led by Andrew.

Stacked neatly next to the report were boxes of photographs Andrew had taken to document the atrocity, letters of appreciation from the victims' families and clippings from

The Times crediting his coverage of the story of wartime horror in Malaya. They'd wanted him to go back to England to a staff job, but he'd turned the offer down.

'This is my last photographic work,' he'd said when the letter from England arrived. 'My photo-journalism days are over, so it's nice to go out on a high.'

'Are you sure you don't mind,' she'd asked, 'giving it all up to help me here at the mine?'

'No.' He shook his head, smiling down, his arm around her. 'My life is here now. All things change and all things must pass.'

Ella picked up a copy of the *Malay Tribune* that Naseem had placed there earlier: there was trouble in the south. Chinese workers, encouraged by communist rebels, had set fire to a rubber plantation. The outbreaks were happening with worrying frequency, and she knew it wasn't safe to go anywhere without a gun. There were so many roadblocks and terrorist attacks recently, and there had been rumours of possible disruptions from supporters of Chiang Kai Shek. *Malaya for Malaysians – Asia for Asians!* was a slogan she heard everywhere. The tide was turning against the British colonialists and they might yet all drown beneath it.

When she had finished reading, she put the paper down. Scattered around the room were the boxes and tea chests that had arrived months ago from England. There was one that Ella hadn't yet had the courage to unpack. It contained *The Cuckoo Dance* – the painting she had created for Polly and James but which they had insisted should be in Malaya, to honour their son. Today, she knelt down beside it and started to lift the precious work from the straw that was protecting it. At last! She couldn't wait to show Andrew what she had created.

'Come to my office at twelve o'clock,' she had told him earlier as they lay in bed, their fingers intertwined. They could hear the macaques calling in the trees and the parrots squawking. 'There's something I want to show you.'

Time passed quickly as she unwrapped the painting. Before she knew it, the clock was chiming twelve. She stood up with pins and needles sparking in her knees as she brushed down her skirt.

Her nerves fluttered like a million butterfly wings as she checked the time on her watch, then at last she heard Andrew's footsteps before he knocked on the door. When she opened it, he stood framed in the sunlight flooding through from the hall. Her heartbeat quickened as she welcomed him inside.

'So, what is it?' he asked, his voice teasing as he pulled her towards him and kissed her gently on the lips. 'You said you needed to show me something.'

'Just wait.' She led to him over to the large canvas she had propped against one wall and covered with a sheet.

He stood with his hands in his pockets, head tilted to one side as she revealed the painting. He glanced up at her briefly then swung his gaze back to the canvas.

'Goodness. Is this your work?'

'Yes.' Nervousness fluttered through her. She waited for his considered reaction.

'Oh, Ella,' he said, his eyes still fixed on the picture. 'It's beautiful. I'm so happy. I can't believe you've started to paint again.'

'Well, I haven't really. It was something I did in England – for Polly and James originally. I've decided it is the best thing I've painted and therefore I want it to be the last. But really, do you like it?' She smiled at him, warmth filtering from her core.

'Of course I do. Tell me about it.'

She relaxed. It had been much harder than he knew for her to share this with him 'When I learnt Johnnie had died, it seemed the best way of honouring him and comforting his parents. But they told me to bring it home. That it belonged here.'

'Well, I'm glad they did.' Time seemed to stand still as she waited for Andrew to turn fully towards her, and when at last he did a smile radiated from his face, transfixing her. 'It's magnificent. You should put it somewhere special. Have you thought where?'

She nodded. She knew precisely where she was going to hang it.

Ella stood in the blistering afternoon heat wearing a black linen dress and a black hat with a veil covering her face. From this vantage point at the top of the hill, she could see miles of jungle below her, the tin mine, paddy fields and tea plantations. In the distance, bamboos rustled and a macaw screeched, but she stood in silence as beads of perspiration slithered down her neck, along her collar and down the grooves of her spine. Toby, who was settling into life in Malaya, although he still missed Polly and James, stood like a soldier to her left. Tall and upright, he held her hand, not really understanding what was happening. She squeezed his fingers, looked down at him and gave a reassuring smile before turning her attention back to the priest who stood in front of the tiny gathering. The memorial, a simple column of stone, had been erected there earlier in the week.

Grace stood to her right, and then Noor, while a little further back she could sense Rupert and Andrew. She could feel his gaze fixed on her back as he watched and listened to the priest telling them all to join with him in prayer.

'Dear Lord,' he said, 'today we remember our dear brothers now departed . . .'

Ella closed her eyes and listened to his words. When he had finished, she took off her crucifix and laid it on the ground. In silence, she read the list of names that had been carved there: twenty-one in total, listed in alphabetical order – all the men equal and united now – until her eyes rested on the name Johnnie McCain.

At last, she turned and made her way slowly back to the car and down the bumpy hill all the way to the villa, a mile or so below. She knew that Andrew, Grace, Noor, Rupert, Lian and all the others would follow, but for now she was glad of the silence in the car as the driver took them home.

She hadn't invited many guests to the reception, for there weren't many left to grieve. Twenty or so had already arrived and were spilling out onto the newly relaid lawn. She could see Dr Gibbins, who had retired after leaving Changi, and his wife Edith who had said she couldn't wait to get back to Malaya – her home. Ella continued to make her way to the drawing room where the shutters had been opened wide, creating a continuous space between the inside of the villa and the garden.

Golden light flooded the room and birdsong filtered in from the trees. She could hear the long mournful cry of a monkey, the chatter of the guests on the lawn, then a moment later the sound of plates and cups being brought from the kitchen on a trolley for afternoon tea. Noor came into the room with Rupert, her face lifted towards his. Both of them were smiling while she rested her hand, on which a new diamond ring glinted, gently on his arm. She looked every inch the efficient school administrator she had become, as well as the sister Ella had always wanted, perhaps the only person she knew who also understood the significance of the villa, the mine, and of being Eurasian in Malaya.

Ella turned her gaze away to the white chrysanthemums in tall vases that stood everywhere. The room looked clean and fresh now that the sofas and chairs had been reupholstered in a pink-and-blue chintz, the walls repainted a brilliant white and all the carpets cleaned. The chandelier glittered, sending rainbows of light across the ceiling, while fans turned gently, cooling the damp surface of her skin.

And now, she turned to look at the corner of the room, for there, far away from the damaging sunlight, stood Johnnie's piano. Today, it was polished and gleaming. On the wall above it hung her painting of him – *The Cuckoo Dance*, the sun catching the gold-flecked paint at just the right angle, and the score of Liszt's *Liebesträume* positioned on the piano stand in pride of place. Earlier, she had placed a single red rose in a bud vase and it stood on top of the piano, surrounded by photographs of Toby, Grace, Polly and James.

Dear Polly, she thought, how kind you were to me, how strong you are. I wish you could be here today.

Andrew brought her a cup of tea. 'Here,' he said. 'How are you doing?'

She said nothing, merely nodded and took the cup, grateful for his thoughtfulness, knowing that he would understand her need at this point more than any throughout the day to be alone.

And then, as planned, Grace in a black tea dress made her way to the piano. The room fell silent as she pulled out the stool and settled herself down. She coughed, then lifted her hands and played.

Ella closed her eyes. How she had longed to hear this piece of music again. She counted the rhythm: the first beat of each measure was accented, corresponding to an extended, highly stretched set taken on the first count, followed by two short steps. One, two, three – one, two, three – the melody rose and fell, swooped and swayed. It was smooth and confident, elegant and beautiful. She lost herself in it, and when it had finished, all too soon, she opened her eyes reluctantly. It felt as though she was lost in time; she could see Johnnie looking at her through Grace's eyes, as though for one last moment they were reunited across the lost and distant years and he was telling her: *All is well.*

*

When everyone had left, she and Andrew sat on the verandah waiting for the sun to go down.

He took her hand and gently stroked her fingers.

'What do you think will happen now?' he asked.

She recalled how he had asked her that once before and she had been uncertain then, but now she knew the answer with utmost certainty. As she watched the fierce blood-red of the sun going down over the jungle, she felt complete. She knew what she wanted more than anything; that although she would never forget the past or Johnnie, she would always want Andrew by her side. He would help her to rebuild not only what was lost, but her belief in their ability to carry on.

She lifted her face to his and their eyes met. She brought her face closer to his, and he responded with a long kiss. Her heart spun like a pinwheel as he pulled her closer. They stayed sitting on the verandah, holding hands, until the sun had finally disappeared behind the treeline.

And she knew, as they sat there, that for all the days to come, whatever else happened, he would always be there by her side.

Author's Note

In the writing of this novel, I have tried to keep as much as possible to true historical events, although the characters are all people of my invention. In order to produce a flowing narrative, it has been necessary to somewhat condense the incidents that took place and to use a little creative imagination.

In undertaking my research, I have found some amazing resources. In particular, the BBC WW2 People's War Archive, where the real-life experiences of Brian Napper, Bernard de Neumann, the Shuttleworth family, the Foulds family, Mrs Florence Shaw, Doreen Little, Bill Harvey and many others enabled me to understand the horror of the Japanese Occupation of Malaya, as well as the realities of escaping to England and what life during WW2 was like for those who suffered it.

The internet continues to be a golden source of information: from facts about rationing in England to the lives of women, fashions, recipes, the bombing of Coventry, newspaper reports, YouTube videos of life in Malaya during the Japanese Occupation – the list goes on! The lot of women always interests me, especially how much has changed and how much we have fought for those changes. It intrigued me to find out that, prior to WW2, women would never have been required to bear arms, but the National Service Act of 1941 made conscription legal. Almost 90 per cent of women aged 18–60 were employed in essential work, which is why my main protagonist, Ella, is called up, even though she is a single mother of a young child.

Books that continue to give me inspiration include the *Nella Last's War* series (housewife, 49) – her accounts of life during WW2 are captivating and unique; *Singapore, A Pictorial History 1819–2000* by Gretchen Liu, which is still providing me with many hours of fascinating browsing; and *Wartime Kitchen: Food and Eating in Singapore 1942–1950* by Wong Hong Suen, which enabled me to illustrate my narrative with authentic recipes and allow my characters to eat surprisingly well during the most trying of times.

Acknowledgements

I'd like to thank so many people for helping me with the writing of this book. The majority was written during the first national lockdown of 2020, and I wouldn't have been able to manage it without the love and support of my daughter and husband.

As usual, my agent, Caroline Hardman of Hardman and Swainson, has been a rock – just full of sensible and helpful advice, and for gaining me a book deal to start with: thank you, Caroline, you have made my dreams come true.

I'd also like to thank all my editors, past and present, as well as the whole team at Penguin for everything you have done in producing my novel in what was a very tough year for everyone. Thank you for getting my book out into the world!

I'd also like to thank those people who helped me with snippets of information or for just being there throughout the pandemic via Zooms or email. Firstly, the entire body of writers known as the Debuts2021 Facebook group – our Zoom meetings were fabulous; and the D20s, who seemed, during lockdowns, like the older, wiser cohort of writers a year ahead of us. I'd like to thank Gayle Farr for her wonderful photographs of Malaysian tin mines and her stories about what it's like to live in Southeast Asia; along with Liz

Alexander, who responded to a Twitter call-out from my agent regarding geographical logistics in Malaysia.

Thank you to everyone who has helped me and encouraged me. Your love and support is there in my text, woven in the lines.